# BLEEDING LONDON

# BLEEDING LONDON

## GEOFF NICHOLSON

**THE OVERLOOK PRESS**
WOODSTOCK · NEW YORK

First published in paperback in the United States in 1998
by The Overlook Press, Peter Mayer Publishers, Inc.
Lewis Hollow Road
Woodstock, New York 12498

**Library of Congress Catalog-in-Publication Data**

Nicholson, Geoff.
Bleeding London / Geoff Nicholson
p.      cm.
1. City and town life—England—London—Fiction.
2. London (England)—Fiction. I. Title.
PR6064.I225B58 1997      823'.914—dc21      97-10215

Originally published in the United Kingdom by Victor Gollancz

Manufactured in the United States of America

ISBN: 0-87951-886-3

9 8 7 6 5 4 3 2 1

# STRANGE MEETING

It is shortly after midday on one of those slate-grey, mid-January days when it seems never to become fully light, when dusk starts to coalesce in mid-afternoon. The cold, sheer air is pierced with panels of artificial light, and a forty-year-old man in a cashmere overcoat walks beneath a railway bridge in this frayed, nondescript part of east London. Water runs down from the girders overhead. He sees the yard belonging to a car dismantler, some of its stock parked in the road. He sees an off-licence with bars on the windows, a minicab office as narrow as a corridor. It is all alien territory and yet he is not in any ordinary sense lost. He looks pleased with himself, as though he has something to celebrate, as though he might already have been drinking; but above all else he looks out of place. The wrong man on the wrong street at the wrong time; a confluence of errors, of bad luck and hard lines.

Suddenly someone speaks to him. At first he's too self-absorbed to take any notice but then he sees that the speaker is one of six boys, men, who are walking along in the same direction as him: three black, three white, three beside him, three hanging back. He sees that they're younger than he thought, very big, dressed in slick clothes that are encoded with American names, references to basketball and gridiron teams, and a voice repeats, 'I said I think you're lost.'

'No,' the man says firmly and advances his pace, enough to show determination but not, he hopes, panic.

'Yeah, I really think you're lost.'

Two boys behind him each grab an arm, restraining and immobilizing him, and the one who spoke, a black kid with a big, broad, intelligent face, wiry adolescent fluff on his top lip, starts going through his pockets. The man in cashmere looks unusually philosophical, as if he has no objections to being mugged, as though he has been expecting this, as though it is what he's been waiting for. He stands still, doesn't struggle, lets them get on with it, whatever it is they have in mind. He doesn't even bother to look at his assailants. Instead his eyes stare off into the distance. The street appears utterly, improbably empty, not that he believes the presence of other people would help him.

And then he realizes he is wrong. The street isn't empty at all. He sees someone else, someone standing in the shadow of the railway bridge, just another mugger, he thinks at first, a lookout maybe. But as strange hands invade his clothes and body, removing objects – keys, a handkerchief, a London *A–Z* – and throwing aside those things that are judged valueless, this new character steps forward. He looks bad, as though he has been in the wars, in a serious fight that he did not necessarily win.

He is a white man, maybe twenty-five years old, tall, broad, tough-looking. But his face is roughed up, the integrity of the skin broken through, made ragged and livid; a cut lip, an eye bruised black, raw grazes on all the face's hard, sharp, vulnerable edges. He's wearing a petrol-blue suit that once must have looked immaculately sharp. Now it's flayed out of shape, torn at the knees, streaked and clotted with ominous substances. And under the suit there's a white T-shirt stained with dark islands and archipelagos of what can only be blood.

The bloody man is watching the mugging with a weary interest, walking towards it, involved yet bored by the spectacle. The black kid now has a wallet in his hands and is examining its contents with a quick, dismissive precision.

6

The bloody man says loudly in a northern accent, 'Give him his wallet back, there's a good kid.'

The six muggers hear and laugh. Partly it's the accent, partly it's the absurdity of the request. They turn, let go of their victim having winkled out his valuables. That's over. They're on to a new, more compelling engagement.

'Say that again,' says the boy with the wallet.

'I said give him his wallet back, there's a good darkie.'

The silence seems bottomless.

Then one of the white guys says, 'Are you insulting my friend, you racist cunt?'

'I don't think he's much of a friend.'

By this time they've taken in the appearance of the new arrival, read at least some of its meaning: the suit, the face, the blood. One of them, more observant or less brave than the rest, sensing something dangerous and feral, says to the others, 'We don't have to get involved with this, you know.'

But the holder of the wallet isn't listening and says, 'Why don't you make me give it back?'

The man runs his hand through his hair, pulls a face that conveys mostly ennui.

'I'm really so tired of all this,' the man says, referring to a history they cannot know. 'All this macho, violent nonsense. I don't need it. Neither do you.'

Then, as if absent-mindedly, he pulls a gun out of his pocket. It could be real, it could be a replica, but the young muggers will barely have time to wonder about that. The man with the gun looks unsteady on his feet, faltering, unstable. Then he says, 'Actually I don't need this gun either.'

He drops the gun thoughtlessly towards the pavement and as it lands it goes off. A single shot is unleashed, the violent noise amplified and made metallic by the confines of the bridge. The bullet lodges in one of the parked cars but it could have gone anywhere, into flesh and bone. The muggers make a run for it but the bloody man grabs the nearest one and hits him across

7

the face with the back of his hand, then repeats the action five or six times.

'Don't you dare accuse me of racism, you stupid little piece of dung,' he says.

And then he hits the boy again before tossing him down on to the pavement in front of him, as though dealing with a bag of household waste. He starts kicking the boy, but then feels an intrusive presence at his shoulder. He turns, ready to deal with whoever, whatever it is, but it's only the man who was mugged, the victim.

'Stop it,' he's saying. 'What are you doing? You're going to kill him.'

As though this is a brand-new thought, the man stops his kicking. He composes himself, straightens his unstraightenable jacket, and takes half a dozen paces away from where the boy is lying. The boy warily reassembles himself, drags his body across the pavement, gets to his feet and starts to run. The two men watch him go.

'You're right. He's not the one I want to kill. Let's get out of here. Where are we?'

The man who was mugged bends down to the pavement and gathers up his keys and handkerchief, redistributing them around his pockets. Meanwhile his saviour picks up his gun, the stolen wallet, which the muggers abandoned in their flight, and the *A–Z*. He peers around him, looking for a street sign to tell him where he is. He finds nothing, but opens the man's *A–Z* nevertheless. It doesn't help. The map itself is an absurd puzzle, a conundrum, a maze. Thick black lines have been drawn through every single street, through every single road, avenue, place, bridge, mews, on every single page of the map. By this method every street name has been made illegible as if the whole of London has been scored through and obliterated, made theoretical and anonymous. The map has been reduced to a pattern, to decoration and ornament, an abstract design with London as its distant organic inspiration. It will not guide them home. Far away a police siren claws through the air.

The man in the bloody T-shirt looks at the man in the cashmere overcoat, the owner of the useless map, and says, 'You're going to tell me there's a really simple explanation for this, aren't you?'

# THERAPY

Judy Tanaka and her therapist sat in an awkward though not especially hostile silence for almost all the first half of the session. Winter sun streamed into the basement room, and the shadows cast by the window frames cut the carpeted floor into sharp, bright diamonds of light. Judy's therapist, a slender, youthful but grey-haired woman who wore big rings and yellow silk stockings, stared out of the window at the overgrown Kentish Town garden beyond, but she had the trick of letting her clients know that her attention was still in the room with them should it be required.

Judy Tanaka had spent a lot of time wondering about her therapist, chiefly about her sexual orientation, whether or not she was gay, and whether or not there was some sort of unprofessional hostility to be found in the cold way she greeted Judy at the beginning of each session. Maybe the therapist hated her because she wasn't gay, because she had a lively hetero sex life that the therapist couldn't hope to emulate. Maybe she was jealous. Maybe she wanted to seduce her patient. But Judy had concluded that this sort of speculation was an understandable but nevertheless irrelevant and all too obvious evasion of the matters at hand. She did her best to stop thinking about her therapist and start talking about herself.

At long last she said, 'I think something very strange is happening to me.'

'Something good?' the therapist asked, slowly turning her

head towards Judy, and untangling her attention from the garden.

'I don't know exactly,' Judy replied. 'But I definitely think I'm changing.'

'And in what way or ways are you changing?'

Judy wriggled in the big, creased, leather chair and thought hard before answering.

'I think I'm becoming more complex,' she said. 'More dense, more full of noise and pollution, more beset by problems of organization and infrastructure.'

The therapist looked at Judy dumbly, suspiciously, and Judy was dismayed by her unconcealed lack of interest and understanding.

'Sometimes I feel bombed and blitzed,' Judy said. 'And sometimes I feel plagued. Sometimes I feel like I'm on fire, and other times like I'm lost in a fog, in a real old-fashioned pea-souper.'

'I think you're a little young to remember pea-soupers, Judy,' the therapist said, kindly enough. 'The necessary clean air legislation was passed well before your time.'

'Maybe I have a race memory,' Judy insisted.

'What race would that be?'

Oh dear. Here they went again. Judy was used to this tactic. It had been tried often enough before. People, even professional helpers, wanted to believe that all her angst and confusion stemmed from the simple fact of her foreignness, from being half-Japanese, a stranger in a familiar London landscape. Judy regularly dismissed such cheap and easy explanations.

'The race memory would be English,' she insisted to her therapist. 'I was born in south London, for Christ's sake.'

The therapist demurred and Judy continued, 'And these problems I have with men. Out-of-towners. They're all just tourists, just day-trippers. They come and gawp at my tourist attractions, leave a pile of litter, then go on their way.'

'It's an apt metaphor,' the therapist said.

'It's not just a metaphor,' Judy insisted. 'Look at me. Don't I remind you of anything? I display signs of both renewal and decay. Strange sensations commute across my skin. There is vice and crime and migration. My veins throb as though with the passage of underground trains. My digestive tract is sometimes clogged. There are security alerts. There's congestion, bottlenecks. Some of me is common, some of me is restricted. I have flats and high-rises. It doesn't need a genius to see what's going on. Greater London, *c'est moi.*'

The therapist coughed to hide a snigger of derision, but she failed to hide it completely. Judy knew she was foolish to come here to these expensive sessions in a part of town she never otherwise frequented to be mocked by a woman she neither knew nor trusted.

'I'm sorry,' the therapist said. 'I don't mean to be insulting, but I'm used to dealing with people who are disturbed or dysfunctional, not with people who fear they are turning into major world cities.'

'Then it appears I may be with the wrong therapist.'

'That may very well be true,' she agreed. 'Perhaps you should think about what kind of therapist might serve you better: a town planner, a local government official, a property developer.'

Judy started to cry. This too was a regular occurrence at these sessions, and in a way she welcomed it since it helped her to feel that they must at least be fiddling around in the right general area. The session was nearing its end and Judy could sense the therapist wanting to draw things to a professionally reassuring close.

'Judy,' she said, and she seemed to be doing her best to sound like a favourite, kindly aunt, 'it's always very pleasant to talk to you at these sessions of ours, and I would never turn you away if I thought you were in serious need of my services. But frankly, you're one of the saner people I've met in this insane city. And I'm not just talking about my clients now, I mean everyone, the entire population.

'So why not save yourself some money? Why not stop trying

to invent interesting symptoms for yourself? Why not cancel next week's appointment, and the one after that? And why don't we agree that you'll only come back to see me when there's something really dramatically, spectacularly wrong with you?'

# STATION TO STATION

It was late, nearly one in the morning, a cold, hard, winter night, and the lights of Sheffield Midland Station glowed bright and blank. The last train from London was long overdue and Mick Wilton was one of twenty or thirty people waiting to meet it. At the taxi rank at least the same number of Pakistani taxi drivers were sitting in their cabs, a boring wait for a cheap fare. In the car park Mick stood patiently beside his car, an old Mercedes. He was only partly aware of the image he presented, tall, broad, tough-looking, a low-rent character in a high-priced petrol-blue suit, worn now as ever with a spotless white T-shirt. He fought hard not to show the irritation he felt. Waiting was not his style, not in stations or anywhere else.

At last the train slunk on to the platform, indolent and heavy, ground to a halt and disgorged its passengers. Of course she was one of the last to emerge. He saw her coming down the concrete steps, small but conspicuous, a taut redhead in ankle boots, a short skirt and a gold leather jacket. She looked hard, much harder than him. Christ, he thought, she looks like a stripper. Then again, she was; Gabby, his girlfriend, his other half, or whatever you wanted to call it. But tonight there was something not right about her, a stress, a dishevelment that was caused by something more than just tiredness or a lengthy train journey, more even than the drink or drugs he suspected she might have been putting away the moment she was out of his sight. She walked over to the car, scarcely looking at him.

'All right?' he asked.

'No. Not all right.'

She got into the car but she didn't want him to take her home, not now, not yet, so he drove somewhere they could talk, up on one of the hills above the station where the big high-rises stood.

Gabby said, 'So I did the strip like I was supposed to and it went pretty well really. In this sort of club, restaurant, in this private room. It was a stag night and there were six of them and obviously they were rich, stuck-up, posh bastards but at first they didn't seem too bad really.

'So they gave me some champagne and made me do an encore. And one of them grabbed my arse and another one grabbed my tits, which you know can be all right if it's done the right way. And in any case, I can handle it. Then one of them tried to kiss me, which is obviously completely out of order, so I smacked him and then another one got into the act and, you know, we had a bit of a wrestle and basically they all raped me.'

Mick said nothing. He tried to keep his face as still and inert as a waxwork, but inside his head all kinds of pornographic loops flickered into life; six nameless men in a dark dining room, hunting prints on the walls, masked waiters. Gabby is naked except for a few erotic accessories, suspenders, fishnets, elbow-length gloves, and she's in tears, pursued by half a dozen savage, thick-necked, in-bred toffs, evening dress in tatters on their bullish frames, trousers down, cocks up.

'All of them?' he asked. 'All six?'

'Yeah,' she said. 'In turn. While the others held me down. It was pretty much your standard gang-rape.'

He put his hand out to stroke her face. It was meant to be reassuring, unthreatening and unsexual, but she pulled away and shuddered.

'Which act did you do?' he asked.

'Cleopatra.'

'Did you get paid after all this?'

15

'Yes.'

'That's something.'

'Not much.'

'Did they hurt you?'

'Yes.'

'Big guys?'

'A couple of them.'

'Not very bright boys obviously. Any idea who they are? Got any names?'

'Yeah, actually I have.'

She reached into the side pocket of her leather jacket and pulled out a flimsy piece of paper with handwriting on it.

'One of the waitresses saw what happened,' Gabby explained. 'She took pity on me. She knew them. They're regulars.'

Mick looked at the handwriting and saw it was a list of six men's names.

'Only names,' he said. 'No addresses?'

'Won't that be enough?'

'I hope so,' Mick said.

'I hope so too. What are you going to do?'

'I'm going to deal with it, right?'

'Good,' she said, and her whole being softened with relief. 'I knew you would.'

He got off the train at St Pancras, a lone man without luggage, the same suit, a new white T-shirt beneath. Pale winter sun leaked in through the grey glass vault overhead and made him feel both depressed and determined. He moved swiftly through the crowd and went out of the station to the open air where the black cabs waited. He got into the first one and said, 'Dickens Hotel, Park Lane.'

The couple of days he'd spent in Sheffield getting ready to leave had been bad. There was no living with Gabby. She wouldn't let him touch her, wouldn't let him near. He took it for granted that she'd want him to stay with her but she'd sent him back to his own flat, wouldn't even let him sleep on her couch. He'd tried not to be angry. He wanted to be sympathetic. He knew that she'd been through a lot and was hurting. But he had feelings too and he was thrown by the way she kept her distance. She said she didn't want to talk about it, and the sooner he got to London the better.

The driver started the meter and the cab chugged into life. The driver was not a talker and Mick was glad of that. He looked at the adverts lining the inside of the cab, one for a laptop computer, one for a plastic surgery clinic. Then he looked out of the cab window at the thick traffic, the motorbikes weaving in and out, at the blurred air, the people hurrying along the pavements, late for something. He hated everything he saw, and he allowed an expression of condescending disgust to settle on his face. London.

It felt strange to be here but it also felt inevitable, as though he'd had no choice in the matter. If somebody you cared about got hurt, then you did something about it. You came to their assistance. You protected them if you could, but if it was too late for that then you took your revenge. You handed out punishment. You made sure it would never happen again. It wasn't some complex code. There was no sense of chivalry or honour involved. It was just cause and effect. You did what needed doing. And when you got right down to it, maybe it didn't even have all that much to do with Gabby being 'his', with affection or attachment. Probably he'd have done the same for someone he cared for much less than he cared for Gabby. He might even have done it for a bloke.

He wanted to keep it simple and efficient. He didn't want to involve innocent people. He didn't want to prolong the agony. He just wanted to get the job done. There were six men out there who had it coming to them, and it was coming express delivery. The only thing that threatened to delay him, to make his life unnecessarily difficult, was the nature and complex unfamiliarity of London itself. If those six bastards had been Sheffield lads he'd already have finished the job by now.

At last the cab driver spoke. He said, 'What hotel did you say, mate?'

'The Dickens,' Mick replied.

The driver scratched the rolls of flesh at the back of his neck. 'I don't know that one.'

'I thought you London taxi drivers knew everything.'

The driver seemed undecided whether or not to take offence, but simply said, 'I know Park Lane but I don't know any Dickens Hotel.'

'Is that right?' Mick said, unhelpfully.

'OK,' the driver said, 'we'll find it when we get there.'

They got there and Mick was quietly impressed. This looked much better. This was a more pleasant version of London. There was still too much traffic but at least there was a park and the hotels looked moneyed and comfortable. He looked at their names, and they all seemed vaguely familiar, places heard about on television or read about in the papers: the Dorchester, the Inn on the Park, the Hilton, but there was no Dickens. The driver stopped the cab before the road dragged him into the currents of traffic swirling round Hyde Park Corner.

'I didn't like to say anything,' he said, 'but I didn't think there was a Dickens Hotel here.'

Mick sat impassively.

'I don't suppose you know what number Park Lane?' the driver asked.

As a matter of fact Mick did. He had a business card from the hotel. He took it out of his breast pocket and without saying a word handed it to the driver who looked at it for less than a second and then shook his head in mocking, disbelieving sympathy.

'You from out of town?' he asked.

'So?'

'You want bloody Park Lane, Hackney.'

'Do I?' said Mick. 'Take me there then.'

'I'm not going to bloody Hackney.'

'What's wrong with Hackney?'

'When you find someone to take you there, you'll find out. That's a tenner you owe me. Now on your way.'

'You're taking me there,' Mick said.

'No, I'm not, pal.'

Mick sat still and imperious. He wasn't going to lose his first argument in the big city.

'Out,' said the driver and he stepped from his cab. He opened the rear door and Mick could see he was carrying a baseball bat. That amused him.

'I said out. Or else.'

Mick, unruffled, said, 'You'll need more than a baseball bat,' and he exploded into violence. He grabbed the bat from the driver's hands, swirled it round and hit him across the nose twice. He leapt out of the cab, knocked the driver aside and went to the front where he kicked in both headlights. He was thinking of smashing the windows with the bat, puncturing the radiator, thinking of giving the driver a proper going over, when a sudden change came over him, as though a fatherly restraining hand had been put on his shoulder, sanity returning. He threw the bat aside and began to walk slowly away. 'I hate this town,' he said, and he broke into a run, dashing into the streets behind the big hotels before the driver could find any allies.

He soon stopped running. Running was no more his style than waiting, but he continued to cover ground, walking fast, determinedly, foolishly, lost. He had no idea where he was or where he was going. He felt furious and humiliated, and for a while at least the simple performance of looking as though he knew where he was heading was enough to help disperse the anger. The streets of Mayfair confused him. He had imagined that every street in London seethed with activity and population, yet these streets were more or less empty. The buildings were big and imposing but they had sucked in all the crowds from the pavement.

He walked for half an hour or more, in a straight line when

19

he could. His sense of direction was good enough to make sure that he made some progress and didn't backtrack on himself, but whether that progress was any use to him, whether his sense of direction was taking him anywhere worth going, he didn't know. At last, his anger all but gone, his pace slowing, Hackney still an undiscovered country, he grasped that he was truly lost.

He asked one or two people for directions, but they had no idea what he was talking about and he wasn't sure whether it was their foreignness to blame or his. The people he asked had no idea how to get to Hackney. It was a distant province, a place beyond the remit of cartographers, off the edge of the known world. At last he settled for asking a simpler question. 'Do you know where I can buy a map? A newsagent or something?'

He was addressing a tweedy, bearded, middle-aged man. He looked like a Londoner (whatever that meant), that was why Mick had chosen him. The man said, 'You're only round the corner from one of my favourite shops, the London Particular. They'll be able to sort you out.' And he gave directions that even Mick could follow.

Mick arrived at the London Particular, a bookshop of sorts, an old-fashioned, bay-windowed place, narrow at the front but opening out into a large, deep, sky-lit area at the rear. Mick went in a bit reluctantly. He sensed he was entering a specialist establishment. A newsagent would have been more welcoming and easier to deal with. The sheer quantity and density of stock in the shop was overwhelming; books, maps and guides, new and secondhand, were crammed into bookshelves of immense height and depth. They towered up to the ceiling, higher than a man could reach, and they were stacked two rows deep on some of the shelves. On the floor there were boxes, crates and sometimes just loose piles of guide books and magazines. In the centre of the shop was a table stacked high with precarious piles of books. He felt clumsy, out of place, his every movement threatening to knock over some carefully arranged construction.

There were a couple of browsers inside but he could see no assistant. He was tempted to walk out, but where would he walk to? He would wait until someone appeared. Meanwhile he continued to look at the stock, and only slowly and belatedly did it dawn on him that every single book, guide, map and magazine in the place had London as its subject. There were history books, memoirs, biographies, books on London architecture, on town planning, on immigration and riots and insurrection. The guide books, plenty of which were antique or written in foreign languages, offered specific and specialized routes through London. There were guides for rock music fans, for lesbians, for cemetery enthusiasts. Even the maps were specialized, being designated for walkers or motorists, parking maps, 3-D maps, 'murder' maps. A simple map, capable of getting him from A to B, from wherever he was now, to the Dickens Hotel, Hackney, seemed simultaneously too much and too little to ask for.

Then an assistant appeared and Mick's heart sank. There behind the counter was a Japanese-looking woman, young, attractive, smart, but very, very foreign. Mick shook his head, not at all surprised by his bad luck, and was heading for the door when he heard her call after him, 'Can I help you, sir?'

The voice didn't sound as though it could possibly have come from her. It was clipped and projected, without any trace of a foreign accent. In fact it was a posh, English, upper-class voice, far more pukka and correct than his own. It was the kind of voice he had been taught to dismiss and distrust: superior, middle class, southern.

He turned to her and said, 'You speak English.'

'Just a tad,' she replied.

'I'm lost,' he said. 'I need a map.'

Given the number of maps to choose from it would have been easy for her to treat his request dismissively, but she didn't. She was helpful, easygoing, not at all the snotty bitch that her voice had made Mick expect. She set him up with an

*A–Z*, even showing him the pages on which Hackney was to be found.

'First time in London?' she asked.

'No,' Mick said proudly. 'Third.'

'Do you think you might need a guide book?'

Well, he was going to need guidance, though he couldn't see exactly what kind of guide book would offer the sort of information he wanted. He said, 'Maybe,' and she directed him to the modern guide book section where he was duly baffled.

'Any recommendations?'

'How about this one?' she said.

She handed him a book called *Complete London*.

'Complete?' he queried.

'Yes.'

He looked puzzled and doubtful.

'Well, how can it be?' he said. 'If it was really complete it'd have to contain all the information in all these other books, wouldn't it? In fact, it'd have to contain all the information in all the books in the whole shop. Right?'

'I suppose that's true,' she admitted graciously.

'And all the information in all the books on London that you *don't* have in the shop. The book'd have to be bigger than the shop. In fact the book would probably have to be bigger than London itself, wouldn't it?'

'I'd never thought about it in quite that way,' she said.

'Well, think about it,' he said.

She pretended to think, but she did not pretend very hard.

'Maybe I should just pick one at random,' he said.

She bowed her head a little, submissively; the customer was right. She watched as without looking he reached out towards the bookcase. His fingers riffled the air and landed on the spine of a book called *Unreliable London* and he hooked it out. He stared at it curiously. Although it wasn't a secondhand book it was well battered as though it had sat neglected on the shelf for a very long time. The photograph on the cover, which was a little faded and a little out of focus, showed a dull shot of Tower Bridge.

'I can't vouch for that particular volume,' she said. 'Perhaps you should choose again.'

'No,' said Mick. 'I've made my choice. I was obviously meant to have this book.'

He said it with complete earnestness, but she wasn't sure whether he was joking or not. An English trait. They both smiled uncertainly at each other.

'What's your name?' Mick asked.

She hesitated before saying, 'Judy. Judy Tanaka.'

'Very exotic,' he said.

'Not really. In Japan, Tanaka is the equivalent of Smith.'

'But we're not in Japan, so it's still exotic, OK?'

'Fine,' she said, and she took the book and the map from him, rang them into the till and put them in a bag.

As he was paying he said, 'And where are you from?'

'Streatham,' she replied.

'Oh, right,' said Mick, as though the name meant something to him. It didn't, of course. It was just a foreign place that he'd never heard of. It might have been in Japan for all he knew.

A long time later, footsore but refusing to acknowledge it, he arrived at the Dickens Hotel, Park Lane, Hackney. It had been a long walk and he had passed a number of hotels on the way. A part of him had thought about abandoning the Dickens and checking into one of these. But he'd decided against it. You had to be careful in London. There were serious rip-offs waiting round every corner. A bloke he knew in Sheffield had recommended the Dickens, and that was good enough for him. You didn't want to go somewhere you didn't know and where they didn't want you.

Park Lane was a wide, busy, residential street, full of potholes and jammed with parked cars, although from what Mick had seen so far most London streets were like that. There was a boarded-up pub on the corner and a take-away offering dumplings and fritters.

It didn't look the kind of street that would contain a hotel. The houses were tall four-storey buildings that must once have belonged to the rich, but a look at the long row of doorbells outside each front door confirmed their rabid subdivision into flats.

A part of him would have been happy to know that he'd come to the wrong place for a second time but on the front of one of the houses he saw a polished brass plaque that said 'Dickens Hotel'. He had arrived. Yet it took more than a plaque to make a hotel and this place looking like nothing more than a boarding-house with misplaced and unconvincing pretensions. And after he'd climbed the half-dozen steps to the front door and rung a bell, he was immediately confronted by a woman who could only be a landlady.

Her age was hard to guess and you could tell she wanted to make guessing difficult. The hair was dyed jet black, the clothes could have belonged to a brash eighteen-year-old. The make-up was plentiful and a little old-fashioned, suitable, say, for a forties Hollywood musical. He couldn't stop staring at the beauty spot that he felt sure had been painted on her right cheek.

In return she looked at him only fleetingly, then said, 'I was expecting you hours ago.'

'I came by the scenic route,' he said.

'What?'

'I walked.'

The entrance hall wasn't badly kept. The carpet and wallpaper were new, there was a big gold-framed mirror and a couple of reproduction chairs. But Mick was taken to the third floor, a place of streaked walls and lino and chipped paintwork. His room, situated next to the shared bathroom, was small, with a candlewick bedspread and wallpaper that erupted with pink roses. There were only a few stains on the carpet, only a couple of cigarette burns on the bedside table. The mirror on the wardrobe had only a small crack and the lace curtain across the window had definitely been washed within living memory. He pushed it aside and looked down into the street.

The woman said, 'You must be very fit if you walked all the way from St Pancras.'

'Yeah, I'm in training.'

She was impressed. Mick viewed the street scene with disdain. Across the road a man was committing major surgery on a collision-damaged BMW. A female crustie was walking down the street dragging a skinny, grubby Dalmatian behind her. It was a struggle since the dog was doing its best to shit as it walked and was leaving a line of long slender turds along the centre of the pavement.

'What do you call this area?' Mick asked.

'I like to call it Stoke Newington,' said the landlady. 'Why?'

'I wanted to make sure I hadn't entered the twilight zone,' Mick replied.

But he took the room. What else was he going to do? It was just a room. It held no horrors, and he wasn't planning to be there long. Night was falling. He sat on the bed and watched the gathering darkness drain the pink roses of their violent hue. He wondered if he could face fritters and dumplings. He opened the door of the wardrobe and found that someone had left a girlie mag lying there face up. He thought the model on the cover looked strangely like Gabby. He slammed the wardrobe door shut, spread himself out on the bed and stared up at the cracks in the ceiling. Before long he could make out faces and the outlines of mythical countries.

# THE WALKER'S DIARY

# THE PENULTIMATE DAYS

I was worn out today as I walked the city. The weather was bitter and my overcoat was barely warm enough. My feet and my back and my head all ached. As the task nears completion, it becomes more frustrating. The need to be finished, to be at an end, is overwhelming. I have worn myself out on this city. It has eroded me. I have left no mark on it but I have been worn down like a pencil, reduced to a stub.

I have seen it all, the rotting hills, the hungover squares. I have been through the shy neighbourhoods and all the half-deserted streets, and I have been left drained and evacuated.

I have been to the boundary, to the wall, to the places where the city ends, where the train tracks knot together, where the pylons hiss and fizz their dissatisfaction, where the workings show, the innards, the guts, the secretions, to the place where we hone our taste for fragments. Here in this kaleidoscope of ruins, here where the fabric develops stress fractures, where the plots unravel, and the old stories get forgotten, where oral history is speechless, where myth dies, I have been both lost and found.

I have seen history and nostalgia. I have seen love and death and their pale companions sex and violence. I have seen a fine town, a nation, a great cesspool, the modern Babylon. In Phillimore Gardens, South Kensington, I looked in through a basement window and watched a heavy woman dressed only in a corset as she kissed a man in a suit and tie.

I saw statues of Boadicea, John Kennedy and Bomber Harris. I saw a minor road accident in Windmill Road, Mitcham. I saw a woman pissing in the street in Wandsworth. I took my stand on a broken arch of London Bridge to sketch the ruins of St Paul's. It was a day like any other. I walked and I watched. I did my best to be everybody's blue-eyed boy.

I'm not naive enough to believe I know the whole story, but I think I have seen both the broad sweep and the particulars, annihilation rolling in like a fog, as comic and as zany as consumption; all those forgotten diseases: apoplexy, dropsy, canker, spotted fever, palsy, scrofula. I have developed a nostalgia for sedition, for mob rule, the burning of gaols, the contagion of fury.

I saw the solid, sturdy monuments to trade and its names, the Hoover factory, the Oxo Tower, the Tate Gallery; sweet and sour reminders of empire. I went along wandering roads that waste everybody's time. I saw a lost London of public executions, of coffee houses, the Euston Arch, Newgate, Bedlam. I heard the unfamiliar poetry of extinct trades, a poetry that speaks of a city's past, of a long-gone culture: cinder-shifters, tallow-chandlers, ballad-sellers, hawkers of fish, soap-boilers, hammermen.

I listened too to the plots and rhythms of place names. What was in them? I heard the cracked narratives of the clothed city: the Mozart estate, not famed for its prodigies or genius; the unsnake-like Serpentine; King's Cross, Queen's Park, Prince of Wales Road – places not much frequented by royalty. I saw the slew of history, of kings and pretenders, developers and reformers, visionaries and bureaucrats, martyrs and wide boys. I read the obvious eponyms, the roads named after Cromwell, Wellington, Addison, Albert, Mountbatten, Mandela. I saw little pieces of London which are forever foreign: Maida Vale, Trafalgar, Waterloo, Mafeking Road, Sumatra Road, Yukon Road, two Ladysmith Avenues, six Ladysmith Roads. I saw the quixotic and quaint: Artichoke Hill, Quaggy Walk, Yuletide Close, Pansy Gardens, Evangelist Road.

Often the city felt alive, as though it had flesh and blood, arteries, nerve centres, beauty spots, scars, guts, a heart, parasites, an anus. But which was which? Where was the soul? Where was the cloaca?

I followed in their footsteps; all the great Londoners, the native and the adopted: Dickens and Pepys and Boswell and Johnson and Evelyn and Wat Tyler and Guy Fawkes and Betjeman and Nash and Wren and Newton and Marx and Dick Whittington and, well, you name them.

I went to St Anne's Court in Soho, a little paved alleyway where, according to her autobiography, Marianne Faithfull sat on a wall every day for several years, strung out on heroin. Her only solace was when Kenneth Anger or Brion Gysin came along and fed her. Not exactly the life of our normal street addict.

In Hertford Road, Edmonton, there was a man wheeling a little girl in a pushchair and he kept saying to the child, 'If I give you some sweeties you'll be my friend, won't you?' He said it over and over again, love and desperation endlessly repeated in his voice.

I saw the City, a place of deals and commodities, of money and electronic transfer, a place that believes in futures, that thrives on confidence, a place where markets are made, where fortunes are composed and dissipated, where chaos is not simply a theory.

In Lupus Street, Pimlico, I saw a traffic warden. He was wearing a little peaked cap, and a blue nylon anorak with the collar turned up. He didn't look like much, but the way he prowled down the street, muscle-bound and dangerous, you'd have thought he was the villain in a James Bond film.

In Regent Street, in the window of Dickins and Jones, a display assistant was painting the lips of the mannikins a pale cherry red.

I found myself on the bridge, between the shores, connected with the past yet living in some poorly imagined future, in this new place of somebody else's making, futuristically quaint perhaps with cars like Bakelite radios, men with jet packs strapped to their shoulders, dressed in skin-tight silver synthetics, helicopters and monorails full of commuters. We thought it might be like this, the London of Dan Dare. We were wrong to expect the expected.

London (a city only passingly like hell) is not everything. It is not even all things to some men, but in a certain way it's more than enough, definitely more than enough for me. It contains all the data from which the ideal city might be constructed; a visible, hard city, a city of forking paths, no city of angels. This also has been one of the dark places of the earth, a place where I have looked to be a victim of someone else's vengeance, where I have looked for the metropolitan assassin. The city of cross words.

Sometimes I got lost, or perhaps I was always lost, lost before I started and more lost as I travelled. But it was never a matter of geography, not a malaise that the cartographers could rid me of. I developed a taste for spaces cleansed by plague and fire, by blitzes and bulldozers.

Soon I will no longer have use for a map. Maps are euphemisms, clean, clear, self-explanatory substitutes for all the mess and mayhem, the clutter and ambivalence and blurring and intermeshing weft and warp of the real places they purport to describe. They are fake documents, pathetic simplifications and falsifications. They're no longer necessary since I have created a new London, not one made out of stone and brick, tarmac and concrete, but a London created out of memory, imagination and shoe leather. I have dreamed it. I have made my dreams come true.

Even in the beginning it did not feel like a quest, much less like a journey, though I always suspected there was a destination, a final still point. Although I knew this was not an adventure story, although I did not believe I was paddling up-river, I knew there were things waiting for me in the darkness, in unfamiliar manors, walls with ears, with eyes, with teeth, with everything, things that were unknown and certainly nameless, marked cards, new geographies, bullets with my name on them. Tomorrow I find them or they find me. The end is in my sights.

The London Walker is his own worst enemy.

# SCROLL

Anita looked at the words on the screen and scrolled through the text again, trying to decide exactly what she was looking at. In one sense the answer was easy enough. She was looking at the contents of a computer disk she had found in a desk drawer in the study in her own house. It had been hidden under a pile of envelopes, but it seemed to her that it had been hidden in a way that guaranteed it would be found sooner rather than later. There was a label on the disk in her husband Stuart's handwriting, but all it said was 'UNFINISHED'.

She had come home today after barely a couple of hours at work. She had claimed to have a headache, but it was a condition more metaphorical than medical. She needed room and time to think about work, something she could only do when not actually *at* work. There was a new crisis just around the corner and she would soon have to make some very big and difficult decisions. She wished she didn't have to make them alone. But business matters seemed irrelevant the moment she found the disk.

The discovery had been so casual yet it seemed so vital to her. It was, in a sense, what she had been looking for all along, although her searching had been barely conscious. Yet now that she had made her discovery she knew she had expected more and she had expected worse. She had feared there would be something shameful, something sick and violent and possibly pornographic, something perverse and destructive, something

31

she might be able to understand but would possibly never be able to forgive. Instead she had found something she simply did not fully understand, pages of some sort of journal or diary, perhaps a confession, though she couldn't work out exactly what it was her husband was confessing to. If anything it seemed to be a text that relished obfuscation, that was trying hard not to give up its meaning too easily.

She read the words again but remained confused. It was not what she wanted it to be. It was not an explanation. She wanted a document, a manifesto, that would make sense of what she increasingly thought of as her husband's recent 'absence'. That was what she called it, though it was not the most obvious term. It was not any sort of physical absence. He was there every morning and evening. They worked together in a manner of speaking. He spent time with her, talked to her. They slept their nights in the same bed. They had sex as often as any couple who've been married for ten years. He spent most of his time behaving like a good husband.

Nor was there any easily identifiable emotional absence. Stuart was attentive and loving. He was there for her. He supported and encouraged her when needed, and he knew when to leave her alone. He was doing nothing wrong and yet she had a terrible sense of his being not quite there. She wanted to know where he was and why. And perhaps, she now thought, he was in these words.

Stuart's working day was the sort that entitled, indeed required, him to be away and out of touch for many hours, and that had never bothered her before; in a sense she'd arranged it that way, but now it *did* bother her. The unaccounted parts of his life had become an intolerable mystery to her, and for a long time she'd had no idea how to solve the mystery. She couldn't ask him. She could hardly follow him, could hardly employ a private detective. People like her didn't do things like that. She didn't want to make a fool of herself.

She had thought it just possible that he was doing something as innocent and banal as attending a gym or health club, for one of the strangest things about Stuart was that he was looking so healthy. He'd lost weight recently, nothing dramatic, just a gradual slimming down. And his face had colour. He looked good, he looked younger.

A less confident wife would have suspected an affair but Anita did not, and even if she *had* suspected, even if she'd had proof, it wouldn't have worried her the way she was worried now. She was secure enough, and she knew her husband was responsible enough, that she didn't have to fear his walking out. He'd had at least one affair that she'd known about. It had been with a very junior employee. Anita hadn't liked the idea, hadn't liked the reality, but she'd lived with it. She'd gritted her teeth and waited for it to be over, and sure enough it soon had been.

But the unfaithful Stuart's behaviour had been nothing like this. This was something quite new, something she suspected and feared had nothing at all to do with sex or love or betrayal, nor with anything else with which she was familiar.

She'd tried gently asking friends and colleagues whether they'd detected anything different about Stuart and they'd all said no. But even if someone had been prepared to humour her, they would surely have thought the changes were for the better. Stuart had seemed happier recently. In fact he had seemed positively serene. In theory he had no less than the usual number of worries but they no longer threatened or disturbed him. He looked like a man who had achieved wisdom and contentment. No wonder she was terrified.

She realized that the few pages she'd been reading on the screen explained very, very little. Stuart had, of course, always been a great fan of London, had always gained energy from the city. But this strange poetic ramble did nothing to justify his serenity, nor her feelings about him. However, she had read only one file. She knew that the disk contained a great deal more information, apparently a great many more of her husband's words. She looked at the other file names. They were intriguing but unrevealing: WRAPAROUND, DISCOVERY, V & D. She knew she would have to read them all. She always hated reading screens. She wanted hard copy. She found another file, set up the printer, then went downstairs to make coffee while the machine churned out the next instalment of Stuart's diary.

# PARTICULARS

Two lost, frustrating days passed before Mick Wilton returned to the London Particular, days in which he came to fear that he might be making a fool of himself in this alien, overpopulated capital. They were days in which he'd not even known where to start. He had drifted the streets, aimlessly, idiotically, a man without direction. At last he'd decided that the bookshop was his only hope. He found it using the *A–Z*, and the address on the paper bag the book had come in.

Again the bookshop contained few customers and Mick was pleased to see the same assistant behind the counter. It was odd to think this complete stranger was the person he knew best in the whole city. She recognized him and half-smiled.

'Hello there, Judy!' he said quickly. 'I need some assistance.'

'Yes, sir, what were you looking for?'

'Don't call me sir. It's Mick.' Then he hesitated, embarrassed to be admitting need. 'Hey, are you really English?'

'It depends what you mean by English. It depends what you mean by really.'

'OK,' he said, happy to accept that there were any number of things that might be meant by those words. 'But how well do you know London?'

'I know London,' she said.

It was the answer he wanted. He moved closer to the counter and leaned on it conspiratorially.

'This assistance that I need, it's not really very complicated,' he said, and he took a deep breath. 'You see there are some friends of mine who I've lost contact with, old college pals kind of thing. And obviously I know their names but I don't know their addresses any more. I mean they've moved since I last saw them. So like, for example, I look them up in the phone book and there's maybe six Graham Pryces and four Justin Carrs, and the addresses mean nothing to me because I'm not a Londoner, and I don't want to have to go round to every single address looking to see if I've got the right one. So I need some local knowledge.

'You see, I happen to know that these old friends of mine have done pretty well for themselves. And I'm sure somebody like you, who *is* a Londoner, could check these addresses and say, yeah, that's the sort of place a well-to-do person would be living.'

He finished, took another breath, and looked at her hopefully.

'Why don't you just ring all the different numbers until you find the right person?' she said.

'I want it to be a surprise.'

Her glance told him she was completely unconvinced.

'That's why I wanted to be sure you really knew London,' he said.

'I know London,' she repeated.

'So are you going to help me or not?'

Out of his pockets he pulled a list of names and several folded pages torn from telephone directories.

'It sounds fishy,' she said.

'I realize that, but it's not. Honest. What can I do to convince you?'

'Frankly, I don't know.'

He looked around as though the setting itself might offer some chance for him to prove himself. Then he caught sight of one of the other customers in the back of the shop and the opportunity came straight to him.

'You see that guy over there,' he said very quietly, nodding

36

towards a bald, skinny man in a raincoat. 'He's hiding a hundred quid's worth of atlases underneath his coat.'

'You saw him?' she said, shocked.

Mick nodded and the man turned his head a little towards them, just enough to indicate that he knew he was being talked about. He waited a moment then started for the door, his progress marked by an elaborate casualness. Mick took two steps away from the counter and stood blocking the exit.

'Put the books on the counter,' he said to the shoplifter.

'What books?' the man asked.

'Don't get me angry, you little twat,' Mick said, and the man immediately produced the atlases and placed them on the counter.

'All right,' he said, and he shrugged. 'You can't have me for nicking them 'cause I hadn't left the premises.'

Mick stared at him with bored contempt. 'Now pay for them,' he said.

'I don't want to pay for them,' the man said.

'I know you don't, but you're going to.'

The man decided to make a run for it, and he launched a determined effort to get past Mick and through the door. Mick made only a perfunctory attempt to stop him, apparently letting himself be shouldered out of the way. The shoplifter accelerated down the street in a panic and Mick turned to Judy who asked, 'How did you know he was stealing books?'

'Well, I could tell you it was because I used to be a store detective.'

She did not look convinced, even less so when Mick placed a wallet on the counter and offered it to her.

'What's that?' she asked.

'The guy's wallet.'

She shook her head in disbelief, amused despite herself.

'It's OK,' said Mick. 'He won't be coming back for it.'

'You're a pickpocket as well as everything else.'

'What's everything else?'

'I don't know yet.'

37

'Surely I've earned myself something,' he said winningly. 'A bit of help? A bit of information?'

Half an hour later Judy Tanaka was on her break and they were drinking coffee in an Italian caff and she was doing her best to help him. She turned back and forth between the list of names and the torn pages of telephone directory, and occasionally she consulted the index of her *A–Z*.

'This isn't as easy as it looks,' she said.

'It doesn't look easy at all.'

'Like here you've got a Jonathan Sands, and there are six people called J or John Sands in the phone book. Four of them I think we can rule out but that still leaves one in Hampstead, one in Chelsea, both pricey addresses, you know? It could be either.'

'I can see the problem,' Mick said.

She continued to concentrate on her task, but she asked distractedly, 'What are you going to do when you track down these people?'

'We're going to have a reunion party.'

'Are you a private detective or something?'

'Something,' he said.

'Are you some sort of criminal?'

'Would it make a difference?'

'I don't know. Would I be an accessory?'

She smiled as she said it. The idea didn't particularly displease her.

'Accessory to what? Partying?'

She smiled more broadly. She knew he had no reason to be honest with her, and that was probably for the best. She found the prospect of his criminality intriguing but she didn't necessarily want to know any detail.

'Really,' she said, and she sounded disappointed, 'there's only one of these people I can be absolutely certain about: Philip Masterson. For that name there's only one address that fits the bill at all. It's in Maida Vale, whereas all the other Philip

Mastersons live in Walthamstow or Peckham or areas like that. He has to be the one.'

Mick looked at her unsurely. These were all place names he'd never heard before. They evoked nothing for him, had no ring to them, no connotations. But he nodded willingly enough. He believed her. He trusted her to the extent that he had to. She was his only ally, his only source of favours and information. She handed back the pages of directory and pointed out the address that fitted.

'You're good,' he said.

'Not bad for someone who looks like a foreigner, eh?' she said. 'Do you know where Maida Vale is?'

'It's OK,' he said triumphantly. 'I've got a map, remember.'

# CONSERVATORY

I f there was one thing above all others that made Sally
Masterson and her husband Philip decide to buy the maisonette, it was the Victorian-style conservatory; an iron-framed
structure with spangles of red and blue stained glass and french
windows that opened out on to the elegant and well-stocked,
if pocket-size, walled garden. The conservatory was lovely,
bright, spacious, atmospheric: a special place, an arena.

They had no complaints about the rest of the property. They
liked the fact that it provided living accommodation on two
floors, ground and garden level. Sally liked the living room,
especially the fireplace with its reproduction William De
Morgan tiles. Philip was more impressed by the generously
proportioned bedrooms, the wide hallway and the spacious en
suite bathroom. All these factors had been persuasive enough,
but it wasn't until Sally saw the conservatory that she completely lost her heart. In fact, she loved it so much she had been
prepared to postpone their honeymoon for the pleasure of
moving straight into their new home.

Sally had not wanted to change much about the conservatory.
She knew there were times when a space had to be left to
express its own essential personality. Nevertheless she had felt
the need to express her own personality at the same time, hence
the huge bunches of dried herbs, her collection of novelty salt
and pepper shakers and a kind of totem pole from somewhere
in Canada. Apart from that all she'd had to do was get a few

panes of glass replaced and have the frames painted. Decisions about furniture had been easy enough: a rattan sofa, a small perforated steel table and a couple of Rietveld zigzag timber chairs. The conservatory was now perfection, although she sometimes wondered about blinds or curtains to keep the neighbours at bay.

She would always vehemently deny that she was a snob. For example, it would have been possible, in fact it would have been all too easy, to claim that their new home was in Little Venice, but she made no such claim. She was quite happy to say she lived in Maida Vale. She knew that before long she would soon be moving on and up, but for now it would do, at least so long as she had her totally perfect conservatory.

It was early; seven in the morning. She had risen, showered and had put on only underwear and stockings. She was now seated at the steel table in the conservatory drinking laceratingly strong black coffee. Philip was out taking his daily early-morning jog. She looked at her watch and saw that he was a little behind schedule. A familiar irritation surged through her.

Sally was a trim, well-groomed, slightly boyish blonde. Her hair was cut into a short no-nonsense bob. Her breasts were small and her legs were long. Her eyes were a soft blue and her mouth was thin-lipped though pleasantly curved. When not in her underwear and stockings, her style of dress could be a little severe, and it was possible to think she was, austere, asexual, but that would have been a terrible mistake.

At last, with some relief, she heard the front door open and close, heard Philip's weighty feet on the ground floor landing, heard him descending the stairs to the lower level. He stood in the doorway between the breakfast room and the conservatory, breathing a shade heavily. He was sweaty and oxygenated. She loved it.

He said, 'Now?'

She said, 'Yes. Now. Of course. Here and now. Quickly.'

Philip Masterson was a good-looking man, not film star good-looking, not good-looking in a way that meant he, or

Sally, would ever have to fight off women; but when she first presented him to her girlfriends they all agreed that she had got herself a chunky handsome husband. He was dark and hirsute. There was thick hair on his head, arms and back, and there were many occasions when he needed to shave twice in a day. He was perhaps a little overweight for some tastes, which was surprising given that he took so much exercise; squash and swimming and occasional football, as well as the jogging. But he had a strong, big-boned frame and Sally thought he carried his bulk easily.

He smiled roguishly and went into the conservatory to where Sally was ready and waiting for him. He went up to her, slid his hand inside her white lace briefs and pressed his big hot palm against her belly. She quaked with familiar expectation. She helped him off with his T-shirt, shorts and jock strap. She let him kick aside his own shoes and socks while she lowered her panties, folded them and placed them neatly on the unused chair. That was all she would be taking off. He would be hot and unshaven, laced with sweat, and she would be cool in white bra and sheer stockings. They wouldn't do any kissing, since that would destroy her make-up, but she was happy to be, in fact insisted on being, mauled, thrown around, thoroughly fucked.

He began by pulling her to her feet and dragging her over to the rattan sofa. He touched her neck, breasts, stomach, and moved himself so that his penis came into handy proximity of her mouth. She took it in her hand, firmly and quite fondly, but she pushed it away to avoid smearing her lipstick, then she got up from the sofa, finding it too soft and comfortable.

Philip took her by the wrists and spun her round. He squeezed her bottom before pulling her to him, snaking his hands around her and directing her towards the french windows. Her finely manicured hands grabbed the door handles. She braced herself, her head arched forward and Philip eased her thighs apart, stroked her investigatively before penetrating her.

His actions were athletic, strong, purposeful, deeply felt. Sally's face was tight, grimacing, fierce. You might have looked at that face and thought she wasn't enjoying this very much, but that would have been another mistake.

And she enjoyed herself even more as Masterson prised her away from the doors and they inched their way slowly, a little awkwardly, into the centre of the conservatory. They had to disconnect briefly and Masterson took the opportunity to sink to his knees and Sally went dog-like in front of him, her buttocks high, her legs wide apart. His hands gripped her hips as though they were conveniently placed handles of flesh and bone. His rhythm remained slow and constant, unhurried but insistent. He was prolonging the experience rather than hurrying it along and bringing it to its conclusion. This was not quite right for Sally.

She turned her head to make brief eye contact with him, and as she fixed him with her glance she said, 'That's not hard enough, you bastard,' and that spurred him on no end. He pushed her head down with the flat of his hand so that she fell all the way forward, her torso flattening and slipping against the cool smooth expanse of the conservatory's pink sandstone tiles. He dragged her back towards him in a charade of savagery and mastery and he finished off with a few hard, ferocious strokes, not great in number but putting all he'd got into each of them and into her. When she knew he was coming then she could let herself go too, and as she climaxed she yelled, 'Oh, Mummy.'

He withdrew briskly, stood up and made for the shower. Soon Sally would get up too, collect herself and dress for work, but for a few savoured moments she lay there motionless, and if you had been in a position to peer in through the roof of the conservatory you would have seen her looking as happy as she ever looked, having been had briskly and sweatily and uncomplicatedly on the floor in her very favourite place.

★

43

Mick Wilton was, in fact, in just such a position, lodged in the middle branches of a mature horsechestnut tree that overlooked the Mastersons' conservatory. And having watched the floor-show with great, perhaps indecent, interest, he moved from his vantage point, and climbed easily through a couple of the neighbouring gardens so that he was there at the front of the house, ready for Philip Masterson's departure for work.

Less than ten minutes later, now shaved and showered, Masterson bounced out of his front door. He was wearing a navy wool pinstriped, three-piece suit and he was carrying a full briefcase, but he still looked intensely athletic, as though the day would be a series of sporting contests, jousts; not just business as usual. He repeatedly tossed his car keys up in the air and caught them as he walked along the tree-lined street, along the row of residents' parking spaces until he came to his own car, an E-type convertible, a low-slung, racing-green slab with personalized number plates. The hood was up and even though it was a cold winter morning he intended to lower it before driving to work. That was the sort of chap he was. But as he got closer he saw that someone had cut three long, jagged slashes through the thick black material of the hood.

'Fuck,' he shouted at the world. 'Fucking hell.' And he ran up to the car, threw down his briefcase and looked as though he might stamp his feet and throw a full-blown tantrum.

Then, out of nowhere, Mick appeared. He was someone who would always be better suited to the night than to the early morning, but he was trying hard to look like a man who was on his way to work, a man who had heard the shouting of a neighbour and had decided to help.

In what he took to be a neighbourly fashion he said, 'Car trouble?'

'You could say that,' Masterson replied. 'Some bastard's done this,' and he pointed at the hood.

'That's a rotten dirty trick,' Mick sympathized.

'If I ever get my hands on them . . .' said Masterson.

'Yeah,' said Mick and he went over to have a closer look at

the damage. He inspected the cut material and said, 'How much does a new hood cost?'

'I don't know,' Masterson said. 'Enough. But that's not really the point.'

'Are you insured?'

'Of course I'm insured, but . . .'

Masterson calmed down a little, not because he felt any more philosophical about the damage but simply because he knew there was nothing he could do about it at the moment and because he had to get to work. 'I'll worry about it later,' he said, and he began to undo the catches that held the hood in place.

'Need any help?' Mick asked.

'No.'

But Mick took no notice and started grabbing at the edge of the material.

'I can do it quicker myself,' Masterson insisted, in what he generally knew to be a commanding voice.

Mick said, 'Oh, OK,' and he stopped fiddling with the hood. Instead he stood back and stared at Masterson as he completed the operation, rather clumsily since he was angry and because he didn't like being stared at. Then, when Masterson was finished and had got into the driver's seat, he watched in disbelief as Mick opened the car's passenger door and slid in beside him. The leather seats didn't fit Mick's body very well but he tried to get comfortable and he reached for the seat belt to strap himself in.

'Excuse me,' Masterson bawled. 'Excuse me. What exactly do you think you're doing? Get out of my fucking car. Now. No argument. All right?'

Mick shook his head. 'I cannot tell a lie, Masterson. It was me who slashed your hood.'

'What?'

'It was a bit juvenile, I know.'

'What? Did I hear you correctly? Who the fuck are you? And how do you know my name?'

Masterson raised his clenched fist as though he was about to punch Mick in the face.

'Bad idea to do that,' said Mick. 'I have this thing in my inside pocket. It's a 9 millimetre, fifteen round EAA Witness. Solid steel construction, three dot sighting system, combat trigger guard, staggered high capacity magazine. I got it from America. It's nice. It gets the job done. Honest.'

He opened his jacket so that Masterson could see the hard outline of the gun against the lining. Masterson's fist still hung futilely in mid-air, then his fingers unclenched and he gingerly put his hand on the huge, wooden steering wheel.

'What do you want?' he asked, moving and speaking with a new-found, meticulous precision.

'That'll become obvious,' said Mick. 'But for now just drive.'

Masterson obeyed, and as he set the car in motion Mick admired the vehicle: the short black gear lever and silver hand brake, the serious sculpted dashboard, the long snout of the car pushing out in front of them. Then he looked out at the street they were driving along, still Masterson's street.

'London,' said Mick. 'Just like I pictured it. Skyscrapers and everything.' But Masterson didn't know what he was talking about.

'I don't know much about London,' Mick continued, 'but this looks like a nice enough place to live. Wide streets. Plenty of trees.'

'We like it,' said Masterson.

'What would a house like yours cost?'

'We don't have the whole house actually, just a maisonette.'

'Still, it can't come cheap.'

'I don't see that it's any of your business, actually.'

'Well, I'm the one with the gun.'

'I'm not frightened of you, you know.'

'No? Then you're very stupid. So what's the house worth?'

It took Masterson no time at all to realize the significance of the gun.

'About two hundred grand,' he said. 'It's a very nice maisonette.'

'Well, yeah, it'd need to be. In Yorkshire that sort of money'd buy you a mansion.'

'Unfortunately I happen not to work in Yorkshire.'

'What line of work are you in anyway, Philip?'

He thought about telling Mick to mind his own business again, but he knew it would be useless.

'I work in the City,' he said.

'Yeah? Which city?'

'THE City. The City of London.'

'Yeah, but what do you do?'

'I do the kinds of thing you do in the City. I buy and sell. I deal. Brokerage. OK?'

'Oh right, I'm with you. You mean the CITY. People use the term all the time, but nobody knows what it means.'

'Some of us do.'

'Go on then.'

Patiently as if explaining to an insistent but not very bright child Masterson said, 'Historically the City has been the most important financial centre in the world, a place where money and markets are made. And even though its power has declined in the face of Tokyo and New York, it still ranks in many ways as the leader in global finance. Geographically the City is the square mile of London that contains international banking institutions such as the Bank of England, Lloyd's of London, the Stock Exchange, the Baltic Exchange et cetera, et cetera.'

'Must be handy having them all so close together.'

'In the age of the computer, less so, but for various historic reasons, mostly to do with monarchy and empire, we're all there together, yes.'

'So if you were a member of some terrorist gang and you planted a couple of bombs in the City, it wouldn't matter if you missed one target, you'd still be bound to blow up something worth destroying.'

'Arguably, yes.'

'So maybe you should all split up, some of you go to Land's End, some to John o'Groats, some of you come up to Sheffield.'

He said it drily and he didn't laugh, and yet he wasn't taking himself absolutely seriously. But he seemed to be demanding some reaction from Masterson. In the event Masterson said, 'What do you want?' There was a little desperation in his voice. 'Is this a mugging? You want my wallet?'

Mick was non-committal. 'OK, I'll have your wallet,' he said, but he said it as though he was doing Masterson a favour.

Masterson handed over a smart grey pigskin wallet and Mick flicked through it, extracted a few twenty pound notes but left the credit cards in place.

'I wouldn't normally take your money,' Mick said, 'but this is such an expensive town. City.' And he handed back the wallet.

'If you want the car, you can have the car too,' said Masterson.

'Yeah, why not? It's insured after all.'

'I'm not going to fight you,' said Masterson.

'You're telling me,' Mick agreed. 'Nah, I don't want your car. I don't think I could cope with London traffic. It scares the life out of me.'

'Then what do you want?'

'I don't really know. I'm new here. What did I ought to see?'

'What are you talking about?'

'Go on. Show me some sights. Take me on a tour of London.'

'This is rather stupid.'

'You think so?' said Mick. 'OK then, pull over.'

Masterson pulled over and stopped the car. He looked greatly relieved as if the ordeal was over, as though this brief encounter with a madman might now be concluded. He would soon be at work, maybe even joking about it with his colleagues. His hand rested on the gear lever and he waited for Mick to say something, make some move, to get out and leave him alone.

But Mick didn't get out. He reached over for Masterson's left hand. In one brisk movement he took the little finger and jerked it back as far as it would go. There was a little resistance, then a soft, brittle snap and Masterson screamed with pain as the finger broke. He looked at his assailant in utter disbelief. This couldn't be happening to him.

'Don't accuse me of being stupid,' said Mick. 'Now drive on. I want to see Big Ben.'

Wincing with pain, Masterson clicked the car into gear and they set off again into traffic.

'Is this rush hour then?'

'Yes.'

'Well, where's all the traffic? I mean, this isn't so bad, is it? I've seen worse traffic jams in Bramall Lane, that's in Sheffield, where United play. And what about the pollution they're always talking about? I mean, it can't be all that bad, can it? Not if people like you drive around in open-top cars.'

'I suppose you're right,' Masterson said.

'That's the spirit,' said Mick. He was friendly now. 'You must be a bit of a tough guy,' he said reassuringly. 'A lot of men faint when you break their finger.'

Masterson did not receive the compliment with any grace. He watched the road, tried to be neutral, to do nothing that would rile Mick. They drove in silence for a while, Mick watching the passing scene with interest. When they drove into Trafalgar Square Mick recognized it at once and sat up in his seat, alert and excited. He gawped up at Nelson's Column, as beguiled as any tourist.

'Can't they do anything about those pigeons?' he wondered aloud.

Then they went down Whitehall until the Houses of Parliament came into view, but this time Mick didn't see anything he recognized.

Masterson said, 'What now?'

'What?' said Mick. 'Are we there?'

'That's Big Ben over there.'

49

'Really?' said Mick in surprise. 'No. Get away. Surely Big Ben ought to be bigger than that.'

'No, that's how big Big Ben is.'

'Well, I have to say I'm a bit disappointed. I was expecting more. Maybe I was expecting too much. I thought it'd be a huge thing like a skyscraper.'

'Sorry,' said Masterson.

'No, it's not your fault. OK, let's try again. Where next? How about Kew Gardens?'

'That's really a very long way from here.'

'Really? How far?'

'About an hour's drive, I suppose.'

'That's no good,' Mick said. 'How about Hampton Court?'

'That's even further.'

Mick shook his head, perturbed and concerned. 'That's inconvenient, isn't it? You'd think they'd put all the famous places next to each other, wouldn't you?'

Masterson looked at him dubiously. He still couldn't tell whether Mick was really as naive and obtuse as he was acting. There was no hint of irony, no sense that he was making jokes, and yet Masterson didn't think he was dealing with a stupid man.

'OK then,' Mick said. 'You choose. Show me something that's nearby. Some important sight.'

'Do we have to do this?' Masterson pleaded.

'Yes, we do.'

'Right then, how about St Paul's?'

'Is that big? Is it impressive?'

'I think so.'

'You're on then.'

'Look,' Masterson said, a curious blend of hopelessness and forced, unfelt, pacifying patience, 'if all you want is a sightseeing tour of London, why don't you get on one of the tourist buses?'

'And why don't I break another one of your fingers, yeah?'

'No, no, you don't have to do that.'

'Don't get funny then.'

'I'm not being funny, but my finger's killing me actually. The pain's terrible. I think I ought to get to a hospital.'

'You'll be all right. I've done it before. It hurts but it's not serious. I mean, cricketers break their fingers and then go on to score centuries, so don't get too dramatic about it, OK? And incidentally, I don't *just* want a sightseeing tour of London from you. What I want is to punish you. And breaking your finger's only part of it, right?'

'Why do you want to punish me?'

'I can't really tell you that,' Mick said thoughtfully. 'Not yet. But everybody's done something they need punishing for, haven't they? Everybody's done something they've got away with that they shouldn't have. I'll bet you can think of something.'

Masterson shook his head but didn't try to argue. He simply drove in the direction of St Paul's.

'You're married, Masterson, yes?'

'Yes.'

'Happily, of course.'

'Yes.'

'That's great. I find that really touching, I do. In a world where nothing lasts, and nobody's faithful, and people just shack up together and move out when things get a bit tricky, somebody who's prepared to say till death us do part, well, I think you have to admire that. How long have you been together?'

'Not long.'

'Newlyweds. Sweet.'

'Look, you can do what you like to me, but leave Sally out of this, please.'

'I'm only *talking* about her. Sticks and stones. I wouldn't hurt her, that'd be cowardly, wouldn't it? But she *is* a looker. She is a great-looking woman. But I was wondering, does she always keep her bra and stockings on while she's being shagged, or was that just today?'

51

A chilling, incapacitating anger crept over Masterson. All he could ask was, 'What did you see?'

'I saw the lot, the pair of you, at it on the deck. It was worth watching. But I admit I was more interested in seeing her than in seeing you.'

'You sick fuck,' said Masterson. He slammed on the brakes and the car lurched to a halt on a double yellow line. 'I've just about had enough of this.'

'You haven't had anything yet.'

Mick pulled out the gun. It was as he'd described. He released the safety catch and pressed the snout against Masterson's temple. Masterson began to tremble.

'I know what you're thinking, Philip,' said Mick. 'You're thinking, this is London, this is England. This sort of thing can't happen here. But it can, believe me. You're thinking men don't have their brains blown away in broad daylight just because they refuse to do what they're told. But they do, Philip, they really do. Believe me.'

Masterson bowed his head, partly in agreement, partly in genuine submission. He was still trembling. Mick motioned for him to drive on. He was about to ask whether Masterson had had a good stag night but he stopped himself; that would have been giving far too much away.

Instead he said, 'When I saw the two of you together on the floor like that, obviously a couple in love, I felt sort of envious, but at the same time I couldn't help thinking how long will it last? How long before you start getting bored with each other? How long before you start pretending you're too tired? How long before you start thinking about someone else while you're in bed with your wife? How long before you're both unfaithful? It made me feel a bit sad.'

Masterson watched the road intently, tried hard not to listen or respond to what Mick was saying.

'In fact I wondered if it mightn't have started already. Does she always want it from behind? Is that so she doesn't have to look at you? Doesn't she ever let you kiss her? Doesn't she ever take your cock in her mouth? And is it always that quick? That orgasm she had, I suppose it looked convincing. It looked very good really. I just wondered if it was real.'

For a second Masterson looked as though he was about to speak, about to fight back, but Mick waved the gun in his direction.

'Don't say anything silly,' Mick said, then as though there was no conflict or enmity between them, 'How about having a drive down Carnaby Street?'

'You can't drive down Carnaby Street. It's a pedestrian precinct.'

'Then how about Selhurst Park?'

'I don't know that.'

'It's the football ground where Crystal Palace play.'

'Where is it?'

'I don't know. You're the Londoner.'

'I'd need directions, or at least a map.'

'Forget it. How about Buckingham Palace?'

'Yes, we can drive past that.'

They drove to Buckingham Palace, but again Mick was disappointed. It was a grim building and you couldn't get anywhere near it. And so it went on for the rest of the morning, an increasingly pained Masterson forced to drive an increasingly unimpressed Mick around a version of tourist London; or rather around Mick's own idiosyncratic version of London, those places he simply happened to have heard of: the Monument, Stamford Bridge, the Old Curiosity Shop, the Post Office Tower, Portobello Road, Soho, the Hammersmith Flyover. And as they went he asked lots of questions.

'So what's the population of London?'

'I really don't know.'

'Come on, I bet you do.'

'Isn't it about nine million these days?'

'Yeah? And what percentage of those were born here, do you reckon?'

'I honestly don't know.'

'Fifty per cent, would you think?'

'I really have no way of knowing.'

'But I'm asking you to make an educated guess, aren't I, you prat.'

'Well yes, fifty per cent sounds about right to me.'

'You're not just trying to keep me happy are you? Not just humouring me. How many black cabs are there in London? Go on, guess.'

'I don't know, ten thousand?'

'How many buses? Go on. Guess.'

'Two thousand?'

'How many privately owned cars? How many motorbikes? How many milkfloats?'

'I've absolutely no idea, I'm sorry, I'm sorry.'

'You're rubbish, aren't you?'

'Yes, I'm rubbish. I'm in pain. I'm scared to death. When is this going to end?'

Masterson looked as though he might be about to cry, as though he feared he had offended Mick again and that Mick was about to inflict new pain upon him.

At long last Mick said, 'Fair point. But I've got to say that I'm still a bit disappointed. Basically London looks like a big slum with a few famous landmarks scattered through it. Wouldn't you say?'

'Yes,' Masterson said numbly. 'That's exactly what I'd say.'

'Good. OK, I think I've just about seen enough of London for one day. It's been a nice enough outing. But now, if you'll take me to the bridge . . .'

Masterson looked blank. 'Which bridge?' he asked.

'London Bridge. Where else? Then I'll let you go on your way.'

Masterson wanted to believe him but he couldn't allow himself that luxury. When they stopped at a traffic light, Mick said, 'I want you to take off your tie, OK? And I want you to take off your jacket, and I want you to take off your shirt, and if you're wearing a vest that'll have to come off too.'

Wearily, resigned, scared, Masterson nodded and began to undress. 'Anything you say.'

He wriggled in his seat as he stripped off his clothes and handed them to Mick who effortlessly tossed them out into the street. Masterson sat bare-chested behind the wheel of his car, too frightened to feel the cold.

'Is there a reason for this?' he asked.

'Yeah, you're going swimming.'

Masterson grimaced and drove on until at last they came to London Bridge.

'What's this?' Mick demanded.

'It's London Bridge,' Masterson said.

Mick looked at it with disdain. 'No,' he said. 'London Bridge is the one that opens in the middle for ships to pass through, isn't it?'

'No, that's Tower Bridge.'

'Are you serious?'

'Yes. It's over there.'

He indicated downriver, and sure enough there was Tower Bridge, no distance away.

'Well, bugger me. Sorry about that, Philip. You probably think I'm a complete prat.'

'No, no, it's an easy enough mistake, anyone—'

'OK, stop here anyway.'

Masterson stopped the car when they were precisely halfway across. London Bridge was wide enough to accommodate six lines of traffic and their sudden stop caused little disruption. Nor was anyone much concerned when the two men got out of the car and shinned over the metal railing that separated the road from the pavement.

'Now, off with the shoes and socks, the trousers,' Mick said. 'But keep your pants on. We don't want to cause offence.'

Masterson was far beyond embarrassment. He stripped off his remaining clothes as bidden. The pavement was sufficiently empty that such passers-by as there were found him easy to ignore.

'Now,' said Mick, 'up on the side and in you go.'

Along the edge of the bridge was a balustrade made of broad, smooth, speckled granite blocks linked to each other by a flat continuous metal railing. It was low and no obstacle at all. It wouldn't have held back even the most timid jumper. Hesitantly, but making sure he showed no resistance, Masterson got up on the balustrade, positioning himself as though sitting on a fence. He looked down at the flat, brown, metallic surface of the freezing water below him and shuddered. The river banks looked a long way away, though the north side looked marginally less forbidding. There was a wooden jetty and metal ladders. On the south the buildings seemed to jostle right up to the water's edge, flat faced and inhospitable.

'Look,' Masterson said plaintively, 'I don't know who you are, or who you're working for, or who you think I am, or what you think I did; but I didn't, I really didn't.'

'That's not very logical is it?' Mick snapped. 'If you don't know what I think you did, how can you be sure you didn't do it?'

'That's true I suppose logically, but in any case, I'm sorry. I'm really, really sorry for whatever you think I've done.'

'Even if you didn't do it.'

'Yes, I'm just so, so sorry.'

There was no doubting his sorrow. There were tears in his eyes, his lower jaw was malleable as dough.

'Fine,' said Mick. 'I accept your apologies. Now in you go.'

'No, don't ask me to do that.' Masterson looked down at the water again, contemplated the drop and the width of the river and let out a bovine moan. 'I could kill myself,' he said.

'You'd have to be very unlucky,' Mick said. 'You'd have to fall badly, hit your head or something, get a lungful of water.'

'I could still really hurt myself.'

Mick tapped the gun in his pocket and said, 'Whereas I might only blow your balls off.'

A sightseeing boat went under the bridge, the rows of orange seats meticulously laid out on its upper deck. From somewhere

Masterson seemed to be gathering a few last grains of bravery and defiance. He said, 'I don't think you want to shoot me. Not here, not like this, so publicly. If you'd wanted that you'd have taken me somewhere else. I don't think you're totally insane.'

Mick reached over to where Masterson's damaged hand was resting on the metal parapet, and he took the broken finger and stirred it around as though it were a spoon in a cup of coffee. Masterson lost all power of speech or sense.

'But you're not quite sure how insane I am, are you?'

'No,' Masterson gasped.

'So I think you're going to have to jump, aren't you?'

'I'm too scared to jump,' Masterson said wretchedly.

Mick slapped a hand on Masterson's bare, hairy shoulder, left it there like an epaulette and then pushed. There was no adhesion between Masterson and the smooth surface on which he was sitting, and he simply slipped into space. He went out of sight and Mick had to peer over the parapet to watch the body falling swiftly and straight into the inert waters below.

Masterson hit the surface and the sound of his splash was thin, distant and undramatic. Once his head had appeared above water, and after he'd started a forlorn, weary . breaststroke towards the bank, Mick turned away, vaulted over the railing into the road and went back to the car. There was something else he wanted. He reached behind the driver's seat for Masterson's briefcase. He opened it, emptied out the contents until he found what he was really looking for; Masterson's address book. That was all he needed. It would contain five vital addresses belonging to men whose names he already knew.

Mick left the car, became just another man walking along London Bridge. He was heading north though he was unaware of the fact. That direction simply looked more inviting, more dense and alive. The buildings looked grand but anonymous, distinguished and heavy with money. He suspected he was a long way from the Dickens Hotel.

# A PHONECALL HOME

That evening, from an old-style, red, urine-tainted telephone box, its walls tiled with prostitutes' cards, and empty Nourishment cans on the floor, Mick rang Gabby.

'It's me. I'm here in London.'

'Yeah?' she said. 'How is it?'

A trail bike with a metallic, unsilencered engine note blasted its way past the phone box.

'It's OK,' he said, after the noise had gone. 'It's big and dirty and it's not easy finding your way around.'

'I wasn't asking for a postcard home. I meant the business.'

'Yes, well, I'm taking care of it.'

'Don't do anything silly.'

'I'm not a silly person.'

'I know, but don't get hurt.'

'OK. But there's stuff I need to ask you, stuff I need to know.'

The deadness at the other end of the line was so abrupt that he thought he might have been cut off.

'Are you there?' he asked.

'Yes. What do you need to know?'

'Well, for a start, the bloke who was getting married, was he called Philip?'

'We didn't get formally introduced.'

Mick acknowledged the stupidity of his question, then asked, 'But was he a big bloke?'

'I guess so,' she said, sounding willing to agree.

'And sort of sporty with it?'

'Sure.'

'And did he have a hairy back?'

'How the fuck would I know?'

'I thought it was the kind of thing you might have noticed.'

'I was trying hard not to notice anything at all at the time . . .'

'I can see that, but still . . .'

'And in any case, he didn't take his shirt off. And even if he had I wouldn't have touched his back, would I?'

'OK, I can see that.'

Mick fell silent. There were other things he'd have liked to ask but he didn't want to make Gabby any more angry.

She said, 'I don't find this very easy, you know.'

'I realize that.'

'Or very pleasant.'

'I'm just trying to work something out, that's all.'

Mick noticed a couple of black girls standing outside the call box waiting to use the phone. Their presence was hard to ignore. He was aware of their laughter, their long legs, the can of lager they passed back and forth. Their intrusion made him want to talk more softly to Gabby, more intimately, but with the background roar and clatter and road noise he would have made himself inaudible.

'Did this Philip guy have any distinguishing marks?' he asked as gently as he could.

'I don't know, Mick, all right? I had my eyes shut. Is that good enough for you? What's the matter with you?'

'I just want to be sure I gave a pasting to the right man.'

'Gave?' She sounded puzzled, then delighted. 'You already did it?'

'The first one, yeah. It wasn't that difficult. He said he was sorry.'

'Bastard.'

'Yeah, but he did look genuinely sorry by the time I'd finished with him.'

'I bet he did. Did you tell him who you were?'

'What do you think I am?'

'Did you say anything about me?'

'Oh sure.'

'This is excellent,' she said. Her voice was giddy with excitement. She sounded grateful and exhilarated and loving. 'Look, Mick, I appreciate this, I really do. When you've sorted all this out then I really want us to be happy.'

'Yeah?'

'Like we used to be, you know.'

'You mean sex.'

'Yeah. Like it used to be.'

He was pleased to hear her saying this, and he hoped she meant it, but he couldn't resist adding, 'But not till all this is sorted, right?'

'That's right.'

'OK,' he said gamely. 'So there's only another five to go.'

The moment he put down the phone, one of the two girls outside opened the door and they both tried to get in before he'd left.

'Hey,' he said. '*Excuse me*. That's a phrase we have in the English language.'

'Oh, fuck off,' they said in unison.

Mick stared at them. They didn't look like such terrible girls. He considered wrecking the phone box just to annoy them, but it was just a thought. He knew he'd never do a thing like that. Meaningless violence was not his style.

# RADIO

It was late and if he could have had his way Mick Wilton would have been sound asleep. Instead he was bristlingly awake in the airless room at the Dickens Hotel. He sprawled on the bed, propped himself up on one elbow, feeling the ruts and craters of the mattress; a relief map of enemy territory. There were ugly noises reverberating through the building; slamming doors, coughing, bad plumbing. What was it about London that could make a man feel so miserable, so melancholy? Mick was not as a rule given to thoughts of self-destruction but he understood how the grey murk of a room like this could seep into you and make you decide you'd had enough.

Things got so bad that he went to the wardrobe and fished out the girlie magazine. It was fairly soft. Ignoring the Gabby lookalike on the front, and in truth he wasn't sure she really looked that much like Gabby after all, he opened it at the centrefold and looked down at the pink, polished image. She was a bright-eyed, broad-mouthed girl, thickly permed auburn hair, completely naked, reclining on straw bales in front of a painted backdrop of fields and sky. Her head was thrown far back but she managed to maintain eye-contact with the camera. Her legs were open, more like ten to two than quarter to three, and one hand was raised to her breast. She was pretty enough under the make-up, though no way was she the country girl she was trying to appear. Mick thought for a moment that she

61

didn't look the type to be posing naked in girlie magazines, but checked himself quickly enough. He reminded himself that he knew nothing about types.

There was a black felt-tip pen in his free hand and he started doodling on the centrefold. First he drew in the outlines of a bikini, see-through (as it were) to start with, and then he shaded in the outlined area until the model was decently covered. The picture lost its meaning. Why were her legs arranged like that if not to expose herself? He continued shading, turning the bikini into a one-piece swimsuit, then into one with a halter neck, then with sleeves, then extending into a full catsuit with only the girl's hands and face showing. But somehow the exposed hands and face were enough. The way the fingers were held, the expression in the eyes and mouth, they still said, 'I'm naked. I'm showing myself off so you can look at me.' He no longer wanted to be part of the bargain. He closed the magazine and dropped it on the floor.

There was no TV in the room but there was a clock-radio with a fake wood case. It was tuned to some light jazz station but he wanted to hear speech. He spun the dial until he found a woman's voice, low, husky, deliberate, and it was talking over the Stones' 'Let's Spend The Night Together'. When the music ended the voice said, 'Hello, London, you sexy city.'

He scanned his room again, thought about the colourless, ugly, sexless streets that lay outside and wanted to turn the radio off, but there was something in that voice, a warmth, a compelling quality, that kept him tuned in.

There was another slice of music, '"Let's Talk About Sex, Baby",' and then the woman's radio voice said, 'Yes. Let's. This is Marilyn Lederer talking to London, talking frankly about sex, about hang-ups and cock-ups and let downs. I'm no doctor but I do have a certain expertise in these areas. Give me a call, and for the fans of coprolalia among you (and you know who you are), bear in mind that we do have a licence to keep. Other than that the lines are completely . . . open.'

Of course there was no phone in Mick's room either but it

would have made no difference. What would he have said? 'My girlfriend was gang-raped by six men recently and now she's lost interest in sex. What do you think I should do?' He couldn't understand why anyone would ring these programmes, what they got out of it, what need was fulfilled by speaking on the radio. But he was happy enough to listen to other people's confessions.

'You know,' said the woman's voice on the radio, 'a lot of people call in and say, "What are you wearing, Marilyn?" and I always answer, "What would you like me to be wearing?" Because, you see, this is the joy of radio. It's the medium of the imagination and you can dress me up any way you want. Whatever you need you can get. It's like TV, only the pictures are dirtier.'

The voice sounded so close, so intimate, and whether it was natural or not, or whether it was a case of successful voice coaching or of electronic manipulation, didn't matter; it made Mick feel less alone, and he could easily imagine it doing the same for others, for a slew of lonely listeners all over the city. He would have expected them to be mostly male, yet when the calls started to come in at least half were from women.

The programme functioned partly like a problem page. People called to discuss specific personal difficulties; women whose men came too soon, or who weren't romantic enough, men whose partners wouldn't perform certain necessary and desirable acts. Commonplace tortures. Marilyn Lederer handled the calls breezily, warmly. She was serious but not solemn, like a sexy older sister. But not all the callers had problems. Some were more celebratory. A sixty-nine-year-old woman rang in to say she was still enjoying a good sex life, and this was rapidly followed by a sixteen-year-old girl who called in to say she'd recently, i.e. within the last half-hour or so, lost her virginity, and she thought it was fantastic and she needed to tell someone.

'You've just told about three-quarters of a million listeners,' said Marilyn Lederer.

Mick found himself smiling, an unexpected activity in this

room. As the programme went on he saw that it wasn't a show directed solely at sad, desperate insomniacs, and for a while he felt better about himself simply because he was a listener to such a good, open-armed programme. Then came the crucial call of the night, from a man who identified himself as Bob from Fulham. He said he was fifty-seven years old and he sounded working class, ordinary, essentially cheerful but with something on his mind.

'And what do you want to share with us, Bob?' Marilyn Lederer asked.

'Well, I'm having a bit of difficulty with the wife.'

'In bed or out?'

'That's just the problem,' he said and he laughed uncomfortably. The laugh died and he kept quiet and Marilyn Lederer let the silence last as long as she could, waiting for him to speak, but in the end she had to say, 'Are we talking about performance, Bob?'

'Yes.'

'About what you're doing?'

'No. Not about what. About where.'

'OK!' She sounded thrilled. Here was something that was going to create sparks. 'Where are you doing it at the moment, Bob?'

'Er . . . in bed.'

'Nowhere else?'

'Not really, no.'

'And your wife's not happy with this?'

'That's it. She doesn't just want to do it in bed.'

'That's fine isn't it, Bob? You don't object to that, do you? You wouldn't mind trying it on the carpet or in the bath, would you?'

'She doesn't just want to do it outside the bed. She wants to do it outside the house.'

Marilyn Lederer gave a low whistle of appreciation.

'Right, Bob, your wife wants you to make love to her in the

open air. And I take it that when she says outside the house she doesn't just mean the back garden.'

'We haven't got a back garden, but that's not the real problem. I love my wife, that's fine, I want to make her happy, I'm game for a bit of al fresco sex but I don't know where to go and do it, and I was wondering whether . . .'

He hesitated, and his silence spoke volumes about sexual reticence and awkwardness. Then he forced himself to continue.

'. . . whether any of your listeners could ring in with suggestions about where to have sex in London out of doors without getting caught.'

Bob lapsed into confused silence again. He was glad to have got it off his chest, even so his embarrassment still blushed down the line. Fortunately Marilyn Lederer let him off the hook. She addressed her audience on his behalf, telling them to call in and help out poor old Bob of Fulham. Mick lay back on his bed and listened, hardly imagining that anyone would call in. But they did, in their hundreds.

At first the suggestions were mundane. Callers recommended parks and heaths and commons and recreation grounds and car-parks, but it soon got much more personal and anecdotal. People started to give details of dark alleys and shop doorways where they'd had particularly enjoyable bouts of sex. Station platforms were recalled, churchyards, telephone boxes, bridges, embankments, towpaths, tunnels. It appeared there was no part of the city that hadn't been used as a venue for sex.

The idea seemed to please the callers and it especially pleased Marilyn Lederer. She egged on her audience fervently. A woman rang up to talk about all the many, many places she'd had sex. For a moment her voice reminded Mick of Judy Tanaka, but that was probably because all posh voices sounded much the same to him. She was quite a caller. It seemed there was no district or borough, no location or postal district anywhere in London that she hadn't performed. She was proud

65

of it, as though she had something to prove, was going for a record.

Mick found himself inexplicably incensed. He thought of ringing up and saying that in Sheffield at least, sluts kept quiet about the precise details of their activities, but of course he didn't. The programme raced by without any intervention from him and at two o'clock when it ended the lines were still stacked up with callers.

In his room in Hackney Mick wasn't sure whether to be pleased or dismayed. The show asserted that sex was fun, easy, commonplace, but right now it didn't seem like any of those things. It occurred to him that it was quite likely someone might have had sex in this room, on this bed. He didn't find the thought celebratory or involving. It gave him the creeps. He was not in London for anything so trivial as sex. He did not find it a sexy city, whatever the people on the radio said. He found it hard and scruffy and cold and affectionless, a place where terrible things happened or were made to happen; and the sooner he could cease contact with it the better.

# NAMES

Once it would have been easy enough for Stuart to blame his parents. They were the ones who had given him his name; a painfully absurd name that he hated. The name Stuart was innocuous enough, and so in most contexts was his surname. It was inherited in his father's case, acquired through marriage in his mother's; and he would have conceded that there was nothing inherently absurd about having the surname London. The last time he'd looked in the London telephone directory there were twenty-five or thirty others in the same boat. There were famous Londons, Jack for instance, and Julie. And he would also have admitted that if one had to be called after an English place-name London was clearly preferable to a great many others: Worksop, Diss, Looe, Foulness.

But surely his parents should have had enough common sense not to join the name of a capital city with the name of a period in history. They should not, they should so obviously not, have given him the name Stuart London. He despised it. It was a chapter in a history textbook, the title of an exam paper, the name of a historical map, scarcely a person's name at all.

What had depressed him even more was that for a long time his parents hadn't even realized what they'd done. They were not stupid or simple people, but they were not students of history either. The Tudors and Stuarts were unknown quantities to them. So for that matter were the Romans, the

Georgians, the Victorians. It was only when little Stuart, a short-trousered schoolboy, came home from class, confused, laughed at, mocked to the point of tears, that his parents had some inkling of what they had done. They saw, too late, how their son's name might be considered laughable.

His father tried to make light of his son's misery and said how much worse things might have been if he'd called him Norman London, but this didn't help at all. Besides, his father pointed out, it wasn't one of those totally ludicrous names that every Tom, Dick and Harry would find hilarious. It wasn't Eva Brick or Eileen Dover. No, people had to have a certain subtlety of mind and a certain level of sophistication to find his name a joke. His father implied that this would make things better. Stuart knew it only made things worse.

Alas, he was now no longer a schoolboy, and was therefore no longer able to blame his parents for anything. He was a forty-year-old man, who, in serious consultation with his wife, had decided not to have children. But if he'd had children he'd have called them something plain and simple, Bill, Alice, something like that. They wouldn't have had to go through what he'd been through.

Stuart had suffered long and hard but he had never quite had the confidence or the desperation to change his name. He'd considered it many times, had even considered some serious alternatives, but had not taken the final step. And then one day it was far too late. He found himself in a position, in a profession where his name might even be construed as beneficial; albeit a position and profession for which he no longer had much respect or tolerance.

He hadn't intended to find himself here. In so far as he had ever possessed any ambitions at all they were about becoming an architectural scholar or a historian, or possibly some sort of curator, something like that. But none of that had worked out. Instead, after several interrupted courses of study, after a number of career changes and crises, he had found himself as a part of the tourist industry, as managing director (he still found the title laughable) of a company called, with what these days seemed to him a ravaging lack of originality, The London Walker. London by name, London by nature. And he wondered if in some sense his name had preordained this fate for him.

You would pick up The London Walker catalogue if you considered yourself to be the more discriminating, more cultured kind of tourist, the type who wanted to get off the tour bus and walk the streets of London in the company of a knowledgeable and articulate guide. The catalogue had a quotation from Samuel Johnson in it, not the obvious one, but instead, 'By seeing London I have seen as much of life as the world can show.' If you liked what you read you might well find yourself signing up for one or more of the following guided tours: the Bloomsbury Walk, the Boswell Walk, the Christopher Wren Walk, the London Crime Walk, the Holmes and Watson Walk, the Art Gallery Walk, the Docklands Walk, and so on and so forth, *ad nauseam* in Stuart's opinion.

Stuart, even though he had never wanted to be a business man, knew that any kind of business was a series of only partially solvable problems, a series of headaches that didn't wholly respond to treatment. There was no business that had ever 'run itself', but for the time being at least The London Walker ran without any input from him. That was because he had a wife, and she ran the business for him, for herself too, and she ran it better than he could. It would have been nice to think he could have sat back and grown fat and rich on the profits. In fact he sat back and felt utterly useless and depressed.

Stuart was not a native of London. He had been born in Colchester in the mid-fifties, but London had always seemed a magical place to him. His father had war stories from when he was a fire watcher in London and, before she was married, his mother had been a great fan of West End musicals and she still talked about them as part of her golden past. When he was a child there had been family excursions, days out in London, an aunt in Finsbury Park who was occasionally visited, but these jaunts were never enough for Stuart. From the earliest age he'd known that he wanted to move to London, live there, be a student there. He'd driven himself to pass O-level Latin so he could study English at UCL, even if his interest in English literature hadn't survived his first term there.

As a student in London, the city had drawn him in like a benign spider's web. He'd sit in the student bar with a copy of *Time Out* and see what films were showing, what bands were playing, and it would always be the most distant cinemas, the most far-flung venues that attracted him. Whereas other students were attached to the West End by an inelastic tether, he found himself free to bounce around the most inaccessible and provincial parts of the city.

The majority of these trips had to be solitary. It was generally impossible for him to persuade any of his student friends to come with him to what they called the outer limits, but he was not deterred. Sometimes he would have girlfriends and if they liked him enough they would be prepared to indulge his whims, his urge for the margins. But none of his girlfriends ever lasted very long. His longest relationship was with a girl whose parents lived in Spitalfields, and he sometimes thought the relationship only survived at all because he responded to some archaic poetry in that place-name. Being able to say he was going out with a girl from Spitalfields had, in his own mind if nowhere else, a certain glamour to it. He was profoundly disappointed when in due course he discovered that the 'spital' part of the name was a contraction of the word hospital and not some archaic spelling of spittle, as in saliva.

But when he had no girlfriend, and when he travelled the city alone, he never felt lonely. The city supported him, engaged him and kept him company, and he was very grateful to it.

His student years passed rapidly, and although he wasn't a bad student, he was only interested in what he was interested in. Having abandoned English he dallied with history, then with history of art, with philosophy and anthropology. He got a degree, but only just. He wouldn't have minded becoming an academic, but his learning was too patchy, and it was impossible to imagine what he would have researched. Instead he found himself doing a series of 'real' jobs; working first on a travel magazine, then for a small advertising agency, then as a technical writer for a computer firm. While all his friends seemed to conceive of themselves as over-qualified and unemployable, he found himself constantly facing a working future that promised promotion, security, responsibility, challenge.

Several years went by in this way, then one day he woke up, knew he was in absolutely the wrong place, the wrong job, the wrong industry, and decided he'd better run. He walked out of his job, moved into a much cheaper flat, lived on his meagre savings and wondered what the hell he was going to do next.

He knew that he still liked London, that he liked exploring it, walking through it. He knew he wasn't too bad at talking to groups of people, and surprisingly he found that he quite liked foreigners. He wondered how these interests might be turned into a means of making a living.

With a recklessness and a nerve that he later found amazing, he set up a series of walking tours of London: the Architectural Walk, the Mob Walk, the Sculpture Walk. He was their only begetter. He led the tours, devised the routes, tore the tickets, made the phonecalls. He had some leaflets printed and strewed them around hotels and tourist information centres, got himself mentioned in the listings magazines, and he was only slightly surprised to find that he soon had a thriving little business, which he called Stuart's Tours.

As anticipated, a lot of his work was with groups of American tourists. They were his best audience. His insights, his quirkiness, his jokes, didn't go down so well with non-English speakers, especially not the Japanese. But his youth and enthusiasm went a long way. Tourists were charmed by his manner and impressed by the depth of knowledge in one apparently so young, although at the age of twenty-six he didn't feel young at all.

He quickly honed his skills. Those who took the tours said

he was a natural communicator, that he should write a book, have his own TV show. Modestly, and accurately, he said they were wrong. Nevertheless, he could see that he was enough of a communicator to be able to make a living this way. Some seasons of the year were better than others, some years were better than others, but he soldiered on for three summers and winters, and he didn't go broke.

He was always concerned to give value for money and he never treated his tourists with anything other than respect, but as time passed he was aware that he was losing some of his original charm. He wasn't becoming cynical exactly, but he was getting weary.

The business was a one-man show and that made for a solitary if simple working life. But he had never been very good at the paperwork or admin and he was pleased when the business became busy enough to justify advertising for an assistant. He needed to import some organizational skills but he also needed company.

The ad must have been badly worded. He only received one reply, from an ambitious, friendly, outgoing, thoroughly business-like young woman called Anita. She had recently returned from a round-the-world trip and said she wanted to be involved in the tourist industry. She also said that she wanted to start at the bottom and work her way up. Stuart was unaware that he was at the bottom, had no idea what the way up might be, and was even more baffled when she talked in the interview about the enormous potential she saw in his business.

In the absence of competition he employed her, but she would probably have beaten most other candidates. She was obviously going to be good at the job, but what really clinched it was her name. She was called Anita Walker, a name he found as absurd as his own. It was a frivolous reason for employing someone but he never had reason to regret it. Anita could handle the accounts, could handle people, could conduct a walking tour if necessary, could do just about anything she set her mind to. Within six months she had made herself indis-

pensable and within a year she had married the boss, not that
Stuart had ever felt like her boss. She became Anita London.
'A neater London.' Well, few people ever picked up on that,
but her name lived on in the company's new title. They
combined their names to become The London Walker.

Right from the beginning she told him that a business must
expand or die. He didn't particularly want it to do either, but
he settled for expansion. Anita's idea was simple enough.
Instead of having one man devising and conducting all the
tours, she saw that they could find any number of cheap,
capable people to do the work of guiding: students, resting
actors, retired academics, bored but intelligent housewives.
They could be trained quickly and easily and sent on their way
to do the job, creating much more work, more turnover, much
bigger profits. She also suggested that some of Stuart's tours
were, how could she put it, a little recherché. Why not go for
a broader market? Why not the Shakespeare Walk? The Royal
Walk? The Rock 'n' Roll Walk? Stuart briefly objected that
this was not what he'd had in mind when he started the
business, but, in the face of Anita's developing business plans
and cash-flow forecasts, this was no objection at all. At the time
it seemed like a risk and a diversion but he couldn't deny that
it worked.

The company progressed. There was a new office, a pool of
employees, bigger and better business plans, loans, a lot of
meetings with bank managers and freeholders. There were
times when it all looked very precarious indeed but at the end
of each year the accountants, who never appeared to have had
any confidence whatsoever in the enterprise, declared that The
London Walker was doing surprisingly well.

Meetings with bank managers and accountants were still not
Stuart's forte, however. At first he continued to lead walks. But
Anita had been right. His knowledge of London was detailed
and profound, his love of it real, yet as the years went by he
had an increasing distaste for the obvious. He genuinely wanted
to reveal London to the people who came on the tours but he

was bored with its more obvious features. He wanted to show its eccentricities and unknown quarters. Rather than take them to the Tower of London he'd have preferred to take them to the abandoned Severndroog Castle near Oxleas Wood. For Stuart it increasingly wasn't enough to tell a few old anecdotes and point out a few sights and locations. He felt that truth was more profound in the obscure corners than in the grand sweeps. And on a good day he would find these corners, even while ostensibly showing punters the more orthodox aspects of London. His tours became increasingly abstract, free form, improvised, often turning into a sort of mystery tour. A crowd that had signed up for a canal walk might be treated instead to a tour of sites connected with leprosy. There were a few complaints, some dissatisfied walkers who demanded their money back.

He organized a walking tour called Stuart London's London – The City That Nobody Knows. Of course, he saw there was an absurd contradiction in the title of the tour. If it was a London that literally nobody knew then clearly he wouldn't have known it either. But the real problem was nothing so philosophical as that. Quite simply, nobody ever signed up for the tour. Weeks passed and the other tours did good business. People wanted to see the Beatles' London, and Virginia Woolf's London, Pepys' London and Hogarth's London, but nobody wanted to know the London they didn't know. They wanted to know better the London they already knew. Stuart was profoundly depressed.

It was Anita who eventually told him he should stop pounding the streets and take a more consultative role, maybe have a less hands-on approach. What she meant, simply, was that he should stop conducting these obscure tours that nobody wanted or enjoyed. He was quietly devastated but he agreed to take a four-week break and see how things went. Ostensibly he would use the time to brush up on his already encyclopaedic knowledge, but in reality he sat around the office watching how efficiently the business worked without any help from him. Young, fresh-faced guides who didn't know too much actually gave the punters far more of what they wanted than he did. It was a terrible revelation but one he couldn't ignore.

He agreed to stop leading tours. He stayed in the office and desperately tried to think of a role for himself. He sometimes interviewed potential members of staff but his instinct for spotting potential was fallible. He sometimes trained new guides, but he knew so much about his subject that often he found it impossible to distill information of the right sort and in the right quantities to be useful to new recruits.

For a while he conceived of his consultative role as thinking up new and original ideas for tours, but this was not an area where novelty or ingenuity were particularly welcomed. The Henry VIII Walk and the Jack the Ripper Walk were always likely to do better business than Stuart's fancier inventions such as the Thomas Middleton Walk, the Post-Modernist Walk, the Anarchists' Walk. In fact it was a guide in her first week with the company who came up with the idea of the London Lesbian Walk, which for a while was one of the most popular tours.

So Stuart began to withdraw even further. He was no longer sure what his job was, but whatever it was, a lot of people seemed to be able to do it better than he could. He had lost something, a spark, an enthusiasm, a common touch. He felt becalmed. He started to work from home, a situation that rapidly turned into sitting around the house not working at all. He knew that madness lay that way. He was not suited to inactivity. If he wasn't needed by The London Walker then he wasn't the sort of person who could simply put in an appearance and pretend he was working when he wasn't.

There were some ways of disguising his uselessness. There were people he could have meetings with in the name of business, working lunches that could become boozy and pro-longed, extended to absorb half the day. But Stuart always felt ashamed to be returning home or to the office half-cut at four o'clock, and by five a fierce alcoholic melancholy would have

75

set in. It felt terrible. There was no way he would be able to pursue a career as a professional London drinker.

More harmlessly he sometimes slipped away to see a movie. That felt only mildly shameful, but the pleasure it brought was outweighed by the guilt he felt, knowing that his wife and his employees were out there working while he wasn't.

He toyed, very briefly, with the idea of becoming a womanizer, of spending his afternoons having affairs, and he succeeded in going to bed with one of the young female guides. But no, it was more than just going to bed. It had very nearly been a full-blown affair. It had been nice enough in its way, intense and exciting and all that, but it really wasn't nice enough to risk your marriage and therefore your business and livelihood for, and it certainly wasn't nice enough to want to make a habit of. Once it was over he hadn't had the energy or the inclination ever to do it again, but the memory of it stayed with him, both sweet and threatening.

The only kind of clean, simple, honest pleasure that satisfied him was using London in the name of research. Any increase in his knowledge of London must surely be of benefit to the business, or so he told himself. He would spend afternoons in the Museum of London, the V and A, the British Museum. There was nothing academic or systematic about these visits. In fact he would sometimes see other people apparently doing much the same as him, and for them it was obviously nothing more than killing time, sheltering from the cold or rain. But time needed no killing for Stuart. While ever he was engaged with London it passed very swiftly and happily.

On other occasions Stuart needed nothing so organized as a museum. He got pleasure simply from walking the streets of London. Certainly some streets offered more than others. Some were full of interesting sights or people, others were places he knew well or liked a lot. Sometimes he experienced the pleasures of familiarity, sometimes those of novelty, but it was always a pleasure.

He didn't give much thought to what precisely he was doing,

but if he'd been compelled to think it through he would undoubtedly have said this phase was a temporary one, a period of transition before he worked out his new role within the firm. But gradually, and it hardly took a genius to work it out, he saw that no such role would ever materialize. He was, in the most ordinary sense, redundant. The London Walker was no longer going to be part of his life, of his self-definition. He would have to find some different reason for being. He thought of trying to get a new job, of starting a fresh career, but he felt far too jaded and old for that. He needed something that connected with his own deep interests, something that was simply more him. He needed a Big Idea, and sure enough, eventually, it came.

Once it had arrived there was an inevitability about it, something undeniable. He was sitting in the coffee bar of the Museum of Transport in Covent Garden thinking how much he disliked buses and tubes when the idea finally struck, and the moment it was there he couldn't see why it had been so long coming. It felt so completely and perfectly right. What he had to do was utterly clear. He was going to walk down every street in London.

The reasons why a man might choose to walk down every street in London seemed many and obvious to Stuart. It could for example be explained simply in terms of curiosity, in a man's urge to see new things, to investigate those parts of the city that were off all the tourist maps, that were known only to locals and the more intrepid explorers.

He would, inevitably, go to places he'd never been before, that was at least partly the point, but he would also find himself in places he didn't especially want to go. He didn't think there were any areas in London where it was simply too risky to walk, but he knew he would be going to districts that he had until now consciously avoided – and probably for good reasons – but that was the nature of the beast. Perhaps then his walking would be an act of reclamation, a way of taming the city, a way of saying that London was open and accessible to everyone, that it held no secrets, no unknowable horrors.

Obsession also fitted the case. A man who walked down every street in London could be considered a superior, more abstract sort of trainspotter, with the obsessive's desire for completion, for having the whole set. He would walk past every school, every gaol, every theatre, every hospital, every pub, every solicitor's office, every used-car lot, every folly, every MI5 safe house, every brothel and crack den, every plumbers' merchant, every delicatessen, every law court, every sports stadium, every everything. He would have been there, seen there, done that. And even if he missed certain things, markets that were only held one day a week, parades that were only held one day a year, great buildings that were hidden behind scaffolding, nightclubs that were known only to members, well, at least, he'd have walked past them, been in the streets where they took place.

And maybe this could be explained as part of a simpler desire just to show off, to say look at me, look what I've done, what I've achieved, aren't I a fascinating if eccentric character? That made perfect sense.

Yet he didn't want to make London his. This would not be anybody's particular version of London, not Dickens', not Pepys', not Betjeman's, and certainly not his own. Since every street was to be walked down, every street would have equal value and importance. He wouldn't spend extra time in those streets that were attractive or steeped in history, neither would he dismiss streets that appeared to be featureless or uninteresting. He sensed something profoundly egalitarian in all this, a belief in a sort of democracy, a belief that all places, all things had merit and were to be equally cherished and respected. And perhaps there was a spiritual, maybe Buddhist element in that, a belief that all places were one, but he didn't want to run too far with that idea or there'd have been no point in setting off at all.

And yet, convincing though these reasons were, he was not

quite convinced by them. His real motives seemed other, and far less reasonable or explicable. In the end he didn't know why he was going to walk down every street in London. In truth he felt compelled by a force he didn't understand. It wasn't logical and he wasn't sure he really had a choice. It was just something he had to do. The city was mysteriously leading him on, drawing him in; it was a mystery that he relished. Perhaps it had to do with love or sex or self-knowledge, one of the 'big issues', but although he was only intermittently eager to understand his own motives, he did genuinely believe that if he walked long enough and far enough he might eventually work out why he was walking at all.

For the moment it was easier to think about practicalities. Stuart tried to lay down some rules of engagement for himself. His desire to walk down every street in London required him to make some definitions. First there was a need to define exactly what he meant by London. He decided that his London would be synonymous with the London boroughs, although he was aware that this increased the size of his task. The boroughs included outrageously distant areas like Croydon, Bromley, Ruislip. Once these places would have been in, respectively, Surrey, Kent and Middlesex, and even now they remained outside the London postal districts. But what was London if not its boroughs? If you didn't define London in the broadest possible way, you might as well restrict yourself to walking, say, round the square mile of the City.

Then he had to decide what he meant by 'street'. His dictionary defined it as 'a paved road (esp. Roman): a road lined with houses, broader than a lane.' He was immediately suspicious of a definition of street that found it necessary to use the word road, but he obviously intended to walk down roads too. He also intended to walk down roads that weren't necessarily lined with houses. For that matter he intended to walk down lanes too. Alleyways and courtyards, mews and closes, avenues and walks were certainly on his map, as were embankments, bridges and towpaths.

On the other hand, there were some paved roads where he didn't intend to walk at all; along stretches of London motorway, for example, through underpasses and road tunnels, along flyovers. Public parks presented another problem. After a lot of thought he decided he would walk around the boundaries of every London park and common, but only go into them where there was what might be construed as a genuine road. So he would walk along Rotten Row in Hyde Park but he wouldn't be compelled to walk along every path that cut across Hampstead Heath or London Fields or Wimbledon Common.

In the same way, he felt he wouldn't need to cover the roads that went through retail or business parks or through industrial estates or which were service roads for factories or warehouses. If roads claimed to be private he was quite prepared to respect their privacy. And, in a rather different way, he would apply much the same rule when it came to council estates; a walkway between two tower blocks could remain untrodden, but a genuine road where cars or milkfloats or dustbin lorries could pass would have to be walked down.

There was to be nothing macho or Herculean or competitive about his project. He had nothing to prove, and there would be no time limit. He wouldn't have to cover vast distances in a single day. There would obviously be a certain amount of endurance, patience and determination involved, but it wasn't to be anything so crude as a simple test of stamina or staying power.

He decided he would undertake his walk in sections of ten miles per day. That felt like a suitably modest figure. At a brisk pace he would be able to cover that distance in no more than two and a half hours, which would represent a relatively minor intrusion on his day. But perhaps he'd be walking more slowly than that. He wanted to give himself the time and freedom to observe and appreciate his surroundings. He would allow himself to rest if and when he wanted to, and he'd certainly be able to stop for a coffee or even a beer. And if someone tried to engage him in conversation, then he wanted to have time for that too.

A fitter man might have found ten miles a wholly trivial distance, but for him at his age, with his low level of fitness, ten miles a day seemed on the limit of what was easily achievable, especially since it had to be done day after day. He might have managed to cover twenty-five or thirty miles in a single session but he'd have been crippled the next day. He didn't want to be crippled, yet he did want to feel the basic physical effort of covering the ground on foot. He wanted to feel the solidity of the pavement. He wanted the slog and the weariness of it.

He had to make sure this didn't just turn into gentle strolling and sightseeing, into a series of days out. To that end he decided that he would not be allowed to enter any gallery or museum or tourist attraction. He would be allowed to go into shops only if he had something specific to buy that he needed for his walk: a drink, shoe laces if his current set broke, Elastoplast for his feet perhaps, but he couldn't enter any shop simply to browse. If it rained or snowed he was entitled to take shelter, but not for more than half an hour; after that he'd have to continue walking, whatever the elements. If he was passing the house of a friend he would not be allowed to call in and break the journey. If he happened to run into somebody he knew and they suggested some social venture, he would have to decline.

He considered taking a camera with him to photograph the things that caught his eye, to create a visual record and an *aide-mémoire*, but he decided against it. He feared that the presence of a camera would turn his walking into a photographic expedition, into a quest for the picturesque. Besides, taking photographs would make him conspicuous, and there were all sorts of places where a man with a camera would be unwelcome.

If he had been homeless and rootless, a street person, it might have been very different, purer in a sense. He could have started walking, continued for as long and as far as he saw fit and then he could have stopped and spent the night wherever he happened to be, then started again the next morning. That way there'd be no crossing the city to get back to base. Not everywhere would be equally hospitable. Doorways in Hampstead or Kensington or Chelsea were not welcoming to the homeless, and on some estates a man sleeping in a doorway might have found himself in all sorts of trouble, but as a methodology this homeless version had a lot going for it. Or perhaps, less dramatically, he could have taken to the streets in a camper van and completed daily circular walks from where it was parked, returned to spend the night, then moved on to a new starting place in the morning, gradually covering the whole city.

But, of course, he wouldn't be doing it like that. He had a home to go to, a wife, a job of sorts and, as far as possible, he didn't want that life interfered with. Each day, using either his car or public transport he would need to travel to a spot from which to begin his walking, and at the end he'd either return home or go to work. He wouldn't be able to walk at weekends, either. He'd just do it on weekdays as though it were a job. Then there'd be family holidays, Christmas, days when he or Anita might be ill and at home. There might even be days when he was required to do something for The London Walker, though of all possible disruptions this seemed least likely.

He had no intention of telling Anita what he was doing. She would not have disapproved exactly, not even thought he was mad, but she was an all too practical woman and she would simply have pointed out the immense difficulties he was going to face, the sheer size of the enterprise.

He was well aware of the vastness of what he was proposing, but at first it was hard to find the exact parameters of that vastness. He spent a lot of time trying to find out just how many miles of road there were in London, but he failed until he consulted an HMSO document called *London Facts and*

*Figures*. There it all was in black and white, in both miles and kilometres. It told him there were 8,318 miles of road in London, 37 of them motorway, 1,080 of them trunk and principal roads, and the rest were 'other'. If he walked ten miles a day, fifty miles per week, 2,500 miles per year, he would have covered London in less than three and a half years. That was a daunting task but certainly not an impossible one.

Then he realized that the 8,318-mile figure assumed he would never have to walk the same street twice and that was clearly not to be. For one thing there were culs-de-sac and dead ends. In order to walk along them at all he'd obviously have to walk along them in both directions. But even without such obvious difficulties the asymmetry of London streets was such that covering an area with a single, continuous walk that never covered the same ground twice was next to impossible. Take the simple case of a set of parallel streets running east to west that connected with streets running north to south at either end, a shape that looked like a ladder. There were such configurations all over London. He looked at his map and immediately found examples in Wimbledon, Battersea and Catford. Say you began walking along the east/west streets; there was no way to get around such a pattern without either missing sections of the north/south streets, or without repeating certain stretches. Given the nature of his enterprise, only the latter was acceptable, which meant he would cover a lot more than the simple mileage of London streets, and the ladder configuration was one of the simplest. As the pattern of streets got more complex, it became even harder to cover efficiently.

Then, like all cities, London was in flux. Even the most recent maps couldn't keep up. New building created new roads. By the time he'd completed 8,318 miles of walking there would be a new set of streets that hadn't been in existence when he'd started. He would have to mop these up at the end.

He bought a map, an *A–Z*, but he chose the colour version because it was printed on smooth, unabsorbent paper. He wanted no blodges, no seepage. He also bought a black marker pen, for he intended to draw a thick black line along all the streets he had walked so that the whole map would eventually become black and obliterated, no street names visible, London reduced to an abstract linear design. The map would become increasingly less useful and one day it would be completely useless and meaningless. That would be a very special day, the day when it was all over, but he knew it would be a long time coming.

The task loomed bigger and bigger, but in a strange way it didn't matter how big it was, because whatever its exact dimensions it was certainly finite. The task, like London itself, had limits. It was achievable. It was only a matter of time and persistence. There was a goal, an end in sight. For a long time starting seemed like much more of a problem than finishing.

He knew he had to begin somewhere and he knew that in one sense any place was as good as another, but he scanned the index of his *A–Z* looking for a street name that sounded appropriate. His eyes fell on a line that read North Pole Road. Next day he went there and started his walk.

He had no idea what to expect in North Pole Road. He knew there would not be frozen wastes, igloos, polar bears, and yet he couldn't imagine what a street with this name would be like. It was situated in west London, not far from Notting Hill, not far from White City, very close to Wormwood Scrubs.

He looked at his *A–Z* and then at a tube map and he decided he would have to drive there. He parked in a leafy street called St Quintin Avenue. On the corner were three young teenage girls and they had a baby with them. He assumed it belonged to one of them but he couldn't really tell. They held the baby up as though he were an aeroplane and made him fly through the air at head height, then every now and then one of the girls would pretend to headbutt him. It looked like a form of torture but it was obviously done with affection and the baby didn't object.

Stuart made the short walk to North Pole Road. He was

84

glad he hadn't hoped for too much. It turned out to be an ordinary local high street, with a railway bridge at one end, and a small public garden at the other that served as a traffic island. The street consisted of two parades of shops facing each other: Roger's Bakery, Mick's Fish Bar, Jackie's Flowers, Marion's Hairdressing, Varishna's Newsagent, Charig's Wine Shop. There was a butcher, a greengrocer, a bookmaker's, a few take-away food places, a pub called the New North Pole. Everything felt small-scale and decent and unexceptional. It was represent-ative of a certain sort of London, not rich, not poor, not pretty, not ugly, not hostile, not hospitable. He was pleased to have started with somewhere so mundane yet so typical. But try as he might he couldn't find much to keep him there, so he walked towards Wormwood Scrubs, a place he had never been to before. It was the name both of the gaol and of an area of open land with playing fields. He walked along Ducane Road, past a school and a hospital until he came to the prison.

In some ways it was much as expected, with forbidding brick walls and towers and barbed wire, but its location was not at all as he'd have pictured it. He somehow felt that prisons would be located in the middle of nowhere, away from people and civilization. Wormwood Scrubs, however, was situated on a main road, on a bus route, near shops and a housing estate and a railway line. The prisoners could probably look out of their cells and see the buses and trains going by. It felt all wrong. The sheer proximity of daily life would be part of the punishment. The high walls meant there was little for him to see, but at one corner of the prison site there was what looked like a house (although surely the gaol didn't contain workers' cottages?) and there was a walled garden with a huge rose bush climbing up over the brickwork and escaping.

He had to go back more or less the way he'd come and as he passed the school he watched some fairly talented schoolboys doing catching practice on the playing field. It was then he realized that this first foray was in danger of turning into an aimless ramble. He pressed on determinedly. It took a long time to walk all the way up Scrubs Lane, past the industrial estates, across the bridges that took him over railway lines and canals, and at last he came to the Harrow Road. He wondered why some roads merited a definite article (the Old Kent Road, the King's Road, the Edgware Road), while others of apparently equal status and nature (Oxford Street, Essex Road) did not.

He followed the Harrow Road on its long, eastward course. It was wide and windy and it rattled with traffic. He saw a tyre centre whose frontage had a mural depicting members of staff. He thought about setting foot in Kensal Green Cemetery but he resisted. Further along, nearer town, he left the Harrow Road, and took a footbridge over a canal and headed towards the Trellick Tower. He thought of Hugh Casson, frightened by Ernö Goldfinger, scared by 'the degree of certainty compressed into a small room.'

He found his way to Ladbroke Grove, passed under the Westway where he saw two drunks standing on top of a prefabricated toilet doing some kind of dance. There was also a hairdresser nearby called Have It Off. Then back through the leafier part of Notting Hill, or perhaps it should have been called North Kensington, he wasn't sure, and he returned to where his car was parked.

He sat in the driver's seat feeling both footsore and pleased with himself. He knew his walking could have been more purposeful but he'd done a reasonable ten miles. Not bad for a beginner. He opened his *A–Z*, took out a marker pen and drew black lines through all the streets he'd walked along that day. When he was finished he tossed the *A–Z* on to the passenger seat and drove home.

He knew he should have felt good, yet as he drove he had a profound sense of emptiness and dissatisfaction, and it wasn't simply because he'd occasionally lacked purpose in his walking. Rather he suspected that something fundamental was wrong with his method. Somehow he couldn't imagine completing another thousand days like this. Simply scoring out streets after he'd walked along them wasn't going to be enough. It marked his passage but it didn't record his presence. Even as he sat there with the day's walk fresh in his mind, he knew it was already starting to fade away. He could no longer quite picture the prison towers, and he'd forgotten the name of the hairdresser in Ladbroke Grove. Before long the whole day might just as well never have happened. There was nothing to say he'd been there. His experience was disappearing and he knew he had to find a way to reclaim and retain it.

The solution was obvious enough. In order for his experience to feel real and meaningful it wasn't going to be enough just to do the walking. And if he didn't have a captive audience of tourists to whom he could describe what he saw, he realized he was going to have to write about it.

# PLAYERS

Mick Wilton liked to think of himself as one of nature's aristocrats. The world obviously saw him as a plebeian, so he had to rely on nature for a second, higher opinion. When it came to cars, suits, women, that sort of thing, he liked to think that he knew quality, even if he didn't always have enough money to indulge in it. In his fantasies, for instance, he went from one exotic, expensive location to another, in a chauffeur (or, in a better fantasy, chauffeuse) driven Roller, never having to engage with the grime and irritation of the city streets.

He had decided he would not be travelling again by black cab. He didn't want to be ripped off by some cockney wag who insisted on broadcasting his views on queers, blacks and women, especially if they weren't prepared to go to Hackney. You had to admire them for knowing their way round the whole of London, and you had to admire them for even keeping their sanity, given the number of hours they spent negotiating London traffic, but they were still people he didn't want to deal with.

The tube wasn't an option. Mick's knowledge of the system was patchy, gleaned from a couple of daytrips, but the experience had been profound and bad. It had been a waking nightmare, everything he feared and despised all in one place; countless faceless people jammed into carriages in factory-farm conditions; people blocking your way, taking up too much room, refusing to let you get past, leaving their bags in the way. Then when the train pulled into the station there was the group grope of people getting on before they'd let other people off. Oh sure, there were heavenly voices trying to control all this mayhem, telling you to move right down inside, the guard on the train (a moron with a speech impediment) saying let the passengers off first, and being ignored, then some stuck-up ponce telling you to mind the gap. And when the tubes weren't full they were occupied by kids who had to put their feet up on seats, by men who thought it was cute to be drinking lager at ten in the morning.

But Mick's real problem was more intrinsic, more philosophical. The very idea of sending packed trains through the bowels of the earth, like turds through a vast, curving gut, appalled and frightened him. It would take so little for these tunnels to get blocked, for the electricity to fail, for a fire to start. The King's Cross fire was a bad dream he'd always been expecting to come true. He could imagine the selfish panic, the fireball, the smell of burning flesh. No point looking to your fellow passengers for help. They were in their own private hells. What if there was a bomb? What if there was a power cut? What if there was a nutter with a gun? Mick wasn't claustrophobic in any ordinary sense but there was something about the tube that could turn him into a sad, screaming wreck.

So Mick didn't travel by tube. He didn't travel by bus, either. He just didn't. It was one of those things that a man like Mick couldn't bring himself to do. The world of bus conductors and bus tickets and request stops, of sharing a seat with some stranger, it wasn't for him. He was too impatient, too cool, too, yeah say it, aristocratic. So Mick walked. He did a lot, a whole lot of walking. He walked a very long way before he found his way back to the London Particular.

Judy Tanaka was standing at the top of a set of wooden library steps, restocking the Ordnance Survey section, when she saw him come in. The shop was as empty as ever. Mick was carrying a plastic bag with a Virgin Megastore logo on it, and it bulged with the oblong shapes of the video tapes it contained. The *A–Z* he'd bought from Judy was in there too. Judy smiled uncertainly. In a way she was glad he'd come back. It would have been strange if she'd never seen him again, as though she'd read only the first chapter of a book she'd then lost, but she was sure he hadn't come just to be friendly. She knew he had to be there because he wanted something from her.

She came down the steps and said cheerfully, 'Can I help you, sir?'

'Don't call me sir,' he said as before, and then he realized she was joking. He felt embarrassed. The encounter had got off to a predictably clumsy start. 'But you can help me,' he added. 'You have a television, right?'

She nodded uncertainly.

'And you have a video recorder, yes?'

'Yes,' she admitted, aware that she might be admitting something else too.

'Good. Can I borrow it?'

She laughed in sheer disbelief. How could he have the nerve to ask to borrow a video recorder from someone he barely knew?

'OK, I can see you don't like that idea,' he said quickly. 'But I don't necessarily want to take it away from you. What might be easiest is if I just came round to your place and used it there.'

'You want to come to my flat?'

'Yeah. But only to use your video. There won't be any funny business. I'm harmless. It's just that I'm living in a dump at the moment, with no video, no telly, no phone. I'd be really grateful.'

'You're crazy,' she said.

'No, I'm not.'

'Well, you have a lot of nerve.'

'That's true.'

'I don't know you.'

'That's sort of true too, but you know I'm OK.'

She wasn't quite prepared to agree to that, not yet. Instead, stalling, looking for a delaying tactic and simultaneously aware that she was putting him on the spot, she asked, 'Did you find your friend Philip Masterson?'

'Oh yeah,' he said enthusiastically.

'Was he glad to see you?'

'He was knocked out. It was a great reunion and I couldn't have done it without you. I'm very grateful.'

She wasn't entirely prepared to be thanked so effusively, either.

'What do you need the video for?' she asked.

'To watch some films,' and he tapped his bag. His face was bright with optimism. 'You can watch 'em with me if you like.'

'I don't know why I'm even considering this.'

'Because you can tell I'm not a bad person.'

'You're asking a lot, you know.'

'Yeah, but I'm asking very nicely.'

She laughed again; at him, at herself, at the situation, at her inability to say no, at her inclination to say yes. He stood silent and puppyish, waiting for her to speak.

'What videos are they?' she asked.

He emptied the carrier bag out on to the counter and lined up the five video boxes. They were films she hadn't seen, that she barely recognized, but from their titles and packaging she could tell they were somewhat obscure, not very popular, not quite mainstream. They weren't in keeping with her idea of what Mick's tastes would be.

'I won't be watching these movies just for the fun of it,' he said.

'No?'

'No, it's research. I'm studying one of the actors in the films.'

'Studying?'

'Yes, an actor called Justin Carr. You know him?'

'No.'

'You might know his face.' And he pointed to the stills on the back of one of the video boxes. They showed a good-

91

looking, lean-faced, brooding actor. He looked very English, very well-bred, yet dark enough and rough enough to be enigmatic. It was a face she was sure she'd never seen before.

'Justin Carr?' she said. 'Wasn't that one of the names on your list? You went to college with him?'

'Kind of thing.'

'And now you're studying him.'

'That's it.'

'I feel very nervous about letting you use my video,' she said.

'Why? You can watch me the whole time, make sure I don't abuse it or anything.'

'And I feel very nervous about being alone with you in my flat.'

'Why?'

'Because I don't know you.'

'You mean like we haven't been properly introduced? Come on. This is the third time we've met. People get married who've met each other less than that. What do I have to do? Catch another shoplifter?'

'That might help,' she said, and for a moment he feared he'd exhausted the small fund of obligation she felt towards him.

'There are five films there,' she said. 'That's a lot of video watching.'

'Yes, but I don't need to see them all from beginning to end, just the parts my friend's in.'

For a moment she seemed less sure than ever. It sounded so suspicious. It sounded like no way to watch movies.

He said, 'Look, I'll meet you after work, we'll go to your place, we'll watch videos, that's all. I'll even buy the take-away. I'll even let you keep the videos. Please.'

She felt sure she was going to say no, but then he smiled at her, said 'Please' again, and completely against her instincts and her common sense she found herself saying 'OK.'

He was there waiting for her when she finished work and although he tried to talk her out of it they travelled by tube to her home in Bethnal Green. He wanted to walk but she said that was ridiculous. So the tube it was. They didn't talk much on the way there and Mick was glad. It took a lot of concentration to keep his claustrophobia in check. For her part, Judy had decided not to worry about what might or might not happen when they got home. She didn't usually get to meet men like Mick, and she suspected he was the sort of man for whom all the usual manners and rules didn't apply. She didn't think he was a threat to her, yet she felt she was definitely letting herself in for something.

She lived in one of a long row of terraced houses tucked away in the streets behind the Bethnal Green Museum of Childhood. Most of the neighbouring houses were neat and cared for, but the one she lived in was mean and decrepit; cracked rendering over dodgy brickwork, paint flaking off the front door, rotten windows, abandoned scaffolding in the front garden.

She rented a place at the top of the house. It was more than a bedsit but less than a flat; her own kitchen but a shared bathroom. The room where she lived and slept was long and thin, low-ceilinged, the eaves cutting a diagonal slice out of one side. There was a small bookcase stacked with paperback novels, a crammed chest of drawers, clothes hung on hangers from the picture rail, fancy lamps and candlesticks, a vase of fresh flowers, and there in the corner were the television and video. The single bed had been partly disguised as a couch with cushions, and although the room was tidy, it was so small that every time Mick moved he felt he was going to knock something over, break something, destroy the careful order.

'Nice place,' he said unconvincingly.

The walls were painted a stark, wintry shade of blue and she had hung no pictures on them, but on one wall, above the gas fire, stretching from the mantelpiece to the ceiling, was a large map of London. It was perhaps three feet by four feet, and it covered an area from Brentford in the west to London City airport in the east; from Haringey in the north to Streatham

93

Common in the south. Mick knew none of these places, and he thought it was an ugly thing with which to decorate a wall. It made the place look unhomely, as if it were an office.

She saw him looking at the map and said quickly, 'It doesn't cover the whole of London by any means. It leaves off all sorts of fringe areas of Greater London. But then there are parts of London that I wouldn't think of as London at all. Still, it's good enough for my purposes.'

He wasn't interested enough to ask what those purposes were, but he noticed a couple of hooks directly above the map, and nearby some sheets of rolled transparent plastic. It looked as though the hooks were designed to hold these transparent sheets in place over the map. And as he looked a little more closely he saw that some of the sheets weren't wholly transparent at all. They'd been marked with mysterious arrows and crosses.

Judy waved a hand at the map and the sheets and said, 'It's just a game I sometimes play.'

That was all the explanation she intended to give, and it was enough for Mick. He thought nothing of it and sat down on the edge of the bed, carefully, as though he might be about to sit on something precious and breakable.

'I'm sorry. It's a slum, I know,' she said.

He didn't disagree but said, 'You should see my place.'

'How come you live in a slum?' she asked. 'For that matter, how come you don't own a television?'

'Too poor,' he said facetiously.

'I don't believe that. I know how much that suit must have cost.'

'You can't live in a suit, can you?'

'So where *do* you live?'

'Sheffield,' he said. 'Sheffield, Sex City.'

'But in London.'

'Park Lane, Hackney,' he said. 'But I'm not living there. Just staying there.'

She went across and looked at her map to see where it was.

'I've never been there,' she said.

'You're lucky.'

'What do you do for a living?' she asked.

'Let's watch some films, yeah?'

The collection of videos that Mick had assembled did not by any means constitute the complete filmic works of Justin Carr, but the examples were representative enough to form a good introduction. They also came from the raunchier end of his catalogue. None of them was remotely pornographic but there was often nudity, even if it was mostly female and mostly tasteful.

The first of them, called *Red Fins*, was a kind of English road movie, and Mick watched intently as the plot unfolded. Carr had a lead part as a wheeler-dealer who imports classic sixties American cars from California. He was even better-looking on screen than he had been in the stills. He was animated yet vulnerable, tough yet boyish.

There was a cops and robbers plot involving drugs and stolen cars and Mick was engrossed by it, but Judy saw the way he became even more involved whenever Carr appeared on screen. It was as though he was an obsessive fan of the actor, seeing only him and only his performance.

In a coda after everything had been worked out, Carr and an actress had sex on the bonnet of a Cadillac while it was parked on a beach in Northumberland. The scene was apparently shot at dawn, the sky was icy blue, and the two actors looked freezing and windswept as they flailed about on top of the car. However, it was shot from a great distance so that although they were both completely naked the scene was scarcely explicit at all.

The moment the film ended, as the credits started to roll, Mick pounced on the machine and put in the next video. This time it was some kind of Australian co-production, called *Roo*, set in the Outback, with Carr the only English actor surrounded by a cast of leathery character actors who all looked vaguely familiar from other Australian films and soap operas. There were a couple of mystical Aborigines who kept staring off into the distance in a knowing manner, and there was love interest in the form of a female photographer who was there taking pictures of the local wildlife.

This time Mick couldn't be bothered to watch the scenes where Carr didn't appear and he hit the fast forward button whenever Carr wasn't on screen. There was a brief sex scene between Carr and the photographer in an end-of-the-world desert motel, while the radio played 'I've Got You Under My Skin'. The lighting was very dim and orange and the actress held a sheet around her most of the time. Carr undertook a little breast-fondling and kissing, but in fact they never got very far with it since they were disturbed by vile animal noises coming from outside the motel.

Once that scene was over, even though it was some way from the end of the film Mick yanked the video out. He'd seen enough.

He slotted in the next video, *Unhappy Jack*, a coming-of-age movie set in an unnamed London suburb in 1980 just before the Falklands War. Carr had an unpromising role as the boyfriend of the eponymous fifteen-year-old hero's older sister. Mick only stayed with it as far as the moderately kinky sex scene in which, after a drunken night out, Carr watched while the sister did a nude dance for him, pouring wine over her breasts so he could lick it off.

'You mentioned something about a take-away,' Judy said as Mick pulled the tape out of the machine.

'Oh yeah, sure,' said Mick and he extracted a twenty pound note from his pocket and handed it to her.

'Any preference?' she asked as she went to the phone.

'No, no preference,' said Mick, as the fourth film began. This time he skimmed rapidly, not even watching the whole of scenes in which Carr had a major part. It was called *Rochester*, and in Mick's opinion it didn't look like a real film at all. The titles, even the packaging, didn't look the way a film was supposed to look.

It was a long, arty experimental movie, a series of 'meditations' on the life of the seventeenth-century rake. It looked as though it had been largely improvised; the dialogue rambled and occasionally died completely.

There was a fair amount of nudity, although Carr was fully dressed throughout, and in his biggest scene he tried with increasing difficulty to read an obscene poem by Rochester while a female skinhead, naked but for black stockings and a ruff, fiddled around inside his trousers and distracted him. But by and large it was all talk and no action. Mick paid it little attention and when the pizzas were delivered he was able to look away from the screen and eat without feeling he was missing much. He ran the final third of the film through on fast forward and found nothing worth stopping for.

The final movie was called *City of Skin* and was the classiest of the bunch; one of those late-eighties movies about corruption in the City, about public and private morality, in which the lead characters lived in opulent converted warehouses, drove Porsches and talked about Docklands development, took cocaine, did ruthless financial deals, and had athletic and empty sex. Carr was the leading man. His sex scenes (there were two) both took place in his massively over-designed penthouse looking out over the Thames. The first scene was shot in daylight and after romping all around the room he pressed his naked co-star up against the flat's big panoramic window, and there was an external shot from the river showing her breasts and belly squashed flat against the glass. The second scene was shot at night and made great use of reflections. The blinds were open and the lights were on in the penthouse so that this time the windows reflected the two people having sex inside the room while the lights of London outside were superimposed over them.

Again the rest of the film scarcely interested Mick, but this time he rewound the tape and watched both sex scenes again. Then, at last, he'd seen enough. He knew what Justin Carr looked like from all angles. He glanced at his watch. It was very

97

late. He hadn't been much of a guest and he reckoned he must have overstayed his welcome. He turned towards Judy and was ready to apologize but he saw she'd fallen asleep beside him on the divan. He looked around and found a coat to drape over her, then without waking her he let himself out and walked home, leaving the videos behind but being sure to take his *A–Z* with him.

# A FUNNY FEELING INSIDE OF ME

With a wide, innocent, slapped-on smile across his other-wise vacant face, Mick rang the doorbell belonging to Justin Carr. He stood outside the white mews house, one of a dozen or so clustered together in a safe, still Kensington enclave. There were a number of untidily parked cars along the mews, a woman was out washing a green Peugeot and two girls were visible at desks in one of the properties that had been converted into an office, but the street was as quiet and calm as any spot in London.

Mick looked up at the first-floor windows of Carr's house. The curtains were open and the overhead light was on to keep away the dark afternoon. Mick rang the bell again. It was a long time before he heard heavy feet on the stairs, descending to the hall, and when the front door was opened, it was thrown wide with uncoordinated abandon, with no hint of the retiring film star.

Mick didn't immediately recognize the actor in the doorway despite having watched so many of his videos. Justin Carr stood there wearing a white bathrobe, his feet in heavy black workboots. His hair was short but tangled, his face unshaven and unwashed. It was hard to tell whether he was drunk or hungover, but something about him wasn't quite steady. He looked fatter than on screen, his face less angular, less defined, less itself. He appeared shorter too, but Mick had expected that.

'Yeah?' Carr said, expressing neither surprise nor interest nor welcome, his voice very different from the warm, trained tones he used professionally.

'Mr Carr, Justin,' Mick said enthusiastically. 'I'm a great fan!'

Carr rolled his eyes in theatrical disbelief, and said under his breath, 'Thanks.' His hand was on the edge of the door ready to close it briskly, but Mick said, 'I wonder if you could do me a favour?' and his foot was in the door before Carr could take any further evasive action.

'That all depends,' Carr said.

'Of course,' said Mick, the smile still on his face, but now with an additional look of soft, supplicating humility. 'I only want an autograph.'

'You have a pen, I suppose.'

Mick did. He held out a pen and a video cassette of *Roo*. The cover showed an illustration of Carr clutching and kissing a blonde, basque-clad actress in a scene that, as far as Mick remembered, didn't appear in the finished movie. Carr took them and said, 'This won't write on plastic,' and he pulled out the insert card and autographed that, scrawling across the actress's bare shoulder. There was little space for a signature and the autograph spilled over on to the dark colours of the rest of the design where it became invisible. Mick looked on disappointedly.

'Maybe if you signed the other side, the blank side of the card,' he said.

Disobligingly Carr turned the card over, signed it, said, 'OK,' and handed it back.

'Much better,' Mick agreed.

'Gotta go now. Got a bath running,' said Carr.

Mick's foot remained in the door, and although the smile stayed on his face Carr was now aware of the threatening bulk and presence of his visitor.

'You don't mind signing autographs?' Mick asked.

'It's very flattering,' Carr replied unconvincingly.

'You do it often?'

'Not in circumstances quite like these, no.'

'You get a lot of fans chasing after you? Women?'

'No.'

'Or aspiring actors who want to know the secret of your success?'

'No.'

'Hey.' Mick spread his arms in a big open gesture. 'I'm being a pest, aren't I? On your doorstep, with you only half dressed.'

'That's right,' Carr agreed.

'So why don't I come in?'

'No,' Carr said firmly.

'Why not?'

Carr's voice changed, became harder, more actorly. 'I've given you my autograph, that's as much as I owe you. That's as much as you're entitled to. I'm going. So if you'd move your foot . . .'

He tussled with the door but Mick's foot resisted the effort.

'He's given me his autograph, aren't I the lucky one?' Mick sneered. The dark clouds rolled across his demeanour for a second, then just as rapidly rolled away, but the sudden darkening was more than enough to disconcert Carr. He continued trying to close the door as Mick asked him, 'What's your favourite film? Who's your favourite leading lady? Who's your favourite director?'

As though he was slipping into character, Carr became strong, forthright, heroic. 'Move your foot,' he said. 'Now.'

It was convincing enough as a piece of acted authority but Mick was unimpressed. Without warning he gave Carr a slap across the face. It wasn't hard, and it was surprise more than anything else that sent Carr staggering backwards into the hallway. Mick followed him in and closed the door behind them.

'I really do admire some of your work,' Mick said. 'But that's not the point. It's not why I'm here. I'm not here as a stalker or some crazed fan.'

'What do you want?' Carr wanted to know. 'What the fuck do you want?'

'An old line. I've heard that before somewhere. And I usually reply that I just want to talk.'

Carr appeared suddenly very frightened and desperate. Mick noticed the actor's hands were shaking but perhaps they'd been shaking all along, and not only from fear.

'OK,' Carr said, trying hard to gain a little control, his voice designed to calm both himself and his assailant. 'Let's talk. You'd better come up.'

He scrambled up the stairs ahead of Mick, the boots making him comically awkward, into the body of the house, a single open space that looked cluttered yet uninhabited. The walls were bare and painted white, the floor was completely covered with pale jute matting. There were no chairs, no table, no sofa, but a mattress was laid out under the windows as though someone was camping out there. Black sheets and a duvet spilled across the floor.

The absence of furniture was countered by a littering of electronic toys: a giant flat-screened television with speakers placed in corners of the room and an integrated stereo system, an electronic keyboard, a fancy telephone with built-in fax machine, a video camera on a tripod, an exercise treadmill, a radio-controlled toy truck. Everything looked pristine and new, expensive and state of the art.

And strewn amid this hardware were empty bottles – champagne, saki, mineral water – stacks of CDs, overflowing ashtrays, Rizla papers, glossy magazines, telephone directories, a couple of movie scripts. It was an adult playroom. Carr looked as though he had been playing for a long time but whether alone or with others Mick couldn't tell.

Carr positioned himself in the middle of the room, accustomed to being centre stage, yet he seemed to be troubled by his lines, and he didn't quite have the measure of his audience yet. He looked over at all the expensive gear he had accumulated.

'If this is a burglary,' he said to Mick, 'you've struck very lucky indeed. I hope you've got a van.'

Mick ignored this, then as if something had been preying on his mind he said, 'I thought you told me you were running a bath.'

'I lied. I was trying to get rid of you.'

Mick considered the answer, deciding how insulted he ought to feel at having been lied to, and whether he should do something about it. He looked around the room, taking it all in, as though he might be asked to make an inventory, then he said, 'Give me your wallet.'

Without a fuss, Carr picked up his jacket which was bundled on the floor, fished out the wallet and handed it over.

Mick said, 'I'm going to take your money because if I didn't I wouldn't be able to afford to stay in the rathole I'm staying in and then I'd be on the street in a doorway or something, so you can look on this as a way of fighting homelessness. OK?'

Mick examined the contents of the wallet. There wasn't much cash in it, but he showed no disappointment. In fact he seemed preoccupied by something else. 'This is what's called a mews house, yes?' he asked.

'Yes,' said Carr.

'Funny word, mews.'

'Not really,' said Carr.

'No?'

'Originally it meant a cage for hawks, especially when they were mewing, which is another word for moulting. In the fourteenth century the king's mews were in Charing Cross but Henry VII disposed of his hawks and used them as stables. The usage spread. Most London mews were stables at one time or another.'

As he spoke he visibly gained confidence and stature. Having lines to say suited him.

'Is that right?' Mick asked.

'Yes.'

'How did you know that?'

'Some research I once had to do for a part I was playing.'

'Well, thank you, Justin, that was very educational,' Mick

said, and he sounded as though he might almost have meant it. 'I suppose there must be mews houses outside of London but I don't think I've ever seen one. By and large people outside of London wouldn't be seen dead in converted birdcages, would they?'

'Probably not,' Carr agreed. He thought it was good to agree.

Mick said, 'As an actor I suppose you've got to live in London, haven't you? No point trying to be an actor in Pontefract, I guess.'

'Quite.'

'Is that your real name by the way, Justin Carr?'

'It is, as a matter of fact.'

'Sounds very actorish, doesn't it? And is that your real voice or do you put on that posh accent?'

'It's real enough.'

'And do you do other accents? Welsh, Geordie, Yorkshire?'

'It's not my strength, no.'

'But they teach you that stuff at acting school, don't they? Go on, do a Yorkshire accent, because I'm from Yorkshire, see, and I'll tell you whether or not it's any good.'

'I really couldn't,' Carr demurred.

'Yeah, you could.'

'I don't want to. OK?'

Mick shook his head. No, it wasn't OK. He slapped Carr in the face again, much, much harder this time, putting his weight behind it. Carr was knocked backwards, and he fell against the television screen before steadying himself.

'Leave the face alone, all right?' he said plaintively. 'I've got a screen test in a couple of days' time. It's rather important.'

'Then be a bit co-operative, why don't you?'

'All right, I'll do a Yorkshire accent if you insist. What do you want me to say?'

Mick shrugged. 'Anything you like. In your own time.'

Carr began to recite Hamlet's 'To be or not to be' soliloquy in a broad Yorkshire accent. Mick let him run through the whole speech. The accent wasn't bad. It wandered a little, starting out somewhere in the vicinity of Harrogate and ending up nearer Barnsley, but it sounded passable enough. Mick had heard much less convincing accents on television. 'Aye, there's the rub,' was particularly authentic. When Carr had finished, Mick applauded and Carr allowed himself a tiny, self-congratulatory smile.

'The sound of applause, that's what it's all about, eh?' said Mick.

'Perhaps,' Carr agreed.

'Must be different with film though.'

'Yes, it's very different with film.'

Carr had a number of thoughtful things to say about the difference between film and stage acting, and there were a number of anecdotes he used in press interviews to demonstrate his points. Despite the inappropriateness of the situation he was thinking of launching into one of them when Mick said, 'One thing I've always wanted to ask an actor. Let's say you're doing a love scene with an actress and you're in bed together and you're naked and you're kissing and all that, well, it stands to reason you're going to get an erection. But supposing you don't fancy the actress, and supposing you don't get an erection, well, doesn't that really piss her off?'

Carr looked at him in a kind of wonderment. How could this man seem guileless, so innocent, and yet be so dangerous? The effects of that last slap across the face were still reverberating through Carr's head. Could Mick really want to discuss acting technique at a time like this, and was he really as stupid as he appeared?

'It doesn't take much to piss off most actresses,' Carr said ruefully.

'Yeah, sex scenes,' said Mick. 'They must be really tricky. What's that old theatrical adage? Never be filmed having sex with animals or children.'

'Never *work* with animals or children.'

'I knew it was something like that.'

'You think you're a bit of a funny man, don't you?' Carr said boldly.

'Do I?'

'Maybe you should be on the stage.'

'Should I?'

Carr was feeling braver, a little more in charge.

'Look, I'd be really grateful if you'd just get on with whatever it is you're here for,' he said.

'Well, your gratitude really means a lot to me, Justin, but I'm not yet ready to get on with it, and you should probably be grateful that I'm not.'

He moved towards Carr and gave him a full-blown back-hander across the face. Carr jerked sideways as though an electric shock had been sent through him. His jaw snapped shut and his teeth bit into the soft flesh inside his mouth. He tasted blood.

'You see, I don't care very much about whether or not I spoil your screen test,' Mick added; then, as though returning to a subject they'd been discussing previously, 'Of course you've never really shown your penis on celluloid, have you, Justin? Have you?'

'No,' Justin said, pain marbling his voice.

'Don't blame you,' Mick said. 'I mean when it comes to showing your penis on screen it's no good saying size doesn't matter, is it? These days you know your audience are bound to have seen some pretty hefty guys. These days everybody's seen some porn movies, haven't they? And who the hell can compete with those lads? Not that I'm comparing you with them professionally. You're an artist. They're just porn stars.'

Carr said nothing. He was not going to engage with this new, crazy turn in the conversation.

'You know,' Mick said, 'a lot of struggling young actresses find themselves having to make porn films to pay the bills, and these films can come back and really hurt an actress's career, can't they? How about you, Justin, have you got some sordid little movie stashed away somewhere that's going to come back and haunt you?'

'No,' Carr insisted.

'But then you would say that, wouldn't you?'

'Look, please,' said Carr, no longer at all brave, no longer able to put on much of an act, 'can't we stop this absurd performance? Can't you please just get on with whatever you're here for.'

Mick looked around the room again. It might have been that he was looking for something to steal, but his eyes settled on the video camera.

'Does that thing work?' he asked.

'Yes.'

'OK, set it up for me. Let's make a movie.'

Carr hesitated just for a moment and Mick took half a step towards him. That was enough to dispel any hesitation. Carr quickly set up the camera so that it was pointing towards Mick, and so that Mick's high-contrast image, swathed in a blue aura, appeared on the screen of the television. Then Mick noticed there was a cassette in the video machine and that it was recording.

'Hey,' he said. 'Wouldn't it be ironic if you managed to get my face on film and then hand it over to the police?'

He half pushed and half kicked Carr across the room, only stopping when one of the walls blocked his way. Carr fell to the floor and Mick booted him in the stomach a couple of times, driving him into the skirting board, before leaving him to lie motionless. He walked away, grabbed the cassette and waited until Carr was in a state to listen to him again.

Mick said, 'You know what they say about some actors, Justin, they say so and so's such a great performer you'd be happy to hear him recite the London telephone directory. You must have heard people say that. OK, let's try a little experiment. Let's see if you're that kind of performer.'

He grabbed the collar of the white bathrobe and pulled Carr to his feet. He yanked the robe down and aside, then completely off so that the actor stood naked in front of one of the room's bare white walls. Mick turned the camera to face Carr. The image on the television screen looked pale and inert, bleached of line and colour, and Carr looked a pathetic, abused creature, poorly framed at its centre. Mick threw a telephone directory at him. He caught it ham-fistedly and desperately turned to the first page.

'Don't bother with that section,' Mick said. 'Forget the dialling information, the codes and all that. Start where the names start. And Justin . . . do it with feeling.'

Carr found the appropriate page and was surprised to find that the entries all began with numbers, the 1st Royal Eltham Scout Group, the 5th Putney Sea Scouts, the 15th Wimbledon Scout Group, but he read out the names, addresses and phone numbers as clearly and correctly as he knew how. He'd read perhaps half a dozen entries when Mick screamed at him, 'No, no, no, Justin. There's no drama, no light and shade, no passion.'

Carr said he was sorry and began again, making a determined effort to bring drama, light and shade and passion to his absurd reading, though he was far too frightened to really know what he was doing. Mick let him continue for a while before interrupting again and saying, 'No, Justin, it's just not working for me. I tell you what, let's try the Fs.'

Carr nodded and awkwardly skimmed through the directory till he found the Fs and began again. He'd read out entries for Faal, Faas, Faasen, Fabb, Fabbicatore and Fabrini before Mick yelled that this was supposed to be the London telephone directory, not the Roman one. He didn't want to hear all those foreign names. Carr moved on rapidly to Faber but Mick remained unimpressed.

'No, no, Justin, it's still very, very lifeless. I tell you what, since it's London, why not read it in a cockney accent? I know you can do accents.'

Carr nodded agreement and started to read the entries for Fagan. 'Broader cockney,' Mick shouted. Carr tried to broaden the accent as he read out a few Faheys. 'Broader, much broader,' and Carr exaggerated the accent still further as he read out some Fairbairns and Fairbanks, while Mick shouted, 'And louder with more projection and more fire. I want to feel the hairs standing up on the back of my neck.'

In a loud, projected, fiery, broad cockney accent Carr did his desperate best to read out the Fairley and the Fairman entries, but his voice was trembling with fear and effort, his adopted accent was slipping, and before long Mick was bawling again. 'Are you trying to defy me, Justin? Are you deliberately refusing to take direction?'

'No, no,' Carr assured him. 'I'm doing my best. I am, I really am.'

'OK, Justin, forget the cockney. How about a different kind of London accent? How about Finchley? Can you do a Finchley accent?'

'I'll try,' Carr said desperately, and he read a few more names and phone numbers in a nondescript north London accent before his voice became caught up in his throat, and he stopped and began to sob, his head lolling forwards, his shoulders heaving and shuddering.

'I don't know what you want from me,' he said. 'I'm sorry, but I just don't.'

Mick looked at the poor, naked wretch on the television screen and said grandly, 'I want scale. I want nobility and pathos and dignity and tragedy. I want the magic to shine through these names and addresses. I want the whole of London, all its many facets and characters, all its rich culture and history, to come alive through your performance, Justin. Am I asking too much?'

'I think you're mad,' Carr sobbed.

Mick crossed the room and scythed Carr's legs from under him so that he fell heavily to his knees. Mick stood beside him and produced his gun. He held it to Carr's head, then turned slightly so that he could see the television screen. The gun looked inky and blurred in the image, and bigger than in reality. Mick's face looked fleshy and unformed, while Carr's was a picture of real, not acted, terror. Carr could feel the gun being moved across his temple and he began to shudder uncontrollably.

'It's OK, Justin,' Mick said. 'We're not making a snuff movie here. Not today. Not if you behave yourself, anyway.'

Mick looked around once again, as though hoping that a chair might somehow magically have appeared. He walked out of range of the camera and settled for the windowledge, leaving Carr to weep and kneel and shake on screen. Mick looked into the quiet mews below. If anyone down there had heard the shouting and the acting they had chosen to ignore it.

Mick said to Carr, 'Do you know that song "Maybe it's because I'm a Londoner that I love London town"? Do you? Well, you know, I've always thought it's a really poxy song. I mean it's not good enough to love a place just because you happen to come from there, is it? Loving it just because you're a Londoner is rubbish. It's not a reason, it's just a prejudice. What do they know of London, who only London know? You follow?'

Justin was beyond following or replying, but Mick continued.

'Why not say you love London because of its architecture or its culture or its people? But just because you happen to be a Londoner . . . well, I think it's crap. It's like me saying, maybe it's because I'm a northerner that I think all southerners are soft nancy boys who deserve to have their faces kicked in. Yeah. It may be true, but it's not a *reason*, if you see what I mean. Tell me Justin, can you sing?'

Justin shook his head vehemently to say that he couldn't sing at all, definitely not.

''Course you can sing,' Mick insisted. 'Don't be modest. Don't they teach you anything at RADA? Come on, give me a few choruses of "Maybe It's Because I'm A Londoner", otherwise I'll come over there and knock eight kinds of shit out of you.'

Softly, sadly, boyishly, Carr began to sing the song. It was a frail, paper-thin rendition, but Mick appeared to be finding it very effective.

'That's lovely,' he said. 'A voice like yours deserves a much bigger audience. Tell you what, Justin, I want you to go down into the street, into your mews, and I want you to sing that song, not just for me but for all your neighbours and for all your fans and for anyone else who happens to be passing by. Some of them may think it's a bit eccentric of you to be singing in the street stark naked, but you're an actor, Justin, you're entitled to a few eccentricities. Why don't you do it in the road? And the thing is, while you're down there performing, I'll be up here watching you and I'll have my gun trained on you, and if the performance slips below par in any way, if I detect a lack of commitment, a lack of respect for the audience, I'll shoot you. Got that? Sorry if it seems a little harsh, but everybody's a critic these days, aren't they, Justin?'

Carr sobbed and nodded, and somewhat to Mick's surprise he left the house, went down into the mews and began to sing. He sang the song much more loudly than he had before, with a kind of fierce, tuneless passion, and as he sang he walked the full length of the mews, giving the performance his all, turning the song into a desperate showstopper.

The two girls in the office stood at the window staring and giggling in disbelief at the naked man in the street, a man whose face looked oddly familiar from television or somewhere. Meanwhile, the woman who'd been washing the Peugeot stepped back into her house the moment Carr appeared. Once inside she phoned the police, and though they didn't consider it an emergency, although they didn't rush, they did eventually arrive.

Carr was still naked and still singing when the police car pulled up. As the police threw a blanket around him and escorted him back into his own house, he began to talk wildly about an intruder, about Hamlet, about being forced to read aloud from the telephone directory, about having a gun put to his head. But the police looked over the house, saw the empty bottles, the unmade bed, the Rizla papers, and concluded that Justin Carr was a man who had been working and playing far too hard for his own good.

# STRIPPING

Gabby would never have said stripping was an art, she didn't say things like that, but she'd have insisted there was a definite knack to it. Not everybody could do it, that was for sure. Having a reasonable body, having no problems about getting your kit off in public and being prepared to go through a few lecherous dance moves was only a part of it, and not really the most important part. It definitely wasn't something you could train for, and although it was a thing you generally got better at the more you did it, there was a whole category of girls who did it night after night, year after year, and never got the hang of it at all. If your heart and instincts weren't in the right place you were wasting your time. But if you had a certain native talent for it and if you were willing to put in some effort, then you could keep on working, getting well paid, and winning over audiences long after glamour girls with much better bodies had been booed off the stage.

It was a funny thing though, and she'd seen it dozens of times, there was a certain sort of girl who got less sexy the more clothes she took off. They'd come on doing the dance of the seven veils or whatever, and they'd look really hot with these seven flimsy bits of costume draped around them. But by the time they were down to the last veil you'd lost interest, and by the time they were completely naked it was about as sexy as looking at a diagram in a school biology book.

Gabby wasn't like that at all. There are some people, possibly many people, who consider the naked human female form to be a chaste, wholesome, natural, decent thing. But these people have never seen Gabby. There was something truly, darkly indecent about her nakedness. It came partly out of the inherent lines and shape of her body; a skinny rib cage, big unsiliconed breasts, dark nipples, a patch of pubic hair that waved itself at you. And there was also the matter of what she *did* with this body. She was not a great dancer and she knew it, yet she had the knack of moving in a sensual, sexy, rhythmical way that managed to display and flaunt every intimate surface and crevice. When Gabby danced, everybody in the place, from the keen salivators in the front row to cool determined drinkers leaning against the back wall, they all got an eyeful, and they took notice of what they saw.

There was also the face. Some strippers make a living out of looking innocent, meek, virginal, the nice, sweet girl who doesn't look the stripper type. But Gabby *did* look the type — in spades — and she worked hard at looking that way. She had big, black-ringed eyes, a wide painted mouth, long, shaggy, red hair. She looked like a slut and that suited her audiences just fine, and it had always suited Mick too.

Mick had had a big influence on her look and on her performances. When she'd first met him he was a bouncer at a club where she performed. She'd thought he was just a tough guy, a bit of a thug, hard but brainless. But after they'd been out together a couple of times she realized she'd been very wrong. He was full of surprises. He occasionally read books. He knew things. He'd got some imagination and he was a bit of a thinker.

He came up with the idea of her doing a routine as Elizabeth I, complete with full Elizabethan gear including a crown and sceptre. The costume had cost a fortune and the act hadn't gone down noticeably better than when she'd just stripped off her ordinary stage gear, but Mick was really into it by then. He fancied himself as a stage director. He came up with a Cleopatra routine and a Florence Nightingale routine, and he'd wanted her to do Boadicea but Gabby didn't think anyone would know who Boadicea was. Mick was disappointed and they'd argued about it, but in the end he'd seen it her way. He'd had the good sense to realize you can't do an act you don't believe in.

Gabby was grateful to Mick. A stripper needed a gimmick and you had to be very careful these days. The schoolgirl routine had been part of the stripper's repertoire for as long as anybody could remember, but in recent times you couldn't walk on stage dressed as a schoolgirl without stirring up all sorts of feelings about child abuse. You couldn't carry a whip because there'd always be some daft bastard in the audience who'd find a way of leaping up, grabbing it and using it on you. Wildlife was even worse. She'd known a few girls who'd used snakes in their acts, and one who'd had a pet monkey. But now if you appeared with an animal the audience felt cheated if you didn't have sex with it.

Yeah, Mick had been good for her but, at the same time, she found his interest a bit strange. A lot of her previous boyfriends had wanted to stop her stripping altogether, either by trying to coax her out of it or by laying down the law and threatening her. She wasn't having any of it. Stripping was her. It was what she did. She'd lost a few decent men because of it, but that was a price she was willing to pay. With Mick, however, the fact that she stripped seemed to be part of what he was attracted to. He liked to watch her perform. It turned him on. The knowledge that he'd be going home with the woman who was parading naked in front of a room full of men was a big thrill for him.

That was weird, but it seemed weirder still, since in lots of ways Mick was so incredibly straight. He didn't drink much. He didn't do drugs. He didn't even like Gabby to smoke dope, and he'd have gone mad if he'd known about all the stuff she snorted and swallowed when she wasn't with him. She needed it. She didn't like to be too clean when she performed. The right combination of chemicals could really help with the act, could make her more confident, wilder, could give her that necessary sharpness and edge. She'd never injected though. He'd have seen the needle marks. He still got mad when he thought about the Celtic cross she'd had tattooed on her right arm, and she'd had that done long before she met him. The way he talked you'd think that tattooing was a kind of sacrilege. He didn't even like the fact that she had pierced ears, which was pretty funny considering that half the strippers she knew had pierced nipples.

There were also the razor marks on her wrists and forearms, half a dozen per arm, not very deep, not very convincing really, just a lame, hapless attempt at hurting herself. There hadn't even been that much blood and nobody at the hospital had been at all surprised. These scars, for some reason, he didn't mind. Maybe they even appealed to him. They showed that she was weak and in need of him. They also meant that she always wore gloves when stripping, never took them off however naked the rest of her became.

Mick's smattering of history was enough to pass for originality in the world of stripping, and he was the one who'd come up with the idea of the Beefeater. He'd turned up at her flat one day carrying a Beefeater's tunic and a hat. That would only cover the top half of her body but he reckoned that was fine. Stockings and high heels on the bottom half would get the rest of the job done. She pointed out that Beefeaters were always men but Mick said that was part of the point. The next day he turned up with an eight-inch plaster model of Big Ben that he'd found in a junk shop and he suggested she could use it in the act if the occasion demanded.

By then she was performing in London quite regularly, and she'd said she thought it might be carrying coals to Newcastle, that they'd seen enough of Beefeaters down there, but in fact the act was a success and went down as well in London as anywhere else.

Gabby had the ability to work a crowd, to vary her act so that it hit them where they lived. There were strippers who went through the same tired old routines regardless of the circumstances. They'd do the same act whether they were performing for a hundred drunken squaddies or for a coach party of retired vicars. Gabby liked to be flexible. She liked to pick up on the crowd's energy, provoking them, being egged on by them, improvising like a good jazz musician, finding herself doing things that she didn't know she was capable of.

Of course, money came into it. A point would come in her act when she'd circulate the room holding an empty pint glass in her hand, asking for money, getting the men to dig a little deeper, prising and teasing the cash out of them, telling them that if they filled the glass then she'd go a bit further with her act. This inevitably meant audience participation. If the glass filled up the way she wanted it to then she'd sit on men's laps, unbutton their shirts, rub their chests, or spray canned cream across her breasts and have punters lick it off. Shoving the plaster model of Big Ben into herself was another little extra, but she had to be careful with it. That point on the top looked as though it could be lethal.

But mild audience participation and a bit of self-penetration was as far as she ever went. There were some girls who'd do anything on stage. Anything. They always said they were only doing it for the money but Gabby thought it was more complicated than that. They'd go down on their knees, suck men's cocks, they'd fuck them, they'd let themselves be whipped. They didn't seem to be actually enjoying it, not in any straightforward sexual way, at least, but they were definitely getting something out of it, satisfying something that needed to be satisfied, and not just the need for money.

Gabby had never been tempted to go that far. You might as well be a prostitute. She'd met people who talked about 'the sex industry' as all one big happy family, but she didn't feel that she had anything in common with people who fucked for money. She'd even turned down the chance to be in a blue movie, which would have meant an amazing amount of money. But that hadn't tempted her either. Once they'd got you on film they'd got you for good. Someone might recognize you. Your father might see it. At least with a live show the audience was as implicated as the stripper, and once the show was over it was over. Nobody could replay it. Nobody took away anything that was yours.

Mick had never really wanted her to go stripping in London. He thought London was a city where anything could happen, where any sort of horror might afflict you. But the money was good and she'd done quite a few gigs down there and she'd had no trouble at all, so Mick had gradually got used to the idea. There were times when he offered to come with her, offered to drive her there and back, but she'd always refused. She liked to be alone there. It gave her a feeling of independence and sophistication. She liked to make a day of it, do some shopping for clothes and shoes, and that had always been enough to deter him. He wasn't the sort of man you could drag around women's clothes shops. But when she got back she always had to give him a painstakingly detailed account of how the gig had gone, what the place was like, what she'd done in her act, how the crowd had reacted.

Unlike some strippers, Gabby didn't hate men, but she did find them comical. They were so easy to read. You knew exactly what they'd do in any given circumstances. The sight of a naked woman, the mere *promise* of the sight of a naked woman, was enough to make them do almost anything you wanted. And even though he was a strange one, it was pretty much the same with Mick. All the way back from London she'd rehearsed what she was going to tell him, what she was going to say about the gang-rape, so that he'd react in precisely the way she wanted. She knew that if she did it right he'd immediately head down to London, start tracking down six men, and start kicking heads. It was strange to think how much power she had over him, how much he was her creature. But then, she thought, we are all somebody's creature. And predictably enough he'd gone, just like that, so quickly, with such determination, just as she'd wanted and planned.

Life was different without him. Their affair wasn't big or serious or permanent, but they'd seen a lot of each other and there was something missing when he wasn't around. Still, a woman could find ways of entertaining herself. For one thing she could carry on stripping, working on the local circuit that she knew best. It was strange not having him there to watch the show and offer some comments on her performance. She realized how good he was, how he had never put her down, only ever said how she might improve what she was already doing. In his absence she hoped she could keep up his high standards.

She tried to imagine him in London, a place that she barely knew and yet had a powerful attraction towards. She felt for him, a danger to himself but more of a danger to others. Either way she would be glad when it was over, when he'd done what he'd gone to do. She hoped he didn't get hurt. She hoped he didn't get caught. She wished he'd get on with it, do it quickly and efficiently, but more than anything else, she wished he'd stop telephoning her.

# A SECOND PHONECALL HOME

Mick stood in a different phone box, about to ring the same Sheffield number, Gabby's number. The floor of the phone box was wet and it stank of urine. Was that a thing that happened only in London? Maybe it happened everywhere but he wasn't sure. He rarely used phone boxes back home but he had no memory of them being as foul as this one.

'It's me again,' he said the moment the line connected.

'Hello, Mick.'

She sounded bored, weary, not especially pleased to hear from him, as though she found him a bit of a pest.

'Two down, four to go,' he said.

'Really?' And she perked up considerably. 'Any trouble?'

'Not for me,' Mick said serenely. 'Do you want to hear some details?'

'No, not really,' she replied.

'No? I thought you might. I mean I'm punishing these guys, but I was thinking you might want to know precisely how I'm doing it.'

'I'm sure you'll be doing it just right.'

'I might be doing it too little or too much.'

'I don't think you will be.'

'These guys walk away after I've finished with them, you know. They're wounded but they're still walking.'

'That sounds OK to me,' Gabby said.

'If it doesn't sound right I can fix it so they never walk again.'

'I don't mind them walking, I just don't want them doing what they did to me, not ever again.'

'That's a different sort of problem,' Mick said thoughtfully, 'and I've been giving it some consideration. I mean, here I am beating up these guys, but so far they don't know why. I reckon they just think I'm some nutter. I could tell them why I'm doing it, of course. I could say it's because of what they did to you, and there'd be some satisfaction in having them know why it's happening to them. The downside is that the ones I'd attacked would then be able to warn the others and they'd be ready for me and able to protect themselves and that's definitely not what we want, is it?'

She was very quiet at the other end of the phone and then she said hesitantly, 'No, it's probably better if you don't tell them. Let them work it out for themselves.'

'If they worked it out for themselves they'd still be able to forewarn the others, wouldn't they? So what I've been doing is dishing out the punishment in such a way that I don't think they're going to be very eager to go telling anybody about it.'

'I'm sure you're doing right,' she said.

It seemed he could do nothing wrong in Gabby's eyes.

'What you been up to?' he asked.

'Working.'

'Really?'

'Yes. I thought I'd better get back to it, like when you fall off a horse.'

'Very brave of you.'

'It didn't seem all that brave.'

'Weren't you scared?'

'Of what?'

'That it might all happen again.'

'For obvious reasons I tried very hard to put that thought out of my mind, OK?'

'OK. Which act did you do?'

'The Beefeater.'

'The oldies but goodies,' he said.

'The act went well,' she said with finality, before he had a chance to ask.

'I'm glad. No trouble?'

'No, of course not. This is Sheffield. It's not like down there in London.'

'No, it's certainly not,' he said.

'Mick,' she said, sounding suddenly intimate, 'I want you to be careful. I want you to hurry up with what you have to do, don't get into trouble, get it over with and come home.'

'That's exactly what I have in mind.'

'London, it's a dump, isn't it?' she said, and he didn't really think she meant it but he agreed with her anyway.

'Yeah,' he said. 'It's a dump, a slum, a zoo, an armpit. Whatever.'

She made a contented noise down the phone.

'Another thing I was wondering,' Mick said. 'When you went through your ordeal, did you recognize any of the guys?'

'Why do I need to recognize them when you've got their names?'

'I mean, did you recognize any of them at the time, like before they raped you, while they were just watching you strip. Because it turns out one of them's quite famous. This Justin Carr character; he's an actor, he makes films, he appears on television. He's a bit of a sex symbol. He's a familiar face to some people, apparently.'

'Not to me.'

'Me neither,' Mick said. 'But fame's an interesting thing isn't it? I mean if you'd been raped by Roger Moore, you'd have recognized him, wouldn't you? Or Keanu Reeves or Rowan Atkinson. So he's not *that* famous. But I was thinking, he was taking quite a risk, wasn't he? It wouldn't have done his career much good if it had got out that he took part in a gang-bang, would it? You could have gone to the papers or anything.'

'He probably wasn't thinking very straight at the time,'

Gabby said. 'He was drunk. He was crazy. The others were egging him on ... Look, Mick, I know you're there sorting this business out for me, but really I find it very difficult to talk about.'

She started to cry loudly and forlornly. Mick had no possible defence against it.

'I can understand that,' he said sympathetically. 'I'm sorry.'

'Isn't your money running out yet?'

'Oh yeah, maybe it is. Look, before I go—'

The phone went dead and Mick was left wondering whether the money had really run out or whether Gabby had hung up on him.

# JUDY TANAKA REDRAWS THE MAP

Her letter of application had been irresistible; elegantly handwritten on thick, textured paper, and submitted along with one short page of word-processed CV. It said the sorts of thing Stuart wanted to hear, that she'd lived in London all her life, that she'd travelled extensively abroad, that she was an enthusiast for London, its people and its history, that she wanted to share her enthusiasm with the rest of the world.

It sounded to Stuart as if her ambitions might be pitched a little high for someone wanting to be a tour guide with The London Walker, but he recognized that anybody can get carried away when they're trying to get a job. He wanted to meet her. But it was Anita who got particularly excited by the application. She noted that the girl had an interesting Japanese-sounding name, and she had an idea that finding a Japanese-speaking guide would be a great thing for the business, and she told her husband that he really had to interview Judy Tanaka. Stuart did as he was told.

It was at the time when Stuart was trying hard to 'redefine his role' at The London Walker. Anita, by contrast, was looking around desperately, simply trying to find something for him to do. Fortunately she knew that an ad placed in *Time Out* or the *Evening Standard* asking for new tour guides could be guaranteed to bring in scores, maybe hundreds, of applications. The job of sifting through the letters, compiling a lengthy shortlist and then interviewing a lot of candidates could be arranged so that it soaked up massive amounts of Stuart's time. The need for new guides was genuine enough and a truly good one was always worth grabbing even if you weren't in absolute need at that moment. Anita had felt some relief when Stuart took to the task with enthusiasm. He might not have. He might have thought it was beneath his dignity. She was delighted to see that dignity was no longer part of his make-up.

At the interview Judy Tanaka seemed disappointingly taut and awkward. Her long black hair was scraped back, leaving her forehead vulnerably high and bare. Her clothes were beige and tight, uncomfortable-looking, as though she'd bought or perhaps borrowed them specially for the interview and would never wear them again. Stuart introduced himself and tried to make a little joke about his name, but she didn't laugh. Yet the moment she began to talk her real self came flooding out, something much looser and livelier than her look suggested. The voice took him aback, these very correct English tones coming out of an oriental-looking mouth, but he soon got used to it.

He talked her through her CV and that was all fine by him; in most ways far in excess of requirements. The only disappointment was that she didn't speak any Japanese. She was only half-Japanese, it turned out, and her Japanese father had discouraged her from learning the language, in some dubious attempt at integration. Stuart wasn't really disappointed at all, and he thought it served Anita right for jumping to such easy conclusions. What was in a name? He started on some basic questions. He asked what was her favourite London park, and she said Green Park. Her favourite museum, the Horniman. Favourite pub, the Cheshire Cheese. Her favourite mews, Grafton. Her favourite market, Leadenhall.

Before long it didn't feel like an interview at all, but rather like a conversation between two people who had discovered a shared interest. But it was when they started to talk about London follies that he really lost his heart to her.

Stuart mentioned the Pagoda at Kew and wondered if she

preferred the Peace Pagoda in Battersea Park built by some Japanese Buddhist sect. The Nipponzan Myohoji, she said. But no, she didn't love it particularly. She said that when it came to phallic excrescences she was more partial to the Walthamstow 'land lighthouse', built by the United Methodist Free Church in the nineteenth century, as a source of spiritual light. He'd heard of it but never seen it. He asked her if she knew the folly tower off Clapton Common, formerly in the grounds of Craven Lodge, and he felt a certain relief when she didn't. He had started to fear he would have nothing to teach her, that she might know more than him.

Together they fretted about the fate of the Roundhouse and of Battersea Power Station. They wondered whether Marble Arch could now be considered a folly. Or how about the new MI5 building? She said that perhaps 'folly' referred not to any real or imagined lack of utility but rather to the kind of imagination that designed and produced a certain sort of architectural style.

The conversation flowed, went back and forth, and before long Stuart had no doubt that she should be offered a job, though he had some doubts about whether or not she would take it. The role of tour guide seemed far beneath her, and the pay was insulting. He was reluctant even to make the offer in case she turned him down, because, strange as it might be, he would have found that hurtful. He didn't want the interview to end but there was no point delaying or pretending that he had to think about it or consult with somebody else. He offered her the job there and then, and could hardly believe how good he felt when she immediately accepted. Having Judy Tanaka as one of his employees felt like a great step forward, and not simply in the life of the company.

'The people who come on these tours,' he explained, 'they're here to see sights, the Tower of London, Big Ben, Nelson's Column, and in one sense, of course, they've already seen them. They've seen them in books and on postcards and on television, and most importantly they've seen them in their mind. What they're usually doing when they come on a tour is having those images reinforced, making sure that the Tower of London is the way they always imagined it. And in most cases it will be. You may regard that as unfortunate or you may not.'

'I think it's sort of sad,' she said.

'I knew you would,' he replied. He felt that he already knew how she would feel about a lot of things. 'There will be times when you may find yourself unable to resist subverting those easy expectations.'

He smiled and she smiled back, though she didn't really understand what he meant.

Stuart decided to start her on the Whitechapel Walk. This was generally regarded by the other guides as a hardship posting. The number of people on the tour tended to be small, hence there was less chance of making good money from tips. And the people who took the tour were an odd bunch. Some were Jack the Ripper freaks with all the weirdness that involved. Others were genuine East End enthusiasts who often wanted more information than the guides could provide. Others still had simply signed up for the wrong tour, or taken a chance because the Royal London Walk was full, or they had mistaken Whitechapel for Whitehall. Furthermore, the streets of White-chapel contained plenty of local people who thought the spectacle of someone guiding a group of tourists through their manor was an absurd and offensive one that deserved to be loudly mocked and shouted and laughed at.

These competing forms of difficulty could be tricky to deal with, but Stuart didn't doubt that Judy would be able to cope. He knew she had the right stuff. But she still needed to be trained and that was his responsibility too. Sometimes training could take place in batches. If two or three new guides started at the same time, then they could be taught simultaneously. But there was nobody starting at the same time as Judy, so Stuart had her all to himself. He wanted it that way. He looked forward to seeing her again, and spending time with her. In fact he knew that he was looking forward to it far too much. When the morning came to train her he was in a state of ridiculous nervous excitement, an excitement that he hoped he was managing to hide from Anita.

He met Judy at Aldgate East tube station on a chilly April morning. She had abandoned her prim interview clothes and looked much happier in jeans and a stylishly battered suede jacket. He walked her round the prescribed tour route and gave her the script that he'd written for the walk. If a newly recruited guide was awkward or apprehensive he would tell him or her to stick to the script as though it were holy writ. In Judy's case he told her to use it only as a jumping-off point.

He stressed how easy it all was, how basic the level of information had to be. Of course, Jack the Ripper had to be dealt with but Stuart told her he wanted it to be only a small part of the tour. There was more to Whitechapel than that. He said she should quote Charles Booth who in the nineteenth century called Whitechapel the Eldorado of the East, then she should move swiftly on to the Whitechapel Bell Foundry, which had been making bells for Westminster Abbey since 1565. She should take the group to Cable Street, talk briefly about Mosley, and say something bland about continuing racial tensions. He said it was worth mentioning that the *Spitting Image* workshops were nearby.

If the tour took place on a Sunday morning, then it would include Brick Lane market; the only place Stuart had ever seen a stall selling secondhand, partly used candles. If the group was interested in art and if there was a free exhibition on, they could be taken to the Whitechapel Art Gallery. If she liked she could mention the literary connections with Whitechapel: Walter Besant, Peter Ackroyd, Iain Sinclair, but she should go easy on this, since she could be certain that nobody on the tour would ever have heard of any of these people.

Stuart's attitude towards tourists had hardened considerably over the years. He was sure most of them were perfectly sane and rational when they were at home, but there was something about becoming a tourist that robbed them of their basic common sense. There'd been a woman on one of his tours, for instance, who'd asked him where she should go to see the Fire of London.

He told Judy that ending a tour wasn't always easy. Finding the right note of finality could be strangely difficult. There would always be those walkers who lingered on and asked a lot of questions at the end simply because they wanted to prolong the tour in order to feel they were getting more for their money.

If the group had been a particularly hideous one, he recommended taking them to a pub in Commercial Road called, inevitably, Jack the Ripper, a sort of theme pub with murder and sexual mutilation as its subject. If the guide did it just right he or she could slip away quietly before the group realized they'd been dumped in a strip pub.

At the end of this particular morning, however, Stuart took Judy to the Blind Beggar, up the far end of Whitechapel Road, the pub in which Ronald Kray committed the murder which eventually led to his downfall.

'The dangers of telling the truth,' Stuart said enigmatically. 'George Cornell called Ronnie Kray a fat poof, so Ronnie and Reg tracked him down to this pub and Ronnie shot him dead. But George Cornell wasn't lying. What did Ronnie object to? To being called fat or to being called a poof? In fact he was both.'

'Maybe he wanted to be called a big-boned poof,' Judy said.

They had a couple of drinks and they ate their ploughman's lunches and Stuart continued to talk about the joys or otherwise of being a tour guide, and more enthusiastically to talk about the joys and otherwise of living in London. Judy was attentive in a professional sort of way but to Stuart she felt like a long-time colleague, not a raw trainee.

They were getting along better than he could ever have hoped for, and he was not sure whether it was courage or recklessness or simply impatience that drew him on and led him, as if inadvertently, to say, 'Look, this has nothing to do with work, it's not any sort of blackmail, or coercion or sexual harassment or whatever, but something tells me you and I might find ourselves having an affair, don't you think?'

Having said it, he clenched himself, his whole body tensing up, waiting for the terrible consequences, the slap in the face, the drink poured over his head, the sound of breaking glass.

But she said, 'I think so, yes.'

He wanted to cheer, to punch the air like a goal scorer, but instead he said, 'I don't know if it's altogether wise or sensible. Obviously I'm married, very married, and it's not as if I can really offer or promise you anything or . . .'

'Let's just get on with it, shall we?' she said.

He nodded and smiled, and began running through his mental diary to see when and where the consummation might be arranged, but Judy was settling for nothing so organized or so delayed. She stood up, took his hand and pulled him out of his seat and started to walk towards the Ladies. The pub was empty, nobody was looking, and she dragged him in after her, into a cubicle, where she slipped down his trousers and her jeans, and they had rapid, raging and not really all that satisfactory or comfortable sex, but to a large extent it was the thought that counted, and the thought was pretty terrific. Stuart didn't know what had hit him, but it was something big and powerful, like a speedboat.

The next time they met she invited him to her flat. He had offered to pay for a hotel room but she found that inappropriate. They went by taxi to Bethnal Green and he had stepped into her small attic room with some trepidation. The horrors of cheap, rented London accommodation were behind him, though not so far behind that he didn't have horrible memories of rooms and shared flats in places like Bethnal Green. But the room was nice enough, and Judy was there in it and, in any case, as soon as they entered the room she had his clothes off and was humping him ruthlessly on the thin nylon carpet.

She reacted so intensely, so passionately when he made love to her that he knew it couldn't simply be a matter of his touch or his personality or technique. She was reacting to something in herself, a need and a hunger that was largely independent of him.

Afterwards as she lay panting on her back, still naked, legs still splayed, she said, 'I want to be fucked everywhere. In every hole. In every position. In every London borough. In every postal district.'

Stuart grunted uncomprehendingly.

'You know, when sex is good,' she continued, 'when it's really, really good, I feel as though I'm disappearing, being pulverized, being fucked into oblivion, so that I'm nothing, just particles of air pollution, debris, smog, particles of soot and skin floating through the air and settling on the city.'

Stuart didn't know what to say. He dressed slowly and went to the kitchenette to make coffee. As Mick would do later, he had noticed the wall map of London the moment they'd walked into the room but hadn't had much time to comment on it. Now he could look at it more closely and see that there was a sheet of transparent plastic hanging in front of it, marked with a series of hand-drawn coloured crosses. When he'd made the coffee, when Judy had put some clothes on, he asked her what the map was all about.

She didn't give a direct answer. Instead she took down the existing plastic sheet and replaced it with another that hadn't been drawn on. She got a couple of coloured marker pens, a red and a blue, and handed him the latter. Then she asked him to make a cross at every spot on the map where he'd ever lived.

He considered that by most people's standards he'd moved around a lot in London, especially in his early years there, and had lived all over the place. That fact seemed to please Judy. He stood in front of the map and found himself making a dozen or so crosses. The pen skidded over the slick plastic surface leaving behind thick, rather imprecise marks. There were some strange, distant scatterings, one in East Dulwich, one in Lee, one in Hendon. Even while he was living in these places they'd seemed wrong, like excursions away from the locations where he really belonged. However, there was a definite clustering around west London, half a dozen or so crosses within a trapezoid that had Notting Hill, Marylebone, West Hampstead and Swiss Cottage as its corners, what he thought of as his area, the place where he now lived with his wife. A dust cloud of guilt suddenly blew through his mind and he had to fight hard to sweep it away.

Then Judy gave him the red pen and told him to mark the transparent sheet with all the places he'd ever had sex. Only slightly embarrassed, he did as asked. Initially the pattern was the same as the previous one. With the exception of one rough, shared flat off the Goldhawk Road, where he'd only stayed for a couple of weeks, he'd managed to have sex in all the places he'd lived. But soon the pattern became very different indeed. There were now marks in all sorts of outlying districts, places where girlfriends had lived: places like Gipsy Hill, Crouch End, Elephant and Castle. There were occasions when he had slept with women on other people's floors, after parties in Brixton and the Old Kent Road. He had a clear but disconnected memory of being at a very dull dinner party, and of slipping into one of the bedrooms for a tremendous quickie with a woman called Lynn. He was fairly sure this had been in Acton and he drew a cross accordingly, but its positioning was necessarily vague.

By now there appeared to be no patterning at all in the placement of his crosses. A truly critical eye might still have seen a preference for west London and for north of the river, but it was only a slight preference. Beyond that, the marks looked as though they might have been made more or less at random.

Stuart counted up the crosses and discovered that he'd had sex with women in twenty-six separate locations around London: not twenty-six different women, he was quick to tell Judy (he hadn't changed girlfriends nearly as often as he'd changed flats), though he had no idea whether she'd consider that many or few. And he really had no idea why he was counting, why he was making these maps, except that Judy had asked him to.

She looked at the finished map, apparently approvingly, and said, 'I think we've still got a lot of ground to cover.'

He liked the way she said 'we'.

One day she showed him some other plastic sheets, maps that had been drawn on by other visitors to her room, by other lovers, for all he knew. He saw how the city was overlaid with the patterns of where other people had lived and had sex. And he saw how these patterns resembled or differed from his, how they sometimes intersected his own map, sometimes seemed to complement it, other times seemed to have been drawn in strict opposition. There were people whose maps centred intensely around Kensington or Belsize Park, others who were concentrated on south London, others who had lived and fucked all over London at every point of the compass. In one or two cases the patterns appeared to be not merely promiscuous but systematic and exhaustive. He wasn't sure whether he found this depressing or not.

Soon, not much to Stuart's surprise, Judy turned herself into a valuable and well-liked employee. Even Anita liked her, though she continued to show a slight and totally unreasonable resentment because Judy didn't speak Japanese. Stuart took a certain pleasure in his wife's resentment. On the other hand he sometimes felt acute pangs of jealousy. It was strange to think of Judy going around London with groups of strangers, leading them, talking to them, performing for them, charming them. He thought it wouldn't take much for some single male tourist to entice her into conversation about art or history or architecture and then offer to buy her a drink and say that he was alone and lonely in London, in need of company, and then . . . Stuart tried hard not to think about it. He knew what a wasteful, hopeless emotion jealousy was.

He had never imagined that an affair with Judy would be useful as a piece of industrial sabotage and yet she was able to enlighten him about all sorts of things that went on in his business. Most of it was fairly tame stuff, tour guides who cut corners, who found ways of taking money from tourists without issuing tickets. But the thing he liked best was hearing how much the employees disliked Anita, and hearing that they had a pet name for her: Boadicea.

Several times he asked to see Judy's own personal 'map' of London, the plastic sheet that showed where she'd lived and fucked. She was uncharacteristically coy but immovable. She wouldn't show him. And yet in the weeks that followed, Judy did reveal her own personal, singular version of London to him. She took him by way of the Piccadilly Line to try to locate the pissoir in the Holloway Road that Joe Orton wrote about in his diaries. By his account it was 'the scene of a frenzied homosexual saturnalia' on at least one occasion some time in 1967, and presumably far more often than that. The diary said the toilet was under a bridge, but they failed to find anything that could be positively identified as Orton's old haunt.

'Thirty years is a long time in the life of a cottage,' Judy said philosophically.

More satisfactorily they went to 28 Charlotte Street, the home of an eighteenth-century whipping brothel presided over by a Mrs Theresa Berkeley. It was a place where, in general, customers were flogged with birches, cat-o'-nine-tails, and even fresh nettles. But customers could give as well as receive. There were prostitutes there who were prepared to be whipped, including, for two hundred guineas, Mrs Berkeley herself.

They found two doors in Charlotte Street, both marked with the number 28. One belonged to offices on the upper floors of the building, and the other was the door to a bookshop called the Index Bookcentre. A copy of Trotsky's *In Defence of Marxism* was displayed in the window. They browsed briefly in the bookshop and afterwards had a Greek meal at the Venus Kebab House.

They took Stuart's car and drove to Waterloo Road and

Judy recalled a passage from Flora Tristan's *Promenades dans Londres*, in which she describes how in the late 1830s the entire road was filled with prostitutes, leaning out of windows, sitting on doorsteps, many of them bare-breasted, raucous and cheerful, arguing with each other and their pimps. Judy took Stuart to Waterloo Bridge where Tristan had later stood and watched as a great tide of women crossed the river, heading into town for the brothels, the parks and theatres and 'finishes' of central London, where they would stay and be debauched till morning, when they would return south of the river, used and sated.

One day Judy and Stuart went to Fleet Street and looked for Fleet Alley where on 23 July 1664 Samuel Pepys took 'a turn or two with a most pretty wench' in one of the doorways. But Fleet Alley was not to be found. It appeared no longer to exist. Similarly there was no sign of Axe Yard in Westminster where he had lived.

On another occasion they went to Gray's Inn Road, to a distinguished, four-square, redbrick building now called Churston Mansions. In a previous incarnation it was Clevelly Mansions and had been the home of Katherine Mansfield and her lover Ida Constance Baker, known as L. M. Here, in a three-roomed flat that had as its centrepiece a stone Buddha surrounded by bronze lizards, Mansfield and Baker had committed sexual acts that were for the times, and in the public imagination, genuinely shocking. Here too, at least one of Mansfield's male suitors had threatened to shoot himself for love of her.

Judy and Stuart walked the streets of London trying to pick up on the mass of erotic energy, the afterglow of these coming togethers, these acts of desire, of love and transgression; acts of defloration and perversion, acts stemming from diverse needs, psyches, cultures. But it wasn't just sexual tourism. Judy did her best to participate in this afterglow, to make it glow that little bit brighter, and Stuart was her willing, if somewhat self-conscious, accomplice.

Whenever they visited one of these places with an erotic history, Judy insisted that they make love, if not actually there on the very spot, then in a park nearby, or in a dark corner, or at the very least in the back of Stuart's car. Stuart found himself in a state of horny amazement. He didn't think he was the sort of man who did things like this. He was also aware that these acts, these couplings, were changing the shape of the maps that could be drawn for them. Each time he returned to Judy's flat he added a cross or two to his map, but Judy still refused to reveal hers.

She said, 'There are an infinite number of maps that could be drawn of London; not just sex maps but death maps, crime maps, drug maps, maps of resistance and insurrection, of liberation and oppression, murder maps, suicide maps.'

'Walking maps,' he said.

'Imagine being blind in London,' she continued. 'Imagine having to negotiate the streets, or travel on the tube, having to listen to all the noise, the traffic, the building work, the buskers and beggars. What kind of map would a blind man use? How would he use it?'

Stuart shrugged to show his ignorance about these things, although he did vaguely remember reading about someone who'd made a sort of 'sound map' to help the blind recognize parts of the tube system.

'Sometimes I think I'd like to be tattooed,' Judy said. 'All across my back. With a map of the London Underground system. Or perhaps not just a tattoo, more a form of scarification, so that the scar tissue would be raised, a little like Braille, to represent the lines and the stations. And I could stand naked in the entrance halls of tube stations and blind men and women would come up to me, and run their hands over me, over the tattoos, until they'd worked out their routes. Maybe they wouldn't even need to be blind.'

She made him stand naked in the centre of her room, a map of London placed on the floor at his feet. He looked down at the shadow he cast over the city. She stood behind him and her hands curled around him, caressed his chest and his belly, then found their way to his cock. With a few strong, rapid strokes she made him come. His semen eased out of him, seemed to float above London for a moment, like liquid bombs, then fell to earth in thick, scattered splashes. She knelt down and peered at the map. In the places where his semen had landed she could just read through the cloudy translucent liquid the names of Belgravia, Walworth, Angell Town, Brockwell Park.

'More places we have to visit,' she said. Then she lowered her head, snaked out her tongue and meticulously licked his semen from all the places it had fallen.

Stuart had never imagined it would be like this. He felt that things were getting out of hand. He had seen something attractive and vital and, of course, sexual, in Judy Tanaka. He had not thought she was an ice-maiden but neither had he imagined she would be nearly so wild and rash. A part of him was thrilled by it, but increasingly it worried him. He feared that her recklessness might produce a similar recklessness in himself and that was no part of his plans. He didn't want to get into trouble. He had every intention of remaining completely in control, and above all of remaining married.

Meanwhile Judy revelled in being indiscreet. A woman who dragged you into the Ladies at the Blind Beggar or who insisted that you have sex with her in an alleyway off Tottenham Court Road in the middle of a Tuesday afternoon, or who insisted on delivering blow jobs while you sat in your car at a parking meter in Jermyn Street, was not someone who would be very understanding when you explained to her how you needed to be careful in order to protect your marriage.

Of course he hadn't told Anita about Judy; Stuart and Anita had a frank and civilized marriage, but it wasn't quite as frank and civilized as *that*. Stuart was careful to cover his tracks. Discovery mightn't spell total disaster. Anita was tolerant, forgiving, actually not all that concerned with sexual faithfulness, but she wouldn't stand for a fuss, for being made to look a fool. Being betrayed by her husband and a junior tour guide would not go down well.

Once, to Stuart's almost heart-stopping alarm, Judy stripped her clothes off in the corner of a not particularly deserted churchyard in Clerkenwell. He had tried to cover her up but she was determined not to be covered.

'Which way round is it?' she asked as she stood there naked. 'Is the body like a city or is the city like a body? Which is the metaphor? Which is the real subject?'

Stuart was far too embarrassed to offer an answer.

'There are some cities you wouldn't want your body to resemble,' she went on. 'Pompeii, Coventry, Milton Keynes. Hiroshima.'

He felt oddly offended. He walked off, left her to her nakedness. It was a bad joke, if she had intended it as a joke.

'Sorry,' she called after him. 'I guess you can't joke about Hiroshima. Not even if you're half-Japanese. Not even if you're naked.'

The affair continued for a good few months. Stuart savoured all the usual excitements and guilts, the usual pleasures and the usual sense of risk, but with Judy everything was heightened, as though she was constantly wanting to raise the stakes. He did what he could to avoid analysing his feelings, and he had no urge to categorize the nature of their affair. It was more complex than lust, less nourishing than love. There was respect for the other partner and yet a dizzying sense of transgression, of doing wrong, of going to hell in a basket.

But even though the affair took him all over London it was obviously, in the most colloquial sense, going nowhere. He knew it would have to end sooner rather than later, that the end would be sweetly painful, and that the decision to end would be his not Judy's. Yet he still surprised himself when he suddenly, abruptly decided it was over.

Judy had taken him to Hampstead Heath, scene of all sorts of sexual encounters, perhaps rather few of them heterosexual. Stuart and Judy were tangled together, standing up, only semi-naked, in a copse that promised to provide adequate cover. Suddenly a small black dog, rapidly followed by its owner, discovered them. The dog owner, a lean, white-haired, soldierly-looking man, stared at them with as much pity as disgust and said, 'You dirty buggers. You deserve all you get.'

It seemed an odd thing for him to have said, but in a peculiar way it struck home with Stuart. As he buttoned and zipped himself up he knew that his affair with Judy had finished. Comic and trivial though this particular discovery had been, he realized they'd been lucky to get away with it for as long as they had. Discovery by the man with the dog had been somehow symbolic. If it went on much longer it would be Anita doing the discovering, and the consequences of that could be far more terrible than the simple pains of an ended affair.

The next time he saw her he told Judy as swiftly, as diplomatically as he could that it was all over. She did not take it well. She screamed at him, called him every bad thing she could think of, threatened obscure and terrible revenges. He told her she was being absurd. It had been an affair, he said, nothing more, fun while it lasted and surely not so terrible now it was over. But Judy wasn't having any of that. She was wounded in a way he had never imagined, never bargained for. All he could do was say he was sorry, even though he wasn't particularly. And when she began to say that she thought she was deeply, desperately in love with him, he was more convinced than ever that he'd done the right thing by ending it.

Judy Tanaka disappeared out of his life, left the job at The London Walker without giving any notice, something that both infuriated and perplexed Anita. Judy hadn't seemed the kind to leave them in the lurch like that. It was said by other members of staff that there must surely be some pressing reason for her departure, and perhaps she'd return one day with a full explanation.

For his part, Stuart spent several weeks thinking Judy might exact some terrible revenge on him. The most likely, he thought, would be telling Anita about the affair. But it never happened. She was gone for good. Only months later did Stuart hear that she was working in a bookshop, a job that seemed far too dull and undemanding for someone of Judy's talents.

Once it was all over Stuart felt little more than a profound sense of relief. He'd had a lucky escape. He'd got away with something that he probably hadn't deserved to. Until Judy came along he had not been consciously looking for an affair. He'd known something was absent from his life, something that he needed rather badly, but he certainly hadn't thought it was extramarital sex, and it seemed he was right.

Once Judy had gone the need for that something was greater than ever, it multiplied, grew exponentially; but a new affair, a new mistress, certainly wouldn't have helped. If it would, there were plenty more new tour guides, replacements for Judy in every sense. But he knew that was not what he was looking for.

The affair was over and he wanted to get back to his old ways, back to the way things were before, and yet it didn't seem to be an option any longer. Something, and possibly Judy was the agent here, had changed him. The old dissatisfactions were still there, but now mutated.

For a while he threw himself into trying to be a better husband for Anita but that gave neither party much pleasure. It was just as well he discovered what it was he needed to do. Even when he'd discovered it, he found it hard to understand exactly how the end of an affair could produce in a man the need to walk down every street in London; yet undeniably there was a connection.

He couldn't see how this was any more convincing a reason than the other, more prosaic ones he'd previously tried for size. But somehow it fitted better even if it seemed more bizarre. Judy had made the whole of London come sexually alive for him. Now it appeared that he had ditched Judy but was continuing his affair with the city, pursuing it, wanting to possess it. He found himself bitterly amused at the absurdity of this latest 'explanation', but at least, he thought, he was no longer being unfaithful to Anita. Anita, however, when she eventually got to read the diary, might not see it that way at all.

# THE WALKER'S DIARY

# THE FIRST ENTRY

So I have decided to keep a diary of my London walks; nothing too ambitious, nothing too pretentious. I'm simply going to describe what I see, although of course I know that the process of seeing is a highly selective one. What I see will reveal as much about me as about London.

At first I thought I might make an entry for every single street in London, set down what I observed in each one, what was special and unique about it. But I immediately realized the folly of that. You can't force it. You can't make yourself see things. There'll be unremarkable streets where I see nothing worth remarking on. That's fine. London has to offer itself up to me and I have to offer myself to London.

I have decided that I shan't write anything down while I'm actually doing the walks. I shan't be taking notes. I don't want to look like a spy or a journalist, and I don't want the act of note-taking to get in the way of seeing. Then, when I get home, I'll type up my recollections of the day as best I can. I only want to remember what I remember. If I forget things, then so be it.

Once the information is on disk I'll find a place to hide it, somewhere that prying eyes like Anita's can't find it. Why this urge for secrecy? I'm not sure, but it feels very real. For that matter, I wonder why Samuel Pepys wrote his diary in code? I'll check on that.

★

Oxford Street – Not my favourite bit of London but this enterprise is not about playing favourites. De Quincey refers to it as a stony-hearted stepmother who drinks the tears of children, which I think is going a bit far. Certainly on this weekday morning Oxford Street was completely free of children. At nine-thirty few of the shops were open. Outside the shoe shops staff were waiting for their bosses to arrive with their keys to let them in. In a doorway two homeless men were in sleeping-bags, fast asleep, showing no signs of waking despite the daylight and the presence of people. You'd have thought the homeless would be early risers.

Outside Tottenham Court Road tube station a dark girl, maybe Spanish, maybe Italian, was handing out leaflets advertising a language school. She gave one to an old, stocky, grey-haired Londoner who looked at the leaflet and reacted furiously.

'You're telling me to learn English?' he ranted. 'You're telling *me*?'

The girl who'd handed him the card didn't know what he was talking about. Maybe she didn't even know what he was saying.

A young black man with a woolly hat and sunglasses came down the street making odd movements with his left hand, a strange sort of action somewhere between mime and martial arts, and he was talking to some invisible companion as he walked along. When he got level with me he half looked at me and said, 'That's all right!!' and swept away.

I saw a man in a tam-o'-shanter. And a boy in a long, dark sinister-looking mac whose head was shaved except for a turd-shaped lump of blue hair on the very top of his skull. He looked like a maniac yet he was with a girl dressed in perfectly ordinary clothes, looking like a secretary, though she was carrying a yellow balloon on a stick.

A sad-looking, camp young man with a pierced ear and nose was holding a Polaroid camera, trying to get a picture of the window display in Top Shop. He was waiting not very

143

patiently. There was a stream of people passing by. You couldn't imagine when he'd ever get a clear shot.

At Oxford Circus a little Hare Krishna procession with an amazingly mixed group of people, painfully skinny young lads, a very county-looking woman, a fat middle-aged Asian man in a suit and overcoat.

A well-dressed man with a light Australian accent was handing out leaflets. He said, 'I'm giving these to people who are into health and beauty around the world.' But he didn't give one to me.

I realized there were more bureaux de change in Oxford Street than you would ever have imagined possible, tucked into tiny thin premises no wider than a doorway.

There was an 'authentic Indian buffet' advertised at the Cumberland Hotel.

Outside Littlewoods there was a busker playing an accordion. In front of him was a strong metal collecting box with the word 'Blind' painted neatly on it in four-inch-high letters. I noticed the box was chained to the man, to make sure someone didn't steal it from him. Are there really people in the world who'd steal money from a blind busker? Then I realized of course there are. Thousands of people. There are people who'd steal his money, his accordion, his white stick, his guide dog, his false teeth.

Finally Marble Arch, which I couldn't see at first because the traffic was so dense and blocking the view. The arch looked monstrous yet unimpressive, run aground on a traffic island, surrounded by the swirl of buses and cars.

This part of Oxford Street, formerly Tyburn Road, was the end of the route along which prisoners were brought to their place of execution, an obscene parade, the road lined with drunken, jeering crowds who threw stones and dirt and dung at the condemned, there but for the grace of God. Maybe De Quincey was right.

★

144

I walked along Chester Row, not far from Sloane Square. Charles Dickens used to live at number one, and T. S. Eliot used to live at number five. I don't know if Thomas Stearns was much of a walker, but he could definitely describe the experience of walking home late at night through certain half-deserted streets.

Dickens too was something of a night walker. He wrote an essay called 'Night Walks' in which he described the noise of the city as a 'distant ringing hum, as if the city were a glass, vibrating.' When his father died he walked the city on three consecutive nights from dusk till dawn.

But Dickens was a walker, full stop, not just at night. In his era my daily ten miles would have been paltry stuff. People must have thought nothing of walking ten or fifteen miles just to go to work and back, but even by the standards of his day Dickens was an excessive, not to say obsessive walker. Friends who stayed with him would be invited out for a stroll and would return hours later, exhausted, Dickens having taken them twenty-odd miles and walked them into the ground. But he didn't do it just to impress others. He did it because he needed to. At one point in his life he believed he had a moral duty to spend as many hours walking as he did writing.

And I'm not sure whether he used walking as a way of meditating on his feelings or as a way of escaping from them. Certainly he must have thought about his work and his characters as he walked, maybe he even found material he could use, so it wasn't wasted time, but more than that he seems to have used walking as a way of driving away melancholy.

For myself, I'm not sure exactly what I feel as I walk. I've not got as much on my mind as Dickens had, and yet the walking has rather the opposite effect that it had on him. If anything, London amplifies my melancholy rather than rids me of it. Fortunately the act of writing about what I've seen then dispels the melancholy. Does this sound glib?

★

At the corner of St Swithin's Lane and King William Street; the place where a hoard of Roman coins was discovered in 1840. They were forgeries, but *Roman* forgeries, eighty-nine silver denarii; but only silver plate, a thin veneer layered over copper. They dated from Boadicea's time and had perhaps been buried for safe keeping, to be dug up later if only Boadicea hadn't done such a thorough job.

In Fellows Road, NW3 (I'd call it Swiss Cottage but maybe it was Belsize Park), there was a gaping yellow skip in which a fridge, a cooker and a washing machine had been rather carefully deposited, lined up neatly, side by side. A man in a flat cap came out of one of the houses carrying a gas fire which he placed painstakingly in the skip, being careful not to spoil the neatness of the design.

In Winchester Road I saw what from a distance looked like an art gallery showing miniature silver and gold sculptures, carefully arranged and spotlit on glass shelves. But when I got nearer I saw the shop was an architectural ironmonger's and the 'sculptures' were gold and silver bath taps.

In Lambolle Road, a narrow street, cars parked tightly on both sides, I saw a sixties Cadillac convertible with its hood up, bright red, huge threatening fins. It was so large it looked too wide to get through the gap between the cars. But it did, making slow, stately progress, growling like a motorboat.

In Merton Rise I saw a building called Villa Henriette.

At the top end of the stretch of Finchley Road that runs from St John's Wood to Swiss Cottage, the road became a sort of dual carriageway, but the median was no more than two feet wide. However that was wide enough for someone to have set himself up as a flower-seller, buckets of flowers arranged in the middle, selling to drivers of cars stopped at the traffic lights.

A little lower down the road, at a zebra crossing, there were bunches of flowers tied to the illuminated bollards and to the column of the Belisha beacon, and a yellow police accident sign that asked 'Can You Help?'

I went to 7 Cavendish Avenue because I knew it belonged to Paul McCartney. It was a huge, forbidding, square house, with a high garden wall, solid green gates. There were closed white internal shutters at all the windows. It looked utterly uninhabited. I'd read there was a sun-house in the garden in the form of a geodesic dome, but the walls were too high to see in.

A little way down the road, one of the houses had a bust of a classical god in the window. It was bigger than human size, and maybe that was appropriate it being a god, but the bust had its back to the street and so you could look up into the rear of the head and see that it was completely hollow.

In Eamont Street there was a place called Gorky Park which advertised itself as a 'cruise bar'. It was boarded up and available to let.

In Circus Road I saw a very smart woman in late middle age who was standing in the street not wearing a coat despite it being a cold day. A taxi pulled up, someone got out, and the woman ran over and I heard her say in very clear, clipped tones, 'Excuse me could you tell me what day of the week it is. You see I've been abroad.'

In Broad Lawn, New Eltham, I saw a workman sitting in a van eating his lunch. I was surprised to see he was gnawing a raw carrot, which didn't seem like standard workman's fare. But then I saw the sign on the side of the van that said he was a piano tuner and that seemed perfectly in keeping.

In Mapesbury Road, Willesden, I saw six disused, uprooted telephone boxes lined up in the garden of a semi-detached house.

I walked down Waterloo Passage, Kilburn, a narrow lane behind the Iceland supermarket. There was a sign stating that this was a public walkway and rubbish wasn't to be dumped there. Needless to say, it was almost impassable because of bags of rubbish. Someone had sprayed 'IRA Wayne was here' on a door. I hadn't imagined that IRA members had names like Wayne.

Kilburn; a lot of people in the High Road looked beaten up by life, by drink, by each other. I saw a fancy goods shop that was having a 'pot pouri clearance', and a music shop nearby had a ukelele for sale in the window, but there was a handwritten sign on it saying 'Junior Guitar'. Someone was going to be very disappointed come Christmas morning.

In Cambridge Avenue I came across a disused church constructed from sheets of corrugated iron, with a sign on the tower that said 'T. S. Bicester'. I had no idea what that meant, but there was another sign on the door, a sort of wanted poster, asking for people to come along and help with the Willesden Sea Cadets. The T. S. stood for training ship (not Thomas Stearns), and there were two circular holes in the doors meant to look like portholes.

In Golden Square there was a man carrying a pair of tom toms. He went into a phone box, made a call and started talking to someone at the other end of the phone and I heard him say, 'Hey, I've bought some tom toms, listen.' And he played the tom toms down the phone to his friend.

I was in Roman Road, Bethnal Green, not that far from where Judy used to live; still does for all I know. Judy – the best sex, the wildest sex, pure London sex, I always think of it as.

I'd done my ten miles and it was beginning to rain, so I felt free to bend my rules and go into the Bethnal Green Museum of Childhood to take shelter. Inside I was struck by how many of the exhibits were miniaturizations of London. There was a nineteenth-century peep show, a large black box with a tiny eyehole into which you peered and saw the Thames Tunnel, made up of receding planes of paper figures and arches; a pedestrian tunnel then, a train tunnel now, I think.

There was a German model of the Monument and its

surrounding buildings, printed on paper to be cut out and constructed. There was Buckingham Palace printed on thick wooden blocks as a backdrop for toy soldiers.

There were also various board games involving London, some very obscure, some as familiar as Monopoly. I've never understood Monopoly. The London it refers to seems to bear no relation to the London anybody knows. There's a story, almost certainly apocryphal, that Waddington's, who were based in Yorkshire, sent a secretary down to London on a daytrip. She wandered around and jotted down the names of places she saw almost at random, and these names were used on the board.

I don't see how this can be literally true. It would be a pretty arduous daytrip that took in Whitechapel Road, the Old Kent Road, the Angel, as well as Bond Street, Whitehall, Park Lane, Fleet Street, plus all the train stations. Still, the sense remains that Monopoly was devised by someone who didn't have much of a grasp of London geography. There are plenty of those about.

Park Lane, Hackney, a wide ugly road, cars jammed in tight, a derelict pub, boarded-up windows that burglars or squatters have unsuccessfully tried to break into. There was an old lady walking along the road: blue beret, a short rain coat, a flowered skirt. Suddenly she lifted up the hem of the skirt and reached underneath for her slip, which she then raised to her face and blew her nose on, good and hard.

Nearby an ugly, uncared for three-storey building and by the door a plaque announcing that this was the Dickens Hotel. The plaque was the shiniest, cleanest, most polished thing in the whole street. I wonder what kind of people stay at a hotel in Park Lane, Hackney. Maybe sad people who come down to London from Yorkshire and don't have much of a grasp of London geography.

# JIGSAW

It was eight in the morning and Mick Wilton was in the cold, shared bathroom of the Dickens getting himself washed and shaved, when he heard a light tread outside, footsteps walking along the corridor in the direction of his bedroom. He'd left the door unlocked since, with the exception of his gun, Mick owned nothing that anybody would wish to steal. The gun, however, was not a thing he left lying around in his room, not even while washing and shaving. It was now tucked into the waistband of his trousers and he couldn't help feeling its presence. He listened to the intruder arriving at the door of his empty bedroom, knocking once and immediately entering.

Mick wiped the foam from his half-shaved face, moved the gun to his pocket and touched it for reassurance, then he silently left the bathroom to return to his bedroom. The door was open a couple of inches. He couldn't see round it and no sound came from behind but he knew someone was inside. He took a deep breath then sharply kicked it wide open and charged into the room, ready for most things, but in the event quite unprepared for the sight of the housecoat-clad landlady setting something down on his bed.

She spun round, startled and terrified. The blue, quilted housecoat flapped open to reveal more chest than Mick wanted to see, and the landlady's newly made-up face gawped at him open-mouthed and wide-eyed. Then the shock evaporated on both sides. It was only her. It was only him. The bathos of the moment produced apologies from each of them, hasty and mutually unfelt, and the landlady said, 'I was only bringing you your post.'

She pointed towards the thing she had placed on his bed, a neat, brown-paper package; harmless-looking, but Mick's alarm returned. Who would send him a package? How many people even knew he was here?

'It's got a peculiar rattle to it,' the landlady said. 'Why don't you open it?'

But Mick would not touch or even investigate the package until she had left the room. When, with some reluctance, she had gone, he picked it up cautiously. It was light and not solid and as he shook it gently he could hear the contents rattle together. The sound was dry and brittle, unthreatening. Once Mick had removed the brown paper he was not too surprised to find that the package contained a jigsaw puzzle. That was pretty much what it had felt and sounded like. But who the hell would be sending him jigsaws? Who would be sending him anything? He searched the wrapping and found a sliver of paper, a compliment slip from the London Particular with a note that read, 'Something to do in the evenings besides watching second-rate videos.'

A part of him felt insulted. OK, he realized she thought she was smarter than he was, but did she really need to rub it in like this? What kind of idiot, what kind of child, did she think he was that he'd want to play with a jigsaw? He was about to toss the present away disdainfully when he looked at the box for the first time. It didn't contain a picture as such, no rural English scene with thatched cottages and a duck pond, instead it showed a highly detailed map of London. He still thought it was a pretty stupid present but at least he could now see the point of it, the joke.

Grudgingly he opened up the box and looked at all the myriad pieces of London meshed together inside, pieces that were asymmetrical yet with a reassuring sort of regularity; distant and diverse parts of the city fragmented and brought into improbable contact. He picked out a couple of pieces at random; on one completely green piece he saw the word Crystal (of Crystal Palace), and another piece, entirely blue, part of Barn Elms Water Works. He let them drop back into the box and they left a few filaments of cardboard dust on his fingers.

He looked at the lid and checked the dimensions of the completed puzzle and saw that it would be much too big for any of the flat surfaces in the room. Having so recently felt insulted he now felt oddly deprived. He wanted to make a start. Regretfully he placed the lid back and gently put the box away in a drawer of the bedside cabinet. He left the brown paper on the floor, but he took the compliment slip, reread it, then folded it carefully and put it in his wallet.

As he left the Dickens a little while later, the landlady was in the hall, dressed now, obviously waiting for him yet wanting the meeting to appear accidental.

'It's always nice to get presents, isn't it?' she said, and Mick couldn't disagree.

'From an admirer?' she continued.

The word admirer struck him as comically inappropriate. He didn't believe anyone had ever admired him.

'Yeah, sure,' he said.

'London postmark, I see,' she said. 'Only been here five minutes and already he's breaking hearts. I'll have to watch myself.'

'You do that,' he said.

Mick went into the street and began his day, his work. Things were a little strange at the moment. Since dealing with Justin Carr he had hit a slight hiatus. Revenge on Carr had been so sweet and so appropriate that Mick now wanted to deliver equally fitting acts of vengeance to the four men remaining on the list. Simply tracking them down and giving them a good kicking was no longer enough for him. He had not lost his sense of urgency but there were some things that couldn't be rushed. They had to be done right.

Days and nights were therefore spent in what Mick liked to think of as reconnaissance. He knew all his victims' addresses. It was simply a matter of checking them out, seeing how they lived, following them sometimes, seeing how they came and went, what time they left for work, when they got home, seeing what they did in the evenings, determining whether they were married or single, seeing whether they were gregarious or solitary. Sooner or later he knew that in each case the proper opportunity and occasion would present itself, and he'd be there, ready to take it.

The four victims lived some way from each other, one in Chelsea, one in Fitzrovia, one in Docklands and one in Islington, so he found himself covering many miles of the city going from one location to another, still avoiding public transport whenever humanly possible. And he was surprised to discover that he was starting to know his way around parts of London. Sometimes he'd find himself in a place he'd heard of, a famous place, with a recognizable name, familiar from the news or Monopoly, or just from a pop song (Walworth Road, Pentonville Road, Baker Street), and he'd feel simultaneously disorientated and at home. He couldn't quite square the fact that these places, which to his eyes looked so ordinary, so workaday, also carried such a weight of history and fame with them, and yet he felt good to find himself using such famous streets in his daily wanderings.

Already certain routes through the city were becoming his own. He was discovering the logic and connectedness of the streets, discovering short-cuts, but he would still have been lost without the map he'd bought from Judy. At first he had hated it, had hated having to carry it. Either he tried to cram it into one of his pockets in which case it destroyed the lines of his suit, or he carried it in his hand in which case he looked like a hick from the sticks. But what was the alternative? Wandering around lost.

So he carried his map and soon he didn't feel too bad about it at all, largely because he saw so many others like himself, also carrying maps. Some of them were obviously tourists and out-of-towners, but he'd see quite ordinary people, people who looked like they belonged here, who looked like Londoners, who also obviously needed to use maps in order to get around. He saw van drivers driving along with maps held open across the steering wheel. He even saw a black-cab driver consulting an *A–Z*.

Because he was carrying a map, people would sometimes stop him and ask for directions. Suspicious and irritated at first, he gradually took some pleasure in being able to help. People tended to be friendly and open towards him because they wanted something from him and he responded decently to them. Occasionally he found he could help with directions simply from his own knowledge of the city. It was strange how these passing, issueless encounters with strangers could produce an enduring feeling of well-being. Helping people to find their way made him feel oddly at home and accommodated.

On one bizarre occasion, as he was approaching Covent Garden tube a woman, also carrying a map, greeted him with a big smile and asked him if he was Emil. He shook his head and quickly said no, but when he thought about it later he realized he'd been needlessly honest. The woman was attractive, and he reckoned she must have been meeting a blind date or a lonely heart, and the map had been some kind of signal. From the way she'd approached him she obviously didn't mind the look of him, had obviously hoped that he was Emil, and if he'd said yes, then she'd probably have happily gone off with him. It would have been a laugh. Then he remembered he wasn't in London to have laughs.

He was standing in Chelsea, outside the house of a man called Jonathan Sands, the next most likely candidate on his list, when someone asked him for directions to Hackney. Mick offered the use of his map but the enquirer, a Turkish immigrant by the look of him, saw the length and complexity of the journey and walked off in a mean sulk as though it was Mick's fault.

154

Mick was reminded of his own journey home. It was mid-afternoon, cold and dank. His shoulders were soaked with rain. He knew very little about Jonathan Sands, but he knew that despite having a wife and young child he didn't come home much. He knew that he had a lot of magazines delivered, mostly about things maritime, and that he kept a boat moored in Chelsea Harbour. At present the house was dark and uninhabited. A cleaning lady had come and gone an hour or so earlier but now there was nothing. The wife and child were out. It would be hours before Sands came home from work. Mick decided to return to the Dickens. He knew there'd be better days than this.

He got back to Hackney in late afternoon. It was already dark and he had a long evening ahead of him. These winter days were short and they disappeared all too quickly but sometimes the nights seemed endless and torturous.

As he got close to the Dickens he saw a skip full of building rubbish on the other side of the street. He crossed and dug around in it until he found a big piece of discarded hardboard. It was jagged-edged and irregular and spotted with tacky stains, but it was good enough for what he wanted, for what he now felt he wanted rather badly; a flat surface on which to do a jigsaw.

He took the wood up to his room, laid it on the bed and started the puzzle. He found it totally impossible at first. It entirely dispelled the sense of belonging he had begun to feel. All the streets and place names were suddenly foreign to him. They sounded simultaneously alien yet quaint: Hatch End, Barking, Tooting Graveney. They did not belong to the London he knew. And when he came to locations he'd heard of, places he'd been to, he no longer had any idea where they were in relation to anywhere else. The map was even more confusing than the reality.

But he persevered and gradually found that bits of the completed map were starting to coalesce. The edges were the easiest, followed by the river, and these fixed points seemed to offer clues as to how he might proceed. He put together large patches of recognizable green space, then motorways and arterial roads. He made some progress. But when it came to assembling networks of short, dense city and suburban streets, he had to rely on trial and error and occasional strokes of good luck.

It might have been frustratingly, maddeningly difficult, yet he enjoyed the difficulty. He was glad it wasn't the child's play he'd first thought it was going to be. The act of joining up the city, making it complete and solid, gave him more pleasure than he would have thought possible. As the map came nearer to coherence and completion he felt oddly proud of himself, as though he was gaining mastery over this once wholly unfamiliar territory.

He worked on diligently into the evening, and London took shape before his eyes, but eventually a terrible moment came when it dawned on him, with a kind of aching deflation, that there was a piece of the jigsaw missing. He could see there were a dozen holes remaining in London and only eleven pieces left with which to plug them, and as he slotted in each of the eleven, it became clear that the missing piece was the one that had Park Lane, Hackney, on it; his street.

He searched the box, the bed, the floor, but it wasn't there. He could barely believe the disappointment and depression that overtook him. The piece's absence seemed to be telling him something, that he had no place here, that he didn't belong, that he barely existed, that his existence was a blank. This sleazy, crummy place and situation he inhabited was just a hole in the map. Then he realized that the significance must be quite other. The piece's absence surely could not be accidental.

He was tempted to throw the whole puzzle up in the air, to reduce London to fragments, then put it back in its box. But instead he held himself in check and sat silently and patiently and more than a little dispiritedly, waiting for what he knew would come. Her timing wasn't bad. He'd only been sitting there for three-quarters of an hour. He had worked more quickly than she'd expected.

And then the knock; cautious, feminine (half-Japanese?), and he opened the door, knowing it would be her, and she stood smiling at him and held out her closed hand. She unfurled her fingers to reveal the jigsaw piece cupped in her pale, flat palm.

'I thought you might need this,' she said.

'Yeah. I'd be lost without it. What if I'd decided not to do the jigsaw?'

'Then you might still be pleased to see me.'

He reached out to take the piece of jigsaw but she closed her hand and withdrew it. She entered the room and he was so surprised and pleased by her arrival that he didn't think to be apologetic for his surroundings. She glanced around, interested but uncritical, and then he did feel the need to apologize, or at least explain.

'You were right,' she said. 'It is a slum.'

'Yeah, well, if I'd known you were coming I'd have had the decorators in.'

'You're just passing through,' she said, quoting him back to himself.

'That's right,' he said.

'Working away from home.'

'Yeah.'

'And what kind of work do you do exactly, Mick?'

It was a difficult question, one he didn't welcome, but if she was so determined to know how he lived, Mick had no intention of deceiving her. Patiently and not untruthfully he said, 'I do security, protection, debt-collecting, bouncer work. It's not that exciting.'

'You're a bad guy?'

'Not that bad.'

'You're a crook?'

'Well, the judge said I was a petty criminal, which I thought was a bit unnecessary. Obviously I was a criminal otherwise I wouldn't have been in court, but *petty*, I mean, there was no need to be hurtful, was there?'

She smiled, sure that there was at least some truth in what he was saying, but sure too that his way of telling it hid more than it revealed.

'And how are your reunions going?' she asked.

'OK,' he said.

'I thought maybe you'd be out celebrating with your old friends.'

'No, you didn't,' he said.

'You're right,' she agreed. 'I didn't. I thought you'd be home.'

'This isn't home,' he insisted. 'This is how I live in London, but it's not my real life.'

'I know. Your real life's in Sheffield,' she said. 'You probably have a mansion there, and a doting wife and two lovely children and a dog and a pony.'

'Got it in one,' he said.

She smiled. 'Married?' she asked.

'No. I've got a girlfriend.'

'Is it serious?'

'What is this?'

'Just a question.'

'Yes, it's serious. I take these things seriously.'

'And are you faithful to her?'

There was no simple answer to that question and in the time it took him to come up with a complex one she drew her own conclusions.

'Tell me, Mick, have you ever slept with a foreign woman?'

'No,' he said. 'Have you ever slept with a Sheffielder?'

'No,' she said.

'I don't blame you. They're overrated.'

She liked that. She liked self-deprecation, especially in someone who looked like a bad guy.

Mick asked, 'Which half of you is Japanese?'

Playing it straight she replied, 'My father. My mother comes from Streatham. Like me. My father's an artist. He teaches art. He was a sort of performance artist. He was famous for about

158

three months in the seventies. He'll tell you he's a footnote in art history. The bigger the history, the bigger the footnote.'

'Yeah?' said Mick. The idea of having a father who was an artist seemed at least as strange as having a father who was Japanese.

'His best-known work,' Judy continued, 'was sending three hundred anonymous love letters to women all over London, women he'd never met, complete strangers whose names he'd got out of the telephone directory, telling them that he was their secret admirer and too shy to speak to them. But if they'd meet him under the clock at Waterloo Station at seven p.m. on a specified Friday he'd reveal himself. When the women got to Waterloo on the appointed day they found a dozen Japanese men, heads shaved, their bodies painted grey, naked except for loin-cloths, singing, "I'm in the mood for love".'

'How many women turned up?'

'A lot. There were several arrests.'

'Yeah?' said Mick.

'The newspapers said it was a piece of art commemorating the bombing of Hiroshima, but that was only partly true. My father was born in August 1945, the same month the allies dropped the bomb, but he was a long way from Hiroshima. His parents were in a transit camp in California. That's where he was born.'

'So he's really a Californian.'

'No, he's really, really Japanese. Like I'm really a Londoner.'

'Why did you send me the jigsaw?'

'Because I wanted you to have something to do in the evenings.'

'Why did you bring the missing piece? Why are you here now?'

'Because I wanted you to have something else to do in the evenings. I came because I wanted to sleep with you.'

'That's nice,' he said thoughtfully. 'But I don't think I can.'

'Because of your serious girlfriend?'

He thought about explaining the whole damn thing, the rape, the nature of his reunions, how difficult it was to think about having sex with anybody while ever his head was full of imaginary pictures of Gabby being gang-banged by six chinless wonders. But he couldn't. He said, 'The landlady doesn't allow strange women in the rooms.'

She said, 'That's the worst excuse I've ever heard.'

'It's the best I've got.'

She sprang up, angry and insulted, and started to leave.

'Fine,' she spat. 'We'll do lunch some time.'

'That'd be nice,' he said as she slammed the door behind her, and she found herself standing in the corridor, unsure of whether he'd really meant it.

After she'd gone he looked at the jigsaw and saw that it still had a hole in it. She'd taken the missing piece away with her. He turned on the radio and found himself again listening to the phone-in programme where Londoners discussed prurient details of their love lives and sex lives. The tone of the programme was different from the last time he'd heard it. It was now more serious, mostly anxieties and complaints. There were men and women who didn't like oral sex, but whose partners did, or they liked to give but not receive or they *would* like to give but weren't sure of the correct method. Girls of fifteen called in, worried because they were still virgins, men of a much greater age called in with exactly the same problem. There were men whose penises were too small or too large, women whose breasts ditto. There were people who fancied their boss, or their same-sex best friend, or their doctors, or who fancied group sex. Women called in who'd lost their husbands, their sex drives, their G spots. Men called who'd lost potency, erections and hope.

He realized the absurdity of lying there listening to these other problems when he had plenty of his own. His rejection of Judy which might have felt like an act of faithfulness, or at least of well-intentioned self-denial, in reality felt like an act of neurosis, aggression and self-destruction. He kept listening to the radio, hoping it would stop him thinking about what a fool he'd been.

The last caller of the night was identified as Judy. The voice was now unmistakable. She said she'd called last week about al fresco sex but now there was something else she wanted to talk about. She was told to state her problem as briefly as possible because the show was nearly over.

She said, 'There's someone I want to sleep with but he's not interested in me. And I think it's because of where I'm from.'

The hostess seized on the topic excitedly.

'That's terrible, Judy,' she said. 'Sexism, racism, homophobia, they're all part of the same mentality, aren't they? And they're all terrible, and in some small way we on this programme are doing our best to fight them. And where do you come from, Judy?'

'I come from Bethnal Green.'

'Yes, but where do you come from originally?'

'Streatham.'

'Yes, but your ethnic background?'

'Oh, I don't think it's got anything to do with my ethnic background. I think he won't sleep with me because I'm from London.'

Suddenly the closing music was playing and the hostess was saying, 'And I'm sorry we don't have more time to discuss that one. Maybe next week. For now it's good night, London, sleep wisely and not too well. *Ciao.*'

Mick was not sure what he'd heard and he wished he didn't care, but later that night his dreams proved otherwise. They were full of images of jigsaw pieces, naked Japanese men, Judy running all over London following the dictates of some sexual game she had devised for herself, and there at the centre of it all, for no reason other than dream logic, was Jonathan Sands, a man on whom Mick urgently intended to take revenge.

# MARINA

Mick Wilton sat at the bar in one of the expensive, laughable hotels at Chelsea Harbour. He was reading a leaflet he'd picked up. It extolled the virtues of the Thames Barrier, both as an engineering feat and as a tourist attraction. It went so far as to claim that the Thames Barrier was the 'Eighth wonder of the world'.

Mick, naturally enough, had never been to the Thames Barrier, though he did remember seeing something about it on TV, and he thought this leaflet might be overstating the case. He read how the barrier was the world's largest movable flood barrier, though it didn't name any of the world's other flood barriers, movable or not. The barrier was said to be a great triumph for British designers and constructors although apparently some 'Dutch specialists' had also been involved. And then the leaflet said that a visit to the barrier was a 'memorable experience'. He thought this was pretty weak. A visit to Madame Tussaud's might be a memorable experience. A visit to the eighth wonder of the world ought to be something a lot more dramatic.

Mick was bored, by the leaflet, by his surroundings, by the waiting. It would soon be time to deal with Jonathan Sands, but it was only fair to wait, to give him a chance to finish the business he was currently engaged in. Mick looked at his watch. Another ten minutes then he'd have him.

With its new hotels and restaurants and blocks of flats,

Chelsea Harbour looked like a resort out of season, deserted, ominously clean and ordered, something futuristic and authoritarian. There were lumps of modern sculpture dotted about, all new, all looking as though they had been bought off the peg to give the area a bit of class.

Mick felt out of place, but who wouldn't? There were only two other people in the bar, otherwise everyone he saw was an employee of the harbour, carrying tools, buckets, bundles of electric cable.

He looked towards the angular, irregularly shaped marina. It was small, no wider across than an easy stone's throw, and that was where the boats were moored, not many of them either, not more than fifty. The jetties were new and recently swept and well endowed with 'Keep Out' signs. The marina connected to the river via a long, narrow lock and Mick was amused to see a traffic light on the marina side. To Mick it looked like no more than a car-park with water, but the boats themselves were a lot more impressive than the kind of thing you'd find in most car-parks. Some were sleek white wedges of state-of-the-art machinery, with great tangles of navigational gear atop them. Others belonged to the classic school, older, more soulful craft with varnished wooden cabins, teak decks, curls of gleaming brass.

Mick had always detected something nautical about the way Jonathan Sands dressed out of work hours. He'd seen him wearing bright red and blue waterproof jackets with too many zips and pockets, with elasticated cuffs and storm flaps. Sands' boat was a motor cruiser, about forty feet long, sleek, all white and silver and angled glass. Inside it was spacious, with a central wheelhouse saloon, and two separate cabins, one fore, one aft, each of these spaces being considerably larger than Mick's room at the Dickens.

Mick had followed Sands to the harbour a couple of times previously. Sands seemed to go there for some sort of solace for peace and quiet, away from his wife and child. Once there he usually simply sat inside the boat, lounging on one of the

163

padded benches in the wheelhouse saloon, doing nothing except sit and stare. It would have been easy enough for Mick to pick him off on these occasions but the perfect moment hadn't yet presented itself.

Tonight the pattern had changed. Sands had returned late from work, stayed in the house just long enough to change his clothes, then gone out again. But instead of heading for the harbour he'd gone to an expensive bar off the King's Road that was done out like a Mexican cantina.

Sands was a good-looking man. In certain ways he was more classically handsome than Justin Carr. His face was more conventionally that of a film star, and he carried himself in a manner that advertised his wealth, his style, his self-confidence. He would never have trouble picking up women. Nevertheless, Mick was surprised when Sands left the bar after only an hour or so with two girls in tow. They were very young, very drunk, very King's Road, and Sands had one on each arm. He hailed a taxi and Mick watched as they drove away. There was a great temptation to get into another cab and pursue them but Mick resisted. He knew Sands would be taking them to his boat, and Mick certainly intended to follow them, but the time it would take him to walk there would be just enough for the party to get into full swing.

Sure enough, as Mick entered the marina he could see that the lights were on in the aft cabin of Sands' boat, and that the curtains had been hastily drawn, so hastily that they didn't quite meet, and once he'd positioned himself directly outside the window, he was able to see in through the thin gap.

He peered in. The cabin was done out as a bedroom, with wood panels and brass light-fittings, and most of the floor space was taken up by the bed, the foot of which was curved to fit into the specific contours of the boat. Sands was at the centre of the bed, naked and happy, looking regal, lordly, captain-like, and he still had a girl on either side of him, but now they were also naked, lying flat on their stomachs, their firm little buttocks raised and taut as they wriggled around and took turns sucking Sands' cock.

Mick thought of Sands' wife alone in that big Chelsea house, looking after the child. He thought what a shit Sands was. It was easy enough to feel disapproval, distaste, but at the same time Mick found it impossible not to be a little envious. *He'd* never been to bed with two girls at once, never had two girls take turns sucking his cock. He tried to stop himself thinking about it. He couldn't allow himself to be envious. He had to be a better man than Sands, so that he retained the authority to hand out punishment.

As Mick continued to watch, the two girls started kissing each other, started touching each other's breasts. He had to walk away. It was too much for him. He felt unbearably cold and alone. He saw himself as though from a distance. He was a sad outsider peering in at somebody else's good time, desperate for warmth and having to make do with revenge.

And yet he knew that when the moment came, punishing Sands would be particularly sweet. But that moment hadn't arrived yet. It would only come after the girls had been finished with and packed off home. That was why he had to wait. That was why he was in the hotel bar, reading a leaflet about the Thames Barrier, waiting for Sands to finish.

When the time was right Mick downed his drink and sauntered back to the marina. He was on time. When he got to the boat the girls had gone, the light was off in the aft cabin and Sands was again to be seen sitting alone in the wheelhouse saloon. He was wearing a nautical T-shirt, jeans, no shoes, and even though the hatch was open to the cold night he didn't seem to feel it. Mick walked up to the hatch and said cheerfully, 'Nice boat.'

'Oh, well, thank you,' Sands replied.

He was not surprised or startled by Mick's sudden, unannounced presence but the politeness of his response was automatic, not to be taken as a willingness to talk. His thoughts were a long way away.

'This is the Turbo thirty-six, isn't it?' Mick asked, having read the name on the side of the boat.

'That's right,' Sands said.

'What's your top speed?'

'It's very happy doing twenty-five, twenty-seven knots,' Sands said, then realizing he might be sinking into an unwanted conversation with a dodgy stranger he said, 'Do you own a boat here? If not I should point out that this is a private jetty and we have very good security.'

'That's my boat over there,' Mick said, and he gestured with all possible vagueness towards the boats in the centre of the marina.

Sands was not convinced but he didn't intend to cross-question this intruder. He just wanted him to go away. He decided to ignore him. He turned his body, said nothing and sank back into his brooding silence, and Mick seized this moment of weak acquiescence to step on to the boat and in through the hatch.

'I wonder if I can borrow a cup of sugar,' he said as he entered.

'What?'

'Isn't that what new neighbours are always supposed to ask for?'

'I think you should get off my boat at once,' Sands said.

He moved towards Mick, his intentions vague though hostile, but Mick only smiled. He continued to smile as Sands tried to grab him by the arm and frogmarch him off the boat, but Mick wasn't having any of that. He turned, slipped out of Sands' grasp and kneed him in the balls with neat, well-directed force. Sands crumpled. He sagged. Mick took Sands' out-stretched arm and dragged him across to the wheel, and in one sharp, dexterous manoeuvre he handcuffed him to it.

'OK,' Mick said. 'What's going to happen is this. You're going to get your boat in motion, get it on the river, point it upstream. Then I'm going to start asking you questions about London, twenty questions in all, from out of this book.' He waved the copy of *Unreliable London* that he'd bought from Judy's shop. He'd always known he'd find a use for it. 'Then, each time you get an answer right we'll go forward to the next bridge and so on. If you get one wrong, don't worry, there's no penalty, you don't have to go into reverse or anything.

'And so it goes on for twenty questions. Now, for our purposes I'm going to call the Thames Barrier a bridge as well, the final one, like the winning post. And I'm not going to count Hungerford or Cannon Street 'cos they both look like poxy little bridges on the map. And if we've arrived at the Thames Barrier by the time you've answered the twentieth question I'll ask you to put me ashore and you can go happily on your way. Look at it another way, there are eleven bridges before the barrier, so if you can answer twelve questions right out of twenty you're home and dry. OK?'

Sands looked at him in frightened bafflement. He had no idea what was going on, but the handcuff on his wrist told him it was serious. Coming so soon after the session with the girls it had a preternatural air of divine retribution about it.

'I can't do that,' he said.

'Oh yes, you can,' said Mick, and he clubbed him round the back of the head with his fist.

'It's not that I don't want to,' Sands said wretchedly, 'but the fact is, the tide is out.'

Mick thought for a moment. He knew nothing about rivers and tides and Sands had no reason to be telling him the truth. But then he remembered that when he'd done a circuit of the marina earlier he'd walked past the lock and it had indeed been dry, and the river end of it had opened out on to nothing but a wide mud bank. It dawned on him that Sands *was* probably telling the truth.

'Oops,' said Mick. 'Bit of a balls-up, I'm afraid. I'm going to have to think about this.'

He began to think, looking round the cabin for inspiration. He saw a stack of nautical charts and immediately saw that they offered possibilities, since a couple of them showed the Thames in a scale that he could deal with.

'OK,' he said. 'It's a shame about the tide, because I was really looking forward to the boat trip, but I guess we're just going to have to do it theoretically, do it in miniature like a board game, OK? And I think we're going to have to conduct it in one of the cabins so that you can't try anything funny like attracting a security guard.'

Mick unlocked one end of the handcuffs and Sands immediately launched himself forward away from Mick, trying to break free and escape from the boat. Mick yanked him back, grabbed his hair, smashed his face against the wheel, and dragged him into the aft cabin. The bed was still unmade from when he'd been there with the girls. The room smelled of women's perfume, not cheap. Wine bottles and drug paraphernalia were scattered about the tiny area of unused floor. Mick clocked them with disgust and knocked Sands about a little more harshly as he handcuffed him to a suitable light fitting.

He stripped the covers off the bed to give himself a flat surface on which to lay out the charts. Sands felt the blood running out of his nose and watched Mick in continuing confusion.

'OK,' Mick said, jabbing the map with his finger, 'you're here. If you answer this first question right, then off we go upriver to Battersea Bridge. Here, I'll make it easier for you to see where you are,' and he reached into his pocket and produced a tiny model ship, a counter from a game of Monopoly, which he placed in the centre of the river, outside Chelsea Harbour.

'Number one,' Mick began. 'Who said that when a man is tired of London he's tired of life?'

Sands looked at him suspiciously. Could he really be asking such a ridiculously simple question? Well, possibly. Perhaps that was only an overfamiliar quotation if you happened to be a Londoner.

'What on earth makes you think that I'm going to play this ludicrous game?' Sands asked.

Mick looked hurt, as though Sands' failure to understand was a personal slight and a great disappointment to him.

'You're going to play out of fear,' Mick explained. 'Because if you don't play then I'll inflict all sorts of terrible pain on you, and I assume you'd rather I didn't do that. Why not play a ludicrous game if it saves you getting a beating?'

Sands nodded. He wasn't stupid. There was already no doubt that Mick could inflict a very efficient beating on him. If playing along was going to gain him even the smallest advantage he realized he might as well do it. He said, 'As a matter of fact the answer is Samuel Johnson.'

'I've got Dr Johnson down here,' Mick said, 'but I guess that's near enough. That's very good. How did you know that?'

'My expensive education wasn't a complete waste of money,' Sands replied.

Mick moved the tiny boat along the chart, sat it on Battersea Bridge and said, 'Then you'll probably get this one. Question two: in which London square will you find a statue of Mahatma Gandhi?'

'No idea,' Sands said dismissively.

'Don't want to guess?'

'Not really.'

'It's Tavistock Square. Hard lines.'

Sands shrugged to show it meant nothing to him. Mick thumbed through the book looking for another question and said, 'It must be nice coming here of an evening, watching the ships roll in and then watching them roll away again.'

'I like it,' Sands replied.

'But it must cost a packet to keep a boat here.'

'Yes, mooring fees aren't cheap.'

'You ought to tie your boat up in Filey or Robin Hood's Bay, somewhere a bit more scenic.'

'Unfortunately, I happen to live and work in London.'

'What line of work are you in then?'

'Insurance,' he said.

'We have insurance in Yorkshire too,' said Mick.

'I'm in marine insurance. You need to be in London if you're in marine insurance.'

'Yeah. Obviously. Because you see so many boats in London, don't you?'

Sands gave a lightly exasperated sigh. In his current circumstances he was not inclined to embark on an explanation of the workings of the marine insurance industry.

'Forgive my ignorance,' Mick said. 'Right, question number three: how many black cabs were there in London in 1982? It's an old book. I assume they must have had a recount since then, but go on. Have a guess, to the nearest thousand.'

'Twelve thousand,' Sands said.

'Hey, not bad, I'll give you that. Was that a guess? The answer's 12,560, and they were all diesel except for seventeen of them. You're doing well. Now tell me, how do you get two girls to go to bed with you just like that, the way you did with those two tonight? This isn't one of the twenty questions by the way. I mean, what do you say to them? How do you get the conversation round to the subject of three-in-a-bed sex?'

'Charm has something to do with it,' Sands said. 'And offering to give them drugs.'

'You give them drugs?'

'I *offer* them drugs. I don't slip them a Mickey Finn.'

'Drugs,' Mick tutted. 'Don't you have any respect for your sexual partners?'

'I have as much respect for them as they have for themselves.'

'Don't you worry about them, don't you ever think what you might be doing to them?'

'What is this? Do you know those girls? Are you a boyfriend or brother or something?'

Mick made a gesture that said neither yes nor no. He was happy to have Sands remain uncertain.

'I mean, if you are, then what can I say except sorry.'

'Sorry's not enough,' said Mick. 'Now, question four: what is the origin of the place name Soho?'

'I know that,' Sands said. 'It's a hunting cry, like tally-ho, from the days when the area was still parkland and used for hunting.'

'That's amazing,' Mick said. 'It's an amazing fact, and it's even more amazing that you should know it. So, what about your wife? What would she say if she knew what you'd been up to with those two girls?'

'She'd be very glad that I'd had sex with somebody else so that I stopped bothering her.'

'It's like that, is it?'

'As a matter of fact, it is.'

'Have you tried charm and drugs on her?'

'Not recently, no. But I know what the result would be. You're not a friend of my wife's, for Christ's sake, are you?'

'I'm everybody's friend,' Mick said. 'I seem to be able to establish this easy rapport with people. They tell me all sorts of things. I mean, you're probably wondering why you're bothering to answer these questions about your sex life. Is it because you're scared I might kill you?'

Being killed was not one of the options Sands had so far considered. He fought against it but he couldn't stop a shudder running through his body. Mick pretended not to notice.

'No,' he said, 'I don't think that's the reason. I think the real answer is that you realize how good confession is for the soul.'

'I'll remember that,' Sands said.

'OK, question five: what was the subject of John Evelyn's *Fumifugium*, written in 1661?'

'I don't know. Smog, fogs, London particulars?'

'I can only accept one answer,' Mick said.

'London fogs,' Sands said, sorry to be dealing with an idiot.

'Very good. I didn't think you were going to get it. What were you going on about London Particulars? That's a bookshop.'

'It's also a name given to London fogs.'

171

'Get away!'

Sands looked exasperated as well as scared. Mick wondered if it was time to hit him again in order to make him more compliant, but he decided to wait a little longer, see how it went. He moved the toy boat one bridge up the river.

'Question six: the name of which London district contains six consecutive consonants, one after the other?'

Sands looked at him as though he was being ridiculous, as though there was no way any English place name could possibly contain such a configuration. Then suddenly it came to him.

'Knightsbridge,' he said triumphantly.

'Very good.'

'It's a bit of a cheat actually,' Sands pointed out. 'I mean, obviously it was once two separate words and the s would have had an apostrophe.'

'What does it matter?' Mick said. 'You got it right. You ever paid for sex?'

No longer surprised by the turns of Mick's mind, Sands replied, 'Only when I was very young and living abroad.'

'Doesn't count then. You ever forced yourself on somebody? You know, like date-rape or whatever they call it.'

'Of course not.'

'How about when not on a date, just straightforward rape?'

'Don't be ridiculous.'

'OK, question seven: whose last twelve symphonies, and that's numbers ninety-three to one hundred and four, are known as the London Symphonies?'

'That's Haydn,' Sands said immediately.

'Very good. Haydn it is. Twelve symphonies written between 1791 and 1795. I don't suppose you can whistle any of them.'

Sands made a brave attempt to whistle a passage from one of the symphonies.

'That's good,' said Mick. 'I'm tempted to give you a bonus mark, but no, I've got to be fair. You're still doing amazingly well. You're at Westminster Bridge already. Let's hope you can keep it up, as the Chelsea girls said to the man in marine insurance. Right, question eight: who, in a song, didn't want to go to Chelsea?'

'I haven't the slightest idea,' Sands said.

'Oh, come on, everybody knows that.'

'Not me.'

'Of course you do.'

'I've said I don't.'

'Hey, don't get stroppy, Jonathan,' said Mick, and he punched him twice, once in the face, once in the stomach. He felt they were both overdue. Sands' stroppiness disappeared, but from then on things started to go marginally less well for him. As well as not knowing that it was Elvis Costello who didn't want to go to Chelsea, he didn't know that Charles II first met Nell Gwyn in the Dove Inn at Hammersmith. Equally he had no idea that Crouch End derived its name from crux, the Roman word for a cross. He made a stab at guessing the population of London at the time of the Norman conquest, but he was nowhere near the right answer, which was somewhere between fourteen and eighteen thousand.

After eleven questions he was still at Westminster Bridge, still some way from the Thames Barrier, and Mick belted him across the face a couple of times in order to encourage him, help him to concentrate, and this time it did seem to help. Things started to get better for him. He knew that Woolwich was the site of the first London McDonald's. He knew that the Marylebone line was the first tube line. He knew that Christopher Wren was a professor of astronomy at the time he drew up his plans for rebuilding London after the Great Fire. To Mick's amazement he also knew that London's Dog Cemetery was to be found in the north-east corner of Kensington Gardens, behind Victoria Lodge.

'Hey, this is too easy for you,' Mick said. 'Maybe I should change the rules, have you go back a bridge for every answer you get wrong.'

'No,' Sands insisted loudly. 'You set the rules at the beginning, now you stick by them.'

'OK, OK,' said Mick. 'Don't get so excited. It's only a game. Question sixteen: whose grave at the church of St Mary Magdalene in Mortlake is in the form of an eighteen-foot-high stone Bedouin tent?'

'Oh shit,' Sands said, angry at himself. 'I ought to know that. Damn it. De Quincey?'

'Well, it says here, Sir Richard Burton and his wife Isabel, which seems a bit rum to me, because I thought Richard Burton was buried in Wales and I didn't know he was ever knighted, and I thought his wife was Elizabeth Taylor, and I suppose that could be a misprint but I didn't think she was dead. Still, you live and learn.'

Sands shook his head; he was not going to educate Mick about Sir Richard Burton. Mick thumbed through the little book, halted at one page, was about to ask a question, then changed his mind, and kept looking.

'Hey, what are you doing?' Sands demanded. 'Are you trying to find an impossibly difficult question to ask me?'

'I can ask you any question I like,' Mick said.

'Yes, well.' Sands hesitated, realizing the truth of what Mick was saying, realizing the absurd weakness of his own position. 'Well, anyway,' he added, 'just ask me questions that I have some hope of answering.'

'Sure,' said Mick. 'Question seventeen: in *The Young Ones* Cliff Richard is the leader of a youth club in which area of London?'

'Oh, for Christ's sake,' said Sands. 'I don't know that. How would anybody know a thing like that?' He took a wild guess and said, 'Paddington.'

'Yes!' Mick said, and they both let out a sort of a whoop, prolonged in Mick's case, instantly stifled in Sands'. Mick moved the toy boat up the river to Tower Bridge.

'Hey,' said Mick, 'you're going to walk this. Three questions left. Get any of them right and you're there. OK, where in

London would you find the death mask of Tom Paine and a lock of his hair?'

'Oh, come on,' Sands said, genuinely angry. 'How am I supposed to know something like that?'

'Maybe you're not,' Mick replied. 'The answer is they're in the National Museum of Labour History, Limehouse Town Hall, E14.'

'That's ridiculous,' said Sands.

'Yeah, doesn't exactly sound like a white-knuckle ride, does it? But it's all right, no need to panic, here's question nineteen: what's the name of Boadicea's father?'

'Oh, for fuck's sake!'

'What's the matter? You wouldn't want me to make it too easy for you, would you?'

'This is insane. Why don't you just say I've lost and have done with it?'

'Come on, try. It says here he died and had his estate taken away from him by the Romans and that was why Boadicea revolted. Does that help at all?'

Sands was livid at the difficulty of the question. 'This has nothing to do with London,' he insisted. 'Boadicea was queen out in the wilds of East Anglia somewhere. She only came to London to burn it down and as for her fucking father—'

'No,' said Mick, 'I don't think you're going to get it. His name was Prasutagus.'

Sands took a deep, chest-puffing breath. He was frustrated and hugely angry, yet determined to retain some dignity.

'Well, that's really good to know,' he said.

'So, the moment of truth, the final question,' said Mick. 'And I want you to know I'm on your side, Jonathan. I really want you to get this right. OK, question twenty: who wrote those immortal words, "Earth has not anything to show more fair"?'

'Wordsworth,' said Sands at once with a kind of adolescent glee, and he let out a long sigh of relief.

'Oh, Jonathan, that's such a shame,' said Mick. 'I really

thought you were going to do it, but I'm afraid the answer's Flanders and Swann. They're talking about London buses.'

'No, no,' Sands screeched. 'The original line is from "Composed on Westminster Bridge" by William Wordsworth. The line in Flanders and Swann is a parody, a deliberate reference to the Wordsworth.'

Mick looked at Sands disapprovingly.

'Now come on, old chap, play the game. It's here in the book in black and white.'

'Then the book's wrong,' Sands shouted.

'Well, it is called *Unreliable London*,' Mick said. 'But you know this is the book we're using. This is my authority.'

'Then the book's a piece of idiocy. A piece of crap. Ask anybody. Wordsworth wrote "Earth has not anything to show more fair". Ask anyone.'

He was sounding desperate to the point of hysteria. Mick slapped him again to calm him down. Then he slapped him again for luck.

'You'll have noticed,' said Mick, 'that until now I've been very careful not to tell you what I'd do if you failed to get to the Thames Barrier by the twentieth question . . .'

'This is a fix,' said Sands. 'This isn't fair. It never was.'

Mick listened carefully to what Sands had to say, then shook his head sadly, as though disappointed that he was being such a bad sport.

He said, 'It's true that the evening really hasn't turned out as planned. Not for either of us. By rights we should be out on the water by now, somewhere not too far from the Thames Barrier. I really wanted to go there and see it and have a memorable experience. But anyway, it didn't pan out. You were expecting something different too. But the fact is, what I always intended to do if you got the answers wrong was take this gun,' and he showed Sands his gun, 'and I was going to load it with a new magazine . . .' He loaded it with a new magazine.

'Ask me another question,' Sands shouted. 'You nearly gave

me a bonus point for whistling Haydn. Come on, be reasonable . . .'

'And I was going to pull the trigger a few times and empty the magazine, not into you, you'll be pleased to hear, but into the bottom of your boat.'

'No,' Sands screamed. 'This isn't right. You know that. Ask me another question. A decider. Double or quits. Please.'

'And you know the other thing?' Mick said. 'You're right. This isn't fair. It was never meant to be fair. It was meant to torture you a little. The truth is, whether we'd got to the Thames Barrier or not, I was still going to empty the gun into the bottom of your boat.'

'No,' Sands cried out.

Mick was as good as his word, and he was a long way from Chelsea Harbour, and Sands' sinking boat was a terrible, terrible mess, before any of the sluggish security guards arrived to see what the noise was all about.

# MASH

Mick called home again from a pay phone in the corner of an eel and pie shop where he'd just left most of a plate of pie and mash. It was early evening and the place looked ready to close. Gabby's phone rang for a long time, its tone thin and very far away. When she answered her voice sounded breathless and guilty and there was music playing in the background that she made no attempt to turn down.

'I was exercising,' she said.

'Yeah?' said Mick.

'Like aerobics. Got to keep in trim.'

'Yeah?'

'Well yes, and keep in practice, like rehearsing. I've got a couple more gigs at the weekend.'

'Good,' he said. 'You know, at first I thought it was very brave of you to go back on stage after the gang-bang, because I thought you'd be scared of the same thing happening again. But I realized that'd be crazy. What are the chances of it happening twice? I mean, if it had happened again, if you'd got gang-banged again, well, it'd be a hell of a coincidence, wouldn't it? In fact, I think you'd have to say it was more than a coincidence. You'd have to say there was something about your dancing that drove men mad and turned them into rapists.'

'Are you trying to be funny?' Gabby snapped.

'No.'

'Are you trying to say that my being raped is some kind of dirty joke?'

'I would never say a thing like that.'

'Then stop sounding as though you're taking the piss.'

'OK,' he said. 'Sorry.'

It was not normally part of Mick's nature to say sorry. She was surprised and appreciative.

'What's your problem, Mick?'

She meant it to sound concerned, but Mick didn't hear it that way. Slowly, deliberately, he said, 'I think the problem may be something to do with the fact that I'm down in London trying to sort out the blokes who raped my girlfriend, while at the same time my girlfriend's taking her clothes off for strange men back in Sheffield. I think that's the sort of general area where the problem might be.'

'I'm sorry,' she said. 'It's what I do.'

'I know, but I don't have to like it.'

'You never objected before.'

'No, I didn't.'

They slipped into silence, neither of them rash enough to want to open up that particular can of worms.

Then Mick said, 'Actually, I rang up to tell you that number three has been dealt with.'

'Good,' she said.

'Yeah. It was a pleasure, basically. I mean the guy's scum. He's got all that money. He's got a lovely wife, lovely kid, lovely house. He used to have a lovely boat too.'

'What?'

'Never mind. Anyway, he's got all that and he goes around picking up pairs of tarts. He deserves all he gets.'

'What are you talking about? He deserves what he gets because he raped me.'

'Of course he does,' Mick said. 'Of course.'

There was another silence, longer and clumsier than before. Mick knew it wasn't meant to be like this. A phonecall home was supposed to be reassuring, nourishing. Perhaps it would have been better if he'd broken all contact until the job was completed, gone underground, but that would have been stupid. Besides, there were things that he couldn't help asking.

'They're a rum bunch, these men,' he said, articulating something that had been on his mind for a while. 'I mean, I've met three of them now and they're very different from each other. They don't seem to have much in common. They don't look like the sort of men who'd all be friends with each other.'

'What are you saying? That you think you've got the wrong men?'

'They're the ones on your list,' he said.

'Then they're the right men.'

'Yeah, well, maybe I'm mistaken. Maybe gang-rape has this funny way of bringing people together.'

'Is that another joke, Mick?'

'No,' he said, being more placatory than he really wanted to be. 'No way.'

'How much longer before you're finished?'

'I don't know, not long.'

'I'll be glad when you're finished,' she said. 'I miss you, you know.'

'Yeah?'

'Of course I do.'

Mick had no reason to think she was lying and yet she sounded unconvincing. Mick wondered if perhaps he no longer wanted to be convinced.

'You could come down to London,' he said. 'We could have a weekend here together.'

'I hate London.'

'It's all right when you get used to it.'

'I've got a particularly good reason for hating it.'

'It wasn't London that raped you.'

'Well, it feels that way.'

Mick could see there was no point arguing. 'Look, the money's running out,' he said, although this wasn't true. 'I'll go. I'll phone you after I've done the next one.'

Before she could answer he hooked the receiver into place and some coins rattled into the change cup. The owner of the shop was tidying up the chairs, sweeping the floor, ready to close for the night. He looked at Mick disapprovingly though Mick couldn't tell why. Was it because Mick had left the food or because he'd been listening in to the phone conversation?

Mick walked over to his former table and his abandoned plate, looked down at the food and said to the shop owner, 'You know how you could sell more food around here?'

'No,' the owner said, not remotely interested.

'No,' said Mick sadly. 'Neither do I.'

# MR AND MRS LONELY HEARTS

After Stuart ditched her, Judy was left feeling hurt, used, worthless, but above all intensely angry. What had the relationship been about if not excitement, novelty, risk? How could Stuart turn out to be so timid, so cowardly? How could he suddenly start worrying about being caught by his wife, and as a consequence end the most thrilling relationship he was ever likely to have?

She came to the inevitable conclusion that Stuart was not the man she'd thought he was. Consequently he was certainly no longer the man she wanted. Yet she couldn't simply turn off her feelings. She'd have been happy to feel nothing towards him, but that didn't seem to be an option, so she found herself brooding, nurturing her anger. She was aware of a fury boiling inside her. It wouldn't go away, and she wasn't altogether convinced that she wanted it to.

She cursed Stuart and in her day-dreams she saw her curse bearing strange, evil fruit. She saw Stuart mown down by a London double-decker, Stuart struck by a lingering, painful, only at last fatal disease, Stuart's business going bankrupt, Stuart's wife leaving him for some new hunky tour guide.

Sometimes she thought that merely imagining these scenarios could act as a form of therapy. If she stoked her anger long enough it might perhaps burn itself out, but there was no sign of that happening yet. She wanted Stuart to be damaged and ruined and in pain, but she was smart enough to realize that in truth it was she who was all these things. Why else would she have answered the lonely hearts ad?

When it was over Judy realized it was not the sort of thing that a married couple would have been able to get away with anywhere except in London. Out there in the sticks, the boonies, the real world, a married man and a married woman would have had a lot of trouble placing lonely hearts ads to meet single people with a view to having casual sex. In a small town, even in a small city, word would have got out. You would be spotted. Someone, possibly everyone, would know you were married and what you were up to. But London was big enough, diverse enough, anonymous enough, that a couple could place ads, meet strange men and women, seduce them, bed them and never have to see them again.

The newspaper ads were vague but welcoming. They were meant to embrace rather than exclude, to attract all sorts of hearts, lonely or not. They were designed to elicit the maximum number of replies, to give the maximum choice. They implied a lack of involvement, they spoke of fun and good times. The word 'uncomplicated' was often used.

They called themselves Irena and Jack, but Judy couldn't be sure those were their real names. They were helped no end by the fact that they had good looks and attractive personalities. There were occasional failures, of course, but in general there were very few men who wouldn't want to sleep with Irena, very few women who would say no to Jack. There were plenty of people out there in London desperate for affection or closeness or sex, and who were prepared to accept an ersatz version for just one night. Next morning they'd be gone and turned into the stuff of erotic anecdote.

The days were long past when Irena and Jack felt any need to justify or explain themselves to themselves. But when one of them met a new partner, certainly when Jack met Judy, he would say that his marriage was valuable to him, too valuable to risk having it damaged by such a commonplace, understandable thing as adultery. Men and women, he said, are imperfect, they fail to keep their promises of fidelity. They are betrayed by feelings of curiosity, vanity, lust. The world was full of people you might want to sleep with, and failing to sleep with them might lead to boredom and frustration, and these in turn might lead to the breakdown of the marriage. By doing it Jack and Irena's way they did what they wanted with whoever they wanted, but it was essentially a case of kiss and tell, and the telling in itself became an erotic activity. The important thing was no secrets, no furtive phonecalls, no illicit assignations. Jack and Irena's desires, their needs, their fantasies, were laid out on the kitchen table along with the morning post. Judy told Jack that she understood perfectly.

What she had more trouble understanding were her own motives for replying to the ad. She had only recently been ditched by Stuart. As well as the unassuageable anger, she was also feeling lonely in a sad, numb, dull sort of way. She wasn't looking for a replacement for Stuart, and that was why she'd answered the ad. There was obviously something fishy about it. It had clearly been placed by someone who wasn't telling the truth. It advertised the charms of a 'tall, creative, good-looking, cosmopolitan man' who was looking to share 'hedonistic days and nights' with an 'independent, unconventional woman'. Its speciousness leapt up at her from the page. Here was someone who was going to turn out to be something unexpected, and she liked that. She answered the ad, included a telephone number and a photograph, and a couple of days later Jack phoned to arrange a date.

The meeting took place in a crowded wine bar in Covent Garden; safe, open, public territory. He was indeed tall and good-looking, a hint of authenticity that surprised her slightly; she had been prepared for him to be short and snaggle-toothed. His features were angular and regular. His hair was long and immaculately cared for. His fingernails looked as though they had been professionally manicured. He ordered a not bad bottle of white Burgundy and then he talked about himself. He talked about his job (something vague and media-based), about his flash car, his Hampstead house, his little place in the country, and though she wasn't exactly impressed by all this, she was not so unworldly as to think that these things were irrelevant. Neither did she think they were necessarily true.

He did his little speech about marriage and faithfulness. It didn't surprise her that he had a wife. Men with his looks and his patter always needed to have a woman in the background. However, what they didn't need was to place lonely hearts ads, at least not for any of the usual reasons. She looked forward to finding out what his unusual reasons were.

She could tell that he found her foreignness attractive. Along with the prejudice and the casual distrust that her looks had brought her, there had always been those who were drawn to her difference and otherness. Jack let her tell a little of her own story and he was obviously disappointed to discover that she was not nearly as foreign as she might have been. Her voice, her background, her attitude, were in many ways surprisingly familiar. She could see his disappointment. She was not as exotic as he wanted her to be. She thought perhaps she should have lied, invented a more alien past for herself, for her protection as well as for his pleasure, but it was too late for that.

She felt mildly light-headed after the wine and she melted happily into the bucket seats of his car as he drove from Covent Garden to a little Italian restaurant in Hampstead. The place was intimate, pricey, very close to where he lived. She ordered the most expensive things on the menu and he seemed to approve. He said he liked a woman with a healthy appetite.

At some point between the first and second courses he launched into a speech about the horrors and problems of living in London, about how he wanted to live in the country full time, preferably by the sea, but alas his job kept him in the big smoke, close to his media contacts and connections. He complained about pollution and crime and noise and expense. He may have meant it, but it still sounded like a speech, like something learned and recited rather than something felt. Besides, like any Streatham girl, especially one who found herself living in a small attic room in Bethnal Green, Judy didn't think Hampstead dwellers had much to complain about. In fact, she had met comparatively few Hampstead dwellers and that had something to do with why she was here with this strange, intermittently bogus man. She was making preparations, doing the groundwork, for getting laid in Hampstead.

She was prepared to be geographically disappointed. She suspected he might only live in the estate agents' definition of Hampstead, in what might more realistically be called Belsize Park or even Gospel Oak. But in the event she was not disappointed at all. He lived in a converted coach house in what was undoubtedly Hampstead proper. She began to see that Jack was not nearly so bogus as she'd suspected.

As they entered the house he explained, in unnecessary detail it seemed to her, that his wife might be coming in later, probably with her boyfriend, but that it was nothing to worry about, they'd probably come in and go straight to bed and not bother them. Judy insisted that she wasn't at all bothered.

The inside of the house did not look exactly like the home of a married couple. Everything was so tidy and ordered, no doubt by a maid or cleaner. Judy had a sense of pale, neutral colour: pale grey carpet, beige upholstery, magnolia walls. It was tasteful without displaying any taste. It looked designed and yet the designer had been keen not to impose any feelings or ideas on the place.

Jack sauntered around the living room, turning on lamps, drawing curtains, a short expedition to create mood and ambience. Somewhat drunk by now, rather than offer Judy more alcohol he got a bag from a drawer in a console table and lit a ready-rolled joint.

Judy had decided to flow along with events. She accepted the joint and inhaled deeply. Soon this would all be over. The sex would have taken place, she'd be eager to leave and phoning for a taxi to take her home. She knew Jack would not offer to drive her. It wouldn't have been such a terrible night, and when she got home she'd be able to place another cross on her map of London.

Jack sat beside her, stroking her shoulder, and very briefly he kissed her. But he was awkward and restless. This was not to be a slow, melting seduction. He wanted to go upstairs to the bedroom, get the job done there. Judy had no objection.

The sex was better than she had expected, than she had any right to expect. It was athletic and exuberant, and it was not spoilt at all when, in the middle of it, Judy had thought to herself, If only Stuart could see me now. She felt a swift pang of fury, which she immediately redirected towards her current sexual partner. She sank her nails into the flesh of his back, and Jack chose to read this as passion, as evidence that he was doing a fine job.

When it was over Jack was much softer and more playful, a lot more genuine-seeming than he had been before. They lay quietly together in silence and then they heard the front door opening downstairs, a man and a woman's voices, their footsteps, their swift ascent to the adjacent spare bedroom.

Jack and Judy were amused by the sounds of sex that were soon coming through the party wall. They giggled conspiratorially as they listened to the masculine grunts, and the rhythms of intercourse that rocked the bed against the wall, but most striking of all was the loud girlish moaning that gradually transformed itself into squeals of delight and finally into screams of ecstasy. They were so loud, so theatrical, that Judy immediately had the sense that this was a performance being given at least partly for her benefit. Jack, she noticed, found the sounds powerfully erotic.

When the noise had climaxed, when silence returned, Jack got out of bed and left the bedroom. He didn't say where he was going and when he hadn't returned fifteen minutes later Judy wondered whether that was it, whether the show was over and she was expected to slip away without further interaction. That suited her just fine, but she thought he might have told her what was correct form.

She sat uncomfortably on the edge of the bed and heard a door open and close, then a couple of pairs of feet descending the stairs, then voices coming from below, two male, one female. She got up from the bed, dressed, looked briefly at herself in the mirror. Her face was flushed but she looked only slightly dishevelled. She put on her shoes, combed her hair and went downstairs. The voices were coming from the kitchen and they sounded as though they were involved in some sort of negotiation. Judy wanted to leave as quietly and as unobtrusively as possible but Jack spotted her and called after her, 'Hey, where do you think you're going?'

His voice contained a mixture of irritation and command that she immediately resented.

'Home,' she replied defiantly, but she stopped and couldn't resist peering into the kitchen to get a look at the owners of the two unfamiliar voices. She saw Jack and two strangers arranged in a bizarre erotic tableau. Jack and the woman, who was presumably his wife, were almost naked. Jack wore only boxer shorts, the woman wore nothing but a short T-shirt that revealed a triangle of hirsute shadow beneath its hem. The other man was dark-complexioned, big-chinned, glum-looking. He was more or less dressed, however. He had on a cheap synthetic fibre suit, but wore shoes without socks and he was bare-chested under the jacket.

'This is the young lady in question,' Jack said to the man, and to Judy he said, 'and this is Tarek. He's from Syria. He's a . . .'

'Student,' the wife added, trying to be helpful.

Tarek looked briefly, dismissively at Judy, shook his head in sorrow and disgust. Then he hit Jack on the nose. It was very crisp and clean, a trained boxer's punch, delivered with great control and the minimum of force. Jack yelped and held his nose as blood started to seep from his nostrils.

'What was that for?' Jack demanded.

'You are sick. Very sick,' Tarek said thickly, and he walked out of the kitchen, out of the house and into the Hampstead night. If he had ever been the owner of socks and shirt he was prepared to abandon them.

Jack watched him go. He appeared disappointed but philosophical. He turned to his wife and some coded, silent exchange of information took place. Then he turned his attention to Judy.

'Our friend Tarek got angry because I suggested a little group interaction,' he said. 'But just because *he* doesn't know how to enjoy himself, that needn't spoil things for the rest of us.'

Judy was aware that the wife was smiling at her. It wasn't wholly sexual but she felt its pressure, the amalgam of coercion and flattery.

'I don't think so,' Judy said. 'I've got one cross for Hampstead. That's enough for anybody.'

Months later, Jack and Irena would still be recalling this strange, awkward night and wondering what the hell Judy had meant by that cryptic remark.

# THE WALKER'S DIARY

# THE VAST AND THE DETAILED

One of those surprising, bright, sunny March days that make you think the winter's over even though you know it really isn't.

On the Victoria Embankment at Charing Cross Pier. A long row of parked, empty tour buses, hundreds of joggers of all sorts and ages, some looking very professional, some looking as though they were on their last legs, and at one point a man performing the weird heel and toe gait of a road walker. Then an old man riding his bike along the pavement and a jogger shouting at him, 'Get in the road, mate.'

Benches looking out over the Thames, metal griffins for legs. Then benches with sphinxes, then with camels.

Under Blackfriars Bridge, cardboard boxes, folded blankets, plastic bread trays belonging to the homeless, all arranged and stacked with great precision and symmetry, but no sign of their owners.

At Paul's Walk the benches were full of people eating their lunches, most of them couples. I wondered if they were having work romances.

You can't walk straight all the way along the north bank of the river. You get forced up Broken Wharf away from the Thames, into Queen Victoria Street and Upper Thames Street.

I walked down Bull Wharf Lane, a dark, narrow alley leading back to the river, but it was a dead end. There was a black road sweeper working there, and he looked at me like I was daft for entering the street at all.

Under Cannon Street Bridge, a low, bleak concrete tunnel, a place where people don't belong, and yet there were lots of people there, many of them sharp young men in dark blue suits with ties that were loud but not too loud.

In Angel Passage there were empty drums like giant cotton reels that had once had massive cables coiled around them.

On London Bridge, a painted sign, black on white and now looking old and faded. It said, 'Less noise. Please consider offices above.' At that point a hovercraft passed under the bridge, its low, thick engine note reverberating under the broad concrete spans.

Outside a house in Barnes, a huge removal van, the number plates and the name on the side Italian. The van was fully loaded but the back was open and inside, amidst all the packed furniture, two removal men had found a couple of chairs to sit on and they were having a cup of coffee, real Italian espresso, made using a proper metal, screw-top coffee maker, and they were drinking out of rather chic white china cups.

I remember when Christina, the daughter of a friend of ours, was about six years old, and we all went to Brighton for the day. We were walking through the narrow streets up by Kemp Town, when suddenly Christina stopped and looked around her very suspiciously and said, 'This street's in London, isn't it?'

Being a good parent, her father stopped too and asked her to explain exactly what she meant, but that's all he could get out of her: 'This street's in London.' She was very confused, maybe slightly scared by it, and she didn't have the vocabulary to be able to explain herself, so we all shrugged it off as one of those silly ideas that kids get, but afterwards I thought about it a lot, and I think I know what she meant.

She somehow thought that towns, or at least streets or neighbourhoods, were manufactured in large chunks, centrally, off-site. She thought they came ready-made and identical and she'd now encountered a block in Brighton that was exactly the same as a block she'd seen in some part of London. I've asked her since if she can remember the episode, but it's gone.

I sometimes think she had a great idea. Let's imagine you were a town planner; instead of designing and building a whole new city you could say we'll have a new Hampstead or a new Knightsbridge, or you could order two hundred yards of Oxford Street or a couple of acres of Hyde Park.

Or let's say you wanted a whole new metropolis; in that case you'd manufacture a brand-new second London, a perfect replica, identical in every physical detail. Then you could set it up in New Zealand or Dubai or Namibia, move in a population, leave it for a year or two, and then go back and see how much the new London had diverged from the old one.

I realize this is ultimately a meaningless idea. London isn't simply its architecture and hardware. The new London wouldn't, for example, be a financial centre, wouldn't be the seat of kings or government. It wouldn't have any history, wouldn't contain the same ethnic or social mix as the original. The climate would be different. But I still think it sounds like fun. I still think it might be better than starting from scratch every time someone wants to build something new.

This one I hardly believe. It's too strange, too anecdotal, too fictional. It's almost as though someone's setting these things up for me.

I was walking along Magdala Avenue, near Archway, and there were two women waiting at a bus stop. They weren't old but they were dowdy, overweight, looking as though they'd led hard, children-filled lives.

They were deep in conversation, but as I got level with them one looked up and turned to me as though she wanted me to settle a difference of opinion they'd been having.

'Excuse me,' she said. 'You've heard that expression "the seven-year itch"? Well, what does it mean exactly?'

There didn't appear to be any ulterior motive, she wasn't sending me up or taking the piss, she just wanted a second, or I suppose third, opinion on what the seven-year itch was. I didn't feel very articulate, but I said I thought it referred to people who'd been in relationships for seven years, though not literally seven, I pointed out, and one or possibly both of the partners had got bored and had started looking for excitement with someone else.

'Yes, right,' the woman went on, but that obviously wasn't all she wanted to know. 'But if like the man goes off on a seven-year itch he always comes back, doesn't he?'

Not wanting to claim any great expertise on the subject I replied, 'I think sometimes he does, sometimes he doesn't.'

'Oh,' she said, very gloomy and disappointed, and her friend looked on sadly.

I just stood there thinking I'd definitely said the wrong thing and wanting to say something more cheerful and optimistic, but I didn't know how to phrase it. Eventually, noticing my lack of ease, the other woman said, 'Thanks very much, sir.'

The use of 'sir' crushed me. I walked on feeling like some evil squire who went around dashing the hopes of poor, honest, downtrodden women.


In Bentinck Street, Mayfair, I saw a tall, imposing bay-fronted house with a blue plaque in honour of Edward Gibbon, author of *Decline and Fall of the Roman Empire*. I looked at the house and thought what a great place it would be to live and write.

But I read the plaque more closely and Gibbon didn't actually live in *this* house but in a house 'on this site'. I felt a little cheated, and then I realized that this was how it was always likely to be. When we say Edward Gibbon lived here, or this was where Elizabeth Browning met Byron, or this is where Christopher Marlowe was killed, or this is where Samuel Johnson walked, what do we mean by 'here'? The here has gone just as surely as the now. Even if they still exist, the buildings they inhabited have been changed out of all recognition. The streets are no longer the same. They've been modernized, transformed. The men and women of the past did not walk these actual paving stones. Their world looked different, smelled different, felt different. They didn't see the world as we see it now, and it's a great arrogance to believe we're treading in their footsteps.

The city, it seems to me, must always be a palimpsest, a series of erasures, of new beginnings, obliterations, of temporary preservations and misguided reconstructions. Much of it is guesswork. There is no authorized text.

As I walk through London I find I'm moved by history but not by nostalgia, and I wonder if what I'm moved by is perhaps something behind history, behind events and personalities; mythic forms, archetypes, the old, old stories, something older than this city, something that is inherent in the very idea of the city.

I was in Upper Street, Islington, at the Highbury end opposite the Union Chapel, when I heard a man shouting, 'They're fucked. This government is fucked.' I thought it might be some lunatic talking to himself but in fact it was a young, smartly dressed man talking to a woman. He was shouting because his politics were so passionate.

'Just a couple of demonstrations,' he said, 'just a couple of strikes, and it's all over for this government.'

In fact the pair were putting up political posters, cheap, A4-sized, photocopied ones with the slogan, 'Ditch this rabble NOW.' The woman was taping them very neatly to the glass sides of a bus stop and the man was giving her quite unnecessarily detailed instructions on how to do it. I wondered why he wasn't doing it himself. Then I saw he was carrying a white stick. He was blind.

In Uxbridge Road, Ealing, I noticed a pattern, a series of events that I must have seen and heard many times before, but only today did I understand it clearly. It's what happens when traffic grinds to a complete halt because some vehicle, say a delivery van, is blocking the road. The traffic sits there for a while more or less patiently, then one driver decides he has to sound his horn, then another joins in, then a few more. Then someone (you never seem to see the person) shouts something obscene, 'Shut up, you cunts,' or something like that, and then someone else shouts something equally obscene back, and then, strangely enough, the horns stop, the shouting stops, the vehicle causing the problem moves on and the traffic starts to flow again.

The process may take a greater or lesser time but is always very similar. You're tempted to think that patience would have brought about exactly the same result in exactly the same amount of time, that the traffic was bound to have started moving again with or without the shouting and horn sounding. But it seemed to me that perhaps there is something about the sounding of horns and the shouting of obscenities that's necessary for the life and traffic flow of any city.

In Station Road, Upper Holloway, a small boy hanging on a railing. He was angelic, blond, smiling, attractive, and he was with another little boy, a year or two older, dark-haired, much less appealing. The latter kicked the former but the little blond boy only giggled. Another harder kick and the little boy giggled even more. Another kick and the boy went into paroxysms of pleasure. I walked on before it all ended in tears.

In Coventry Street, which leads from Piccadilly Circus to Leicester Square, I looked in the window of a souvenir shop. There were lots of models of Tower Bridge and Big Ben for sale. And I thought these were not such bad icons of London, not bad pieces of architecture, after all. There were lots of models of black cabs and double-decker buses for sale too; things not unique to London but certainly part of the scene. However, as I walked past, a group of twenty or so French kids were each buying plastic policeman's helmets.

In Leicester Square itself, waiting outside the Odeon cinema there were half a dozen young, very fashionable Japanese tourists. One was talking on a portable phone, one was carrying a huge bunch of flowers. They were being quite lively and the two with the flowers and the phone started to have a mock fight, pretending to punch each other with their free hands.

There was an HMV record shop with a poster in the window announcing an EAR OUT SALE. Then I saw that the first two letters were covered up. What it actually said was CLEAROUT SALE.

If certain nineteenth-century enthusiasts had had their way the whole of the south side of Leicester Square would have been taken up by a monument to Sir Isaac Newton. Not prepared to settle for a plaque or a statue, they wanted his whole house to be preserved inside a sort of truncated pyramid, on top of which was to be set a massive stone sphere. His tomb in Westminster Abbey is quite wild enough for most people.

I was in Agar Street, by the Zimbabwe High Commission, and outside was an official limo with the registration number ZIM 1. It was parked and the driver wasn't there, but on the front seat there was a bag of Sainsbury's shopping.

The High Commission is a huge marble building on a corner with the Strand, and set around it at second floor level are eighteen naked sandstone figures. They were carved by Jacob Epstein and are collectively known as 'Men and women in stages between life and death', which seems to me a title you could give to a staggeringly large number of works of art.

The story is that when Epstein carved the figures, the public was so shocked by their nakedness that he had to go back and chip off the genitals. (Only of the males, I assume.) I'm not sure whether the story's actually true or not, but certainly today it's more than just the genitals that have gone. It could be chemical pollution in the air, or erosion caused by weather, or maybe it was war damage, but currently the figures are half eaten away, some of them barely recognizable as figures at all. They look like ancient, crumbling ruins, and in that case I suppose they demonstrate a stage that is neither life nor death, but a kind of continuing posthumous decay.

In Sloane Street I saw four men dressed up like chefs. I say dressed up because they somehow looked as though they were playing a part; not like real chefs at all.

In the King's Road I saw a Chelsea pensioner. I saw a bar done out like a Mexican cantina. I saw plenty of flashy young people in clothes that were either fantastic or ludicrous or both, but I also saw a number of smart old chaps in blazers and trilbys. And I saw an apparently posh old lady walking down the street. She had fiercely permed hair, sunglasses, a black velvet jacket, but she was stopping at rubbish bins, having a root through them. I saw her dig deep into one bin and pull out a discarded copy of *Vogue*.

I went to Cheyne Walk. I hung around there waiting for something interesting to happen. I read the blue plaques, I looked at the house Keith Richard lived in, but there was nothing worth recording. However at the corner of Cheyne Walk and Milman's Street I saw a row of three strange garages, their doors shaped like pointed Arabian arches.

In Ventnor Drive, Totteridge, I saw an abandoned wheelbarrow full of hardened concrete. In the concrete there were half a dozen tiny cat's paw prints and the huge hollow where a man's workboot had stamped.

It suddenly started to hail, as fiercely as I think I've ever seen it, and I had to shelter under a walkway in Handel Street, WC1, by the Brunswick Centre, that ran down into a council estate. I could hear children's voices not very far away and they were telling each other to look at the rainbow. I stuck my head out and sure enough, visible through sheets of hail was a perfect, vivid rainbow. Just then a bustling little girl, not more than six years old, came past where I was sheltering and said, 'I can't stand 'ere lookin' at rainbows, I've gotta find my little bruvva.'

How London resists religious and racial cliché. One: Ridley Road market – the fish stalls and the meat stalls, the groupers and the snappers, the chicken gizzards and the goats' feet. And there was a stall selling records of religious music. The stall was run by a distinguished-looking black man whose stock mostly consisted of black choirs and spirituals, and if you'd been making a movie of this he'd no doubt have been playing some rousing music of that sort, but in the event he was playing a religious record by Jim Reeves, not the very blackest of men.

Two: If you'd asked me when I started my travels would I one day see a man walking along the street carrying a cross, I'd probably have said that it wouldn't altogether surprise me. And sure enough I eventually saw him, a black man, bald, fierce, wearing a smart black suit and carrying a white painted wooden cross, taller than himself and made from two lengths of two by one. But the cliché would have had me see him in Brixton or East Ham or somewhere where the black communities are tight, where religion remains strong. In fact I saw him in Kensington Church Street, that expensive street that's chiefly home to countless up-market antique shops.

Marylebone Road: Madame Tussaud's and the Planetarium built on the site of the old bombed cinema. Also the scene of the only war story my father ever tells.

My map is gradually darkening. I am gradually filling in the streets, making them coalesce. The end seems a long way off, but perhaps this is no longer a matter of beginnings, middles and ends. The kick I get from walking down the streets of London is enormous, but getting home and writing up this diary is better still. If I broke my leg and couldn't do any walking for a while, that would be rough but I could live with it. If I broke my hands and couldn't write the diary that would be a tragedy on the grand scale.

I wonder how big the finished document will be. One is tempted to hope it will be as big, as grand, as detailed, as complex and convoluted as the city itself, but I know that's not possible. All I can say is it will be as big, grand, detailed, complex and convoluted as I can possibly make it.

I'd stopped for lunch and was sitting outside a pub on Clapham Common. The common and the pub were nearly empty. There was an old man sitting three tables away. I thought he probably wanted to start a conversation with me, but I stared intently at my newspaper. Then a friend of his walked past and the old man said to him, 'Do you want to buy a telly? Fourteen-inch colour. I want fifty quid for it, or a pound a week for two years, whichever you prefer.'

'I've already got a telly,' said the friend.

'Yes, but have you got a telly in your *bedroom*?' the old man said, as though he was making an incredibly indecent suggestion.

The friend went in, bought himself a drink and came out to sit with the old man. I couldn't hear all their conversation but at one point the friend said, 'I just don't see the *point* of having a lesbian behind the bar.'

I was walking along Prince Albert Road and I looked into the car-park in Regent's Park, and I saw twenty or thirty men each unloading large quantities of equipment from the boots of their cars. This equipment consisted in almost every case of a chunky box on wheels and a long thin case. At first I thought they might be musicians, that the cases might contain instruments, that the boxes might be amplifiers. But then I realized they were far more likely to be fishermen, the long thin case carrying their rods, the box containing the rest of their tackle.

This was more or less confirmed when I saw them heading for the towpath that runs alongside the Grand Union Canal, which in turn skirts the northern boundary of Regent's Park. I was intending to walk that way myself so I followed them. But they formed a little crowd at the bottom of the stairs and I had to push through to get by.

Then I realized why they'd stopped. About thirty yards ahead of us there was a locked gate right across the path. I was as surprised as the fishermen, but then one of them said, 'Here's a man who looks as though he knows how to get a gate unlocked,' and a few others made relieved, encouraging noises. I looked around and saw they were all turning hopefully towards me. I was the man they thought could get the gate unlocked. Needless to say, they were completely wrong, and I had to tell them so, but I was strangely flattered.

# JAPANESE LUNCH

A smiling, bowing, kimono-wrapped Japanese woman greeted them at the door, then guided them downstairs to the body of the restaurant. They were there because Judy had phoned the Dickens and invited Mick out for lunch. She'd had to steel herself to make the call, and had to deal with the awful landlady, but it was worth it when he accepted, as she'd known he would.

The restaurant was bright, low-ceilinged, with prints of fishermen and kite flyers on the walls. There was a large bar area where lone Japanese men were eating and drinking in silence, but a waitress directed Mick and Judy towards the other side of the restaurant, somewhere more convivial, less inscrutable.

A sort of stage or platform, some eighteen inches high, had been built to cover most of the dining area, but then square holes had been cut into that stage, forming cavities big enough to accommodate small wooden tables, which had been duly set in them, so that their tops projected through the holes and stood some twelve inches above the level of the stage. Diners then sat on the edge of the cavity, on legless chairs, their knees under the tables in the usual western way. It was strange but Mick could see how it worked. Far stranger to him was the row of shoes running along the main aisle of the restaurant, deposited there by the diners. He looked at Judy and said, 'When in Japan,' and he kicked off his own shoes, walked across a stretch of the raised platform and lowered himself into the cavity around their table.

Judy arranged herself opposite him and asked, 'Have you eaten Japanese before?'

'Sure,' he said, but in a way that made her doubt him.

The waitress came with the flapping, laminated menus, knelt beside the table and handed them over. Mick looked at the brightly coloured pictures of food with captions in Japanese. The images were informative enough in terms of form, less so in terms of content. Rice and fish and noodles were easily identifiable but that told only a small part of the story.

'What do you like to eat?' she said, trying to be helpful.

He had to think hard before admitting, 'Junk mostly.'

'I don't think they serve that here.'

He looked at the menu again and said, 'You've got to admit it's slightly strange, coming to London to eat in a Japanese restaurant.'

'Where else would you go? Sheffield?'

'Tokyo?' he suggested.

'It's a long way just for lunch. Maybe we should be in an eel and pie shop.'

'No, I tried that.'

'You like raw fish?' she asked.

'Sure,' he said.

'I love it,' Judy said. 'I'd never even heard of eating raw fish until I read *The Old Man and the Sea*. The old man catches fish and cuts them up and eats them immediately, and I just knew I'd love it. But when your mother comes from Streatham . . . In Japan there are restaurants that have tanks of water set in the kitchen floor like ponds and the chef reaches into the tank and catches a fish when he gets an order for one.'

Mick did not look very impressed by all this talk of raw fish so Judy said, 'Maybe you should have tempura; that's fish and vegetables deep fried in batter.'

He looked even less impressed. 'Sounds a bit tame,' he said.

They studied the menus in silence until the waitress returned.

Without consulting Judy, but with a reckless confidence that Judy admired, he ordered the sashimi. She was pleased. She hadn't intended that this lunch should be a test for him, yet she was glad he was coping so effortlessly.

'What have you been doing?' she asked.

'Oh, not much, listening to the radio.'

'Oh yes?'

'And the reason I won't sleep with you has nothing to do with you being a Londoner, and nothing to do with you being half-Japanese either.'

He was aware that he had been talking very loudly so he clammed up completely.

'Well, that's some consolation,' Judy said with enormous self-possession.

'And, as a matter of fact,' he was now speaking in a loud, hissing whisper, 'I think it's a bit bloody much. I don't know you at all, but I turn on my radio and hear the most intimate details about you.'

'Sometimes it's easiest that way.'

'Why'd you do it? Why do you call the phone-ins?'

'It's cheaper than a therapist. And it's supposed to be anonymous.'

'And I don't want you phoning up the radio and telling them anything about me.'

'I bet you don't.' And she had to stop herself laughing at him.

'And that's another good reason for not sleeping with you. You blab to radio stations.'

As though to prove that she was capable of not blabbing she sat in silence for a long time. Mick, feeling that perhaps he'd been a bit rough on her, finally said, 'You come here often?'

'I've never been here before,' she said.

'How did you know about it?'

'I read a review in the paper. I read a lot of restaurant reviews. It's a London habit, I guess.'

'It would have to be.'

He glanced around the restaurant and he liked its air of formal calm. There was no music and nobody was speaking loudly. There were several pairs of Japanese women eating together. It was a little patch of calm and foreignness in the centre of the big city.

Then, without preamble, he said, 'So what's it like to be Japanese?'

She laughed. Had the question come from anyone else she would have been deeply insulted, but coming from Mick it somehow wasn't nearly so bad or so crass. His naivety carried with it a built-in irony.

'I can't say what it's like to be Japanese any more than I can say what it's like to be English. Could you?'

It was a new and surprising thought for him and yet he didn't have to think very long before he said, 'Yeah, I think so,' and although she probably wouldn't have pressed him on it, he began to describe how it felt.

'Well, we're used to thinking of ourselves as the best country in the world, which is obviously bullshit because we're not the best at anything any more. We don't make the best cars or tanks or aeroplanes, we don't make the best watches or steel or televisions. We don't even make the best television programmes any more. And we're not the best at football or cricket or athletics. And we're not the richest or most democratic country in the world. But, you know, we still think we're the best.'

She smiled. She had expected something much less knowing from him.

'If you're only half-English, maybe you only feel half of that.'

'Or none of it,' she added, and she was ready to end the conversation there, but Mick had hit his stride.

'And, you know,' he continued, 'it's a long time since we lost a war, which is a good thing, I think. I mean, I'm not in favour of wars, but if you do get involved in one I think it's better to win it than lose it, although not necessarily. I mean

'. . . well, Hiroshima, Nagasaki, you must know all about that stuff.'

'No more than a lot of English people,' she said.

'And you know, they say in England we haven't been invaded since 1066, but the way I see it we're invaded every day of the year: American films, French wine, Indian restaurants, German cars, Japanese everything, foreign tourists, foreign immigrants.'

'And how do you feel about that?' she asked.

'That's the point I was trying to make. I feel fine. I don't mind being invaded at all. I really like it.'

'You're full of surprises, Mick, you know that?'

'You thought I was going to say something about bloody foreigners.'

She didn't want to admit it, but, yes, she'd thought he might have displayed some sort of distasteful if amusing xenophobia.

'Maybe you're prejudiced,' he said.

'Aren't we all?'

The waitress returned, knelt again and set two black lacquer trays in front of them on the table. Mick looked at his not with surprise but with enormous curiosity. He handled his chopsticks deftly and began to negotiate the slivers of raw fish. As he put them in his mouth his expression showed thoughtful concern as though the food was a cause of deep contemplation.

'In the shop windows in Japan,' Judy said, 'all the mannikins have western faces. They're not allowed to be the yellow peril with slitty little eyes. Don't you think that's strange, a whole culture that has to misrepresent itself in its own shop windows?'

'Most English people don't look much like English mannikins, either,' he said.

'No, but at least they're of the same ethnic group.'

He nodded to accept her point.

'And in Japan even quite mild sex films are censored and they electronically blur the genitalia of the actors, while at the same time there are phallic festivals where twelve-foot-long papier mâché penises are paraded through the streets.'

He looked impressed and amused and he ate another crescent of bruised-looking tuna.

'And in Japan there are love hotels where rooms are rented by the hour and couples go in and have sex on a bed that's in the shape of a space ship or a Mercedes convertible.

'And if I was properly Japanese, when you mentioned the bombing of Hiroshima and Nagasaki I'd have apologized to you. I would know that the very mention of the bombing would put you in a position where you ought to feel remorse, and that would be very painful for you, so I would have to apologize for making you feel so bad.'

'Just as well you're only half-Japanese.'

'That's right. I don't have to apologize for anything.'

'So what's the best thing about Japan?' he asked.

'Mount Fuji,' she said without hesitation. 'In early spring when it still has snow on its summit and when all the surrounding hillsides are full of azaleas in bloom.'

'Sounds good,' he said. 'How much time have you spent there?'

She smiled as though she was about to prove a very important point.

'I've never been there,' she said, and when Mick looked profoundly puzzled, she added, 'I've only heard about it, read things, seen movies, just the way you have. Japan's no more real to me than to any foreigner. It's like you and London. You had a pretty shrewd idea of what London was like, long before you got here. You created your own version of London. It was just as real as the actual London. Japan's the same for me.'

Mick thought she was wrong, but he felt too weary to argue. For her part she wished she'd never spoken. She should have known he was not going to understand, and it didn't matter. She wondered if he was offended, if he thought she was being too clever for him.

'How's the sashimi?' she asked.

'It's fine,' he said, and then becoming confidential he added, 'But do you know, it's stone cold.'

She was about to explain patiently that it was meant to be cold, when she realized that she was the naive one, the one being sent up. He was laughing at her and at his own joke.

'You must think we're a pretty unsophisticated lot up in Sheffield,' he said.

'I don't know what people are like in Sheffield,' she replied.

'You haven't created your own version?'

'Not yet.'

'Then don't bother.'

She hated this antagonism, though given his reaction to the radio phone-in she was hardly surprised. It was not what she'd had in mind at all. She had brought him here for a good reason, but it had nothing to do with arguing about Anglo-Japanese culture.

She said, 'I've got something I want you to see.'

She opened her bag and pulled out a folded page of newspaper. She unfolded it and handed it to Mick. It was from some weekend supplement and across the bottom of the page was a column called 'Kerry Slater's Restaurant Round-Up'. The name was immediately familiar from Gabby's list. The face was familiar too from Mick's reconnaissance. Mick looked at her in some surprise. She had done well to remember a name from the list, though that was not necessarily a good thing as far as he was concerned. How much more would she remember or work out for herself? And what might she do with the knowledge?

'When I first saw your list I thought I recognized the name,' she said. 'But it took me a while to remember where I'd seen it before. Am I right? He is the one you want to have a reunion with, isn't he?'

'Yeah,' Mick agreed.

'Did you know he wrote for the papers?'

Mick had watched Slater's house, had seen him sitting at a desk in his study, punching words on to a computer keyboard, and he had followed him to some expensive restaurants, but he hadn't quite worked out what he did for a living. Mick shook his head, and Judy smiled, pleased with herself.

'You really don't want to get involved with this, you know,' Mick warned.

'No? Why not? I like reunions. I like parties.'

'Not this sort.'

'I want to be involved,' she insisted. 'I don't know why, but I do.'

'You want to be involved even though you don't know what it entails?'

'That's right. Strange, isn't it?'

Yes, it was, and it was strangely appealing. It was much sexier than her offer of sex had been. Even so, he said, 'No, it's a really bad idea.'

But she said, 'I know where he'll be tonight. I know which restaurant he'll be reviewing. I rang the paper, wormed it out of them. I know he'll be eating alone. At the Morel restaurant, eight o'clock. I thought maybe you could use that knowledge.'

'Could I?' he said. 'How exactly?'

'I don't know. I don't know what methods you use.'

'No, you don't.'

'But I want to know. And I want to be there.'

'You're crazy.'

'Maybe. But I want to watch. What do you do to these men? Do you beat them? Torture them? Have them crawl and beg for mercy? Or do you kill them? Are you a full-blown hit man?'

'Hey,' he said. 'I'm still eating my lunch.'

'Don't dismiss me,' she said. 'I'm not some silly little girl.'

'No, you're a bookshop assistant who suddenly wants to be a gangster's moll.'

'Are you a gangster, then?'

'This is stupid,' he said. 'This is bullshit.'

He started to rise from the table, got hooked up on the edge of the sitting cavity, suddenly felt embarrassed and exposed to be shoeless. His socks looked frayed and worn out. His attempt to storm out in high dudgeon was looking pretty inept and comical. He dropped a couple of bank notes on the table and said, 'Look, Judy, stay out of my work. Stay out of my life. Stay out of my bed. Stay out of my radio. All right?'

She bowed her head in an unfamiliar, almost oriental gesture of submission. And when Mick turned round he saw that the other diners and the waitresses had their heads down too, as though to spare themselves the shame of having to look at him. Mick pulled his shoes on and left the restaurant. The moment he'd walked ten feet along the street he regretted the whole business and felt terrible about Judy, but there was no going back, no point in apologizing. He told himself it didn't matter. Judy was just a distraction. She was no part of his plans. First things had to come first. Tonight, for instance, was the night he was going to deal with Kerry Slater.

# BLITZ

After midnight now, the second year of the war. The soldiers have all gone back to their barracks. Earlier that evening they went to Madame Tussaud's, to the half-empty cinema, to the restaurant where they ate five-bob dinners and the band played from seven till ten.

It was a melancholy place. The waxwork halls contained more dummies than visitors, but a few of the men wanted to come and look their enemies in the face, to see the figures of Hitler and Goering and Mussolini; pale, stiff, immobile figures in the deserted Grand Hall.

London itself feels deserted. The children have been sent away. The young men are at the war. The city is blacked out and the remaining population is burrowed away in air raid shelters and tube stations. This is how they fight the Battle of Britain.

Through the black September night come the planes, ours and theirs, the Luftwaffe and the Few. The sky shakes with metal, a primitive, focused vibration, a death rattle. And on the roof of Madame Tussaud's in the Euston Road stands a timid fifteen-year-old fire watcher. Jim London, Stuart's father, a lone and all too slight figure, looking for bombs that don't have his name on them, doing his bit before the inevitable call up. Better here than in some cramped Anderson shelter, dug into the earth, corrugated iron above his head. Much better here than sleeping in the underground like one of an army of rats.

The night sky is full of litter, not only the aircraft but the beams from searchlights, barrage balloons, the anti-aircraft fire, and, of course, the bombs, invisible as they fall. It is more than the cool autumn night that makes him shiver. Powerless, weaponless he just stands and watches and waits for whatever the cluttered night can throw down at him.

And yet the city has a beauty about it tonight. Scrolls of smoke twirl slow stepless dances around its edges, the bright fire from the incendiary bombs turns the outlines of buildings into noble, fragile silhouettes. London seems so big, so diffuse, such a sitting duck. The turrets and spires, the dome of St Paul's, the tower of Big Ben are like targets, chess pieces waiting to be picked off. There is no way of missing. Every stray bomb will score a hit, will destroy something precious, some landmark or piece of the city's past; if not the docks and the munitions factories, then a Wren church, a row of Georgian houses, a fragment of Roman wall.

Jim London has never felt so alert and open-eyed. Fear has given him an almost hallucinatory sensitivity. His eyes seem to see more clearly than ever before, his very skin is alive to the attack on the city. His reactions feel spring-loaded, hair-triggered. And yet he doesn't see the bomb that does the damage, not that seeing it would have helped.

When it comes it doesn't even feel like an external force that hits the building. It feels more as though half the structure, the west part, the part containing the cinema, has simply erupted, spasmed and thrown itself into pieces. The air around him seems to bend. There is furious, bone-splitting thunder, and he is hit by a shock wave. Then debris engulfs him like a solid cloud of brick and tile and plaster. He is knocked sideways on the parapet where he was standing and he stays there, stays down, his arms cushioning his head, waiting for either stillness or the next explosion. He feels as though he is there for an age, time enough to know he has no injuries, time enough to realize that if he stays down too long others will come in search and see what a spineless coward he really is.

When nothing worse happens, he scrambles to his feet and runs to the end of the building to see where the bomb hit. The cinema has simply gone, disappeared as though a heavy, precise child had stamped its fist on a balsa wood model. He can still see the proscenium but nothing else is recognizable, just rubble and rising dust and a deep bomb crater. He scurries down open metal staircases carrying a torch and a fire extinguisher until he reaches street level. He is the first to arrive and warily he approaches the new-made mound of architectural scrap. The air is still thick with motion, dust particles, pulverized cement, wood splinters, but now he sees fragments that make sense, slashed strips of carpets, wooden mouldings, burst cinema seats, and beyond them a deep, dark hole which the bomb has excavated.

He climbs up on the shaky hillock of ruins and peers over into the depths of the hole. At first he sees only edgeless darkness which he tries to tame with his torch. He is not sure what he is looking for. There could surely be no survivors down there, and in any case he knows the cinema was empty. And yet there is definitely something lurking in the void, something that the wan beam from his torch slowly begins to define.

He sees a man's face, still, lurid pink, incomprehensibly serene. Then he sees another, a second pale, motionless face turned up to the blitzed sky. And then another, and another. And then he realizes there are no bodies belonging to these heads. They are detached and unfettered, all lying together in the crater like so many footballs. Some of the faces are smashed, some are curled into horrible, melting expressions, and yet they are bloodless and do not look as though they have recently been in pain. And as he moves his torch he sees more and more of them, hundreds of these thronging, severed heads, all staring up at him, blank but infinitely knowing. He realizes he has come upon something vile and inconceivable, a plague pit, a murderer's horde of corpses . . . and he promptly faints.

In a more terrifying story he might have pitched forward

into the crater full of heads, but instead he falls backwards to safety, where, a few seconds later, one of the other fire watchers, an old man who lost a leg and an eye in Ypres, finds him. Relieved to discover that the fifteen-year-old is not dead, he brings the lad round, gives him some water and explains that the severed heads are wax moulds that have fallen into the crater from the now demolished storeroom of Madame Tussaud's.

'This'll be a story to tell your kids,' the old man says. Then adds, 'If you live long enough to have any.'

# EATING OUT

Mick Wilton had never watched another man masturbate before and he was a little uncomfortable about it now. It felt intrusive and perverted. He had no problem about intruding on Kerry Slater, indeed that was to a large extent the point of the exercise, but he did not like to feel that he was perverted. Seeing his victims in these naked, intimate moments gave him a raw power over them. He wanted that power and he revelled in it, but he didn't want to have to pay too high a price for it. He didn't want to lose himself or become irredeemably dirtied in the process.

It seemed strange to Mick that a single man should have such a big house all to himself. Slater lived in Islington, alone apart from a trio of plump, long-haired cats. They had the complete run of the house but they didn't account for why he needed so much room. What did he do with it? Not much, as far as Mick could tell. Slater worked long hours in his study, and although he went out most evenings, he usually returned quite early, and always alone. Mick had watched him conduct a couple of dinner parties, quite elaborate meals for six or eight guests, and there had been one occasion when a woman had come round by herself in the evening. Slater had cooked again, but she hadn't stayed the night and he'd given her a brotherly kiss before putting her in a taxi.

The house was a stack of small, untidy, shabbily furnished rooms. The living room was welcoming enough with its collection of old, lived-in, unmatching furniture, but Mick thought a man in Slater's position ought to be able to afford a three-piece suite and fitted carpet. The kitchen was well-stocked and well-equipped, but it was a tip. The cooker was filthy, the sink was full of dirty pans, the huge stinking cat tray was in front of the door out to the garden. The dining room, where the dinner parties had taken place, wasn't so bad since it wasn't used very often, but again Mick thought some new wallpaper and, say, a fancy glass and steel dining table would have done wonders. But the bedroom, in a way, was the worst of the lot. This was the place where Slater was now masturbating, exploring his body with his chubby hands, and it was a horrible, bad-smelling, depressing place. Old clothes were bundled together in corners, dirty cups and glasses lined the bedside cabinets and the top of the chest of drawers. Newspapers, books and junk mail were piled up beside the bed. The windows were locked and it was a long time since fresh air had penetrated the room. This was not a seducer's bedroom, rather the bedroom of someone who had resigned himself to a life in which masturbation was to be the dominant form of sexual expression. He certainly looked as though he'd had plenty of practice.

Kerry Slater was a fat man and maybe that was why his penis looked so small. Its end was livid purple, quite a different colour and texture from the rest of his skin. It looked like an afterthought, something hastily added to the thick trunk of his body. The rest of him was smooth, loose and baby pink, though there was nothing babyish about his prematurely bald head, his spectacles, nor the indecent way he was currently lolling naked on the squashed floral sofa under the bedroom window. He had recently emerged from the bathroom thickly wrapped in towels and a robe, and having slowly, painstakingly dried himself off he had turned to the business of masturbation, a simple enough process that he was making into quite a big production.

He had begun by rubbing some oil into his penis and that

had brought it up and into life. Then he'd opened a drawer in the dressing table and pulled out a magazine. Mick couldn't see exactly what the contents of the magazine were but Slater found them compelling and stimulating and they drove him onwards. He peered over the pages long and hard, and his tongue peeked out of the corner of his mouth and his lips got wet. But the magazine wasn't enough, or maybe Slater just didn't want it to be enough. He reached into the drawer again and produced what looked like a giant test tube, with a fitting at the open neck and a length of attached rubber hose that ended in an egg-shaped bulb. It was some sort of erotic suction device and Slater inserted his penis into the business end of it. The curved plastic acted like a lens, magnifying the organ it contained, and as Slater repeatedly squeezed the rubber bulb it did look as though the erection was becoming stronger, filling more of the tube. Slater's face became a cartoon of sexual pleasure, and Mick had to work hard not to burst out laughing at the comic effect.

One of the cats wandered into the room. Slater shooed it away, then with the penis developer still in place he shimmied across the worn bedroom rug, past the walk-in wardrobe, and turned on the TV set and video. There was already a tape in the machine and at once the image of a naked woman appeared on the screen. She was good-looking, oriental, but definitely not Japanese. Mick could tell the difference these days. She looked as though she came from the Philippines or Thailand, from the sexual proving grounds. She had a smooth, youthful face and she was pleasuring herself in a way that was different from but compatible with Slater's own method. She was putting her fingers into her vagina, swirling them about, then removing them, putting them up to her mouth and licking them clean.

Slater looked ready, more than ready, to come. Time was getting on. Mick feared he might be late for his reservation at the Morel, but even so he didn't rush. With the porn still playing on the screen, his penis still in the suction device, he tottered across the room to the dressing table drawer again and this time got out a pair of women's panties. They were white, creased, not especially small, not especially sexy. Mick wondered for a ridiculous moment whether Slater was going to put them on, and he was relieved when he only pressed them to his nose. He sat down again on the sofa, breathed heavily through the panties, pumped the suction bulb energetically, accelerating all the while, until there was a sudden stop, then a few obscenities said through gritted teeth, and he fell back on the sofa, released and relieved. He stayed there for some time, motionless, breathing very steadily, and Mick thought he might be about to doze off. But then Slater stirred himself, pulled himself together, turned off the TV, put away the pump, the magazine and the panties and proceeded to get ready to go out. His dressing was as swift as his masturbation had been prolonged and he was out of the house in five minutes.

At last Mick was able to emerge from his hiding place in the walk-in wardrobe. He stretched himself a little deliberately and theatrically as he stepped into the bedroom. His sense of intrusion was all the greater now. He was standing in the very space where Slater had so recently stood, naked and sexually aroused. Mick still felt uneasy yet he knew this was the place he had to be. He began to search Slater's house. He had already briefly passed through it on his way to his hiding place, and he had previously spent a fair amount of time staring in through the windows, but now he had time to check it out more thoroughly.

As he searched, Mick discovered all sorts of new information about Slater, though how much of it he would be able to make use of was uncertain. He looked at cheque stubs, credit card statements, share certificates, insurance policies, in an attempt to see how much money Slater had and what he did with it. It appeared he didn't do much. His outgoings were tiny compared to his worth.

Mick looked at Slater's passport to see how far he had travelled. There were no great surprises. He'd been around: to Hong Kong, to Chile, to the States half a dozen times, to India,

Singapore. These places didn't come cheap. Mick wondered if Slater travelled alone, and if not who his companion was.

He found several photograph albums containing pictures of Slater and his friends, and sure enough there were faces there that Mick recognized, Philip Masterson and Justin Carr, though Jonathan Sands was absent. Most of the photographs showed mixed groups of people at parties, weddings, picnics, race meetings, country house weekends, beach holidays. The occasions always looked lavish. There were raffia picnic baskets and bottles of champagne. There were boats and classic cars. People wore blazers, boaters, tweeds.

Slater was not photogenic. He looked old and blob-like in the pictures, moon-faced and surprised by the flash. In almost all of them he had a drink in one hand and plate full of food in the other. In one bizarre, unlikely picture he was on a football pitch, dressed as a goalkeeper, standing between the posts, but he still managed to be holding a champagne bottle.

Mick observed Slater's tastes in books, records and videos: the latest thrillers and biographies, serious classical CDs, Humphrey Bogart, Jean Renoir and the American musical.

There were a few recent postcards and letters that Slater had received, but they were not very revealing, thank-you notes from people he'd taken out to dinner, a card from his mother on holiday in Italy. There were some bills, a couple of uncashed cheques from magazines, but Mick couldn't make much out of them.

In the study there was a good collection of cookery books, books about food, and restaurant guides, the tools of his trade. And in the filing cabinets Mick found sheafs of newspaper cuttings, Slater's own work, generally with his owlish face peering out above the by-line, looking well-fed and self-satisfied.

And so Mick returned to the bedroom, the arena of Slater's solitary, baroque sex act. Hiding in the wardrobe had given him some familiarity with Slater's clothes. They were smart and expensive. He ran to suits and sports jackets, grey flannels, handmade shoes, but they were all neglected. Trousers and coats were casually thrown into the wardrobe and left to fester and crease; there were several wrapped around Mick's feet. A lot of items seemed to have trails of food down them.

The wardrobe didn't really fascinate Mick, however. He'd seen enough of it. He went to the dressing table drawer and found a whole heap of magazines with titles like *Inspiration*, *Teenage Lovers*, *Mirage*. They were a good deal filthier than their bland titles suggested, but nothing particularly illegal.

Mick found a man's wet-look G-string, a pack of condoms perilously close to their sell-by date, poppers, and a couple of ludicrous Polaroids that showed Slater naked. They might have been snapped by a partner but Slater could equally well have done them himself with the help of a self-timer. Mick considered stealing them. They might have been useful as negotiating points, but Mick didn't want naked photographs of Slater in his pocket, and in any case Mick felt his negotiating position was pretty well impregnable. But he couldn't resist having a sniff at the pair of ladies' panties that had brought Slater such rapture. Mick took them from the drawer, held them to his nose and inhaled deeply. He could smell nothing. If they had ever been worn by a woman she was either very clean or it was a very long time ago that her juices had flowed.

Naturally Mick had no idea of what the Morel restaurant was actually like, nevertheless he tried to picture Slater having his meal. For no good reason he imagined a place straight out of forties Hollywood; the tables set in booths, waiters in evening dress, the women in strapless satin and a jazz combo playing in the corner. Mick had never been to such a place, wasn't absolutely sure that they existed outside of the movies, but he thought they must exist in London, if anywhere. He wondered how long a meal there would take, whether professional restaurant critics ate quickly and lightly and then went home to write up the experience, or whether they had a good, long blow out and got completely ratted and only tried to remember it the next morning. It didn't matter. It was only an item of curiosity. Whenever Slater got home Mick would be ready for him.

There was a neglected, dust-covered piano in the living room. The stool and the lid over the keys were solid with books and old magazines. Mick swept the debris away, opened the piano and played a few choruses of 'Chopsticks' before becoming bored. There was still a lot of time that had to be filled before Slater returned.

Mick sauntered into the kitchen and began to make preparations. He went to the refrigerator and transferred its contents to the kitchen table. There was butter, margarine, mayonnaise, some bacon, half a lettuce, a pint of stock, a tub of live yoghurt, some left-over curry, cottage cheese, salami, some bottles of Belgian beer. It wasn't nearly enough so he turned to the freezer and removed frozen steaks, sausages, ready-made stews and sauces, little plastic boxes of puréed fruit. He gave each item a good bashing in the microwave until they were at least defrosted, probably half cooked, then he went to the cupboards. He was pleased that Slater was so well stocked.

Mick found exotic items like juniper berries, dried limes, star anise, cardamom seeds, cloves. He didn't know what half the stuff was but he got it all out of the cupboards and arranged it on the table. There were much more mundane and familiar items too: bags of sugar and flour, macaroni, rice, lentils, all kinds of canned foods. Next came the pickles and preserves: anchovies, pickled walnuts, mango chutney, piccalilli, squid in brine, Gentleman's relish. Finally he arranged the liquids, bottles of flavoured oils and vinegars, ketchup, Worcester sauce, Tabasco, soya and oyster sauce, Angostura bitters. The table looked full and abundant though there were some surreal juxtapositions. Mick wondered what kind of appetite Slater would have after his evening out.

Mick began opening things. He unscrewed the lids from jars and bottles, tore open boxes and packets, took a tin opener to the canned goods. Sharp, distinct, pointed smells began to rise from the table: sweet, acid, vinegar, meat, fish. He found a few cans of cat food, chicken and rabbit, plaice and cod, liver and hearts. Their smells were stronger than the rest of the foods, but not noticeably less appetizing. The odour of the cat food brought the three cats running to the kitchen, and Mick had his work cut out to round them up and keep them out, eventually pushing them into the dining room and closing the door on them. The scene was set. Mick had nothing to do but wait.

Slater came home a little before midnight. He travelled by taxi and he was alone as ever. Mick heard him make several drunken attempts to get the key in the lock of the front door, only succeeding at the fifth or sixth try. Having entered the house he went straight into the living room, poured himself a whisky and sat down to make a few notes about the meal he had recently finished. Mick was in no hurry. He sat in the kitchen and continued waiting but that soon became a very dull pastime. Before long he heard a gentle snoring that seeped out of the living room, and it annoyed him a great deal. The feast was ready. Where was the guest of honour? He took a bottle of HP sauce and hurled it at the kitchen wall. The impact was thick and wet, the viscosity of the liquid muting the sound of breaking glass, but he hoped the sheer violence of the smash was enough to rouse Slater.

Sure enough Slater woke up and dragged himself to his feet. He was used to hearing a few bangs and breakages around the place, that was the price you paid for living with three cats, and as he went into the kitchen he called their names, 'Brûlée, Caramel, Fraîche, what have you destroyed this time?'

He knew something wasn't quite right, but he stood in the doorway for a while, still drunk, looking for the cats, peering under the table and round chair legs, and it took him a long time to realize that something had been going on in the kitchen. Then he looked up, saw all the food spread out, and simultaneously a voice behind him said, 'Good meal?' and Mick slammed the door shut.

Slater turned slowly, with equanimity, and he managed to look at Mick without revealing any sign of surprise or alarm.

'It wasn't a bad meal,' he said with abundant composure. 'But I've had better. I'm sure you have too.'

Mick had to smile. Slater was quite a cool customer and he admired that, although too much cool could raise the stakes to a needlessly high level. If a man was too busy being cool he mightn't realize just how serious you were about things.

Slater surveyed the kitchen more carefully and said, 'I take it this isn't one of your mainstream burglaries.'

'Very observant,' Mick agreed. 'What did you have to eat at the Morel?'

Hesitating only for a moment, Slater said, 'A spiced monkfish and lemon sole terrine, followed by pork loin stuffed with boudin noir.'

'Sounds good.'

'Competently cooked but lacking heart, I felt.'

'How was the atmosphere?'

'Formal, perhaps a little severe.'

'Did you have a dessert?'

'A tarte au citron which I found mundane, although I know that many diners claim to find it absolutely spectacular.'

'How was the wine list?'

'Good on the New World but a shade overpriced,' said Slater.

'Just as well you weren't paying then. How was the service?'

'Efficient, if a little fussy.'

'Sit down,' said Mick.

Quietly, politely acquiescent, Slater sat down at the crowded kitchen table. He tried hard to focus. The drink was still clouding his system. Wasn't the threat of danger supposed to make you instantly stone-cold sober? He tried to settle in his seat.

'I hope you've got room for a little something extra,' Mick said.

'Always,' Slater replied.

Mick took the gun out of his pocket and let Slater get a good look at it. Slater shivered, but still with enormous self-possession he said, 'Unless you actually *want* to kill me, you'll have no need whatsoever for the gun.'

Mick nodded, slipped the gun away then placed an empty white plate in front of the seated Slater. Mick reached for an opened tin of tuna fish and sloughed its contents on to the plate, then took a bottle of maple syrup in one hand and a squeezable bottle of hamburger mustard in the other and doused the fish in these contrasting liquids. When the containers were empty Mick gestured for Slater to start eating. He did so, neatly, efficiently, without complaint or apparent distaste.

'Where I come from,' Mick said, 'we don't go out for meals much in the week. If we go out at all it's only on a weekend and that's only if it's somebody's birthday or anniversary or something.'

'I know,' Slater said, continuing to eat. 'I've written about this. That's why restaurants go bankrupt so regularly in the provinces. That's why the provinces have so few good restaurants.'

'Maybe if we poor provincials had better restaurants we'd go out more often.'

'It's possible,' said Slater. 'But I think it's more a question of culture, in the broadest sense.'

Mick had the feeling that he was being insulted, but he wasn't quite sure in what way. Conversation ceased and Slater could attack the contents of his plate without distraction. He swiftly and professionally cleared his plate, then put down his fork and looked at Mick like a game but sad-eyed terrier.

'How was that?' Mick asked.

'Unusual,' said Slater. 'Piquant, brave, assured. Am I right to suspect a Cajun influence?'

'Glad you liked it. There's plenty more where that came from.'

'No doubt,' said Slater.

Mick watched Slater sitting there at his own kitchen table,

looking so at home, so in control, so poised, and for a moment he thought of coshing him with the gun. How else was he going to get to him? Mick felt as though he was the one being tested. He took the plate away and filled it again, this time with cornflakes, pickled onions, dried figs, raspberry vinegar, a few generous shakes of curry powder and ground ginger, and over the top he swirled thick worms of tomato purée.

'What's your favourite kind of food?' Mick asked.

'Until now I think I would always have said eclectic,' Slater explained, 'but looking at this . . .'

'You like Japanese food?' Mick asked.

'Some of it, yes.'

'I had it for the first time today,' Mick said, and then he stopped himself. Why did he need to tell Slater anything? He motioned for Slater to eat up. He had rather more trouble this time. With each forkful he grimaced, and Mick watched with pleasure as the face became flushed and blotchy. Nevertheless Slater persevered, gulping down everything on his plate. The effort looked brave and painful.

'How is it?' Mick asked.

'Ambitious, spirited, traditional ingredients, though iconoclastically presented.'

'I'll take that as a compliment,' said Mick. 'Something to drink? Sweet sherry? Ovaltine? Bovril? Vimto?'

'I suppose water would be out of the question.'

'Too right,' Mick said. 'But if you need to throw up or anything just say the word.'

Slater swallowed hard and shook his head. No, that wouldn't be necessary. That would be admitting defeat and he wasn't prepared to do that.

'You've got a good appetite,' Mick said.

'It has something to do with the gun in your pocket.'

'Even so—' Mick started.

'Look,' said Slater, 'I don't know who you are, whether you're a dissatisfied reader of my column, or a chef I've insulted at some time, or a restaurant owner I've criticized too harshly, but, whoever you are, I'm sure your actions are justified. I'm sure I deserve it. And believe me, I'm not brave, not a hero. I'm not going to fight you. Tell me to eat my own faeces and I'll do it.'

Mick was disgusted. It was a totally unsatisfactory offer. He was glad he didn't have to deal with someone who was trying to be a hero, yet he had hoped for a bit more conflict than Slater was providing. Slater's desire for a quiet life was profoundly at odds with Mick's desire to see him suffer. Mick certainly had no intention of getting involved with faeces but he served Slater more food: cold stew with marmalade and mayonnaise and a chunk of lard and two heaps of instant coffee granules and a crumbled Oxo cube.

Slater began to eat. He wasn't looking good. He was a man in distress, and yet he was still facing his distress all too bravely. He accepted the latest concoction Mick had given him and got on with it. But that was all wrong. Mick wanted him to be unable to get on with it. Mick wanted him on his knees, choking, gagging, weeping, vomiting, pleading and begging for an end to his tortures. Once those conditions were met, once Slater seemed sufficiently wretched and penitent, then the job would be over and Mick could be on his way. But while ever Slater remained collected and stoical Mick would have to continue punishing him, and he was running out of ideas.

'Unusual,' Slater said as he cleared the plate again. 'What it lacked in poise it more than made up for in flamboyance.'

Furious, Mick assembled a final *mélange* of cat food, cornflour, fish stock, brown sugar, Tabasco, mint sauce, defrosted raspberries, goose fat, mango chutney, gelatine and dried tarragon, then watched in dismay, though not absolute surprise, as Slater determinedly began to eat this too. There were tears in his eyes now, but that was because of the Tabasco, not because he was weak or defeated. Mick had had enough.

'OK,' he said. 'That's it. Time for the final course. Now take your clothes off.'

'Oh, really,' Slater said. 'Do I have to?'

It was a complaint born out of inhibition and natural modesty, not out of defiance. Mick assured him that he had no choice and Slater at once removed his clothes, reluctantly but with the minimum of fuss. He looked even fatter now than he had before his heroic bout of eating, and his penis looked even smaller.

Mick used his forearm to sweep the table clear. He used far more force and violence than was really necessary. Food and its packaging went flying across the kitchen, hitting the floor and the walls and then smashing or breaking open. Mick crunched through the mess to the cupboard beneath the sink and tossed the contents around until he found a washing line and some lengths of rope.

'Lie on the table,' he said to Slater.

Slater moved to obey.

'Face up or face down?' he asked, considerately.

Mick had to think about it. He decided that face up would be more humiliating and Slater assumed this position on the table top. Mick tied Slater's hands and feet to the four legs of the table, so that he was spread like a star fish. Then he stepped back and scooped up food from the floor and began to pour and throw and slap it all over Slater's fat body so that before long he was coated, caked with a layer of solids and thick liquids, powders and emulsions, morsels and chunks, that clung to his shape making his body look as though it was in grotesque ferment.

Mick surveyed what he'd done and felt no great pride in his handiwork, but then went to the dining room, pulled open the door and let out Slater's three cats. They found their way, suspiciously but surely, to the kitchen and began to sniff around the food on the floor, before making a swift ascent to the table, following the trail to where the sludge of food was most dense.

Slater remained motionless, his body tensed as though in a dentist's chair, his eyes closed, trying to keep his breathing steady, unsure whether his ordeal was nearly over or just beginning. Mick wasn't sure either. He couldn't shake the feeling that as an act of revenge this had been a pretty feeble, bodged job. Either way he'd had enough. He walked out of the house, carefully leaving the front door open, a golden opportunity for a more conventional kind of intruder.

# YELLOW

Mick was walking away from Slater's house, his steps swift but unperturbed, his demeanour casual but not studiedly so, when he became aware of a car driving slowly along the road keeping pace a little way behind him. He ignored it, didn't turn round, just kept walking. Even when the driver started sounding the horn he was reluctant to acknowledge the car's existence. But in the end he did look, and with some relief saw it was an old Datsun Cherry, not a car the bad guys drive, and he then felt free to look at the driver, and he saw that it was Judy.

She stopped, waited for him to come over to her. He was still reluctant. A car was much easier to trace than a lone man. He looked up and down the street wondering if there were potential witnesses. Then Judy began honking the horn urgently and persistently, and he realized that getting in would make him less conspicuous than not, so he yanked the door open and climbed inside.

The car was a wreck and as he settled himself in the seat it jerked back and slid out of its runners. He was going to make a remark about the shittiness of Japanese cars, but he stopped himself. Instead he said, 'You shouldn't be here.'

'Where should I be?' Judy asked, as she set the car in motion.

'Tucked up in bed with a good jigsaw,' he said.

'Alone or with others?'

'Alone. Definitely.'

'Actually, I was in a restaurant.'

'Which restaurant?'

'You know which,' she said irritatedly. 'The Morel, where Slater was eating. I saw him arrive. I watched. I waited. I thought you'd be coming too. I thought you'd do whatever you had to do at the restaurant.'

'Oh sure. Very discreet.'

'I didn't know discretion came into it.'

'You don't know anything, and I like it that way.'

'I know a lot more now than I did a few hours ago. As a matter of fact I thought you did a very good job.'

At first he didn't understand the implication of what she was saying. Only slowly did it dawn on him that she was passing judgement on the competence of his work, that she must have seen him operate.

'I saw it all,' she said. 'You're not the only one who can spy on people. I followed Slater home from the restaurant. I saw him go into the house. I sneaked round the back, looked in through the window and saw you waiting for him in the kitchen. Then I saw what you did to him.'

'It's not meant to be a spectator sport,' Mick said.

'No? It was quite a spectacle. I could tell you were saying a lot to him and obviously I missed that. It was like watching a movie without a soundtrack, and it's all the more compelling because you don't know exactly what's being said.'

Mick had no time for her interesting little analogy. This wasn't a movie, silent or otherwise. She wasn't taking him seriously enough.

'OK, so you saw me,' he said. 'You wanted to know what I do, and now you know. Happy?'

Mick sounded defiant. He was embarrassed and maybe even a little ashamed, but he refused to be apologetic. He was ready for an argument, ready to attack in order to defend his indefensible position.

Judy stopped the car, turned to him, smiled at him sweetly and said, 'It's fine. I liked what I saw. I like what you do.'

229

He had no answer to that, nothing up his sleeve with which to defend himself. Nor could he do anything when she leaned over and stroked his face and started kissing him. He was thrown and confused, and he resisted for as long as he could, but before long he found himself kissing back.

The rest of the night fell into place from then on. She drove them to the Dickens. Mick wanted to go to her place, but she wouldn't have that. They spent the night in his bed, wrapped together on the slopes and faces of the crummy mattress. Her body was alien in all sorts of ways, novel because of unfamiliarity, but also obeying a geometry and proportion that was different from the white English girls he'd slept with. The skin looked and felt different, smoother with a different grain, the buttocks and breasts seemed to join the body differently.

She could feel him revelling in the newness and she said, 'So now you've slept with a half-Japanese woman. And with a Londoner.'

And he replied, 'And you've slept with a Sheffielder.'

'And a petty criminal.'

Mick laughed. In one way he didn't find it particularly strange that Judy was turned on by the fact that he was a bit of a villain, by what he'd done to Slater. Women were turned on by the strangest things, attracted to the oddest, most unattractive men. Even when they liked you, you were always surprised at what it was they liked. But he was glad that Judy wasn't appalled, that she didn't condemn him.

It would have been easy enough to tell her everything then, and a part of him wanted to. It wasn't precisely a desire for confession, more the need to explain to someone else what he was doing, and have that person confirm that it had at least an internal logic, that it still made some sort of sense. But he didn't take the opportunity to explain. It would have been too difficult. He would have had to tell Judy about Gabby and this wasn't the right moment. He doubted whether any such right moment would ever come.

Instead they talked about cities. It was easier for her. She was well-travelled. She talked about her tourist adventures in Paris, Prague, Athens, Florence, Vienna. It meant nothing to him, this stream of incidents, these tales of lost luggage, of flea-bag hotels, of visits to art galleries and museums, of strange sleazy men who tried to pick her up. He asked why she only travelled to cities, why she didn't go to the beach, to the mountains, and all she could say was that cities were where the life was. He countered with stories about Sheffield, Doncaster, Barnsley, Chesterfield, and she was amused by his sense of the ridiculous, by his refusal to take seriously her attempts at cosmopolitanism. She said she'd like to visit all his places if he'd come with her as a guide. And she told him about the job she'd had with The London Walker, although she made no mention of her affair with the boss. He said it sounded like money for old rope.

She stroked his chest, pressed her fingers into the depressions between his ribs. Her hands felt cool and long and precise. She said, 'If you're ever present at a nuclear attack, make sure you're wearing long-sleeved white clothing.'

'What?' he asked.

'Obviously if you're at the centre of the heat flash it really doesn't make much difference what you're wearing, because at that range your internal organs just boil. But let's say you're a mile or so away; if your skin's uncovered it'll be stripped away from the flesh like orange peel. If you're wearing a black shirt that's just as bad. The dark material attracts the heat, it chars, probably catches fire, the skin underneath burns. But white clothes reflect the heat. They really do give you a chance of survival.

'And definitely don't wear a white shirt that has a dark pattern on it, because the heat will burn through the pattern. Imagine you were wearing one of those T-shirts with a map of the London Underground, then you'd have the design of the tube lines burned into your chest forever.'

'Are you making this up?' Mick asked.

'It happened in Hiroshima.'

'Yeah?'

'Yes. I read about it.'

She moved her fingertips over his chest again, this time tracing invisible tube lines.

Mick woke next morning, found Judy still sleeping soundly on his shoulder and felt above all else surprised. It took a while for the events of the previous night to rearrange themselves in his mind. Then he started to feel awkward. He also felt that he'd been seduced and coerced. He hadn't wanted this woman in his bed, hadn't wanted even to kiss her, hadn't even wanted to get in her car. He felt guilty that he was betraying Gabby, being unfaithful to her, and guilty too that in sleeping with Judy he was being diverted. This was not what he was here for. The purity of his mission was being subverted. He was wasting time. But what he felt worst about, what made him feel especially bad and especially guilty, was the fact that despite everything he was still very glad to have slept with Judy.

When she woke up he was civil to her, kissed her chastely, told her he had no way of making breakfast in his room, not even coffee. She didn't seem bothered by his distance and he felt some relief that she wasn't being demanding or romantic. Maybe, he thought, her feelings were as complex as his.

It was only after she'd gone that he looked around his room, noticed the sheet of jagged-edged hardboard lying on the floor and saw that the final piece had been added to his jigsaw puzzle of London.

# THE WALKER'S DIARY

# WRAPAROUND

It's come as some surprise to discover just how much pleasure writing this diary gives me. I don't quite know who I'm writing it for, but I have a sense that I'm not doing it only for myself. Perhaps I have half an eye on posterity. I hope that isn't too silly or arrogant of me. I used to try to write when I was a soppy adolescent, and later when I first met Anita she encouraged me. She suggested I write a highly personal guide book to London, but I always thought there were enough unreliable guides to London. I didn't want to add to the pile.

Besides, the problem I've always had with writing was that I could never finish anything. Personally I rather like the idea of unfinished works or interrupted masterpieces ('Kubla Khan', *Edwin Drood*), although I can see how a lot of people wouldn't. But with a diary that's not a problem. It ends where it ends. It can't be a beautifully shaped artificial form. It's the same shape as a human life. It ends because the life of the diarist ends. If you need to have a reasonable excuse for not finishing something, then death seems to me like the best excuse of all.

I was sitting in a square formica booth in a snack bar in the Charing Cross Road, nursing a cappuccino in a worn white cup, pretending to read my paper. It was mid-morning and the place was empty apart from me and someone in the next booth, a woman aged about twenty-five. I am no longer shy about staring at people. I saw she had a sharp, narrow face, completely without make-up, but as I watched she began to apply mascara, eye-liner, eye shadow, eyebrow pencil. Her eyes were set wide apart and they looked tired and sad and innocent, but as she worked on them they became more defined, more hard-edged, sexier. A slick of metallic blue and grey formed itself above each of her eyes, and finally she drew two long kitten points leading away from the outer corners. It made her look a little Japanese (and of course I thought about Judy). The woman worked hard, continually checking progress in a small circular hand mirror, and it took a long time. It didn't look like a labour of love exactly, but it was something she knew she had to do.

I have been trying not to make assumptions about the people I see in London, not to jump to conclusions to reinforce the boring, limiting stereotypes. But if I had been forced to guess I would have said she was not a Londoner, not a native, that she was perhaps a tourist, though not on her first visit to England, or more likely a foreign student. I saw that she had a map on the table in front of her, but it was tattered and well-used.

At last the eyes were finished. I wondered if she was about to start on her lips, but she wasn't. She put her make-up away, finished the coffee she'd been drinking and she was ready to go. As she got up she slipped on a pair of wraparound shades that completely hid her eyes.

Walked along Wimpole Mews, the place where Johnny Edgecombe came looking for Christine Keeler and emptied a gun into the front door when Mandy Rice-Davies wouldn't open it, finally taking a pot shot at her when she appeared at a window. Edgecome was only captured after a long siege at his home, somewhere far less desirable and glamorous than Wimpole Mews.

I think the world is divided between those for whom time passes too quickly and those for whom it passes too slowly.

London is probably more enjoyable for people in the latter category than in the former.

The act of getting from A to B, whether it's by public transport or in a cab or by car or on foot, always absorbs massive amounts of time. Partly it's the matter of distances between places, the density of traffic, the inefficiency of public transport, but I suspect it's more than that. The sheer nature of the city saps your energy and your ability to function. It's fine if you want to kill time, you just make a short journey and before you know it you've lost an hour or more.

However, if you're one of those people who's always short of time the same rules apply, London still takes it out of you and that must be as maddening and frustrating as hell.

In Lord North Street, a sign surviving from the war, painted on brick: 'Public shelters in vaults under pavements in this street.'

In Denmark Street (what used to be called Tin-Pan Alley), a young man with rock star looks and clothes was unloading guitars and taking them into a music shop. His image was very cool and hip and yet he seemed uncomfortable and self-conscious. I couldn't think why but when he went to get the second load I saw that he was taking the guitars out of a Reliant three-wheeler, and a sweet old man, his father I thought, was sitting patiently at the wheel, doing a good turn, to his son's excruciating embarrassment.

In Ilderton Road, Rotherhithe, I saw a red sportscar with six raw eggs smashed on the bonnet.

In New Cross, a shop specializing in chess sets, one of them consisting of London landmarks, with cab shelters as pawns, the Tower of London as rooks, St Paul's Cathedral as bishops, equestrian statues of Cromwell as knights, the Post Office Tower as the king, and Thorneycroft's statue of Boadicea as the queen.

\*

London always seems so strange in old movies. It's more or less the London I recognize but it's only ever half as full. There's no traffic on the roads, there are no double yellow lines, no cars parked bumper to bumper. The hero's car always finds a parking spot right outside Buckingham Palace or the Ritz, and nobody ever has to wait around for change from taxi drivers.

I remember when I was a boy I used to read about India, and how on the streets of Calcutta people slept in shop doorways, and I was always very envious. It seemed so easy and convenient. If I went to London with my parents we had to worry about somewhere to stay, somewhere that needed to be booked in advance, that mightn't measure up to my parents' high standards, where the sheets might not be very clean, where the service might be unobliging, where the food might be bad. Today I see people sleeping in the shop doorways of London and I wonder if this is a sort of progress.

In Amhurst Road, Hackney, a house with a bay window. The curtains were drawn, and there was a photograph of Peter Wyngarde as Jason King tucked into the window frame for passers-by to see.

In the front garden of a house in Navarino Road there was a seven-foot-high abstract black metal sculpture of a man.

The window of a basement in Greenwood Road, no curtains and inside a harsh strip light and several women dressed in white at sewing machines stitching pieces of white material together: a sign outside saying 'Dressmaker'.

In Stoke Newington Church Street the building above a greengrocer's was still painted with advertisements for a much earlier business. The biggest of the advertisements said, 'Have your fountain pen repaired here.' What a wonderful, safe, decent world that invokes; not only a world where people actually used fountain pens (which seems quaint and old-fashioned enough in itself), but a world where somebody found

236

it worth his while to repair them, where he could stay in business and make a living by doing it.

Clanricarde Gardens, W2. I used to live in this road when I first left university. I shared a flat with three town planners. We had a party and the brother of one of them came along and said it was really strange, he'd been to a party in this same flat some years ago when it had been lived in by members of Status Quo. Towards the end of the evening somebody standing in the kitchen had been slashed with a meat hook.

A couple of years after I left, I read there was a fire in the street and several houses had been completely destroyed, quite a few people had died. I always wondered whether my former flat was involved. Today there was no sign there had ever been a fire and I couldn't remember my old address, not even what floor the flat had been on.

In Greenwich High Road, a hardware shop, and in the window amongst the spanners and hammers and paint brushes and watering cans there were half a dozen lurid pink vibrators for sale. A handwritten sign said 'Personal Massager', and the price was very reasonable.

In Straightsmouth, also in Greenwich, the front room of one of the little terraced houses was unfurnished and painted all white, and a bearded young man was pointing an old Super 8 cine-camera out of the window as I passed.

Greenwich, the meridian. You have to be impressed by our ancestors' confidence, the fact that we were able to say to the rest of the world, 'This is where time and space begins. If you want to be in step with us then you set your watches accordingly. If you want to know where you are, measure it from here.' And you have to be impressed, not to say amazed, that the rest of the world agreed. Those (I suppose) were the days.

In a side street in Fulham, narrow, quiet, full of parked cars, I noticed a Ford Escort with steamed-up windows. That seemed only slightly strange but I peered at it, looked in and it was quite obvious that there were two semi-naked people inside having sex. I couldn't make out faces or ages, but there was no doubt that is what was going on. Curiously enough the car had a personalized number plate: BOB 47.

I was walking along Crystal Palace Park Road, and I saw an old woman with an easel and palette, working on a large watercolour. It was very strange, an intricately detailed rendition of the old Crystal Palace as it might have been at the time of the Great Exhibition.

It was very good, very skilfully done, but of course it bore no relation at all to what was visible in front of us. The woman glanced round and for a moment I thought she was about to talk to me or explain herself, but she stared at me and obviously decided I wasn't worth wasting breath on. She returned to her painting and I continued walking.

Later I thought perhaps she was trying to pick up on some sort of ghostly remnant left by the vanished Palace. It had had a long life there, from 1854 to 1936, although if it hadn't burned down then, it would surely never have survived the Second World War.

Or perhaps they'd have dismantled it, like they did the glass roof of Cannon Street Station, storing the glass in a warehouse well south of the river for the duration. The warehouse, of course, was destroyed by a direct hit.

Another painter: at Kew I saw a young woman, an art student, I'd guess, fancy patterned leggings, big boots, hair dyed orange. She had an easel set up and she was gazing out over the river, and I was naively expecting her to be painting some tranquil London river scene, but when I got close up I saw she was making some violent abstract with a sort of crucifixion scene at its centre. Just another vision of London.

★

Mortimer Market, a dark secluded yard off Tottenham Court Road, just a place I'd once had sex with Judy – no shortage of those. The whole of London is dotted with them. It's hard to imagine, given my age, and my uxorious habits, that I'm going to have such wild sex ever again. That's it for this lifetime.

Abney Park Cemetery, where, after great hesitation on my part, Judy and I had sex. Clink Street, close to Southwark Cathedral, where Judy fell to her knees and delivered a spectacular blow job. Heath Lane, Blackheath, scene of a rear entry penetration.

Let's face it, Judy was special. How many girls lick your semen up from the surface of a map of London?

And then I saw her. I don't know why I was so surprised. It was in Dorset Street, not so very far from where I understand she now works. She was on the other side of the road. I waved but she didn't see me, or didn't want to, and so I crossed the road and went after her. I only wanted to say hello. By the time I'd crossed she was quite a distance away and walking very fast. I had to break into a run to keep pace. It felt absurd, like I was chasing her, but I finally caught up with her and touched her, I thought perfectly lightly, on the arm.

She pulled away as though I was some sort of molester, a complete stranger, some London crazy who was bothering her. I don't know whether she knew it was me or not but she let out a sort of scream. Everybody in earshot turned round, but it being London nobody did anything. That must have been when she realized she was going to have to at least talk to me. I just wanted to ask how she was, make sure she was doing all right, make sure she didn't despise me. Unfortunately, she obviously does despise me. I said there was no need to run away from me. She said she'd be the judge of that. Then she told me to get lost, and I waved my *A–Z*, said I'd just been to Clink Street and had been thinking about her, about us. She said, 'Fuck off and die, will you, Stuart.' And when I stood there all wounded and speechless, she added, 'Not necessarily in that order.'

# MISGUIDED

Once Judy had gone, and after he'd seen her car drive away, Mick went out, found a phone box and called Gabby. He knew she wouldn't be best pleased to hear from him at this time of day. It was still only eight o'clock and she wasn't an early riser, but that didn't seem to matter right now. There were other issues. He was the one on his own, the one away from home, the one with needs, and he needed to speak to her. He felt dislocated, not like himself, and he wanted her to offer him something familiar and reassuring, even if it was only a familiar sleep-soaked sulkiness. He wanted to tell her he missed her. He wanted to tell her how guilty he felt about having slept with somebody else, but he would not be doing that. More likely he might have done something silly like tell Gabby he loved her, but he didn't get the chance to do that either. The phone rang and rang, and remained unanswered.

As he walked back to the Dickens from the phone box he thought of all the innocent reasons Gabby might have for not answering her phone. Many of them were quite plausible but he failed to convince himself. When he walked in the door of the hotel he was confronted by the landlady. She was standing in the hall, supposedly sorting out the post, but he knew she was there waiting for him. She was wearing a scarlet jogging suit this morning, though the gold mules on her feet suggested she wasn't going to jog very far.

'Had some company last night, did you?' she said.

'That's right,' he replied. He had no intention of lying about it.

'One of our little Chinese friends?'

'Japanese,' he corrected her. 'Half-Japanese.' Then he wondered why he was bothering to set her straight.

'Maybe you're too young to remember what went on in those camps,' she said. 'But I'm not.'

He pushed past her and started up the stairs. He could hear her still speaking, though now more to herself than to him.

'I don't object to a young man bringing a girl back, but there are plenty of local girls without having to resort to the yellow peril.'

Back in his room Mick looked around for something belonging to the landlady that was worth stealing or smashing, but he could find nothing. He did his best to pace the room but it was too small for that. He had to get out again, immediately. He stormed down the stairs and through the hall where the landlady was still in occupation, and left the hotel in a fury. He was in such a demented state that when he found himself next to a bus that had stopped at traffic lights he leapt on and headed for the West End.

An hour later he was walking along Oxford Street, a place he had been before, a name that he recognized, and at first all he noticed was the rubbish. Not the rubbish in the streets, there was surprisingly little of that. It was more the rubbish in the shops, tacky souvenirs: snow domes, plastic policeman's helmets, T-shirts that said, 'Good girls go to heaven, bad girls go to London.' There were clothes shops selling cheap tat that he wouldn't be seen dead in. London was supposed to be this slick, fashionable place, but he thought he was far too cool for most of these shops.

Then there were all the junk food restaurants, not even English junk but American junk, Dunkin Donuts and Burger King and Kentucky Fried Chicken. Some of the architecture was impressive, big solid buildings with columns and arches and ornate stonework, but at ground level they always turned into C & A or Shelley's or Mr Byrite.

There were men on the pavement selling fake perfume from suitcases, pretending it was stolen. And there were people who wanted to give Mick things: flyers advertising shoe shops and warehouse outlets situated off the main drag, cards for dodgy colleges and language schools, free papers and mags with jobs for secretaries and computer nerds. He accepted everything he was given, looked at it, then placed it carefully in the next bin.

Mick didn't know what he was doing here. He couldn't pretend that this was any sort of reconnaissance. He was just walking. He wasn't even doing very much thinking. He'd done his best to shrug off Judy. OK, so they'd slept together. No big deal, and there wasn't any reason why Gabby should ever hear about it. He also tried to shrug off Gabby's failure to answer the phone. Forget it, he told himself, get on with the job.

But he couldn't do that either. He couldn't concentrate. He'd slept badly having Judy in his bed. He felt tired and out of shape. For now he just continued wandering, looking in the shop windows, at the streets, at the people.

He came to the eastern end of Oxford Street and he let his feet carry him into the narrow webbing of streets around the British Museum. They were unfamiliar, yet not unwelcoming, and the buildings were big but human. He found himself in a Georgian square, tall town houses around its edges, a locked garden at its centre, and there was a group of people gathering in the far corner. He walked towards them and he could tell they were tourists. He would have walked right past but one of them, an old American dude with half a dozen industrial size cameras strapped around him, called out, 'Are you part of criminal London?'

Mick stopped, wondered what he was being accused of here and who by, then it all fell into place. He was witnessing the start of a guided walking tour. If Judy hadn't told him the previous night that she'd once been a tour guide he would never have recognized it. He stopped, looked at the gang of tourists and said, 'London, no. Criminal Sheffield, maybe.'

At that moment an unhappy-looking woman announced herself as Anita, their tour leader. She smiled, trying hard to appear pleasant, but Mick reckoned she thought she was too good for this sort of work.

'Are you coming on the tour or not?' she demanded officiously.

He shook his head.

'No, but if anybody wants a crash course in GBH, let me know.'

Anita didn't smile and Mick slipped away. He wondered if he should have gone on the tour, but no, it wasn't his style. He wondered if it would have been more his style if Judy Tanaka had been leading it, and then with dismay he realized he was thinking about her again. He sat on a bench for a while and felt sorry for himself. He was bored and lonely and the day was far too long. It took a lot of self-control not to invent some reason for going back to the London Particular but he just managed it.

After she left Mick's bed that morning Judy drove her car home from the Dickens and only had time for a quick shower before work. All day as she unpacked books and helped with customer enquiries she thought about Mick. She didn't think she wanted anything from him and she didn't even intend to see him again unless he initiated it. She knew he had a girlfriend back home, that he would have no use for her.

All the same, she kept wondering where he was, whether he was on the trail of his next victim, whether he was even now engaged in beating somebody up. She knew she shouldn't 'approve' of Mick's violence and yet she was aware that her approval was irrelevant. She didn't for a moment think that he was simply a criminal sadist. She knew he must have his reasons for what he was doing, and if the reasons were good enough for him they were good enough for her.

The working day was long and she was eager to get home.

243

She managed to escape half an hour early and she hurried back to her flat where she had important things to do. She took out her map of London and one of the transparent sheets. It was the one that charted her own sexual progress through the city. She added one new cross, placing it carefully in Park Lane, Hackney, in an area of the map that was otherwise quite free of such crosses. Then she took a brand-new overlay sheet, put Mick's name at the top and drew a cross on that too, a single mark that coincided exactly with the new cross of her own.

In the evening Mick finally got through to Gabby. He didn't mention that he'd called that morning and he made no attempt to find out where she'd been. In fact they were both lost for conversation. The urgency he'd felt that morning had completely disappeared.

He told her he'd dealt with the fourth of her violators, though he didn't tell her what he'd done, and she said she was pleased, although she sounded indifferent. Then, only because he didn't know what else to talk about, he told her he'd been walking around Oxford Street, had considered going on a walking tour, and she exploded with anger. What the fuck did he think he was doing there enjoying himself and having a good time? Why wasn't he out doing what he was supposed to be doing, taking revenge?

He took it on the chin, didn't argue, didn't apologize, admitted that he'd been wasting time. Her rage seemed appropriate, something apt and deserved, even if her actual reasons for raging at him seemed hopelessly out of kilter. He promised he'd get back to work without delay. That was all it took to pacify Gabby. The phonecall ended on a note of complete and completely misguided serenity.

After she'd put the maps away Judy felt very, very lonely. She put on a CD but it bored her and made her feel melancholy. She thought of phoning her parents but they would guess something was wrong and how could she possibly explain what? Then she remembered it was time for the sexy phone-in programme. She turned the dial, tried for half an hour to find the station, but the programme wasn't there. It had been replaced by a sombre programme about community needs in London. Judy lay on her back on the bed and dealt with her own needs as best she could, but it only brought temporary relief.

Next morning, on her way to work, between the tube station and the shop she saw Stuart. That was typical. That was all she needed. What was he doing in this area of town? He couldn't be following her could he? And why was he carrying an *A–Z*? There was no getting away from him. The creep had even gone so far as to chase after her and grab her. Her decision to scream and shout obscenities at him had been calculated but quite unforced. It was genuine emotion.

Her ploy had succeeded in getting rid of him but when she got to work she was still shaking with anger. She realized that very little had changed so far as Stuart and she were concerned. She still hated him profoundly. She still wanted to hurt him, to see him suffer. He had always made her feel weak and impotent, and the ways of hurting him seemed so few. Maybe she could have told his wife about their affair, yet she suspected that the cold, business-like Anita would have taken it in her stride, shrugged and got on with making a few work calls.

She'd much rather have punched him with her bare fists, broken a few teeth and bones, smashed his nose open, left him in the gutter, cut and bruised and splitting blood. It was a nice thought, but she knew she was no good at that kind of thing. However, as she unlocked the doors of the London Particular and opened for the day, a blindingly obvious realization came to her: she had just slept with a man who was very good indeed at that kind of thing.

# PEPYS

As he walked, Stuart felt increasingly that he belonged to London, but he never made the ridiculous mistake of believing that London belonged to him. London is not Shakespeare's or Dickens' or Dr Johnson's. It belongs to everybody and to nobody, to the tourists and out-of-towners no less than to the natives. The racist tells the object of his hatred to get back where he belongs, Bombay not the Isle of Dogs. History may leave its stamp but it can't make claims to ownership. Was it only because he started keeping a diary that Stuart time and again felt the enduring presence of Samuel Pepys?

It was Pepys' eye for detail that he loved, that he wished he could emulate in his own diary. As the Great Fire rages and the houses burn, Pepys watches the pigeons on the windowsills of the houses, loath to leave their homes, waiting until it's too late, until their feathers catch fire and the birds tumble into space flapping their now useless wings. Yes, Pepys was there and he simply recorded what he saw, but it took a certain talent to be aware enough to see these things. Sometimes Stuart thought he had this talent, sometimes not, but he knew he wanted it.

As he walked through London he saw St Margaret's Church where Pepys was married, the Gatehouse prison at Westminster Abbey where he was incarcerated. There was Salisbury Court where he was born, St Bride's Church where he was christened, in a font that still survives. There were the Gray's Inn gardens where he walked the same paths that Bacon and Raleigh had walked before him. When Stuart saw Hyde Park he was reminded that this was where Pepys went to show off his new carriage and his new wife.

Above all there was Pepys Street with the house which he lived in while working at the Navy Office and while writing most of his diary. And in the same street there was St Olave's Church in whose crypt he and his wife are buried. Elizabeth Pepys died young, and inside the church Pepys placed a marble bust of her that he could gaze at during sermons. Stuart wondered whether some churchmen would find that idolatrous. He also found it a seriously odd thing for any husband to do. If Anita died would he really want her marble effigy staring down at him? No, and yet he would surely keep photographs of her, the way he still kept a photograph of Judy, though that of course was well hidden.

There were other occasions when Stuart's own history became conflated with Pepys', with the history of London itself. His walking took him to the City, to Pudding Lane, the source of the Fire, and the very moment he entered the street and looked up at the Monument, two fire engines hurtled along the street, sirens raging, scattering traffic and pedestrians.

He became enamoured with Pepys' motto *Mens cujusque est quisque*, 'A man is as his mind is', and wanted to use it as his own. He began to see London through Pepys' eyes, failing eyes at that. But it didn't matter, for it seemed to Stuart that Pepys had created a perfect, mythical city; a city of words.

Stuart hoped his diary could be a fraction as worthy as Pepys', but sometimes he felt disadvantaged. It was frequently said that the end of the twentieth century was a strange time to be living, yet Stuart knew it couldn't compete with Pepys' days. You might say that these were plague years, but Aids had nothing on the Great Plague of 1665. And again, it was frequently said that the major cities of the world were in danger of destroying themselves, but it was tame stuff compared to the destructive frenzy of the Fire of London.

Stuart had the not uncommon sense that he was living a life that was simultaneously grotesque yet bland, cruel yet denied the drama of pestilence, fire, war, invasion, blitz. In these horrors there was undoubtedly anguish, but there were also opportunities for redemption. At the very least there were lots of things to write about. Stuart thought Pepys was a very lucky man. Circumstances and history had smiled on him.

Stuart also wondered to what extent Pepys' fame relied on the mysterious and the partial. For centuries the diary had been indecipherable, and in a way it was also only a fragment. It was a big enough text but it covered a small part of a man's life. The sense of interruption was very beguiling. Stuart recalled those elegiac passages towards the end of the diary where Pepys writes of his failing eyesight, his fear of blindness and the ensuing, gathering darkness. The diary was finished unwillingly.

And Stuart wondered by what means, literary or otherwise, his own text might be given a similarly beguiling resonance. Judy had told him to fuck off and die, and, more politely put, that was pretty much Anita's message to him too. He knew that the death of the author could be a great help to a work of literature. It was a frame that could completely transform a painting. Suicide even more so. He could see the appeal of a London journal that began with high, all-encompassing hopes like his own, and was abruptly completed by the author's suicide. Suppose a man had seen the whole of London, every part, every street, every dark corner, and had become tired of it. What else was there to do but die? It sounded like a fabulous ploy, a great step forward and a great ending. As he walked past St Paul's School where Pepys had been a student, his only regret was that he suspected he was too much of a coward to kill himself.

# FIRE

Stuart was asleep, Anita breathing gently beside him. In spite of everything they still slept together. It must have been three in the morning when the phone rang on her side of the bed. She exchanged just a few words with whoever was on the other end, then lightly replaced the receiver, got up and went to the window. She drew back the curtains and stood there a long time looking out, and although she didn't try to rouse Stuart he was now fully awake and his curiosity pushed him out of bed. He took up his place beside her at the window and together they looked out at a distant, flickering orange glow in the night sky. There was a fire burning across the other side of the city. It looked large and fierce but it was far enough away that they soon felt able to go back to bed, thinking it had nothing to do with them.

When they woke next morning and looked out again there was smoke in the sky and the fire was still burning, but in daylight it was much less dramatic, and if anything it looked further away. It was only when Anita listened to the radio and heard the news that hundreds of Dockland apartments had been consumed by fire that either she or Stuart began to take the situation at all seriously.

Stuart had planned to cover ten miles of Dulwich that day but come mid-morning he was wandering through the City looking for a high place from which to get a better view of the fire. Unwittingly he came to the Monument, built by Wren to commemorate the previous London conflagration. Stuart paid his money and climbed the three hundred and some narrow spiral steps that took him up to the caged-in observation platform. Once there he could look down and see the scale of the fire. It was much bigger than he'd imagined, more intense and spreading like a hot, living stain.

There were others beside him at the top of the Monument. Somebody suggested the fire had been started by a terrorist bomb, others said it was a series of uncontrolled gas leaks. One man said it was the blacks who'd started it, but nobody took him seriously. One thing was clear from up there; the fire was not being even remotely contained. It was out of control and the fire authorities were fighting a losing battle.

As he walked, Stuart saw strange activities taking place. There was a great movement of people and their possessions. Those who had managed to save their belongings from the consumed homes arrived at friends' houses carrying all their worldly goods. They were taken in and for a while no doubt felt safe, but it was clear that before long these new refuges would be no safer than the ones they'd vacated, and they would all have to move again.

Arriving home Stuart realized that if the fire was as threatening as it appeared, his own house was as vulnerable as any other. He began by taking his valuables down to the cellar, thinking that would be the safest place for them. So his collection of favourite books, his stereo, his computer and of course the disk containing his diary, his photograph albums and certain business and personal documents, not least his insurance policy, were all carted down below ground. He felt briefly reassured.

That night the fire was still far enough away for him and Anita to sleep in their own bed, but at four o'clock in the morning he woke and felt that everything was still at risk and needed to be moved again.

He dressed rapidly, and looked out of his bedroom window. There was pandemonium. The police had erected road blocks at every street corner. The use of private cars was forbidden, and many had been towed away to make room for service vehicles, the only ones allowed through the city. If he wanted to carry his possessions to a place of greater safety he would have to improvise with a hand cart or baby's pram.

Miraculously he located a shopping trolley, loaded it with his valuables and launched himself and his possessions into the dubious safety of the night. He moved swiftly, but he wasn't sure where he was going. Then it struck him that Bethnal Green would be safe from fire, and he decided to take his things to Judy's place. He wasn't sure what reception he'd get there but this was an emergency after all.

He pushed on through the crowds but he got nowhere. The streets were too full. There were too many tides, eddies and undertows, all pulling in different directions. He lost his way and before long he had also lost his shopping trolley. He took his hands off it for just a moment and when he turned round it had gone. Somebody had taken all the things he valued most, and yet he realized that he felt surprisingly sanguine about it.

He knew there was no point going home. Anita would certainly not be there and for all he knew their house might already be in flames. He had no way of telling. There were no radio broadcasts any more, no television, the stations and channels were all silent. Soon the phones went dead and the electricity dried up. No newspapers were being printed. There was no information at all except what could be picked up on the streets, those things that he could see, hear and smell for himself. He grabbed a few pieces of waste paper from the gutter and began writing down what he had already observed. He knew it was good stuff, almost Pepysian; banners of smoke rising behind St Pancras Station, rocket trails of cinders falling over Trafalgar Square. In Clerkenwell Road he'd seen a fireman in tears, in Old Street there had been two tiny children squirting each other with water pistols, completely unaware of the danger they were in. This diary business was easy when you had such great raw material.

Stuart headed for the river, to Westminster Pier where he

251

boarded a tourist boat that had put its prices up extortionately but was full nevertheless and was running river trips into the heart of the fire. The boat was crowded and Stuart was the last to get on.

Smoke was thickening the sky, and all along the river they saw large numbers of people continuing to bring their belongings out of blocks of flats, trying to save the contents of their homes, since there seemed little chance of saving the flats themselves. The sirens of fire engines, police cars and ambulances still rang through the city but it was hard to see what good they were doing.

Suddenly a small, regal-looking motor launch pulled alongside Stuart's boat. There was a woman standing proudly at the helm. She was dressed in a heavy ball gown, thickly bejewelled and wearing a facial expression that conveyed concern but not anxiety, and, yes, there was something majestic in her demeanour. Nobody seemed to recognize her but Stuart had no doubt at all that it was the Queen of England. Quite a surprise, he thought, but why shouldn't she be on the river at a time like this?

The two boats were almost touching and the Queen was well within hailing distance. 'Hello there, Stuart,' she called out. 'What do you suggest we do?'

Perhaps he should have been surprised to be addressed so directly, but this was surely no time for formality and ceremony. Fortunately Stuart, having recently reread Pepys' account of the Great Fire, knew exactly what needed to be done.

'We need to pull down some buildings,' he replied. 'We have to create large fire gaps. Nothing else will get the job done.'

The Queen nodded sadly but saw the absolute correctness of what Stuart had said. Then she asked him which buildings would have to come down, and without hesitation he reeled off a list of names: the NatWest Tower, Centrepoint, King's Cross Station, Canary Wharf, Harrods, the Civil Aviation Authority Building, the whole of the South Bank complex, everything ever built by Quinlan Terry.

He wasn't sure where he was getting these names from or why he was so certain that they had to be demolished, but his confidence was enormous and one of the Queen's minions was meticulously writing down his every word. Finally Stuart said, 'And I'm afraid Buckingham Palace is going to have to come down too.' The Queen was close to tears at this news but she accepted Stuart's infinite wisdom. What else could she do? She issued a few commands into a mobile phone and repeated the list of buildings. It would be done. Her word, Stuart's word in effect, was law. Stuart was glad he'd gone right to the top, and not bothered with politicians or corrupt local flunkies.

And so the creation of fire gaps began. Stuart was amazed by the technology of it. In Pepys' day they'd had to use explosives to create the fire gaps, and the explosions themselves had caused as much fear and panic as the fire. These days it seemed they could simply make buildings disappear. One minute The Nat-West Tower would be standing there all solidity and corporate pride, the next minute it was gone, and not just blown up or even pulverized, but gone from the face of the city, instantly and forever. Stuart suspected there was some sort of laser involved.

All over London buildings were disappearing, like pieces being taken off a chess board, and only now did Stuart notice that all the buildings that had gone were all the ones he hated most. There was a moral there somewhere. London was being reshaped in his image. Before his eyes all the fires around London were rapidly shrinking and dying. He had saved the day. A feeling of complete well-being came over him.

The Queen took the trouble to find him again, hailed him as the saviour of modern London, and the last thing Stuart heard before he woke up was the monarch saying, 'If you would see his monument look around you.'

He sat up in bed and looked at the clock. It was three in the morning but the phonecall didn't come. He thought of going to the window and looking out, but he knew that this time there'd be nothing to see.

# DOCTOR

Dr Graham Pryce, number five on Mick Wilton's list, liked to tie up his wife. It was a thing that gave him a curious and largely inexplicable pleasure and he had no desire to have it explained. The textbooks he'd read on the subject suggested that it ought to be the other way round, that he should want to be tied. He spent all his days making serious, life and death decisions. He performed operations, thoracic surgery in the main. It was high stress, intensive care. There were junior doctors, nurses, administrators to be bullied. The failures, though much less frequent than the successes, couldn't be easily shrugged off. There were spouses and relatives, parents and offspring to be dealt with; sometimes they were weeping, sometimes they were litigious. Sometimes they were in need of counselling, more often they were in need of and were prescribed a good dose of tranquillizer. Dr Pryce took a masculine, professional pride in appearing to cope effortlessly with all the above.

So after a hard day he should, if he were following the classic scenario, wish to abandon all power, should wish to submit totally and become helpless. He should want someone, a wife, mistress, *maîtresse*, to take complete control. But he did not. He left the submission to his wife, Louise. Not that the submission was completely straightforward. Within the rules they set themselves she was perfectly entitled to struggle a little, to fight, to beat his chest with her fists, dig her nails into his back, to threaten him with vengeance, police, with the wrath of the BMA. For Pryce's profession was of paramount importance in their sexual games. His wife played the vulnerable, needy, hypochondriac patient and he played the wicked, invasive, unethical swine of a general practitioner. It was a satisfactory arrangement for both of them.

They lived in inherited splendour in a Georgian town house off Fitzroy Square. They liked to think of themselves as Fitzrovians; as heirs to the streets of Augustus John, Sickert, Hazlitt, Charles Laughton; as tolerant historical neighbours of the likes of Dylan Thomas, Nina Hamnett, Marie Stopes. Their living quarters were in the upper reaches of the house, the ground floor being used as a reception area and consulting room for Pryce's growing roster of private patients.

The consulting room was a comfortable, reassuring place, one that spoke of discreet money and good health. The room was warm and richly wallpapered. There were leather chairs for both doctor and patient, a wide Axminster rug on the floor, glass-fronted bookcases containing medical textbooks. There were no images of sickness, no stark posters warning patients about disease and distress. Instead there were framed engravings of London buildings, and although a closer look would have revealed that these were in fact London hospitals: Guy's, Bart's, St Thomas's, the Brompton, this room seemed to offer the promise that associations with such establishments would be cordial and brief. Tucked away close to the filing cabinets was a small engraving of Bedlam, but patients never saw that one at all.

Any transaction that took place here would be costly, and yet the doctor who inhabited this room was clearly rich enough that he wouldn't need to rob you. The service delivered would be expensive and honourable. Inevitably, therefore, this room had to be the venue for the Pryces' erotic games.

Once in a while, as often as their mutual needs and tastes coincided, Pryce would book his wife in for the last appointment of the day, and he would send his nurse home early.

Having been out all afternoon, Louise would come to the house as though she were a bona fide patient, and Pryce would let her in and show her through to his consulting room.

His manner would start out reserved and thoroughly professional, although a patient might notice that his tie was loose and that there was the merest hint of malt whisky on his breath. He would listen sympathetically as Louise Pryce told her story, recounted vague symptoms of tiredness, anxiety, ennui. He would ask a few desultory questions about her diet, her sleep patterns, her libido, and then conclude that she was in need of a thorough examination.

She would go behind a screen and shyly remove a few of her clothes. When she had emerged he would bossily tell her to take off the rest (except for the stockings and suspender belt) and when she was a bit slow about it he'd lend a rough but practised hand to speed the process along.

She would stand before him, denuded, eyes downcast, while he took her pulse, while he touched various parts of her body with his fingers and with the cold end of his stethoscope. He would feel her breasts to make sure 'everything was all right in that department' and, once convinced, he would conclude that her problem must lie elsewhere.

He'd slip on surgical gloves and tell her to hop up on to the examination table where he would brusquely spread her legs and begin an internal examination. The touch of rubber-encased fingers, of swabs and speculum, would make her feel that she was melting. Her husband was taking over and she was blissfully losing power. But when he started peering deeply into her, getting his nose and mouth so close that she could feel his breath on her labia, well, a decent woman surely had to protest. She would express a certain lady-like outrage, but that would only bring out the worst in her doctor.

Before she knew it he'd have abandoned his pleasant bedside manner and he'd be buckling leather straps across her midriff, using lengths of bandage to bind her wrists and ankles to the table. A broad piece of sticking plaster would be slapped tightly and immovably over her mouth. Then, when she was totally restrained, totally vulnerable, totally at his sexual mercy, he would step back, do up his tie, straighten his jacket, and say that was enough for one day. He would turn off the lamp on his desk, gather together a few papers and slide them into his briefcase. Then he would go to the door, turn off the overhead light and be gone. His wife would be left there in the dark, bound and splayed, and she would stay like that in a state of ominous, rising sexual tension until Pryce saw fit to return.

By the time he got back, up to an hour later, they would both be in states of headlong arousal. He would return, rush into the consulting room, flail his clothes aside and fuck her where she was, bonds still in place, her mouth still taped shut. The coupling was blind and short, and afterwards, when the whole act was finished, he would release her, let her dress, say the treatment might need repeating quite soon, and then the game would be over. They would go up into the body of the house, open a decent bottle of wine and have a casserole that she had prepared earlier. Domesticity and decency were once again restored.

Mick had seen only part of the performance, the public side. He'd watched Louise Pryce arriving at the house and he'd found it strange that she had to ring the bell to be admitted to her own home. He found it stranger still that after a while all the lights were turned off and that Pryce then left the building. Mick knew that the wife must still be in there, in the dark, and although it just about seemed possible that she had simply decided to go to bed, take an early-evening nap, Mick felt sure there must be a more potent and enticing explanation, one that he could use to his advantage.

Mick was keen to get on with his task. He would be glad when he was finished. He felt he might be losing his taste for revenge. His life was getting too difficult and convoluted. Sleeping with Judy Tanaka had been a terrible mistake, worse than he'd first thought. Love, lust, affection, attraction, desire, need; these were the things that made life complicated and intolerable. They were traps. They threatened to involve him, to enmesh him in the workings of a city where he did not want to belong. He had wanted to be unknown in London, to be invisible, anonymous, to move in and out swiftly and unobserved. Things had changed. He was feeling bogged down, static, and it made him want to hurry, to detach himself, get away from Judy, and that perhaps more than anything else was what spurred him into a rash, improvised revenge against Pryce.

Having seen the outer manifestations of the Pryces' variety act he now wanted to see the whole story. He had set himself up outside the house. He had watched Louise Pryce arrive and enter, seen the lights go off, seen Pryce leave. Mick decided it was time to go in. He knew this was not strictly wise. He knew that Pryce was not there and it would probably have made more sense to be out in the streets following him. Yet something told Mick that the appropriate act of revenge would take place in the Pryces' own home.

Breaking in presented no problems. Once inside the house he began switching on lights. He'd had enough of subterfuge, of hiding and sneaking. He would have illuminated the whole house and walked freely around all of it, intruding, trespassing, searching for nothing in particular. But there was no need. The first room he came to was the consulting room, and there she was, Mrs Louise Pryce, just as her husband had left her; naked and trussed. Mick had not been expecting anything so extreme, so theatrical as this, and yet in the event it came as no great surprise. It made sense. It fitted.

His first impulse was to untie the poor woman, let her get dressed, tell her he was there for her husband, not for her. But at the same time he saw that there must be possibilities in having his victim's wife bound, gagged and stripped before him.

She looked at him fearfully, but there was far more in her eyes than simple fright. There was disbelief and many, many shades of embarrassment that were quite separate from the natural shock she was experiencing.

'Mrs Pryce, I presume,' Mick said cheerfully.

He looked closely at her body. He liked the look of it, the tight stomach, the small breasts with their dark pink nipples. Her skin was pale, and paler still where a bikini had protected areas from the sun, protected too a neat, wholesome-looking appendix scar close to her left hip bone. The patches of thigh visible above the top of her stockings were smooth and seemed, to Mick, to be crying out to be touched. Her pubic hair was short and trim, and he wondered if it had been cut that way to satisfy her husband's tastes.

'Is there any money here?' he asked.

She was trying to be helpful. She nodded towards her handbag which was lying on the floor by her husband's desk. Mick opened it, explored among the lipsticks and tissues and bunches of keys and found a purse with a couple of hundred pounds in it. He took the money gratefully.

'Thanks for helping to make my stay in London just that little bit more pleasurable,' he said.

Then she tried to be more helpful still. Her eyes flicked round the room, and settled on a metal cabinet with a rolling front. She seemed to be directing him there. Mick opened the cabinet and found it full of drugs samples. He turned away immediately.

'Not my thing,' he said by way of explanation. 'I suppose I could try and sell them but I wouldn't know one drug from another. Would you?'

He hoped that this brief interaction might help to make Louise Pryce a little less scared, but it didn't work. He needed to say more. He said, 'I imagine it must be strange being married to a doctor, knowing that he spends all day messing about with other people's bodies, examining them, poking around in them, seeing all these tits and bums and all the labias and vulvas. And then he comes home to you. It must be weird for you. God knows there are a lot of sick people out there.

'The body's such a strange thing, isn't it, Mrs Pryce? It gives a lot of pleasure but it can give a lot of pain too. I mean, I

259

intend to hurt your husband, and OK, I might think about hurting him mentally or emotionally, but let's face it, the body's what you think of hurting first, isn't it?'

That didn't do much to relax the woman either. He wanted to be reassuring. He said, 'I can see that you're frightened, Mrs Pryce, and I can understand why. There you are, all spread out like a road map, and here I am, and let's face it, the road looks wide open. I mean, if I were someone like your husband I'd probably be right in there, no messing, straight into the Dartford Tunnel. That's the kind of man your husband is, so I hear, or so they tell me. They say he's the kind of man who gang-bangs strippers at private parties, at least that's what they say about him in Sheffield. You look surprised. You probably didn't think people in Sheffield talked about your husband. Well, it came as a bit of a shock to me too.'

The expression on her face was developing, maturing, changing from one of simple fear and confusion to a more complicated anguish, as it dawned on her that she might be in the presence of a genuine, dangerous lunatic.

'Frankly, Mrs Pryce, you're a good-looking woman. No man in his right mind would kick you out of bed. But the problem I have is this: I want revenge on your husband and a lot of people would think that having sex with you would be a pretty good way of doing it. But I don't know. I'd have to put my penis into a place where he normally puts *his* penis and that would be a bit disgusting, wouldn't it?

'Now you might say that since your husband raped my girlfriend I'm forced to put my penis where he's already had his, in any case, so I admit the issue isn't all that clear. And I admit that unless you sleep exclusively with virgins you're always going into a hole where some dodgy prick has been before you, so maybe that's not really the issue, but anyway, the important thing is I'm not a rapist. Really I'm not. I mean, there are a lot of men, men who'd call themselves non-rapists, ordinary petty criminals, burglars, who if they broke into a house and found themselves in this position, well, they just

260

couldn't control themselves. But I'm not like that, you'll be glad to know.

'And in any case, raping you because your husband raped my girlfriend, well, that's not much of a revenge really, is it? If I was really going to rape someone I ought to rape *him*, didn't I? I mean, that would be real revenge. Apparently there's a lot of it about these days, maybe there always was but you hear a lot more about it now. It puts ideas into people's heads.

'Of course, there are other things I could do to you that would be a long way short of rape that might piss off your husband every bit as much. Just having your wife seen naked by another man, that'd be enough to make some husbands feel angry and humiliated. But I was thinking of something more concrete. I mean, maybe if I just touched your breasts, stroked your nipples. Would they get hard, I wonder? Or I could stroke your fanny, only the outside at first and then maybe slip a finger in just for size, just testing the waters. Or maybe I should masturbate while I look at you. A lot of husbands would think that was a bit much. I'd be just standing here copping an eyeful, pulling the old pudding, and maybe just before I came I'd get up on the table and ejaculate all over you so that you got sperm on your belly and breasts and on your face and in your hair. Not in your mouth, of course, thanks to the sticking plaster. And when your husband got back he'd see this spunk all over you and he'd have to help you clean it off . . .'

The thought was so headily indecent that he had to stop talking for a moment. Then he continued, 'But really, Mrs Pryce, you'll be glad to hear I'm not going to do any of that stuff to you, because I think it's morally wrong to get at a man through his wife or his children. I'm not a monster, Mrs Pryce, as you must have realized by now.

'You know, I always wonder about the sort of low-life villains who steal old ladies' life savings, or threaten to kill people's children, or who throw acid in the caretaker's face. I mean, I say to myself, how can they do that? I think in most cases the answer is because they have no imagination. They can't imagine what it's like to be old or to have children or to have your face disfigured, because if they could imagine it they'd have some empathy with the victims and so they couldn't bring themselves to do it. I think I can imagine more or less what it's like to be raped, so I wouldn't do that to you.

'But then I think about real villains, the real monsters. They *do* have imagination. They're good at thinking up tortures that you and I could never ever possibly dream of. I was reading something in the papers, can't remember where it was, Bosnia or Rwanda or Nicaragua or somewhere like that, where they'd capture men, fathers and sons, take them to gaol and then force them to give each other blow jobs.

'To me that's more than just sick, it's actually unimaginable. If I'd been given the rest of my life to think up something horrible to do to one of my enemies I'd never have come up with that. Never. So, maybe I'm wrong, maybe some of these guys do have imagination.'

Mick was aware that Louise Pryce seemed to be watching him closely, listening very carefully to what he was saying. He hardly thought she was interested in the philosophy of criminality, and he wondered if maybe she was just staring at him, listening to his voice, trying to commit things to memory that she could later recount to the police. But no, he couldn't quite see that happening, couldn't imagine the Pryces explaining to some honest constable how it was that she came to be in a position to be such a good observer.

'I'd be quite interested in hearing your replies, Mrs Pryce,' he said. 'But you understand why I haven't taken off the sticking plaster. Because I'm scared you'll scream the place down.'

She shook her head to say that she wouldn't do that, but how could he believe her?

'The simple fact is,' he said, 'I feel tired, Mrs Pryce. I find this city of yours pretty exhausting. It's easy to get lost. And frankly, Mrs Pryce, I'm feeling a bit lost. I mean, when I arrived in London it all seemed very clear; six guys who needed sorting out. No problem. That's the line of work I'm in. That's what I do. And you know, it ought to be easy giving these blokes a pasting. I mean, some of them I'd have been happy to do anyway, that prat Jonathan Sands and his bloody boat, that bloody actor. I mean, I have my share of class hatred. I don't mind beating up rich, posh bastards at all. I'd do that any day of the week. But lately it's not been that simple. I have this funny feeling that something's wrong somewhere.

'Yeah, when I first came here I hated London and I hated the people who lived here; too soft, too rich, too southern. But lately it's not been that straightforward. For instance, I like cars, I find them interesting, and London's full of interesting cars. You see lots of left-hand-drive cars for instance. And you can see more Rolls-Royces in London in a day than you'd see in Sheffield in a year. And you see Ferraris and old Bristols and Maseratis. And obviously it's partly a question of money, obviously there's more cash around in London than in Sheffield, but somehow it's more than that. People here like things that are a bit different, a bit special. Even that twat Philip Masterson had a decent car.

'And women too. You see more beautiful women in London than you'd ever see anywhere else in England. Maybe sheer numbers has got something to do with it, the population of London's so big there have to be a few great-looking women, but it feels like there's a much higher percentage in London. And the way they dress. Some of the clothes they wear – they'd stop traffic if they dressed like that in Sheffield, but in London it's just part of the show. I like it. I'm a sucker for all that.'

He picked up the speculum that Pryce had used to examine his wife and held it up to the light. He closed one eye and looked at the world through the curved, distorting plastic.

'If this thing could talk,' he muttered distractedly, then returned to what he was saying. 'It's funny but I suppose I've started to like this place. London. I like the money and the variety and the river and the desirable properties. I like the pubs and the architecture and the people and the restaurants. And inevitably a bit of me is envious. And you know there was a time when envy would have made me want to destroy things, but it doesn't feel like that now. Now I want . . . I know it sounds stupid . . . I want to join in with it.

'As a matter of fact, I've never really felt as though I belonged anywhere, Mrs Pryce, and it never bothered me. I'm not sure if I belong in London or not, but now I'm here I don't really want to go back to Sheffield. And it's troubling me. You know, how is a petty criminal from up north supposed to fit in to all this?

'Sex is the problem, Mrs Pryce. Sex is always at the back of everything. I slept with a woman, a Londoner, and suddenly I'm all confused. Bodies are such a problem. They say that the human body's like a city, in all sorts of ways, and I'm sure they're right.'

Mick went to one of the glass-fronted bookcases and pulled out a copy of *Gray's Anatomy*. He turned through the pages until he found what he was looking for.

'The first cut is the deepest, eh, Mrs Pryce?' he said.

There was a thick red felt-tip pen lying on Pryce's desk. Mick picked it up, went over to Louise Pryce and, with reference to the book he'd opened, he painstakingly drew a large, red, valentine heart on the surface of her breast and sternum. The skin resisted the pen. The flesh sank beneath the pressure of the felt-tip but Mick was scrupulous in ensuring that only the pen should touch her, that there should be no skin to skin contact.

'Yes, a city can have a heart but I don't know where London's heart is. Marble Arch? The square mile of the City? Knightsbridge? And where are the lungs? Where's the liver? The kidneys?'

He drew sketchy representations of lungs, liver, kidneys and a length of colon on the skin of Louise Pryce's thorax. She couldn't scream and she could barely struggle but something in her eyes showed absolute terror, as if she thought he might be about to slash her open, perform some butcher's incision in search of a heart.

'I'm not going to hurt you, Mrs Pryce,' Mick said again. 'I know that drawing on your chest with felt-tip is a pretty weird thing to do. It's true. I feel pretty weird these days. I am weird. But I'm not a nutter. Thanks for being such a good listener, Mrs Pryce.'

He pulled up a chair, placed it close to the examination table and sat there for a long time just looking at her body. There was pleasure in it. He liked to look but he had no desire to touch. He tried to imagine that he was looking at a city, at a new-found land, but all he saw was flesh and sex.

He was still sitting and looking when he heard sounds from the hall; the front door opening, then a man's footsteps. The return of Dr Graham Pryce. He must surely have realized at once that something was amiss since all the lights were on and the door to the consulting room was open. But even though he was forewarned, he was hardly ready for what hit him.

The moment Pryce entered the consulting room, before he had time to take in the scene, before he was even fully aware of Mick's presence, Mick started to punch and kick him. He did it silently, without saying a word, without so much as grunting. Pryce had no chance to fight back, not even to defend himself. The blows came from some dark place deep inside Mick, a place of cold, frightening, irresistible violence.

Pryce folded under the blows, was driven down to his knees, then to the floor, where he rolled up into a ball, not struggling, merely enduring, waiting for the attack to cease or to drive him into insensibility. And as Mick's right foot made repeated contact with his victim's body, he looked over at Louise Pryce, still pegged out on the table, and he could see she was crying, not much, just enough to make him feel bad, just enough to make him stop kicking her husband.

Mick stood still, trying not to sway, not to fall over, sweat pumping out through the creases in his forehead, an oceanic wash in his ears, and before he made his escape he felt the compulsion to turn apologetically to Louise Pryce and say, 'If it's any consolation I don't really know why I did that.' And even then he still wasn't ready to go. He went over to her and said, 'You know another way the body and the city resemble each other? Answer: neither of them has a soul.'

# WORK

All the next day Mick felt like shit. He didn't think he'd dealt properly or adequately with Dr Graham Pryce. He sensed he'd broken the rules. He'd started to develop a new, highly personal variation of the game, and even if it wasn't cheating exactly, something told him it was going to end in tears.

He got up late and wasted the morning in his room doing nothing. He didn't bother trying to phone Gabby. He didn't much care whether she was there or not, and in either case he had nothing much to say to her, no new questions that he wanted to ask. Her encouragement and approval meant little to him. She was the prime mover but the drama by now was his alone.

His room was as oppressive as ever. He didn't want to be there, yet he felt becalmed. He knew he ought to be out in the city tracking down rapist number six, the final victim, a feeling that was only confirmed when Judy arrived at his door.

'The landlady sent me up,' she said. 'I don't think she likes me. I don't think I pass her high standards of racial purity.'

'Not many do.'

He was embarrassed by Judy's presence. His awkwardness and diffidence sat uneasily with his bulk and strength but Judy knew she had the upper hand.

'I'm sorry I had to come back,' she said. 'I realize you don't want me here.'

He found himself denying that, found himself saying he did want her there, that he was pleased to see her. The words sounded unfamiliar in his mouth but they were undoubtedly true.

'It doesn't matter,' she said. 'I'm here about something else. About work.'

'Work?'

'I want to offer you a job.'

For an uncomfortable moment he thought she had been so horrified to discover what he was doing in London that she was trying to straighten him out by offering him a job in her bookshop.

'You know what I do,' he said.

'Oh yes, although I still don't know why. But that's all right too. I suppose it doesn't really matter. I don't need to know.'

She was thoughtful, preoccupied, and for a moment she seemed to be a million miles away, a long way from job offers and rooms in Hackney, in some distant suburb of the mind where the tubes didn't run and where the taxi drivers wouldn't go.

'I've been thinking,' she said, and her speech slowed with the awkward weight of what she had to say. 'Your list of names, could I add a name to it?'

'No,' he said loudly.

'Just one name. Just one man.'

'Oh, come on!' he said.

'Why not? I've helped you. Why won't you help me?'

'It doesn't work like that.'

'Why not? It's what you do. You've said so. What difference does one more make?'

'You want me to beat somebody up for you?'

'That's it.'

'I can't beat someone up just because you ask me to.'

'Why not? Whatever these men on your list did, this man did something worse.'

'You don't know that. You don't know anything about it.'

'This man broke my heart,' Judy said.

The words sounded so small, so delicate. They seemed so old-fashioned, so fragile and out of place in the world Mick was inhabiting, like a china cup in the hands of meths drinkers.

'I thought I was over him but I was wrong. I thought I didn't care any more but now I realize I still do. And I want revenge.'

'You don't beat somebody up just because they broke your heart,' Mick said.

'*I* would if I could.'

'Then maybe you should go ahead and do it. Maybe it's your job not mine.'

She wasn't listening.

'What do I need to give you to make you help me?' she asked. 'Money? Sex? Japanese lunches? What's your motivation here, Mick?'

He wanted to say it was all to do with love. He wanted to say he was punishing these six men because they had hurt somebody he loved. Rape was a special, virulent form of hurt, but it was a matter of degree not of quality. But he didn't say that because he knew it would sound fake. He wasn't sure that he still loved Gabby and if he didn't, then when had he stopped? Come to that, when had he even started? If Gabby had told him that a man in London, maybe even six men, had broken her heart what would he have done to them?

'What I really want,' he said, 'is to stop beating people up altogether.'

'But you're having trouble stopping, is that it? Like giving up cigarettes?'

'Look, Judy, in other circumstances, a month ago, six months ago, maybe I'd have been the man you're looking for. But right now I'm not.'

'His name's Stuart London,' she said.

'Why do I need to know that?'

'Stuart London. It's an easy name to remember.'

'I don't want to know his name.'

'Maybe you'll come across him.'

'No.'

'Maybe you'll change your mind. Maybe you'll find a reason to do what I ask.'

He didn't argue. He felt there was no need. He felt safe in the knowledge that London was too big a city to allow chance meetings with Judy Tanaka's old lovers.

'London may bring you the very thing you need,' Judy said.

'Hey, don't go all inscrutable on me.'

She smiled and she went up to him and kissed him.

'You'd better go,' he said.

She kissed him again, more persuasively this time, and he didn't need so very much convincing.

'Or I could stay,' she said.

'Yes, you could,' he admitted.

He felt feeble and powerless, and just as he had been too weak to stop himself beating up Dr Graham Pryce, he was too weak to stop himself making love to Judy Tanaka. As he was taking the clothes off her, he said, 'You realize none of this is going to make any difference?' And she said, 'If you say so,' and she smiled, and she seemed to him more inscrutable than ever.

# ADDICTION

Some men expected strippers to be complete slags, to be anybody's and everybody's, to be usable and disposable. However, in Gabby's experience strippers were no different from any other group of women. Some of them were slappers, but some of them were professional virgins. Some were happily married, some were practising long-term celibacy. Some were desperately looking for love, others were looking for instant gratification.

Gabby would always have said that she occupied the middle ground, but she'd admit that faithfulness didn't come easily to her. If a man liked her, flattered her, was nice to her, bought her dinner and a few drinks and then asked nicely for sex, well, how could she say no?

She'd wanted to be faithful to Mick, she really had. In fact she'd wanted to be faithful to all her men, but there'd always been a reason why she'd failed in the end; sometimes it was boredom, sometimes it was too much drink, sometimes it was because a better prospect had come along, and that was partly the case here. A good-looking man with money, a flash car and some high-quality drugs had come along and he'd treated her decently and it had all just sort of happened. What was a girl to do?

His name was Ross McLennan and Gabby first met him at the agency that handled her bookings. Most of her dealings were with a chubby, motherly former stripper called Pat.

McLennan was there in the office when Gabby called in one day to pick up some money and Pat introduced him as though he was an old friend, maybe even part of the business, maybe a sleeping partner. There was talk of him wanting to hire a few girls for a party he was throwing, but he never mentioned hiring Gabby.

She knew immediately that he wasn't a good man. He looked difficult and dangerous, and though he smiled at her a lot, she knew it wasn't a smile she could trust. He was older than Mick and usually that wouldn't have been attractive to her, but he wore his age lightly, he dressed young, he looked like a somebody and she fancied him like mad.

Not that it seemed to matter at the time. She thought she'd probably never see him again. Then one night he was in the audience at a club in Rotherham where she was stripping. He watched her do the act. He looked out of place in the smoke and crush of the club and he didn't appear to be enjoying himself very much and he certainly didn't bother to applaud when she'd finished. Neither did he try to go backstage or try to speak to her as she was leaving. Mick was there and maybe his presence had scared him off, although he didn't look like a man who was scared of much.

Next day he telephoned her. She knew the agency must have given him her home number, which was another indication that he was somebody very special indeed. She wanted to be angry that her number had been given out, but she couldn't summon up the pretence. She was glad he'd called her and she didn't bother to hide it.

He said, 'Why the gloves?'

She was surprised and impressed. Nobody had ever questioned the gloves before. Nobody had ever seen them as anything more than part of a stripper's paraphernalia.

'I spent all night wondering what goes on underneath those gloves,' he said. 'I thought maybe it was ugly old tattoos, maybe an ex-lover's name, but you look too clever to have done something like that. And then I thought maybe you were an old junkie and you were hiding needle tracks, but you don't look like a junkie either. So then I wondered if it was deformity, burns or skin disease, or maybe you're missing a finger or even a hand. So which is it?'

'You'll have to find out for yourself,' she said. 'You'll have to take them off for me.'

Her words sounded too obvious, more salacious and silly than she'd intended, but she knew this man was going to be something in her life whether she liked it or not. What was the point of being evasive, and what was the point of resisting? He had been talking to her on a car phone and ten minutes later he arrived at her door. Ten minutes after that she was being unfaithful to Mick. McLennan peeled off her gloves, looked sympathetically at the scars on her wrists and forearms, and kissed them. She couldn't stop herself submitting and she didn't try. She could tell this wasn't going to be just a one-off, not a case of him trying it on because he thought all strippers were slags. It was not going to be anything nearly so simple.

She never found out what he did for a living. He'd never tell her and she could never quite work it out, although over the next few months she pieced together a few tantalizing bits of information. From things he said it appeared he was involved with property and with gambling and with importing cars from Europe. This might have been legitimate for all she knew. Certainly he employed an accountant and a book keeper like any other business. But he also employed some dodgy-looking heavies, men without job titles, men who were not employed for their entrepreneurial skills.

Gabby knew better than to quiz him about what he did. They were both happy for him to remain mysterious. He travelled a lot, to Birmingham, to Manchester, even to Florida (where he topped up his already radiant tan). But whatever he did, he was obviously good at it and it was obviously extremely profitable. She sometimes thought his business must involve drugs too. He always had the very best dope, speed, cocaine, and he was free with it, at least where she was concerned. But maybe it wasn't business. Maybe he had the best drugs because he had the best of everything; the best house, the best furnishings, the best cars, the best whisky and, as he repeatedly told her, the best women.

He seemed to take it for granted that she would have a boyfriend. It didn't seem to bother him. He didn't tell her to stop seeing him. In fact he was very interested in hearing all about Mick.

Gabby felt disloyal enough just sleeping with McLennan; telling him about Mick was even worse. But she did tell him. She couldn't stop herself, and McLennan seemed to have no ulterior motive. He was interested in a disinterested way, only wanting to know something about Mick, he said, because he wanted to know everything about Gabby. She told him and she was disappointed how little there was to tell, what a nothing he seemed to her now, how she seemed not to need Mick any more, how easy she found it to lie to him.

If she could tell McLennan all about Mick, she knew that Mick must know nothing about McLennan, and so it was. He remained blissfully ignorant. Mick trusted Gabby and he was easy to deceive. She'd tell him she was seeing her sister, staying over at her mother's, and Mick never questioned it. It wasn't that she thought Mick would do anything terrible if he found out. She didn't think he'd hit her the way some of them might. Mick could be a brute but he was never a brute to her. It was more that he'd have been disappointed in her, that he would have valued her at more than she was worth.

She liked having secrets. The drugs were a secret from Mick. Having an affair with McLennan was an even bigger one. She wondered if she needed secrets because her life as a stripper was so utterly revealing. She showed everything to her audience, more than just her body. Like any good performer she revealed herself, gave herself away. And before long she had given everything to McLennan. Their nights were long and sleepless; intense, relentless sessions fuelled by alcohol, lust and drugs.

They left her feeling worn, shaky, wrecked, but at least she knew she was alive.

Some addictions are instant, others take a slow, incremental hold. At first it was easy for her to juggle Mick and McLennan, to balance their opposing demands on her, but she knew that sooner or later she would be wholly McLennan's. Even before he went to London, she knew that Mick was meaning less and less to her.

And when McLennan said, 'You shouldn't be a stripper. You're far too good for that game,' well, it was nothing that she hadn't heard before from other boyfriends, but this time it mattered. This time it meant something. It sounded convincing and true. It felt like the thing she'd always been waiting for, the magic words she'd always wanted to hear. Once McLennan had said that, she was his. She'd do anything for him.

# THE SUICIDE TOUR

S tuart was walking along Bernard Street, not far from Russell Square tube station, when he saw a small group of tourists gathering on the opposite side of the road. He could tell they were mostly Americans; it was something to do with the clothes they wore, something alien in the cut, the fabric, the specific tone of the colours.

They were an older crowd with several very tall but stooped white-haired men, some in baseball caps, one in a sort of straw stetson. The men looked bigger and healthier and stronger than their London equivalents, as though they were farming stock, big-framed, with some whiff of Scandinavia in their back-ground. They had their bright, good-humoured wives with them, and in some cases their wives' recently widowed friends.

And then, surprisingly, although Stuart had ceased to be surprised long ago, for some reason it was always this way, there were a couple of sulky, awkward, long-haired adolescent girls. Stuart never understood why they were there, why they hadn't managed to slip away to McDonald's or Carnaby Street or Camden Market or some place where they wouldn't have to listen to the spoutings of a tour guide and where they might take the first steps towards some sort of tentative holiday sexual liaison. What else was the point of adolescents coming to London? But they never did those things. In the event these two stayed, sulked and made bad listeners.

It took Stuart a surprisingly long time to realize that he was witnessing the start of a London Walker tour: one called The Bloomsbury Walk and Beyond. The guide was a very new, very raw recruit called Colin, a boy Stuart had been forced to interview recently at Anita's insistence. These days the whole business of interviews was an irritating interruption to Stuart's walking plans and after the most perfunctory chat he'd hastily decided that the boy would do. In more usual circumstances Colin wouldn't have stood a chance, but turning him down would only have resulted in Stuart having to interview someone else and that would have been even more of a disruption, so he'd given Colin the job, given him an even more perfunctory training session and thrown him in at the deep end where he was currently both waving and drowning.

Stuart knew this could only be Colin's second or third tour, and when he saw the new boy in action, Stuart realized what a truly rotten choice he'd made. Colin was a suit-wearing, red-faced, Bunterish young man. He had a fussy, put-upon manner, and his voice, although clear and expressive, was never very loud. What was worse, as Stuart now saw, he was completely incapable of dealing with a group. The would-be walkers milled around him, willing him to exercise some control, to offer some direction, at the very least to say something to them, but as he repeatedly cleared his throat, looked at his watch, flapped his arms and ultimately did nothing useful, the group increasingly ignored him, one or two of them would start to wander off. Only then would he mutter something after them, by which time they were out of earshot.

Eventually, despite having been unable to command any attention, he decided to start the tour anyway, using more or less the exact words that Stuart had set down for him. He had been speaking for several minutes before any members of the group realized he'd started, and having realized, they began to ask each other what they'd missed, thereby missing more. The overall effect was of a Shakespearean rabble making crowd noises.

Stuart watched the spectacle and his feelings moved rapidly

from derisive amusement through exasperation to anger. He crossed the street and joined the group, apparently as a spectator. Guides were always warned to make sure this didn't happen. It was all too easy for casual passers-by to join the tour late and avoid paying. Stuart stood close to Colin but it was some time before the new guide became aware of his boss's presence, and the moment he did so his mouth dangled open and although it still moved as though speaking, no sound came out at all.

'All right,' said Stuart loudly, busily, taking control. 'Amateur hour's over. Step back, Colin. Then look and learn.'

Colin, surprised but visibly relieved, retreated several large paces and the group turned towards Stuart. His abrupt dismissal of their guide had established a dubious sort of authority. They were glad to have someone who looked as though he knew what he was doing, but his treatment of the young man had been rather nastily dismissive. Their sympathy still needed to be won even if their expectations had been set up.

Stuart stood silently for as long as he could, milking their attention, then he said, 'Around the corner in Russell Square you'll find the Bloomsbury Hotel. Within it you'll find the Virginia Woolf hamburger bar. Alas, Mrs Woolf's views on the hamburger are not recorded in her writings but we do know that she committed suicide because she couldn't bear to live through the horrors of the Second World War.

'You would probably have to ask to what extent Virginia Woolf was actually affected by the horrors of the Second World War, after all she wasn't exactly on the front line, but then it's no good saying that a person's reasons for killing herself aren't good enough. Arguably, she might have tried to kill herself by wandering the streets of wartime London waiting for the right bomb, or perhaps by driving an ambulance during air raids, or why not by joining some secret show and accepting a suicide mission behind enemy lines? Instead she chose death by drowning and she chose to do it out of London. She apparently thought the country had more tone.'

The group wasn't quite with him yet. Stuart had a feeling that many of them probably hadn't actually heard of Virginia Woolf, or if they had, they thought of Liz Taylor in the Edward Albee play, but at least his talk of hamburgers and death and war had drawn them in.

'There's a story told by Casanova about his stay in London,' Stuart continued. 'He was sitting in a coffee house and heard two Englishmen talking about a friend of theirs who'd recently committed suicide. The first man said he thought the suicide had been a perfectly reasonable action considering the state of their friend's finances. But the other man disagreed. He'd been a creditor of the dead man and had been able to take a look at his accounts. In his opinion the friend needn't have killed himself for another six months.'

There was thin, polite, self-conscious laughter as Stuart concluded the anecdote, not a storm of mirth but enough for him to go on, a sign at least that they knew he was trying to entertain them.

'Yes,' he said, 'London's not at all a bad place to die. Freud did it here. Karl Marx too. Plenty more besides, most of them against their will: Jack "the Hat" McVitie, Charles I, Thomas More.'

'Is this a true story?' one of the women asked, but she was ignored.

'Welcome to London,' Stuart said grandly. 'A city much possessed by death. Come, let's walk on.'

He set off briskly across Russell Square in the direction of the British Museum. He had no scarf or cloak to throw over his shoulder as he went, yet there was something sweeping and theatrical about his progress. It would have been demeaning to look back and make sure the group was with him, but he felt sure they were. As he walked he said, 'You think London isn't a necropolis? Let me tell you it is. And people love it. Our cemeteries are popular tourist attractions. People pile into the British Museum and all they want to see are the mummies. They pack into Madame Tussaud's to look at a population of wax corpses. They go to the London Dungeon to gloat over torture and captivity. They go to the Tower of London. They go to Poet's Corner to walk on the dead.

'Yes, we're not bad at death in London. This is a city where Dennis Nielsen had no trouble finding the endless supply of sexually available young men he needed to take home, drug and murder. This was the home of Jack the Ripper. This is the city where Ruth Ellis shot her lover; nothing very surprising about that you may say, but it is also a city where the bullet holes from that shooting have been lovingly preserved and can still be seen in the wall of the pub in Hampstead.

'But these are rather specialized forms of death. Once death would have been more quotidian, more public. One might have walked along London Bridge and seen the heads of the recently executed. Or one might have gone to Newgate or Tyburn or to Catherine Street in Covent Garden and seen public hangings, drawings, quarterings, beheadings. We have a fine tradition of celebrity executions: Charles I, Ann Boleyn, Cranmer. No more, alas. London has lost many of its historic attractions.

'In London we are not so good at assassinations. It's true that Margaret Nicholson tried to stab George III, and it's true that James Hadfield tried to shoot the same monarch, but these were not very serious attempts. The would-be assassins were considered simply to be mad. Hadfield was confined to Bethlem for thirty-nine years until his death. Margaret Nicholson was despatched to the same place but she spent her forty-two years in solitary confinement. Generations later, Bethlem also provided a resting place for Edward Fox who attempted to assassinate Queen Victoria.

'We do much better with mobs; various clergy torn limb from limb in the Peasants' Revolt, a Catholic genocide in the Gordon riots, various bloody persecutions of the Jews. We are good with plagues; the Black Death of 1348, which killed about thirty thousand souls, roughly half the population of London at the time; and we then had the great bubonic plague of 1665, greater in number but smaller in proportion: 110,000 dead, a mere one-third.

'We have had blitzes. We have had terrorist bombs. We have had martyrdoms, burnings at the stake. But they seem so long ago, and they were generally for causes that no longer stir the modern imagination. We have had literary murders: Christopher Marlowe in 1593, in Deptford to escape yet another plague, killed over the failure to pay his bill in a tavern. You will find many contemporary landlords who think his punishment was about right.

'But death is not a literary form. It is formless and always with us; common and ubiquitous, just like sex. A long time ago I had a girlfriend who said there wasn't a single square foot of London where somebody hadn't had sex. I'm sure she was right and I feel the same must be true about death. Every square inch of the city must be infused with mortality. Boadicea, the plague, the Luftwaffe, queer-bashers, gangland shootings, natural causes; they've all done their bit.

'Men die in the street, of heart attacks, of haemorrhages, of knifings, shootings, road accidents. A passing bomb blows them to smithereens. An arsonist torches a cinema full of porn *aficionados*. Old ladies die in council flats, of hypothermia, of fumes from unventilated water heaters, or they're beaten to death by burglars hunting down their life savings. Faces burned in the King's Cross tube fire, lives lost on the river when the *Marchioness* went down. The hospitals that bury their failures. It goes on.

'London has its share of wife murderers, baby killers, sex killers; odd combinations of the above. We are familiar with casual death, with overdoses, impurities, the air bubble locked in the vein. Drunks falling out of trains, coppers shot in the course of routine inquiries. Londoners killed in the crossfire.

'Dylan Thomas continued the long process of drinking himself to death in pubs not far from here, but he had to go to New York to fully realize his aims. Jimi Hendrix ended it all in London, whether accidentally or not, by choking on a cocktail of vomit and drugs, in a house in Notting Hill next door to where Handel had once lived. Kenneth Halliwell killed himself in London too, having first hammered out the brains of his errant "first husband". Here, in Holborn, Thomas Chatterton poisoned himself with arsenic, finding that preferable to literally starving to death when his literary career foundered; also finding it preferable to accepting a meal from his landlady. These artists are often poseurs as well as everything else.

'London lacks one of those truly great sites from which suicides can propel themselves. The railway bridge across Archway Road attracts a few, but we have no famous lover's leap, no equivalent of the Golden Gate Bridge. The Monument, commemorating the Great Fire, used to be a favourite place but the top was eventually caged in 1842. So suicide tends to be an intramural matter, something domestic, performed in bathtubs and bedrooms, a private ritual. There are a few who choose to end it all by throwing themselves under tube trains, and this is a messy end, traumatic for the train driver and for those who see it, but essentially a trivial end. All one really succeeds in doing is irritating a few thousand commuters and making them late for their suppers or their night at the cinema, though I suppose this offers certain desperate people more power than they ever had while alive.

'So if you were going to do the dirty deed, where would you choose? I've always thought that the Telecom Tower, formerly the Post Office Tower, would be a reasonable place from which to launch yourself; unfortunately it's not open to the public. The Whispering Gallery in St Paul's would surely be a spectacular way to go. Imagine yourself falling backwards through all that space, the great dome receding as the wind whips the back of your head and you accelerate towards the cold, solid floor. You'd have an audience, and there'd be people on hand to pray for your soul; but even the most agnostic of us might fret about committing suicide in church.

'The river is a possibility. They say that death by drowning isn't such a bad way to go, that a strange calm comes over the drowning man. Drinking a couple of pints of raw Thames water might be equally lethal, though far less peaceful.

'One might go to the Isle of Dogs, enter a pub, get chatting to some Millwall fans and suggest that there was a homosexual component to their characters. That would be as good as certain death. Being a black man and entering the same pub would probably have much the same effect.'

Stuart walked and talked for forty minutes or more. His unrehearsed and unstoppable flow had a relentlessness about it that kept most of his audience with him, though he did notice that a couple of the widows had slipped away, the talk of death too much for them. But for the others, his macabre talk had a grim appeal.

When he paused once, for breath and for effect, an old man in a shiny Charlotteville baseball cap got up the courage to say, 'Excuse me, sir, I have the feelin' we may be on the incorrect tour,' but when Stuart stared at him with flaming, intense eyes he added, 'Not that I mind. This is entertainin' as all get out.'

Stuart carried on with his spiel, regaling them with stories about the suicide of Judy Garland in the bathroom of a mews house near Sloane Square, where he'd once been to a party.

Finally, and even he wasn't quite sure of its relevance, he told them about the Plague Piper, an itinerant musician who in plague-ridden London was found asleep in a doorway, tossed on to a death cart, dumped into a mass grave and only saved from being buried alive by his dog who knew what the men of the plague did not, that his master wasn't dead, simply dead drunk.

Two of the group applauded at the end of this story but Stuart stared daggers at them and told them it was no laughing matter.

He said, 'In the end there's no need to *look* for death, much less look for a methodology. The modern London walker need do nothing but keep walking, keep on the move. Wherever he goes death will come looking for him, and it will surely find him.'

The tour didn't so much end as abruptly cease. Stuart had said all he had to say. He looked at the faces of the group; some were blank, some confused, but most were still alert and demanding. They wanted more, but he realized he had no more to give them. He felt empty, a bit of a fraud and a show-off. He had no encore.

Colin was looking at him in appalled awe, and Stuart wondered what Colin would have to say when he got back to the office. Would he describe this little side show to the other guides? Would he tell Anita?

Stuart wanted very much to be somewhere else. At that moment a black cab pulled up beside him and let out its passenger. Stuart turned his back on the tour group, got into the now empty taxi and departed, giving a regal wave as he went.

One of the adolescent girls said to the other, 'You know I bet he'd have been a real good person to ask about the tree where Marc Bolan died,' but it was too late. The walkers were left in some confusion, certain that they'd seen something unusual but not absolutely sure that they'd had their money's worth. Poor Colin, hapless and speechless, fluttered his arms a little and tried hard to get the group's attention.

# COTTAGE

Apart from when he'd been at big football matches or rock gigs, Mick had never seen such a crowded men's public toilet. At first there appeared to be a queue, three or four men skulking about the entrance as though waiting for a urinal to come free, but then Mick saw that there already *were* free urinals, and that the men were waiting for something quite different.

He didn't object. It was OK by him. In a way it was very useful. It gave him cover, a reason to be standing around doing nothing, while in fact keeping an eye on his next victim. For Robin Lawton, the last man on Gabby's list, was in position at the far end of the row of urinals, poised, going about his business. He had his back to Mick but it was apparent from his body language, from the steady, regular movement of his hand, arm and shoulder, that he was masturbating, coaxing himself to an erection that could be displayed to his fellow cottagers.

Lawton was a slight man, short and lean, but athletically built without being muscled. He looked about fifty years old, with cropped hair the colour of brushed aluminium. He had on standard cruising gear, tight blue jeans and a dapper leather jacket. He looked more obviously gay than most of the men in there. He was giving out more signals. The rest of them were a varied and unmatching group, of many ages, many shapes, many skin colours. One or two were advertising their sexuality like Lawton but the majority seemed very ordinary indeed, very straight. They did not look like the sort of men Mick would have expected to find eyeing up other men in public toilets, but it was not a subject he knew or wanted to know much about.

Mick had followed Lawton to this place, followed him along the embankment, under a railway bridge, down the dark concrete steps into the toilet. If Lawton thought he was being followed he didn't show it, or perhaps he didn't mind. As Mick walked into the Gents he was aware that his presence had caused a temporary halt to whatever had been going on. All activity ceased for a moment while the inhabitants made sure he wasn't some sort of invader. But after he'd stood there for a while, immobile and unthreatening, a palpable relaxation spread through the place and the men resumed their activities.

There was a lot of looking around, staring, attempts to make eye contact. All attempts were furtive, some were rejected, but some of them must have been successful since a couple of guys paired up and left the toilet together. Soon after that the action became more intense than just looks and glances. There was a steady rhythm of masturbation, of men playing with their cocks and brandishing them. Then as one or two of the men felt brave or safe or aroused enough, they reached over and touched someone else's.

Mick watched in casual disbelief. He had never seen anything like it. Only in London, he thought, though he suspected this could not be literally true. He felt he should have been disgusted by the spectacle but there was something curiously tame and friendly about the erotic exchange. It had none of the passion or ferocity of good sex. The men were touching each other in a spirit of laddish co-operation, doing each other small but significant favours, like giving someone directions or giving them a light for their cigarette.

Nobody spoke, but a couple of men communicated well enough to take themselves into a cubicle, from which, after a moment, there came a fierce steady banging noise that didn't conform to Mick's idea of the sound sex should make.

Elsewhere action had progressed from hand to mouth. The man next to Lawton, a bearded, enormously fat man in tennis gear, was leaning over and devouring Lawton's cock. Lawton's face showed enjoyment but in a watchful, detached, half-hearted sort of way. He was holding back, not wanting to submit entirely to the experience. He kept looking round the toilet, possibly keeping an eye out for intruders, but also as though he was on the lookout for a better, more interesting offer.

Then he caught Mick's eye, caught him watching. Mick's immediate reaction was to turn away but he forced himself to return the look. At first the expression on Lawton's face seemed hostile rather than sexual, but that, apparently, was part of the game. After a while his mouth curved into a slight, apologetic smile, as though he was well aware of the absurdity of his situation, of this location, of the man now on his knees in front of him.

Suddenly he grabbed the man's head as though clutching a football and pulled it hard towards him. He thrust his pelvis into the man's face, and although these actions now indicated a degree of sexual abandon, his face remained more or less impassive and he kept looking at Mick throughout the whole episode.

When he'd finished Lawton ambled away leaving the fat man still on his knees, wiping his mouth. Someone swiftly moved in to take Lawton's place. Lawton collected himself and walked over to the sinks. For a moment Mick thought his quarry was about to leave but, no, he remained there at the sinks and took an unnecessarily long time washing his hands, constantly looking up at the mirror to check out the continuing action behind him. There was plenty to entertain the most demanding voyeur. A young black man with a radical haircut and a thick cock was letting two grey-haired men take turns sucking him.

Lawton finished washing his hands. There was obviously not going to be a towel or hand drier in a place like this, so he stood shaking his hands, just a couple of feet away from Mick. They looked at each other again. Mick thought Lawton was about to speak, but instead he made a complicated, articulate sweep with his head that said he was leaving now and that he wanted Mick to come with him. Mick nodded. He let Lawton walk out of the toilet, then followed him, let him walk some twenty or thirty yards ahead until he took up position by the embankment railings and waited for Mick to catch up. Mick took his time but eventually sidled up to Lawton and asked, 'You got a place?'

'Yes,' Lawton said a little hoarsely, a little awkwardly. 'It's not far.'

Mick said nothing more to indicate agreement, but Lawton started walking and Mick followed. After a while they fell into step, and although conversation was neither easy nor strictly necessary for what either of them had in mind, Lawton became surprisingly, nervously talkative.

'You get all sorts in there,' he said. 'Talk about "Chance encounters in the illicit crypts of homosexual adventure." Flags of all nations. We had a man in a kilt in there the other week. And a young chap with a ring through his cock. Can't say I found it very attractive but it makes a change.'

He seemed to be waiting for Mick to respond, hold up his end of the conversation, but when Mick was silent Lawton continued, 'Best thing, of course, is the married man. They're in there with a mouthful of spunk, then half an hour later they're home kissing their wives. I love that.'

He looked at Mick in a way that was more enquiring than accusatory. Was he suggesting that he thought Mick was a married man? If so, Mick didn't mind. At least it proved that he didn't look like a poof.

'Do you work out?' Lawton asked.

Mick shook his head.

'But you're a big lad. You must do something to get those biceps.'

Mick was finding this unsettling. He didn't mind a bit of

flattery, and he was quite proud of his body, but compliments from someone like Lawton weren't what he was looking for. He was tempted to give him a good going over there and then. The place was deserted enough, but he decided to wait a little longer.

'This place we're going to,' Lawton said, 'it's a little unusual.'

Mick immediately suspected the worst. He wondered what the hell Lawton had in mind, but he knew that he would have to find out.

'I'm sort of a property developer,' Lawton said. 'I find old buildings with a bit of character, say a warehouse or small factory, occasionally an old church or chapel, and I convert them.'

Mick wondered why he was being told this. Where were they headed? An abandoned abattoir? A dungeon? A sewage works? They walked on, into a network of tight, riverside streets, an illogical conglomeration of new building-sites and ancient masonry, of arches and stairways, barred windows and fire escapes. Then suddenly they had arrived in front of a broad, ugly two-storey industrial building and Lawton said this was the place.

The building, possibly an old machine shop, had large areas of tall, metal-framed windows so that the walls were more glass than brick. There were areas that had been boarded up, other areas that had been patched with corrugated iron. Even if it was renovated out of all recognition, Mick still couldn't imagine anyone in their right mind wanting to live in a place like this. He followed Lawton warily.

A flight of half a dozen steps led up to a pair of heavy steel doors. Lawton rattled his keys in the lock and opened one of the doors for them to enter. They walked into a massive unlit space that Lawton gradually illuminated with a series of spot-lights suspended on metal cords.

The place looked both infinitely worked on and strangely unfinished. The walls had long expanses of unpainted plaster and yet pictures had been hung. Elsewhere metal struts and steel frames had been gleefully exposed, but the wooden floor was new, blond, clean and frosted. A couple of black and white pony skins were laid out at opposite ends of the space and a series of furniture pieces had been arranged as though in an art gallery. The furniture was wild and ugly and looked like it had been bolted together from lumps of concrete, driftwood, glass and scrap metal. The glass had shatter patterns running through it. All the metal had dangerously sharp edges. There was nothing else: no carpets, no curtains, no upholstery, no softness.

'You live here?' Mick asked.

'Sometimes. It serves as a showroom too.'

'Yeah?'

'We sell the whole package, the apartment, the interior design, the furniture, the art.'

Mick stared at a strange metal hump at his feet and said, 'Is that furniture or art?'

'It's both,' Lawton said. 'It's a work of art that you happen to be able to sit on.'

Mick surveyed the space and couldn't suppress a snigger.

'People really want to live like this?'

'Actually, yes,' Lawton said frostily.

'Only in London.'

'No, not only in London. Also in New York, Barcelona, Milan. Anyway, I suspect neither of us is here for a chat about international design.'

Mick nodded agreement and Lawton slapped his hands together to show he meant business. It turned out that the metal hump was a kind of chest. Lawton opened the hinged lid to show Mick the contents, and Mick looked down on a mad selection of sex toys.

They were mostly dildos in all varieties, in pink and black, in rubber and metal and wood, from the slenderly boyish to the truly monstrous. Some were realistic, if insanely exaggerated, attempts to model the human penis, complete with veins and sometimes even balls and retractable foreskins. Others were more abstract, more symbolic, in polished gold and silver. Some vibrated, some had studs and straps and rubber friction pads.

'With a little encouragement I can accommodate any of these,' Lawton said.

Mick looked at the largest of them, a gargantuan model with the girth of a beer can, and found himself impressed. He looked at the rest of the contents, at the butt plugs, dog collars, nipple clamps, whips, and a large tub of something called Sex Grease.

'After that I'm ready for anything,' Lawton said. 'Fists, feet, anything that comes to hand really. You can use your imagination.'

He looked to Mick for some sort of reassurance or at least complicity. None was forthcoming and yet he found something encouraging in the solid, blank meanness of Mick's face.

'I like a bit of chat too,' Lawton said. 'You can call me any filthy name under the sun. But words are never quite enough. Sticks and stones. I have the capacity to take a great deal of punishment. And if I squeal a little, or even a lot, that doesn't necessarily mean I'm having a bad time. But I don't need to gabble on like this, do I? I can tell you understand.'

Having stated at least some of the rules he began to unzip his leather jacket. Mick could see he was wearing nothing underneath, but at first his chest was in shadow, the flesh obscured. Then he turned so that light fell across his body and Mick saw that the skin of his torso was scored with weals, bruises, fresh livid grazes, and what looked like cigarette burns. Lawton stood there, pleased with himself, showing himself off. Instinctively Mick looked away, and Lawton was pleased again with the reaction, pleased that he was able to shock.

'If you don't like what you see,' he said, 'you can always rearrange it.'

Mick considered the offer. Lawton unbelted his jeans and pushed them down his thighs to reveal more of the same, more traces of previous encounters, previous users, as though a diagram of sick desire had been doodled on his flesh, turned into a map of scarred skin and torched nerve endings, a city of delicious pain. Even his cock looked bruised and knocked about, stretched and raw.

He kicked off his jeans but left the leather jacket round his shoulders, stood a few moments in Mick's gaze. To Mick's alarm, though not exactly surprise, Lawton reached for the tub of Sex Grease and started lubricating himself in readiness. He was extremely thorough, and when he'd finished he made a move towards Mick. It was an odd move, somewhere between a lunge and an embrace. In any other circumstances Mick would have found nothing remotely threatening in the action. Lawton was a queasy, feeble thing, scarcely worthy of Mick's attention, and yet Mick did now feel threatened and so he lashed out. He was aware that there was something weak and effete about the punch he delivered to Lawton's face, something emasculated and unconsidered. Lawton felt it too. He stopped in his tracks and he stood still, not unappreciative of being hit, but nevertheless moved to say, 'You can do it a lot harder than that, I hope.'

His words were meant to be provocative and taunting, and Mick was duly provoked. He punched Lawton again, in the stomach this time, and the punch was delivered with much more strength and focus. Lawton doubled up and sank to his knees. His face showed that he enjoyed the blow, but Mick didn't like it at all. Now that he was confronted with someone who wanted to soak up his anger and aggression, he felt uncomfortable, unbalanced. Besides, more crucially, he was having a lot of trouble believing that Lawton had raped Gabby.

'Have you ever been married?' he asked.

Even through his pain Lawton found it a laughable question. 'What do you think I am?'

Mick didn't tell him. He said, 'You ever had sex with a woman?'

'No. I've never put my cock in a tin of stale tuna fish either.'

'What a foul thing to say.'

Mick considered hitting him again but he couldn't link up the right muscles and synapses to make it happen. He wondered what Judy would think if she could see him now. Might she be watching him again? Would she want him to hit Lawton for having insulted her sex? Or would she disapprove of hitting such an obvious weakling? Perhaps, he thought, conscience was no more than this, the simple feeling of being watched, by God or by a half-Japanese bookshop assistant, someone who will judge you, hold you responsible, who might think less of you if they believed you were doing the wrong thing.

'I think homosexuality's really peculiar,' said Mick. 'I mean I can just about understand that two blokes might fall in love. Love is blind, et cetera. It's a sort of inexplicable, abstract thing, and I can see how it might make you fall for a bloke. And if it did then I can see how you might want to be with that bloke, and maybe live together. And I can see why you might share a bed, and I can see you might put your arms around each other. But I really can't see why you would suddenly want to have things shoved up your anus.'

Lawton looked at him sourly.

'I mean, buggery's a funny thing, isn't it? Because some people would say that buggery degrades the person who gets buggered. And in that respect they might say it was like rape; the victim supposedly being the one who's degraded. But I don't think of it like that. The rapist is degraded just as much as the victim, and as far as I can see the one doing the buggering is humiliated every bit as much as the one being buggered.'

Lawton opened his mouth to say something but Mick wouldn't let him speak.

'I know what you're going to say,' Mick said. 'You're going to say that some people *like* being degraded. Now that's a tough one.'

'Oh dear,' Lawton said. 'I suspect you're going to be a bit of a disappointment to me, aren't you?'

'You don't know the half of it,' Mick said, and he walked away from Lawton and prowled around the room in search of a telephone. He found one. It was surprisingly plain and orthodox given the location, and he tapped in Gabby's number. The phone rang a dozen times before it was answered.

'Oh, Mick,' she said, startled. 'Hello. I was just on my way out.'

She could hardly be so very surprised that he was ringing her, yet she sounded astonished, as though he was a long-lost boyfriend calling from Australia after years of absence.

'Going anywhere nice?' he asked.

'Just work,' she said, and he could tell at once she was lying.

'Then I'll not keep you,' he said. 'But before you go, I've just got a couple more questions to ask you.'

'Not again,' Gabby said, and she let out a fake, weary, overstated sigh that accused him of being thick and tiresome, but Mick wasn't going to fall for it.

'These guys who raped you,' he said. 'Was one of them a skinny little guy, cropped grey hair, moustache, say fifty years old?'

'Possibly,' she said angrily.

'You're not telling me you don't remember.'

'No, I'm not telling you that.'

'And maybe he was a little bit camp-looking,' Mick continued.

'Camp?'

'You know, like a homosexual.'

'I know what camp means, all right? Look, this man *raped* me.'

'Yeah, well, maybe he was having a night off from being a homosexual.'

'Are you trying to make some sick joke?'

'It's no joke. It's just that I've got him here and—'

'You've got him where?'

'Here. We're in his flat. It's a right fun house. He's on his knees, just spitting distance away, and you know, I've hit him a couple of times and that's gone fairly well, but I'm not all that sure I'm doing the right thing. You see he really doesn't fit the bill as your typical rapist.'

'He was on the list, wasn't he?'

'Yeah, but couldn't the list be wrong?'

'I don't think so.'

'OK then, but just to make me feel better, just to put my mind at rest, I was wondering if maybe you'd like to have a word with him, see if you recognize the voice.'

'You want me to talk to him?' she yelled. 'Are you out of your fuckin' mind?'

'OK, sorry, I can see why you wouldn't want to talk to him.' Mick was trying hard to sound sane and reasonable, and was well aware he was neither of those things. 'So how about this, since he's the last one on the list, I thought maybe you'd have some special requests, some special punishments you'd like me to hand out to him, because this is your big chance. He's game for anything this boy, and actually he's got some scars you'd be bound to recognize, and I thought you could listen in while I get to work, get the full flavour of the event.'

'What's the matter with you, Mick? Have you snapped or what?'

'Not me,' Mick said, making a great effort to hold himself in check, to prove her wrong. But he didn't find it easy to keep this whole performance together, and part of him suspected she was right. Something *had* snapped, or at least been stretched permanently out of shape. It would have been easy enough to scream down the phone at Gabby, easier still to work out his frustrations on the poor wretch who was kneeling a couple of yards away just waiting for some more punishment. Nevertheless he spoke calmly into the phone.

'I have some doubts, Gabby,' he said. 'I have some doubts about this list of yours. I have doubts about what went on with you and these six men. I have serious doubts about whether I've been doing the right thing here in London. I think maybe you think I'm an idiot, or maybe somebody else does. One thing I'm sure of, if this guy here raped you then I'm a . . .'

He didn't get to finish the sentence. What he'd said had made a big impact down the end of the line in Sheffield. It had

295

caused a transformation. Gabby was suddenly very talkative, very concerned, very eager to be nice to him, to smooth his feathers. He could hear a whole flurry of tender coercion coming from her, and although he wasn't listening very closely he heard her say something about love. He covered the mouthpiece and said to Lawton, 'Bring your arse over here.'

Lawton, naturally, did as he was told, smiled coquettishly, shuffled across the room. He knelt in front of Mick, head down, buttocks raised and spread, and Mick took the telephone receiver and slapped Lawton on the backside with it. Mick could sense Lawton's disappointment. He had anticipated much more and much worse.

'Actually,' Mick said, 'I think some of this furniture's quite good.' Seconds later he was out of the building, while in Sheffield Gabby was left wondering how she'd got cut off.

# THE WALKER'S DIARY

## THE KNOWLEDGE

I think I have at last discovered my real reason for walking the streets of London. Perhaps it should have been obvious all along. It seems I am not looking for adventure, for love, for sex. I am not trying to satisfy my curiosity, not trying to reclaim the city. And ultimately, despite my hopes for posterity, I am not walking London in order to create a literary work. No. Quite simply, I am looking for death: my own.

[Anita laughed like a drain as she read these words.]

Lightermen operating in the Port of London, ferrying cargoes by tug or barge, the aristocracy of the docks, seven thousand of them employed after the war. Large sacks of animal bones, donkey, cow, camel, sent in from North Africa heading for the mills at Bow to be crushed into fertilizer. Sacks bursting open, bones picked clean, alive with green beetles.

A herd of cattle thundering up York Way from King's Cross, being driven to the slaughterhouses in Market Road.

Antique shops, museums, flea markets, boot sales: windows through to the past, conduits through which history leaks out.

Boadicea's Hill, a mound on top of Parliament Hill, said to be where Boadicea was buried, although scholars differ on this one. St Paul's Cathedral built on the site of a pagan temple dedicated to Diana. When Wren built St Paul's he found remnants of a circular temple and ox bones used in sacrifices.

The Tower of London built on a holy hill, Bryn Gwyn, the severed head of the hero-god Bran supposedly buried there.

Mudlarks wading through the Thames, often children, searching for salvage. Shoremen working in gangs down the sewers. Couldn't work singly because of the killer rats. Coins dropped down. Sometimes when it rained the sewers would fill to the top with water. The story of the Hampstead monsters – the offspring of a sow who wandered into the open end of a sewer, found a spot she liked, gave birth to her litter, created a subterranean herd, living in stench and darkness, feeding off sewage, breeding.

I stopped for lunch in a greasy spoon. Behind me there were three young people, at least they looked young to me, two men, one woman. They looked stylish and moneyed as though they might work for a record or video company.

One of the men said, 'So I'm trying to get off the tube, right, and there's this man blocking my way, so I push past him, you know, the way you do on the tube, it was no big deal, and after I've got past him he punches me really hard in the back and says, "Learn to say excuse me, shithead." I was worried. He looked as though he would have killed me soon as look at me.'

Then the other man said, 'Well, I got mugged coming through Soho last week. It was late. I was fairly drunk. I guess I must have looked a bit of a target. These three really young kids appeared out of nowhere, surrounded me and one of them said, "Give me your wallet or I'll kill you." So obviously I handed over my wallet. I mean, I don't think he really would have killed me, but you can't take any chances in London these days, can you?'

Then the woman said, 'Well, a friend of mine, in Putney, a burglar got into her bedroom while she was asleep, held a gun to her head, kept her captive till the next morning and raped her half a dozen times. She's still in therapy.'

There was a short silence then the two men said simultaneously, 'You win, we can't compete with that,' and all three of them laughed very, very loudly.

The coronation of Richard I. The Jews have been forbidden to enter the Abbey and take part in the celebrations. They may be essential to the wealth of the country, their presence may have been encouraged by William I because of their financial acumen, but they are still not like us, and they demand a high price for the help. They are usurers. Their religion demands strange rituals. Their exclusion seems only natural. However, one or two of them, apparently more knowing than the rest, have come to the celebrations, believing that they will be tolerated given that they have come with expensive gifts. And sure enough the king himself is prepared to be tolerant. He indulges them quite willingly, enjoys their company, but he has reckoned without certain zealous elements in the court, who, discovering this Jewish presence, immediately seek physical retribution. A good beating is administered to the Jews right there at the coronation, and what happens in the Abbey soon spreads to the world at large.

What better way to celebrate a new reign than to take part in a pogrom? Soon a full-scale purge is taking place in the streets of London. While coronation celebrations continue in the Abbey, a mob outside is setting fire to the houses of Jewish settlers and murdering the occupants as they run out in terror. The king does his best to ignore what he knows is taking place, and he doesn't find it so hard. After all, the Jews are not true citizens. They do not have the full protection of his laws. And yet the noise from the streets, the baying of the mob and the screams of the victims, is loud enough to quite put a damper on the festivities. The king does what any man might do in that situation. He tells his minstrels to play louder and drown the terrible noise from outside.

Postman's Park, the former churchyard of St Botolph, Aldersgate, and on the wall a series of plaques commemorating heroic

299

but ordinary deaths: Alice Ayres, who saved three children from a burning house in Union Street, Borough, but died in the process. Thomas Simpson, who died of exhaustion after rescuing people who'd fallen through the ice on Highgate Ponds. Mary Rogers, a stewardess on the *Stella* who gave up her life belt and voluntarily went down with her ship.

I look at the Millbank Tower and Centrepoint and I wonder why we in London have never dreamed up a Godzilla, a cheap science fiction destroyer of cities.

John Alington, a British farmer and altruist, took seriously his role as educator of his workers. He created a model of the world in his farm pond and used it to teach his employees geography. Then in 1851 he said he would take them to the Great Exhibition, but before they went he instructed them to build a large-scale model of the streets from King's Cross to Hyde Park, so they'd know the route when they arrived in London. The model was a complete failure, out of scale, the workmanship shoddy. It scarcely at all resembled the London that Alington knew. It was clear to him that if his men were not capable of building a model of the city, they would be quite incapable of finding their way around it. He summarily cancelled their trip to London.

At the top of a distant staircase in the Victoria and Albert, there's an intricate scale model of Vauxhall Gardens. The reality is gone. A hundred years of pleasure, of promenading and feasting, of nightingales and fountains, pavilions and statuary, temples, fireworks and on one occasion a re-staging of the Battle of Waterloo.

In the Museum of London, a model of mid-seventeenth-century London, and as a crowd gathers round the model the lights go down and a voice on tape starts reading from *Pepys'*

*Diary*, describing the Fire, and gradually all over the darkened city little electrical lights begin to flicker, impersonating fire.

Another town with fire gaps. After the American firestorm raid on Tokyo, Hiroshima prepares itself for the worst. Expecting incendiary raids they create a series of fire gaps in the town. Wooden buildings are demolished to leave large blank areas cleared of debris, places where there is nothing to burn. They think they are ready for the coming fire. They have no idea. Oh, Judy.

In Lamb's Conduit Street, an undertaker's. I can see that undertakers must always have trouble deciding what to put in their shop windows: flowers? marble headstones? skulls and old bones? This one had solved the problem neatly; antique maps of old London.

I thought of Xanadu and Troy and Babylon and Manhattan, those mythical cities with their palaces and their projects, their structurings and enfoldings. And I thought that London is mythical too, created in the image of each of its inhabitants, newly imagined with each new citizen, with each new attempt to describe it.

As I walk I realize I am no longer the person I was. The middle-aged man in the cashmere overcoat who looks at his reflection in the shop window would be unrecognizable to the boy, the youth, the young man he has previously been. I think that these younger selves would have been contemptuous of that man, complacently certain that they would never end up like him. Probably I'm no longer even the man that Judy fell in love with. I'm certainly not the man that Anita married.

I know too that it is not merely a question of change and growth, not even of decay, but rather of demolitions, regroupings, blottings out. The opinions, the tastes, the most passionately held beliefs have all disappeared in a blitz of slum clearance and redevelopment. Yes, a man is like a city, a site of erasures, of subsidence, in-fill, subdivision and occasional preservation orders. But there is no blueprint, no foolproof map, no essential guide book.

I feel at home in the city, I feel part of its fabric. It feels as alive as I do, but with a much longer life-span. London wasn't built in a day, and I know that it will long outlive me, though in what, and how recognizable a form, I have no idea.

What do people do when they've fulfilled their ambitions? When they've sailed the Atlantic, or made their millions, won the World Cup, or settled down happily with a wife who loves them? Well, in some cases they do it all over again, so that they achieve extra satisfaction from having sailed the Atlantic in both directions, from multiplying their millions, from having retained the World Cup. But to be settled with a wife and a job and way of life is not simply an act of achievement, not a one-off, rather it's a balancing act, an on-going achievement, a feat of management, maintenance and continuity. And I am no longer capable of balancing.

What could possibly replace my walking? If my walks around London were designed to fill some spiritual void, then what would fill it when the task was at last completed? What can a man do when he's done London? Death seems like an attractive option. Actually, it seems like the only option.

I'd been walking in Southfields and was completely worn out and couldn't face public transport, so I hailed a taxi to go home. He was a talkative driver and I wasn't strong enough or brave enough to tell him to shut up. And after a while he'd obviously convinced himself that I was a man he could share his innermost thoughts with.

He said, 'Supposing a man breaks into your house, a man with a gun, a madman. You're at home, sitting quietly with your wife and one of your kids. The madman makes you an offer, gives you a choice. He tells you he's going to kill someone, either your wife or your kid. But he's not sure which, it's all the same to him. And so he wants you to decide for him.'

'Is this a joke?' I asked.

'No,' said the driver. 'It's a moral conundrum. You have the choice of losing a spouse or a child: which do you go for?'

'What if I don't make a choice?'

'Then he'll kill both of them.'

'What if I don't have any children?'

'Then you have to imagine.'

I imagined, and said, 'I'd let him kill *me*.'

'No, no, no.' The driver was getting quite irritated. 'That's not an option. You have to live knowing that you're responsible for the death of either your missus or your child. And you mightn't have all this time to think about it.'

I gave the appearance of thinking long and hard about it, and then I said, 'You know, I think it's precisely because I've wanted to avoid having to make such a moral decision that my wife and I have never had children.'

He turned round and said sarcastically, 'You're a funny man, aren't you?'

I tried to look as though I saw nothing remotely funny about what I'd said, hoping that would shut him up. But instead he started telling me his views on the problem, which of course was all he'd ever wanted to do in the first place. It had something to do with wives being more easily replaceable than children. I wasn't listening. I was thinking how great it would be to find someone who could end it all for me. I was thinking that I might go home now, walk into my house and there he'd be, this madman with a gun, offering me absurd choices, and I'd say, 'OK, go ahead, pull the trigger. Thanks.'

What would the intruder look like? Big, of course, young probably, demented-looking, cropped hair, low forehead, bull-dog neck. Black or white? Wearing jeans and T-shirt? Leather jacket? A suit? Terrorist gear? And what does he say? Is he chatty in his madness? Does he have an accent? South London? East End? Estuary?

I found it all too easy to picture the scene, but I had no ending for it, no punchline. Did the madman really pull the trigger? Was the gun really loaded? Was it even a real gun? Or was he just using it for effect? Was he just another London loser with an image problem and a chip on his shoulder? I hoped not. I wanted him to be real. I needed him to be efficient.

I realized that the end of my wandering should be, not simply the blotting out of the city, but also the blotting out of the self. When the map was all blacked in I'd be ready to be snuffed out. And I know I don't have to plan it. It's there waiting for me, something suicidal, although the inquest won't call it that, but something that gets the job done just the same. Tomorrow I take to the streets for one last time, the last stretch, the last ten miles. And when it's done he'll be there waiting for me, my fate, my killer. Hello, there. Good to see you. Been waiting long?

When a man is tired of London he's ready for a bullet.

# READY

Anita rubbed her eyes, turned away from the screen and experienced what she would later describe as a failure of the emotions. So that was meant to be the answer, was it, the supposed 'reason' for Stuart's new-found serenity? He was content because he had no more worries, and he had no more worries because he had decided to kill himself. He was on the way to a suicide. He was indulging his own mortality.

She was unsure what her reaction should be. She knew she could have been furious. Suicide wasn't at all the simple, easy thing that Stuart had described. It was always a big, ugly explosion in the life of those who were left behind. How could he do that to her? How could he abandon her? The simple way out for him would be impossibly difficult for her. And how could he find her so easy to abandon? Their marriage wasn't plain sailing, but leaving your wife behind should be a cause for some regret, some pain. Her existence might not be enough to keep him here, but it ought surely to be enough to make the leaving that much more difficult. Yes, she might have reacted that way.

And she knew that she might have felt sorry for him. Anyone who contemplates suicide must, by definition, be in terrible pain. She genuinely did not want Stuart to be in that state. How could she not be saddened? How could she not feel a sense of guilt that her own love and concern weren't sufficient to staunch that pain?

Or perhaps she could have felt worse still that she'd had no inkling of how Stuart was feeling, of what a desperate state he was in. She might have recognized this as a failure in herself, as an inability to know what her husband was feeling, and worse, an inability to be able to do anything about it.

She might have had her own suicidal feelings. She might have felt like a murderess. She might have looked at that last entry and been terrified. The tomorrow to which it referred was now upon them. Stuart was out there somewhere in London, concluding and completing his task; looking for trouble, for a way out, for someone to kill him. She might have feared that London was only too full of such people. And she might have thought it was not too late. She might have thought that she still had time to save him. She might have got in her car and driven wildly, recklessly, hopelessly, across the city, trying to find him and save him.

But in the event she felt and did none of these things. She felt no anger, no sympathy, no guilt, no sense of failure. She simply went back to the computer, checked the list of files in order to make certain that she'd found them all, printed them out, and sure enough she had. The full story, such as it was, was in front of her. She gathered the printed sheets together, stacked them neatly on the desk, lined up the edges carefully. So there it was, her husband's secret diary, his great unfinished work, his confession and suicide note, and she realized that she didn't believe a word of it. She looked at her watch. She calculated that he'd be home soon and she'd be more than ready for him.

# TUBE

Mick sat on the bed in his room at the Dickens. The old melancholy eddied around him. The window was open and the cold air prickled the skin on his bare arms. He looked at his watch. It was late morning. He had been there all night, not sleeping, not even dozing, just listening to the sounds of the city. It had been depressingly quiet. He had wanted to hear the squeal of car tyres, police sirens, screams, gunshots, signs of life, but all he'd heard were a couple of far-away radios and the noise of cats fighting or mating.

He had done what he came to London to do. It was over. He knew he ought to be feeling many things: relief, release, contentment at a job well done. In fact he felt nothing. He was beyond feeling. As soon as he could stir himself he would leave this hotel, leave London and go back to Sheffield, though he knew that things there would not be as he had left them. Still, that was where he came from, and it was the place he had to go back to.

He struggled to pull himself together. He wanted some air. He got up from the bed, put on his jacket and went out of the hotel, and as he hit the pavement he realized he didn't have to go back there at all. He could walk to St Pancras, get on a train and that would be it. His gun was still in the bedside cupboard but it could stay there. He didn't need it. In a way he never had. It had done a job but he felt good to know that he'd never had to fire it at anyone. The gun had been a persuader but everything he'd done, he'd done himself, through his own ability and wit. There was a jigsaw and an *A–Z* in his room too, and a book called *Unreliable London*, but he wouldn't be needing those either.

The street was not empty. There were quite a few people going to work, a builder's van was arriving at a house across the street, a postman was making his round. The day was sweetly ordinary, and Mick realized just how tired he was.

They say you never hear the bullet that hits you, and certainly the car that ran down Mick Wilton was on him before he was even aware of the engine noise. All he felt was a metallic scything of his legs from under him, as though someone had clubbed him behind the knees. The big bulk of the car had caught him only glancingly but it was more than enough to put him on the deck, and then a number of men were crowding around him, each one scrambling for the chance to grab him or kick him. He fought back and reckoned that he landed a couple of good kicks of his own, but there was no way he could win. In the end numbers meant everything. He wasn't even sure his gun would have been any use to him.

Then something short and metallic landed behind his left ear and he saw lights and stars that were no part of the London landscape. He was dazed, close to passing out, but he fought to stop himself. Hurriedly, inexpertly, a bag was put over his head and then he was being stowed into the boot of the car that had run him down. Somebody tried to hit him again but missed, and even as the boot lid slammed shut above him, something told Mick that he was dealing with amateurs.

He could tell by the engine noise that the car was a Mercedes, a much classier job than the one he had back in Sheffield, and not some tarted-up, spoilered, pimp's car either, something more executive, more of a director's wagon. It was driven smoothly, unhurriedly, but from the way it hung on the suspension he could tell it had a full load, five or six men inside and, of course, one in the boot.

The journey seemed endless. Then the ride got rough. They

were no longer on tarmac, but driving over mud and grass, and Mick heard the tyres crunch on gravel. The car stopped, he heard voices and he was fished out of the boot and made to walk a short distance through the open air to a doorway into some sort of building. The air inside wasn't as warm as it would have been in a house or office, and he sensed that he was in a large space – a shed or workshop, perhaps another of Robin Lawton's property developments.

He heard doors closing behind him and he was led across a wide empty floor to a corner of the building, and made to step up into a smaller, more confined space. Once inside, his hands and feet were tied. Again he could tell that whoever was doing the tying up was new to the job and when the ropes were in place he was pushed down on to a small upholstered seat and the bag was removed from his head. He blinked at six faces that were moderately familiar. They were the faces of his six victims, Gabby's six attackers, but before he could look any of them in the eye one of them punched him in the mouth. It was Philip Masterson, the man Mick had forced to jump off London Bridge. Mick saw Masterson's left hand, the one with the broken finger, was still strapped up. The right hand, however, as Mick had discovered, was perfectly usable.

'I've been looking forward to that,' Masterson said.

A voice behind him, one that Mick didn't recognize at first, said, 'Don't get too carried away. We don't want him unconscious.'

'Don't we?' asked Masterson.

'No, we don't.'

Masterson resisted the temptation to hit Mick again, but it was a struggle for him.

Mick had a moment to become aware of his surroundings and saw that they were in the carriage of a tube train. Clearly the train was not in service. The seats were ripped and most of the windows were smashed, and perhaps the carriage had been brought to this place to be repaired and renovated. The automatic doors were jammed open and the lights weren't working. There were some fluorescent tubes far away in the roof of the building, but little illumination seeped down to the interior of the carriage.

Even though it was not a real train, even though it wasn't crowded, even though it wasn't in a tunnel beneath the ground, Mick felt a familiar claustrophobia closing in on him, although he was still smart enough to realize that claustrophobia might be the least of his problems. He caught the eye of Robin Lawton, the man whose backside he'd slapped only a few hours earlier.

'I don't think we should have taken the bag from over his head,' Lawton said. 'Now he knows who we all are.'

'That's right. I want him to know.'

It was Jonathan Sands who spoke, the marine insurance man and boat owner. He had taken on the role of leader, something for which he apparently thought he had a gift.

'Why on earth do you want him to know?' Lawton asked weakly.

Sands said, 'Because we have to show people like this that they can't just attack us, that we aren't scared of them, that we're brave enough and strong enough to fight back.'

Lawton looked around him as though checking for possible exits, getting ready to make a quick escape. He said, 'Look, this really isn't my argument. He didn't do anything to me. He hardly touched me. The worst he did was make a phonecall without paying for it.'

'Oh, come on, Lawton,' Sands said with disgust. 'Don't be such a wimp. You were lucky, that's all. He might just as easily have beaten you up, humiliated you, destroyed your property, the things you've worked for and care about.'

From the way Sands talked it seemed that the damage to his boat had been far more painful to him than the damage to his body.

'But the point is, he didn't,' Lawton insisted.

'Oh give it a rest, Lawton.'

It was Justin Carr who interrupted this time. He was looking far more self-possessed than when Mick had last seen him, not naked, not singing 'Maybe It's Because I'm A Londoner'. He had found a small area of the carriage where he could pace and look good. He smoked a cigarette elegantly and languidly, his manner conveying just the right blend of toughness and sensitivity to win over an imagined audience.

'However, much as I hate to admit it, Lawton has got a point, actually,' Carr went on. 'He *does* know who we are. And those of us with a public profile have rather more to lose than certain others.'

'Precisely,' said Sands. 'That's why we have to teach him a lesson in such a way that it makes an absolute end to this business.'

'Like what?' Carr said. 'Pulling his eyes out?'

'Don't be facetious,' Sands replied.

'Let's get on with it then,' Masterson said, and he braced himself to start hitting Mick in earnest.

'I'm not sure about this either,' said another voice. It was a light, fluting voice that belonged to Kerry Slater, the plump, masturbatory food critic. He was looking tense and flushed and miserable. He was a long way out of his natural environment and he wasn't at all happy about it.

'You talked about getting our own back, and I agreed to that,' he said. 'But what I had in mind was forcing him to eat some raw offal or perhaps a couple of pounds of laxative chocolate.'

'Oh, for fuck's sake,' said Masterson and he belted Mick in the face for the sheer hell of it. It was clear that he would just as willingly have hit Slater.

'Wait a minute!' Sands yelled. 'Wait a minute, can't you? You'll get your chance to hit him. But first of all I want him to answer some questions for me. I want to know why.'

'Why what?' Masterson demanded.

'Why this little piece of slime got it into his head to attack us.'

'Because he's a little piece of slime,' Masterson countered. 'Because he gets pleasure from it.'

'Are you really as stupid as you pretend?' Sands said. 'A piece of slime wouldn't have known who we were, wouldn't have come all the way to London from Yorkshire, wouldn't have tracked each of us down to our homes. He wouldn't have spied on us. He wouldn't have learned so much about us, found our weaknesses, wouldn't have inflicted such specific punishments.'

'What exactly do you mean?' Masterson said dumbly.

'All I mean is that before you get your revenge, let's find out what his motives were.'

A new figure stepped forward from the darkness of the carriage. It was Dr Graham Pryce, his face bruised but his suit immaculate.

'I tend to agree with Philip,' he said. 'I think you can overdo this motive business. This chap is very sick. What he did to me was appalling. What he did to my wife was worse. Of course, being sick doesn't mean that he shouldn't be punished but I think it does mean that motivation might be rather thin on the ground.'

'Exactly,' Masterson said. 'He's just rubbish, the kind of thing that you find littering the street, like dog turds or McDonald's wrappers. We should clear him up.'

'I think you're being incredibly naive,' Sands insisted. 'Do you really think he's a one-man band? Do you think he woke up one morning and thought it would be fun to beat us up? Do you think he's the prime mover, the Mr Big? Don't be ridiculous. He's just the muscle. I want to know who the brains are.'

The good doctor shrugged. He knew that in the end Sands would do what he liked.

'Why not ask him?' Pryce said.

It was a novel idea. Till then they had been talking about Mick as though they thought he wasn't there, or as though he was too stupid to be able to follow their conversation.

'All right, I will,' Sands said.

The six men gathered close, stood around Mick, waiting eagerly to hear what was coming next.

Sands said to Mick, 'I want you to answer some very simple questions. Why have you been doing this to us? Why this? Why us? And on whose instructions?'

Mick considered shouting obscene defiance but rejected the idea and said, 'Nobody's instructing me.' He said it under his breath, and as he said it, it finally struck him that these men really didn't seem to know what they'd done. Could a gang-rape really mean so little to them? Could they have blanked it out so easily and completely? Were they really that callous? Could it never have crossed their minds that someone might want revenge?

They were not happy with his simple, straightforward answer. Masterson hit him again, punching him twice in the face and neck.

'Why?' Sands repeated.

There was a long silence as Mick appeared to struggle with himself, appeared to be considering whether or not to make a clean breast of it.

At last he said, 'I'll tell you something that pisses me off about London: Cup Finals. Now let's say the Cup Final is Liverpool against Chelsea, well, they hold it down in London, don't they, which gives Chelsea an unfair advantage for a start. They're playing in their home town, their fans don't have to come such a long way, they don't have all that expense, they don't have any trouble finding Wembley Stadium, whereas northern fans have all that hassle, having to hire a coach, having to pay fancy London prices for food and drink. It's not fair.

'But then let's say the Cup Final is Liverpool against Man. United, they *still* have it in London so that it's unfair to twice as many people. It can't be right, can it?'

'Hit him again, would you, Philip?' Sands said, and Masterson did as he was asked.

'Oh, come on,' said Mick wearily. 'Stop this crap. Don't tell me you don't remember. Don't tell me you don't know. A stag night. A stripper. A gang-rape . . .'

As he spoke he looked into their faces and the blankness there confirmed something that perhaps he had known all along. They surely had no reason now to keep up a pretence, but talk of rape really seemed to mean nothing to them.

For their part, they continued to think he was simply telling lies, simply trying to provoke them, and he was succeeding. Masterson hit him once again, a good blow this time that rocked him back in his seat. Mick was hurting and it showed, but even Masterson began to see that Mick's ability to take punishment might be more than equal to his own taste for dishing it out. Perhaps he also realized that, insane as it appeared, Mick was actually telling the truth as he knew it.

'This is stupid,' said Pryce. 'He's hurt, he's bleeding. He's not going to tell us anything. We've had our revenge. Let's just end this here.'

A couple of voices mumbled agreement but Justin Carr, perhaps having seen more movies than the others, was alive to other possibilities. He said, 'And how exactly do we end it, eh, Graham? He's rather effectively demonstrated that he knows where we all live . . .'

He let that hang in the air for a while, aware that it wasn't a bad line, and slowly everyone turned towards Sands, who was looking much less like a leader now.

When nobody else said anything, Mick, sweating and in pain, experiencing a sickening sense of metal walls closing in on him, took the opportunity to speak.

'You know,' he said, 'it seems to me you lads have landed yourselves in a bit of a predicament. OK, you've got me here, you've slapped me about a bit, you've got as much sense out of me as you're going to get, so what are you going to do next? Let me go, and call that an end of it? I don't think so. I really don't. I mean, I might agree to it now, but why would I keep my word, eh? I don't think the matter's going to end here, do you? Justin's right. I do know where you all live. I've tracked you all down once, and the moment you let me go I think you know I'm going to do it all over again. All you've done this morning is earn yourself another dose of the same. It's the same game but you've raised the stakes. And I thought you were such smart lads.'

Anger buzzed in the air. The six men were angry because they knew he was right. They had considered themselves clever to have captured him, to have given themselves the means of taking revenge. But now the realization of their stupidity was setting over them like a plaster mould.

'So what do you do next?' Mick asked them. 'Well, you can talk among yourselves, kick ideas around, if you like, but believe me, I know, save yourself some time. Sooner or later you're going to come to the conclusion that the only sure way out of this is to kill me.

'Then two questions remain. Who's going to do it and how? You don't have guns as far as I can see, so which one of you is going to kill me with his bare hands? You, Masterson?'

'Killing was never part of the plan,' said Masterson.

'Absolutely not,' Lawton agreed.

'Maybe it wasn't,' Carr agreed, 'but he's right. He's given us no choice.'

'I'm a doctor, for Christ's sake,' Pryce bleated. 'I'm supposed to save lives.'

'You're a clever bastard, aren't you?' Sands said to Mick.

'No, I'm just the muscle.'

'This is a disaster,' said Carr.

'It's not the best,' Mick agreed.

'There must be a way out of this,' Slater said. 'We're reasonable men. We can negotiate. We can come to an agreement.'

Mick sat up in his seat, stared at each of his tormentors in turn, and did not look at all reasonable.

'This is a nightmare,' said Carr. 'We either kill him, which we don't want to do, or we release him, in which case we just set the whole thing in motion again.'

'I don't know if it's a nightmare,' Mick said, 'but it certainly looks like a stalemate.'

However he was wrong. There had been no sound of a car, no footsteps on the gravel or on the floor of the workshop, but suddenly there was someone outside the carriage. The six men turned, furtively, guiltily, peered out through the dark, broken windows as Judy Tanaka strode in through the central set of carriage doors. She was screaming at the top of her lungs, sounding dangerously deranged, and shakily holding a gun out in front of her. Mick recognized it as his own. Her body was quaking and she extended her right hand, closed her eyes and let off half a dozen or so shots into the carriage.

The six men, as though obeying a strict, well-rehearsed choreography, flattened themselves on the floor. The shots had drilled harmless holes in the carriage's walls and ceiling and upholstery. But when there are eight people in a severely confined space, a woman who doesn't know how to use a gun, who doesn't even look where she's shooting, is every bit as dangerous and terrifying as a fully trained marksman.

'Untie him,' she said, her voice loud but trembling, and Sands got up, cautiously, with infinite care and began untying Mick.

Carr said, 'She's had six shots. I think the gun's empty.'

'It's an automatic, you twat,' said Mick, but it didn't really matter. He knew there wasn't going to be any fighting, any wrestling for the gun.

'We wouldn't have killed you,' Sands said. 'You realize that, I hope.'

Mick considered the statement but didn't reply. He suspected it was probably true. Once untied, he took the gun from Judy's shaking hand. He fired one last shot into the floor of the carriage. It lodged in the boards just a yard from Sands' foot, a yard from Masterson's head, and a yard from Carr's hands.

'Stay where you are,' he said. 'Don't even think about moving till we've been gone at least half an hour.'

He knew they'd get their nerve back much sooner than that,

so he shot holes in two of the Mercedes' tyres. It was a shame. He'd have loved to steal the car, but Judy's Datsun made a much less conspicuous getaway car.

'I saw it all,' Judy gushed as she drove. 'I was coming to see you, to have breakfast with you maybe. I was driving around looking for somewhere to park when I saw you come out of your front door. Then I saw the six of them arrive and attack you and put you in the boot of the car. But what was I supposed to do? Call the police? So I followed them instead. They had no idea I was tailing them but they drove for miles and miles to this workshop place. I'm not very sure where we are, but I saw where they took you and I guessed what they must be doing to you. So I drove back to the Dickens, got the gun from your room, returned to the workshop, and you know the rest.'

'How did you know the gun was in the hotel room?'

'If you'd had it with you, you'd have used it when you were attacked, wouldn't you?'

'Yeah, I suppose I would. Thank you,' he said. 'I owe you a favour.'

'Only one?'

'How many do you want?'

'One will do if it's the right one,' she said. 'His name's still Stuart London.'

Mick laughed in disbelief.

'I can't do that,' he said weakly. 'I'm sorry, but I don't think I'm ever going to be able to do that stuff again.'

He was ready for all sorts of reactions from her. The one he'd have liked best involved her saying that she completely understood his distaste for, his satiation with, violence and revenge. He was not surprised when it didn't come. Instead she simply stopped the car, slapped his face as hard as she possibly could and said, 'Get out. Get out of my car. Now.'

He surveyed the empty, anonymous streets around them. He hadn't the slightest idea where he was, but he wasn't going to argue. He left the car as requested and stood motionless, watching as she drove away. He looked down at his suit and T-shirt, imagined the state of his face, and suddenly couldn't help finding it all very funny. He sniggered to himself and then he started walking again, tarnished and afraid, and with absolutely no idea where he was going.

# THE LAST FLASHBACK

He looks bad, as though he has been in the wars, in a serious fight that he did not win. His face is roughed up, the integrity of the skin broken through, made ragged and livid; a cut lip, an eye bruised black, raw grazes on all the face's hard, sharp, vulnerable edges. He's wearing a petrol-blue suit that once must have looked immaculately sharp. Now it's flayed out of shape, torn at the knees, streaked and clotted with ominous, sick substances. And under the suit there's a white T-shirt, stained with dark islands and archipelagos of what can only be blood.

Then he sees the muggers and the man in the cashmere overcoat. He watches. He approaches. There's some discussion, he finds the gun in his hand, the muggers are running, except for the one he's managed to catch, and then the victim is telling him to stop, and he's stopped, and there's a map in his hand, an *A–Z* with all the streets obliterated and he's saying, 'You're going to tell me there's a really simple explanation for this, aren't you?'

# MOUTH

Stuart could, of course, explain everything and he was eager
to do so. Mick was the perfect person to tell. The perfect
witness, the perfect stranger. But this didn't seem like the place
to do any storytelling. He feared the muggers might be back
and that they might have friends who were a lot rougher and
more dangerous than they were.

'My car's round the corner,' he said. 'I could give you a lift
somewhere.'

'That would be good,' Mick agreed.

They headed for the car and on the way there Mick did his
best to describe where he wanted to go. The Dickens seemed
to be his only option but, in the absence of a usable map, he
didn't know how to get there.

'Well, I can get you to Hackney,' Stuart said. 'Once we're
there, maybe you'll see something you recognize.'

Mick thought that was very unlikely but it was as good a
plan as any.

'So what happened to you?' Stuart asked.

'I was in a fight.'

'Did you win?'

Mick looked down at himself again, at the mess and blood
that was on his clothes.

'Yeah,' he said. 'I suppose I did.'

They got into the car and Stuart started to drive faster than
was either necessary or wise. He kept looking in his rearview

mirror to see if they were being followed but Mick thought they were in more danger of being stopped by the police for reckless driving.

'I don't know how to thank you,' Stuart said as he accelerated through a red light. 'I don't know what might have happened to me if you hadn't appeared.'

'You'd have had your wallet taken,' Mick said curtly.

'Or worse.'

'I doubt it. They weren't going to kill you, were they?'

'No, I suppose not.'

'Don't sound so disappointed.'

Stuart's face tightened with an assortment of unmatching emotions. There was trepidation, elation, relief, a hint of hysteria.

'Are you drunk?' Mick asked.

Stuart had to consider this before acknowledging that he had indeed been drinking. 'Just a little,' he said. 'I've been celebrating.'

'Yeah? What have you got to celebrate?'

Stuart tapped the blacked-out *A–Z* which he had placed carefully on the tray between the driver and passenger seat.

'I've done it,' he said. 'I've covered London. I've walked down every single street in London.'

Mick took the *A–Z* and turned the pages, looking again at the firm, broad, black lines that had obliterated every street.

'And you crossed 'em out as you went?'

'That's it.'

Stuart was clearly expecting Mick to be impressed.

'Yeah, well I suppose it's good to have a hobby,' Mick said mordantly.

'It was rather more than that,' Stuart snapped.

Mick thumbed through more of the obsessively marked pages and it appeared to be true. This did not look like the record of some easygoing pastime or distraction.

'So why'd you do it?' he asked.

'Because I was looking for something, or rather someone.'

'Anyone in particular?'

'Yes. You.'

Mick laughed scornfully. 'No,' he said. 'Whoever you were looking for, it wasn't me.'

Stuart shrugged, perhaps a little sadly. For him it wasn't a matter of argument or debate, but of instinctive knowledge.

'Is this some sort of sexual pick-up?' Mick asked. 'I do hope not. I've already done that number.'

'No, not sex,' Stuart said.

'Thank God.'

Stuart's driving was now very relaxed and very bad. Mick wasn't particularly afraid they were going to crash into another car, but he did think they might hit something solid and stationary, like a phone box or a street lamp or a parked police car.

'Tell me,' he said, 'was that a real gun you were waving around back there?'

'Was I waving it? I was trying to keep my hand very steady.'

'But was it real?'

'I'm afraid so.'

'I've never seen a real gun before.'

'You haven't missed anything.'

'Why do you carry a gun?'

'It's an old habit,' Mick said dismissively. 'But I think I've kicked it.'

'You were in a fight. You said you won. Did you shoot somebody?'

'You don't want to know.'

'You're right. I probably don't. Can I look at the gun?'

Mick laughed. He couldn't believe this guy. Still, if he would go around rescuing mugging victims and accepting lifts from them, what could he expect?

'Not while you're driving,' Mick said.

Immediately Stuart turned the car into a side street and stopped. Mick thought it was kind of pathetic, but he saw no reason not to let him have a look at the gun. He took it out of his pocket and placed it on top of the dashboard.

'Can I touch it?' Stuart asked with childlike politeness.

'If you have to. But don't wave it around. And don't touch the safety catch.'

'Which is that?'

Mick pointed it out to him and Stuart picked up the gun as though lifting something as fragile as a bird's egg.

The street they were in was short and narrow and seemed to lead only to a row of railway arches. Cars were parked on both sides of the road and some were half on the pavement to leave room for other cars to pass. There was a short row of houses with front gardens behind high makeshift fences, and opposite them was a huge, dismal industrial building, some sort of factory for the rag trade. The lights were on inside and through a ground floor window Mick saw an Asian man, desperately thin and exhausted-looking, who was examining a short-sleeved shirt printed with parrots and bamboo designs.

'London is a glorious city,' Stuart said. 'It brings you what you need.'

'It brings you a lot of stuff you could do without, too,' Mick said.

'Do you believe in fate?' Stuart asked.

It was a weird question but Mick replied, 'What do you mean by fate?'

'Your wife, for instance, or girlfriend, or whatever you have, do you think you were destined to meet her? Did fate bring you together?'

'Something brought us together, sure.'

'Did fate bring you to London?'

'That's one word for it.'

'And when I got up this morning was I destined to go out, get mugged, get rescued by a man with a gun? Was that preordained? Did fate arrange things so that you and I would be sitting here like this and I'd have this gun in my hand and . . .?'

For a grim moment Mick thought he was going to be shot. Stuart grasped the gun firmly in his hand and looked as though he planned to use it. He fiddled with the safety catch, released it, but instead of pointing it at Mick he opened his mouth wide, as though being helpful to some invisible dentist. Then he laid the snout of the gun along his tongue, and without hesitation he started pulling on the trigger. He was inexpert but fully determined.

He was also badly disappointed. The trigger clicked repeatedly, the firing mechanism slid in and out of place, but no bullet found its way into the gun, into Stuart's mouth and then into the complex configuration of bone and brain. The gun's cargo had been discharged into the fabric of the tube train carriage and then into the tyres of the Mercedes.

A second later Mick belted Stuart on the side of the head. The gun fell out of his mouth, out of his hand, and Mick caught it.

'What is wrong with you, man?' Mick yelled.

'It's all over,' Stuart said. 'I want it to be all over. I'm tired. I've had enough of London, of life, of the whole damn thing. I want to end it all.'

'With my gun?' Mick protested. 'Get your own gun.'

He knew it sounded stupid, yet there was something profoundly objectionable about this man, this complete stranger, wanting to use the gun for his own shabby purposes.

'I should have ditched it ages ago,' he said.

'But you didn't, did you?' Stuart insisted. 'That's fate too. It was meant to happen. London has always brought me what I needed: a career, a wife, a mistress. Why not a means of death? The day I walked my last London street was the day I knew London would bring me a means of ending it all. And it did. It brought me you. A man with a gun. It has to be. Don't you have any more bullets?'

'No, I don't,' Mick said. 'That's a bit of a miscalculation on fate's part wouldn't you say? But then maybe fate's been pissing you about all along.'

Mick was angry now. He'd always known that London was full of nutters but why did he have to meet such a prize one at a time like this?

'I've thought of a way you can thank me,' Mick said. 'Give me your wallet.'

Timidly, obediently, Stuart handed it over. Mick opened it, took out a few twenty pound notes, and was about to hand it back when he saw the name on the credit cards and then on the driving licence. He looked closely at Stuart's face. It seemed weak, fleshy, boyish. He slapped him on the cheek, just soft enough to appear playful, just hard enough to sting.

'Stuart London, that's a funny name,' he said.

'I know, all my life . . .'

He was about to explain but it suddenly seemed like far too much effort. He was aware that Mick was staring at him with an unwarranted curiosity, as though he were a zoological specimen.

'It's strange,' Mick said. 'You don't look like much of a heartbreaker to me.'

'What?' Stuart asked.

Mick didn't reply. He got out of the car and walked away. As he left Stuart and the car behind he heard a grinding of gears and a wild revving of the engine. It occurred to him that Stuart might be drunk enough to kill himself on the way home. If that was what fate wanted it was fine by him. He walked for a few minutes before admitting to himself what he'd known all along, that he was as lost as ever. He would have asked for directions but there was nobody on the street. Then, as he looked round, a black cab appeared out of nowhere. Mick heard himself shouting, 'Taxi' and he ran after the cab as it stopped twenty yards up ahead of him. He heaved the door open and threw himself into the back.

'I want Park Lane,' he said, and he was about to launch into an explanation about which of the many Park Lanes of London he wanted. But the driver said, 'Is that Park Lane, Hackney?' and Mick gratefully said it was.

'Yeah,' the driver said as they moved off. 'I didn't think you looked the type for *the* Park Lane.'

# BACKERS

S tuart drove home, no longer feeling either drunk or celebratory or, for that matter, suicidal. The day's expedition had been lurid, almost hallucinatory, and already some of the events were starting to slip away from him, their texture becoming more muted and mundane. If pressed he could not have proved that any of it had really happened. It was all behind him. The mugging, the stranger, the gun, the botched suicide attempt; they were all gone and had left no trace.

The traffic wasn't heavy. In fact Stuart thought that London traffic was never quite as terrible as people liked to pretend. By asserting that driving in London was a sort of hell people were allowed to feel that their own driving was brave and heroic. Stuart did not feel even remotely heroic. He felt like a buffoon and a bungler. The attempt at suicide had been laughable as well as futile. Fate had indeed let him down. But why had he needed fate at all? Why this desire to be passive? Why couldn't he have found a high place and taken the matter into his own hands? It no longer seemed to be simply a matter of cowardice. Indeed, if he was keen enough or brave enough he could still do the deed right now, but he knew he wouldn't.

Another problem then occurred to him. Was he going to record the day's events, the day's walk, in his diary? If he did, he would completely destroy his plan to leave a great unfinished work. He had imagined a printed text that would end abruptly and there would need to be some editorial insertion, a scholarly note about the exact circumstances of his death. Now he was in a position to write the final page himself, a page that was much more trashy, much less monumental than he'd wanted. But having survived the rough, confused, shambling events, he felt totally unequipped for transforming them into a diary entry.

He drove on and was home sooner than he wanted to be. As he parked the car he looked up at the house and saw that some of the lights were on. That was strange. Anita should have been at work, and he was pretty sure he'd turned everything off when he'd gone out. Still, a little wasted electricity didn't seem worth worrying about.

He entered the house and shouted hello in case Anita was in. He thought his voice sounded perfectly normal and steady. He thought there was nothing in his demeanour that betrayed what he'd been through that day. The house was silent and nobody returned his greeting, but he wandered through the ground floor, and saw Anita's coat and bag cast aside in the kitchen. He saw signs of coffee having been made, but he still heard nothing and he had to go up to the spare bedroom, the one they used as a home office, before he found her. She was sitting in the swivel chair, but she had it turned away from the desk and was reading a sheaf of loose pages. The computer screen was illuminated and the printer had recently been used.

'Didn't you hear me come in?' he asked.

'I was engrossed,' she said.

'Did you decide to work at home?'

'Yes. Did you?'

'Yes.'

On any normal day he would have left it like that, gone downstairs and found himself something to do. But he wasn't feeling back to normal yet. In fact he was feeling unexpectedly warm towards Anita. He knew that she had been spared. If there had been a bullet in that gun, then instead of dealing with paperwork in the spare bedroom she would now be dealing with the news that her husband had blown his brains out. He couldn't quite conjure up a scene of Dickensian woe and grief but he still felt glad not to be putting her through such an ordeal. She may have been Boadicea to the staff but she could still be a soft, vulnerable thing in his eyes. He wanted to be with her, to stay in the room with her for a while and talk.

'What are you reading?' he asked.

'I'm reading your diary,' she replied nonchalantly.

It took a moment for him to understand what she'd said, but then he looked at the screen and recognized his own words there. Anita had found his disk, and the sheaf of papers she was holding was the print-out. Well, yes, that was all part of the plan. The disk was meant to be found, but not yet. It was intended to be a posthumous discovery. He felt as though he had been punched in the stomach, as though he was falling down a mine shaft.

'It's not really a diary,' he said hastily and awkwardly. 'It's just sort of research I was doing for the business.'

'Don't be ridiculous,' said Anita. 'What possible use could the business make of knowing that a woman in Archway asked you to define the seven-year itch?'

Stuart launched into a number of rapidly abandoned explanations before falling into a judicious silence. He wondered how long Anita had been there, how much she'd read, how many of his secrets she knew.

'I can explain,' he said, and he tried to, he really did. He tried to tell her about his desire for knowledge, for completion and ultimately for obliteration, and Anita listened politely though not with great interest. When he could think of no more to say he picked up one or two of the printed pages, looked at her imploringly and said, 'You believe me, don't you?'

'There should be more of it,' she replied.

For one joyous moment he heard this as a sentence of praise, as though she loved what he had written, and he was starting to say thank you before he realized that the expression on

Anita's face wasn't compatible with a demand for more of his prose.

'What I mean,' she said, 'is that if you've really been walking ten miles a day, five days a week, and if you've now finished, having covered eight and a half thousand miles or so, then there should be a hell of a lot more than this. There would be at least three and a half years' worth of diary here, probably much more. There should be thousands of pages.'

'Not necessarily,' he insisted. 'There were lots of streets I had nothing to say about. There was no point forcing an observation. In those cases all I did was mark the street in the *A–Z.*'

'Ah, yes,' she said. 'The famous *A–Z.*'

Stuart now realized that the blackened *A–Z* was bulging in his pocket. Anita put out her hand for it and he meekly passed it over. She looked at the pages with even less curiosity than Mick had displayed, and when she was done with it she dropped it on the floor like a discarded banana skin.

'Yes,' said Anita, 'the *A–Z* is a nice touch but it's hardly proof of anything is it? Any fool can sit down with a map and pen and black in streets.'

'Any fool can, but I didn't,' he said. He was sounding a little desperate now, a little panicked. He added, 'Anyway, you've only got one disk. There are others.'

'Are there really?' she said. 'I doubt it somehow. I don't make any claims to be a literary scholar, but I can smell a fake when it's put under my nose.'

The room felt smaller and hotter than Stuart had ever known it. The ceiling was lower. The whirr of the computer fan filled his ears.

'Fake?' he said. 'No. Absolutely not.'

He looked as though he might make a run for it, but Anita gave him a placatory smile and said, 'Let me tell you what I think probably happened. I think that in the beginning you genuinely wanted to walk down every street in London. It sounds like you. I'm sure you intended to do it. I'm sure you planned to. But I suspect that before long it got very boring. It was all quite pleasant walking through Hampstead and Richmond and Kensington. And it was just fine walking through Highgate and Blackheath. Wandsworth and Stoke Newington had their problems, Lewisham and Leytonstone you probably didn't like at all. And you knew there was going to be worse still: Peckham and Tottenham and Canning Town and God knows where else. I'm sure you weren't a snob about it, probably you really did visit Brixton and Shoreditch and Wanstead. I'm sure you weren't too delicate to walk through a bit of urban blight. But I imagine that before long you looked at all those remaining mean streets that led you through depressing council estates, and through boring, boring suburbs, and perhaps even into some dangerous no-go areas, and you thought to yourself, I don't belong here. This isn't my manor. This isn't my London. And so you said to yourself, "Forget it." And frankly I don't blame you. Nobody would.'

'No,' Stuart insisted. 'You're completely, completely wrong.'

Unmoved and unconvinced, she went on, 'But you couldn't forget it altogether. You'd set yourself this big target and you didn't want to miss. But by then something had changed. By then you were really into the diary. You realized that writing was much more fun than walking. So you started inventing. Why not? You walked less and you wrote more. You sat in your car or in a pub or in a library perhaps, and you made it up as you went along. And it shows. The people having sex in public in Fulham, the woman doing the painting in Crystal Palace, some of the overheard conversations. They're too neat. They're not quite like life. They're not part of the London I know.'

Stuart's face was looking dangerously red and his fists were gripping imaginary dumb bells.

'Let's face it, Stuart, large parts of your diary are a shade too literary. The passages about that little Japanese tour guide, the sex passages, they really weren't very convincing at all, then walking down the street and just happening to see her, the

330

pursuit, her telling you to fuck off and die. I just wasn't very convinced by that.

'And really, the suicide stuff,' she said. 'I suppose I'm not the best person to judge the literary merits of those passages since I know you too well, but I didn't buy it at all. You have many surprising qualities, Stuart, but I do believe that you're completely incapable of killing yourself.'

At last something they could agree on.

'The idea worked as a literary conceit,' Anita said, 'but not as part of an actual diary. And that's all right too. Fiction isn't to be despised. What you were doing was creating a new London, inventing a new city, a city of words, something in your own image.'

Stuart looked angry, frustrated, lost. The years of marriage had taught him how to argue, how to fight and fight back. He knew all about his opponent's strengths and weaknesses, and often the combat could be a sort of familiar, playful wrestling. But now they were fighting to some new set of rules and Anita was using strange, exotic techniques that left him winded and fumbling.

'It's all right,' she said, warmly. 'There's nothing to be ashamed of. You're looking at me as though I'm your mother and I've found the dirty magazines you keep under your bed.'

He actually felt much, much worse than that.

'You've been dabbling in a bit of creative writing,' Anita said. 'It's strange in a man of your age but it's not so terrible. Look, Stuart, I know things have been tough for you lately. I know you've been feeling useless and left out. I realize your current role in the business is no good for any of us. I know that situation has to change.'

Stuart's head slumped. His body looked defeated. Now it seemed she was going to return to an earlier, more damning humiliation: business.

'What about Japan?' she said.

He didn't respond. He thought she must be about to return to the subject of Judy, though he was quite wrong about that.

331

'You're not the only one who has secrets,' Anita said. 'That's the reason I'm at home. I had some important things I wanted to think about. Here.'

She took a box file from a shelf next to the desk, and opened it to revealed a stash of faxes, plans, maps, business letters, most of them containing Japanese characters.

'A business expands or it dies,' Anita said. 'And I think we're both agreed that The London Walker really doesn't have much room to grow. So I've been talking to people, specifically to some Japanese backers, people in the tourist industry. They tell me the Japanese really love London, but there are a couple of problems with it. First; it's too big, dirty, dangerous and expensive, and second, and rather more crucially, it's too far away from Japan.

'But the Japanese are inventive. They've come up with a solution. They want to build a version of London out there in Japan in a place called Hakkaido, an island up in the north. It will only be a very small version, of course. All the tourist attractions of London will be there on one manageable site. There'll be Buckingham Palace, St Paul's Cathedral, Big Ben, all scaled down to about half-size and all within a couple of minutes' walk of each other. There'll be a miniature Tower of London with fake crown jewels inside. There'll be a section of the Thames with an opening Tower Bridge. Maybe we could have a section with replica modern architecture, the Lloyd's Building or the NatWest Tower, though the Japanese do modern architecture rather better than we do.'

Stuart looked and felt like the hero of a low-budget science fiction movie, the sort where the hero suddenly discovers that an alien intelligence has taken over his wife's brain. He was speechless.

'The thing is,' she continued, 'people want to shop when they come to London, so there'll be versions of Harrods and Selfridges and Aspreys and Haden Brothers. There'll be London buses, London taxis, maybe an underground system with just two or three stops, tour guides dressed up like London bobbies.

There'll be walking tours, of course. There could be re-enactments of the Great Fire, the Plague, maybe even the Blitz, although the Japanese are a bit funny about the war, obviously. And they want us to be involved. Because who knows more about London than we do?'

'Who's us?' he asked suspiciously. 'Who's we?'

'The London Walker. You and me,' she said, and then added as a sweetener, 'Especially you.'

'These Japanese people don't know me.'

'I've told them all about you.'

'It sounds like hell,' Stuart said.

'You'll come round. I felt that way at first, but before long you start to see it's a great idea. All London's attractions in an area not much bigger than Trafalgar Square. You'd be able to walk down every single London street in the course of one afternoon.'

When she looked over at Stuart he was sitting on the floor, his back to the wall, his knees drawn up to his chin, a position that could suggest both prayer and supplication, and he was making a wet throaty sound she had never heard before. She couldn't tell whether he was laughing or sobbing.

# SHEFFIELD

G abby was looking good on the day she met Mick from the London train. There was something newly mature and self-possessed about her. Her hair had been cut into a geometric bob and she wore a tailored, slightly mannish tweed jacket with tight jeans and heels. She hardly looked like a stripper at all.

As Mick detached himself from the rest of the arrivals, he still looked rough. He'd put on a new clean T-shirt but the suit continued to show the effects of his recent skirmishes. He walked stiffly towards her. She went to him, put her arms tightly round him, squeezed and kissed him. The kissing was thorough but it did not seem to Mick as though it was very deeply felt. He was glad. He didn't want to have to feel too much. Her arms felt strange around him and he ran a hand through her unfamiliar hair. It immediately sprang back into place, neat and unruffled. Mick realized it was no longer the same colour it had been when he'd left. Perhaps she'd dyed it, but perhaps she'd let it return to its natural colour.

'Did you bring my car?' he asked.

'The battery was flat.'

'Yeah, well, I told you . . .'

'It's OK,' she said. 'I've got a car.'

She took his arm as though he were an invalid or an elderly relative, and walked him across the car-park in the direction of a white BMW.

'Is that yours?' he asked, not expecting for a moment that it was.

'I borrowed it.'

'What? You hired it?'

'Whatever,' she said, and she unlocked the door and got in behind the wheel. She seemed at home, as though the car was very familiar to her. Mick was naturally suspicious, but he folded himself into the passenger seat and prepared for the worst. Without another word she began to drive. Mick had never liked her driving, it was too erratic and it made him nervous, but today she drove fast and purposefully, though she was heading neither in the direction of his flat nor her own. He wondered if she'd booked them into a hotel for their big reunion. That would have been uncharacteristically thoughtful of her.

'We have a lot to talk about,' he said, as an early warning to her that she shouldn't expect this meeting to be too comfortable and easy.

'Yes, we do,' she agreed.

Yet for the moment it seemed best if they said nothing, if they let the backdrop of Sheffield roll by, first the terraced houses, then the retail parks, then a bit of greenery, then into the posher areas of the city. At last there was no city at all and they were in the countryside and Mick wondered if Gabby was doing something totally naff like taking him for lunch at a country pub, but that would have been even more uncharacteristic.

After a few more miles Gabby slowed down, turned into a narrow lane where the hedges almost touched the sides of the car, then along a dirt track that Mick could see led to a group of converted farm buildings. This was one version of the Sheffield dream: moving into the country and doing up an old barn. There was a big open-sided structure, maybe once an old cowshed but now a garage that housed a line of fancy cars. Opposite was a house, a big two-storey stone building with rockeries, an ornamental pond and a pair of huge mill stones set

335

either side of the front door. There was a covered swimming pool out the back and beyond that a paddock with a couple of horses.

Gabby parked the car on a turning circle of gravel at the side of the house and got out. Still bewildered and still saying nothing, Mick slowly followed her.

She said, 'There's somebody I want you to meet.'

'Jesus,' said Mick. 'I can't face meeting anyone. Not now.'

She didn't stop to argue, just walked up to the front door of the house knowing that Mick would have to follow. She went in without knocking and Mick trailed after her. There was nobody there to meet them, but as he walked through the hall and went into the living room where Gabby was standing he saw that this was the house of a rich man; not London rich like Jonathan Sands or Graham Pryce, but rich nevertheless. It all looked simultaneously antique yet brand new. There were beams, bare stone walls, an inglenook fireplace with a big fire, an oak dresser, rows of copper pans; but they could all have been manufactured yesterday. Everything was spotless, polished, without patina, and there was a snowy white sheepskin rug on the floor. There was also the incongruous smell of cigar smoke in the air.

Mick glared at Gabby, trying to convey a whole world of accusation, hostility and suspicion, but she remained perfectly at ease and unruffled. She had the upper hand, if for no other reason than she knew what was coming next.

After what felt like an age, a door opened in a corner of the room and a man came in. There was an arrogant bounce in his step. The way he entered the room showed that he owned all this and much more besides. He was a broad man, tall and big-chested. He could have been most ages between thirty and fifty, though Mick would have estimated the upper end. The image was somewhere between a bouncer and an ageing rock star. The hair was receding but long and meticulously laundered. The clothes were casually flash, a silk shirt, an embroidered waistcoat, a thick, studded belt. He looked like a hard man, a rough diamond, but not particularly thuggish, more the sort who gets other people to do his thuggery for him. Before Mick could weigh him up any further the guy was shaking him by the hand, putting an arm round his shoulder and laughing as though they shared a long and hilarious acquaintanceship.

'Good to see you, Mick,' he said. 'I've heard a fuck of a lot about you.'

The voice was rough and local, though it had had a few edges rounded off. He was a Sheffield lad but he'd been around a bit.

'This is Ross,' Gabby said quietly. 'Ross McLennan.'

Mick did not look impressed, not even interested, and he said nothing, but that didn't matter to his host who was now going round the room stoking the fire, adjusting chairs, forcing Mick to have a drink. Reluctantly Mick accepted a beer and declined a glass.

'Why am I here?' Mick asked.

'Because Gabby brought you here.'

'And why did she do that?'

'Because I told her to.'

'It's like that, is it?' Mick said haggardly.

'Yeah, it's exactly like that.'

Mick sat back with his beer and decided to let McLennan make the running. For the moment he appeared to have no other option.

'I hear you've been in London,' McLennan said. 'Terrible place, isn't it?'

'Some of it.'

'And I also hear you did a pretty good job while you were down there.'

'Who'd you hear it from?'

'Word travels,' said McLennan.

Mick didn't like the idea that anybody was talking about what he'd got up to in London, certainly not to some man in Sheffield he'd never met or heard of.

'Gabby tells me everything,' McLennan added.

'Is that right?' Mick said. 'How do you two come to be such good friends?'

He could see Gabby tensing up but McLennan answered evenly enough. 'Through business,' he said.

'What business?'

'You're a nosy bugger aren't you?' he said, but he was amused, not angry. 'I do all sorts of business. I do some promoting. I saw Gabby's act. I thought she was too good for that game.'

He was sitting close to her and he reached out a hand and stroked her knee. Mick felt it was being mostly done for his benefit, to test his reaction, see if he'd get angry. In fact he felt a great surge of relief. For a moment he thought maybe that's all this was, an unnecessarily elaborate way for Gabby to dump him, a way of showing him that in his absence she had found a new man, someone older, richer and fancier than him. But he didn't believe it could be that simple.

'I admire what you've done for Gabby,' McLennan continued. 'You saw what needed doing and you went and did it.'

'Yeah, I'm good at that,' Mick said. If McLennan wanted to detect a threat in his reply he was welcome to.

'Defending a woman's honour,' McLennan said. 'That's very chivalrous, very Lancelot. Those bastards deserved everything they got.'

'You think so?' Mick asked.

'After what they did to Gabby, I'd say so, yes.'

Mick took a mouthful of beer before saying, 'I don't know what they did and I don't know who they did it to, but I don't think they raped Gabby.'

The statement hung in the air like the smell of yesterday's chip fat. Mick turned towards Gabby who briefly looked as though she was going to protest, but then she stopped herself. It was as though she couldn't be bothered any more, that there was no longer a need to pretend. She wouldn't look at him and she turned in her chair so that the back of one shoulder was facing him.

338

'Are you calling Gabby a liar?' McLennan asked.

'She's been called worse things,' Mick said.

McLennan laughed. It didn't even sound particularly forced. McLennan was easily amused and he didn't seem to mind at all having his woman insulted.

'Gabby told me you were bright,' McLennan said. 'She told me you'd work out what was going on. But she also said you'd get the job done, and that you'd be a good man to have in the team.'

'What is this? A job interview?'

'No. You've already got the job, we're just negotiating terms.'

'What are you talking about?'

McLennan bristled slightly. He wasn't used to being addressed so offhandedly.

'You've already done a job for me, right?' McLennan said. 'You're smart. You were right about those guys. Maybe they didn't rape Gabby. Maybe you realized that a while ago, but it didn't make any difference did it? You carried on. You knew they deserved what you were giving them, even if you didn't know why. Or maybe you were just having too much fun to stop. OK, so they didn't rape Gabby. But they did do something that really got me mad.'

'So I beat them up because they got you mad?'

'You've got it. Exactly. I mean, if Gabby had come to you and said this bloke you've never heard of called Ross McLennan has got six other blokes you've never heard of and he wants you to beat them up for him, well, you'd have hesitated, wouldn't you? But these guys needed seeing to and I can't do everything myself and Gabby knew you'd do a good job, and if she had to tell a little white lie to spur you on, well, so what? The end justifies the means, right? And besides, it was a good apprenticeship, a good trial run. It gave me the chance to see what you're made of.'

Mick did his best to look impassive.

'So what did these guys do to you?' he asked.

'You don't need to know that.'

That old line.

'Don't I?' Mick asked.

'No.'

'Somebody could've got killed.'

'Not you though, Mick. You're too clever for that.'

'I do need to know what those guys did,' Mick insisted. McLennan took a gun out of his pocket. He didn't do anything so uncool as point it at Mick or even hold it properly in his hand, but Mick could take a hint. Suddenly he didn't need to know at all. He shook his head slowly and dumbly.

'You two just about deserve each other,' Mick said, and he waited for McLennan or Gabby to rise to the bait, to defend themselves or each other, but it didn't affect them, they were immune to such low-level insults.

'So the first thing, Mick, is that I owe you some money,' McLennan said. 'What's your current rate?'

He pulled out a bundle of notes and began peeling fifty pound notes off it. Then he had a better idea, shrugged and tossed the whole thing over to Mick. Money, he was making clear, was not the issue here. Mick caught the bundle with one hand, put his beer down on the floor and held the notes as though weighing them.

'Yeah, have the lot,' McLennan said. 'Have a little on account for the next job I ask you to do.'

'No,' said Mick. 'I think I've done enough for you.'

He threw the money back. McLennan couldn't catch it cleanly and it hit him in the chest. Mick got up out of the chair, and whether it was deliberate or not McLennan couldn't tell, but the can of beer was kicked over and its contents leaked rapidly across the floor towards the white sheepskin rug. Deliberate or not, Mick didn't apologize or try to pick up the can and stop the flow.

'What are you doing?' McLennan demanded. 'What are you doing, you little twat?'

'I'm ending the negotiation,' Mick said, and he took a couple of steps towards the door.

'Where do you think you're going?'

Mick wasn't altogether sure but he had to get out of that house. He needed to put a lot of distance between himself and that place, and between himself and Gabby and the business of violent, bogus revenge.

'Don't turn your back on me!' McLennan shouted. 'Don't turn your fuckin' back on me.'

So Mick turned to face him.

'You know,' Mick said. 'I'm not sure I'm quite as clever as you think I am. I never did work out what the real story was. I never really worked out that Gabby had some other man pulling her strings. If I had, in the beginning, if I'd known that you'd stolen my girlfriend and made me beat up six guys for no good reason then I'd have wanted to come up here and fucking kill you. That's what I'd have wanted as my revenge.

'But I really didn't work it out. I didn't know properly till now. And now that I do know, now that I've seen you, I don't need to kill you at all. It's enough just to have made a mess on your carpet.'

He wished it could have been shorter, pithier, more like in a movie. He walked out of the house, across the gravel, up the track, on to the main road. He started walking in the direction he'd come from, back towards Sheffield, the city where he lived; but it was a direction that led to other places too. At first he planned to walk the whole way home but after a couple of miles he knew it was ridiculously far away, so he began to stick his thumb out at the passing traffic. It wasn't long before he got a lift with a van driver from Leeds who was doing a drop in Sheffield then driving on to London.

'Terrible place, London,' the driver said, 'but I can take you all the way if you want.'

Mick looked around the inside of the cab, at the silt of cigarette packets, empty drink cans, yellowed football pro-grammes, at the two balding gonks on top of the dashboard, and he looked out at Sheffield visible in the near distance. He thought about his scuzzy rented flat, not visited all this time, his faded old car, and then of the more general scuzziness and fadedness of London.

'So what do you say?' the driver asked.

It was a long time before Mick answered.

# NEW THERAPY

Judy Tanaka was in her attic room, kneeling on the floor, on the frayed green carpet, her map of London set out in front of her, perhaps like a board game, perhaps like a prayer mat. Coiled at her side was a loose, unruly heap of rolled plastic sheets that were the same size as the map and transparent, except where they had been marked with crosses. She took the first of these sheets, unrolled it and placed it meticulously over the map. This was her own sheet and she experienced a pang of embarrassment and triumph to see just how many crosses there were, and how many sexual acts and partners these crosses celebrated and recorded. They were not distributed evenly or symmetrically or representatively but they certainly showed how geographically promiscuous she had been.

She placed Stuart's map on top of her own. Although the crosses were far less dense than on hers they too showed a decently wide distribution. Stuart had achieved by accident what she had deliberately strived for, and of course some of them coincided.

She took more of the plastic sheets, maps made by her other lovers, and as they stacked up one on top of another, London seemed slowly to be disappearing, not only under a rain of crosses but also under the accumulating opaqueness of the plastic sheets.

Finally she placed Mick's map on the top of the pile. This too coincided with one of her own crosses, but she thought there was a certain beauty about a sheet with a single cross on it, even if it was located in Park Lane, Hackney. It was the most recent and therefore the most clearly visible. It was not lost in the sheen of the plastic, in the reflections of her own history.

Judy knew how deceptive maps can be, how quickly they can become out of date, how places in the real world can have meanings and significances quite out of scale with their carto-graphic depiction.

It was almost spring. The sun had risen high enough to insinuate its way into the therapy room. The days were lengthening, there were daffodils in the garden and the clocks would soon be moved forward. There was even something spring-like about Judy Tanaka as she walked into the room, as though she had a thrilling piece of news for her therapist.

'Please,' Judy said brightly, 'I'd like you to look at my body.'

'Aren't we getting a little ahead of ourselves?' asked the therapist.

'No, no,' said Judy. 'Please look.'

Before the therapist could protest further Judy had stripped naked and was showing her body, revolving on the spot so the therapist could get a full, rounded view. It was immediately obvious that there was a strange serpentine marking curled around Judy's torso. At a first glance it appeared to be a kind of bruising, but it would have been a strange kind of injury that created such a long, thin, continuous and precise bruise. The therapist looked more closely and saw that in another way it was rather more like a rash, a series of dark-blue spots that linked together to form a long, unbroken line. But again it was the wrong shape for any kind of rash she'd ever seen. For a moment she wondered if it wasn't a series of cuts and cigarette burns, something self-inflicted, but knowing Judy Tanaka as she did she thought that surely couldn't be.

Then Judy began to point out certain features of the mark, how it meandered in certain places, how in one place it formed an almost ninety-degree bend. 'Much as the River Thames does at the Embankment,' she said archly.

And as the therapist looked more closely she saw that there was indeed something strangely familiar about the shape and design of the mark. Judy continued pointing to various parts of it and said, as though she were a tour guide, 'Here we see Chelsea Harbour, here Battersea Reach, here the Isle of Dogs, and here the Upper and Lower Pool . . .' And before long the therapist was utterly convinced. The rash or bruise or scar or whatever it was formed a perfect representation of the River Thames, a depiction so accurate, so detailed, that you could have used it as a navigational aid.

The therapist reached out a hesitant index finger and ran it along the line of the mark.

'Does that hurt?'

'Not at all,' Judy said. 'It's rather nice actually.'

The therapist's finger moved further along the map made flesh, from the source on Judy's left leg, up her flank, across her soft, powdered belly, up towards her breasts, then widening out as it curled behind her back.

'Judy,' the therapist said quietly. 'I can see we may need more sessions than I first thought.'

# BOADICEA'S LONDON

She likes the smell of burning wattle in the morning. She has swept in from the east, from the big skies and the waterlands, with her armies and her allies. She comes fresh from humiliation, deposed, stripped of her birthright and inheritance, beaten like a slave, her daughters raped by Roman soldiers. She has come to the doomed town to do her worst, to enjoy the smell of burning wood and thatch and human flesh, to reduce Londinium to embers.

Perhaps her revenge will not be so very sweet. The Roman governor, Gaius Suetonius Paullinus, moving before her, has done his best to reduce the mayhem. Ahead of the certain destruction, he has urged the population to evacuate the town. This is, after all, no military stronghold, no capital. There are no fortifications here, simply a narrowing of the river, a crossing, a place of trade and exchange, a settlement not more than ten years old.

Paullinus knows he cannot defend the undefended, and so has decided to make a sacrifice, but he hopes it will be a sacrifice of buildings not of bodies. He leaves with as many of the population as he is able to convince of their imminent fate. They move slowly with all their belongings, their furniture, their bed linen, the tools of their trades, all their transportable wealth.

Perhaps therefore when Boadicea arrived in Londinium she entered a wholly deserted place, took possession of a void, cold winds playing through the empty market place, nothing but rats in the abandoned grain stores. Yet even so, as she rides along the untended jetties, as her men search the cleared warehouses and workshops and abandoned former dwellings, she already knows she must destroy all this and much else besides.

Or perhaps, after all, the governor was not so persuasive as he would have liked to be. No doubt there were some stragglers, the sick, the old, the proud, the recalcitrant. These few remaining inhabitants are driven into the streets and easily, if baroquely, massacred. Yet destruction demands more than simple death. All those things that speak of ease and comfort, domestic things like bowls, jugs, lamps, glassware, little markers of civilization, all are smashed, crushed, pulverized, made nothing.

Those things that cannot be so easily destroyed must be purified by fire. Wood and straw is torched, makes excellent kindling. Twisters of black and grey smoke ascend from the corners of the town, rising above the crumbling, infirm buildings. Roofs are consumed, walls fall in on themselves. A great furnace of air burns at the centre, a core of heat that sucks breath from the earth.

Boadicea watches and approves. It is a job well done. After the flames comes the Iceni winter. She sniffs the thin, blackened air. She and her armies re-group, see what they have done, and head for Verulamium, for more of the same. And when she has done her worst she will kill herself, take poison rather than face capture and humiliation.

The settlement dies, becomes the home to charcoal and ashes. It returns to a time before Rome, before empire, before Caratacus came here. London becomes its former self, a humble river crossing set amid marshland and sandbanks. Boadicea will be remembered here. Future archaeologists slicing through the sedimentary crust of London history will recognize a layer of red earth, the ashes she left behind.

Later, very much later, in 1856, Thomas Thorneycroft begins

347

his statue of Boadicea, with her daughters, her horses and her chariot. It is a grand, heroic extravagance in bronze; confident, profoundly English, and yet, one might argue, profoundly anti-imperialist. It was not unveiled until 1902.

Later still, it is situated in the elbow of Victoria Embankment and Westminster Bridge, and groups of the more curious sort of tourist surround it, stare up at the wild, solid figures and suggest to each other that it must be a depiction of Queen Victoria.

And finally here comes Stuart London, a London walker if not *the* London walker, conducting a party of Japanese money men round an eccentric, bite-size approximation of tourist London in preparation for their native theme park aspirations. In the years ahead he will learn to understand and respect and even admire Japanese business practices, but for the moment he wishes the members of the group didn't seem quite so indistinguishable from each other, didn't look quite so much like small suit-wearing tenpins.

He has told them that Boadicea is buried under platform eight of King's Cross Station, and they found that a very good joke. Now he gazes up at the statue of her, at her raised arms, her flowing metal tunic. He looks into the face, surprisingly sensitive for a warrior queen, and is pleased to conclude that she doesn't look a bit like Anita.